THE
ROMANOV
HEIRESS

JENNIFER LAAM

AUTHOR'S NOTE

The Romanov Heiress is a work of fiction inspired by Olga, Tatiana, Maria, and Anastasia, the daughters of Russia's last tsar. The novel presents an alternate future in which they embrace new opportunities open to women in the years following World War I.

PROLOGUE

August 1918

The fugitive lay on her back, bruised limbs pressed flat, hidden alongside her sisters underneath a mound of coarse blankets. As the ambulance rumbled to a halt, gasoline fumes flooded the rear compartment, masking the heavy odor of their unwashed bodies. Her breathing grew labored. She didn't know where they were or who had stopped them. She only knew they must not make a sound.

Over the past weeks, they moved slowly through land held by the Bolsheviks. Every evening at dusk, they ate carefully rationed portions of tinned meat and dry wafers while their two saviors—agents from England with forged papers identifying them as officers of the Red Guard—checked the radio transmitter for word of Allied progress toward the northern ports along the White Sea. Then, during the scant hours of darkness afforded by the short summer nights, they traveled a tortuous course to avoid military checkpoints.

Bundled in tattered sweaters, Olga and her three sisters were gaunt. Their neglected hair hung limp about their shoulders. But their faces once adorned postcards, calendars, and boxes of fancy chocolates. If detained, they would be recognized at once.

The missing daughters of the tsar.

Anastasia's warm body pressed closer, trembling as she tensed her jaw and tried to stifle a cough.

A terrifying scenario unfolded in Olga's mind. Thick boots pounded on the roadway before soldiers with red stars tacked to their lapels tossed the blankets aside and dragged Olga and her sisters back into the hellish world they'd been so desperate to escape. What if this journey had been for nothing? Worse than nothing because they had left their parents and sick little brother, Alexei, behind.

Olga was twenty-two years old and the eldest. It fell on her to get them through this nightmare, no matter the outcome.

She felt around until she located her youngest sister's hand. She held it tight, flinching at the hard calluses and pus leaking from an erupted blister on the pad of Anastasia's thumb.

Deep masculine voices, muddled and indistinct, rumbled outside. The fingers of Olga's free hand balled into fists, rage displacing fear. The Bolsheviks may have stolen everything she held dear, but Olga would confront them as a true Romanov. Unbroken. When they raised their revolvers, she would hold her head high and ensure her face haunted these traitors for the rest of their lives.

The back door of the old field ambulance creaked open. Tentatively, Olga drew the blanket down. After hours of near-darkness, sunlight momentarily blurred her vision. When Olga released Anastasia's hand and sat upright, a cool breeze caressed her forehead.

Before her stood a broad-shouldered gentleman of about fifty, with black brows, a full beard flecked with gray, and brown eyes behind wire-framed spectacles. The man wore a khaki tunic, as Papa had during the war. The coat's golden buttons and belt buckle gleamed in the morning sun.

"Your imperial highness." The gentleman removed his hat and bowed his head. He had spoken in English. She assumed he was the commanding officer. A half-dozen other men stood behind him, each dressed in the same khaki uniform. Some rose on tip-toe to get a closer look at Olga.

None bore a red star on his lapel.

Her sisters emerged from under the blankets. They pressed her shoulders, exhalations warm on the back of her neck.

"I think he's in charge." Tatiana, the second eldest, whispered in Olga's ear. "And waiting for you to speak first."

A spark of hope ignited in her heart, yet Olga didn't trust these strangers. It had been far too long since anyone outside her family had shown her kindness or respect. For months, they had been kept under constant watch: shoved about, subjected to barking orders and humiliating whims, and made to feel they clung to life by the thinnest of threads. Olga remembered the defeated expression on her little brother's face when she'd said goodbye for the last time. Even her once proud father bent under the weight of captivity.

Their saviors, the two men who had rescued them from that nightmare, rounded the vehicle and walked toward the soldiers, broad smiles brightening their ruddy faces.

And then the words fell from Olga's tongue easily, as Mama had always preferred to speak English with her family. "We are here then? We've made it to British soil?"

"We have delivered you to Arkhangelsk. From here, you will be transported to your new home."

"We are in your debt, sir."

Olga waited because she knew he would say more. There had to be more. While they had been rescued, their parents and brother remained imprisoned in Ekaterinburg, along with a handful of loyal servants.

"You will return for the others, won't you?" she said, heart thumping. "My family. Our doctor. My mother's maid. You must promise."

The officer held her gaze. "The Bolsheviks fortified their defenses around the city's perimeter. We can't send our agents back to the house."

Faced with those terrible words, Olga couldn't bring herself to ask anything else. Couldn't bear to hear it was too late. Her stomach churned, but she must not break. Not here. Not yet. As the eldest, she needed to stay strong. For her sisters.

When Olga said nothing more, the officer turned back to his men. Three soldiers joined him, lining up before her sisters to help them out of the ambulance.

"I know you are in pain," the officer told her. "Remember that you and your sisters are safe. You survived. And we have done everything in our power to find a secure place for you. I promise."

Almost to the end, Mama and Papa refused to believe our lives were in jeopardy. Distressing messages arrived while we were under house arrest. Friends of our family buried notes under linens covering loaves of bread and fresh butter from a local convent. The same plea over and over. We might escape, but Papa needed to act quickly.

Papa was a kind man and a good father, but never decisive. First, our enemies moved us from Petrograd to Siberia. Missives continued to arrive in secret, and Papa still did nothing, even after the Bolsheviks seized power.

When they brought us to our ultimate destination, Ekaterinburg, the guards said we were now in a "House of Special Purpose." Our charmed lives had vanished. We might vanish as well, seven more victims of the Revolution.

During our last summer in Russia, a miracle occurred. We could no longer attend church, but were granted an evening service inside the house. Mama prepared a modest altar using her fanciest lace handkerchief and two of our precious candles.

When a young priest in black vestments arrived to lead the prayers, he handed me a cloth-bound prayer book, his thin brows pinched.

Inside, I found a fragment of paper tucked between the last pages: a note dashed off in English. Though banned from speaking the language in that terrible place, we were all fluent. My heart thundered. Had the King of England finally come to our rescue? I waited until Tatiana and Maria were chanting a canticle—and the guards distracted, leering at my pretty sisters—to slide the note under my sleeve. We'd all sewn special pouches inside our cuffs for just this purpose.

After the service, the priest collected the prayer books once more. I excused myself to use the communal lavatory, the one room in the house where we had some measure of privacy.

The guards had defiled the walls with vulgar drawings and lewd jokes. Sadly, I'd grown accustomed to such filth. When I entered the latrine that night, I saw fresh graffiti. A woman meant to be our mother lolled naked in bed. A German Black Iron Cross, the hated symbol of our country's wartime enemy, hung from a chain around her throat. The man depicted next to her had a black beard and grubby hands. Our family's so-called friend. Rasputin. Father Grigori, as we knew him.

Bitter tears stung my eyes. My mother may have been born a German princess, but she was no traitor. Hand trembling, I slipped the note from my cuff and read:

We come at midnight. But only for the girls.

Private Diary of Olga Romanova
December 1921

PART ONE

~

FOUR ENGLISH GIRLS

November—December 1919

CHAPTER ONE

A nastasia had always been a handful, so much so that the last time their mother spoke to Olga, she mentioned her specifically. *Take care of your sisters.* Moisture glistened on Mama's cheeks as she pressed Olga close. *Keep an eye on Anastasia. You know how good she is at finding trouble.*

Her sister only found trouble when she set out looking for it—as she had today. Newsprint stained Olga's hands as she re-read the message scrawled across the back page of the previous night's *Evening News.*

I'm sorry, especially to you, Olga. I know you think you're Mother now. But we spent too long in homes that were prisons, even before the Revolution. I won't spend another minute in captivity. I'm going to America to start a new life.

(Former) Grand Duchess Anastasia Nikolaevna

Olga clenched the paper until the words bled into one another. The shabbiness of it all was so typical. Anastasia's recklessness might have been tolerable years ago, when the worst consequence was a half-hearted reprimand from Papa or a split lip from a tumble off a downhill sled. But that world had crumbled to dust at their feet.

And it wasn't as though Olga *wanted* to assume their mother's role, nor did she wish to keep her sisters under lock and key. Only they had no choice. Olga saved the others from their own worst impulses, particularly Anastasia.

Over a year had passed since their rescue, and they remained trapped. Not as prisoners. Not quite. Olga and her sisters shared a four-room cottage in England, not far from the City of Nottingham. Though sparsely furnished, it was comfortable enough. But Olga made sure the heavy damask curtains stayed drawn over the bay windows facing the street. Willingness to hide preserved their safety. This was a tacit agreement, no less sacred because they never stated it aloud.

To the rest of the world, they must not exist.

Rain battered the windows and wind rattled the panes. As the storm gathered strength, a familiar chill prickled the back of Olga's neck. She fancied her mother stood behind her, forever looking over her shoulder, fingers pinching her skin. Her soul had departed from this earth, and yet Empress Alexandra remained disappointed with her eldest child.

Olga had failed to save Alexei and her parents. Now she'd failed Anastasia as well.

That wasn't fair. Her sister was restless. They all were. Anastasia might have moped about, and she clearly detested the gloomy weather, but Olga had no reason to think she would run away.

Or did she?

Once a week, never on the same day, Olga woke to the *chug-chug* of an idling motorcar engine. Unmarked cardboard boxes appeared on the doorstep. They contained groceries, toiletries, clothes, magazines, sweets, and some mad money. With the help of her sisters, she unloaded everything and wrote requests for new items on a slip of paper that was then deposited in the empty box and left on the doorstep.

Last Wednesday, Olga had caught Anastasia at the front window, pulling the drapes back to stare at the sleek motorcar outside. That should have been a clue. She could never lower her guard. Not with Anastasia.

"I'm a grown woman! Let go!"

For the first time in months, Olga crossed herself. *Praise the Lord.* Tatiana had found her.

Olga peeked around the tri-paneled room divider separating the dining nook from the foyer. The front door swung open, blasting cold air and a shower of drizzle into the cottage. Tatiana strode inside. She held their youngest sister by the crook of her elbow.

Anastasia wore a newsboy cap drawn low over her face and a trench coat two sizes too big and spattered with mud. She was soaking wet, rain dripping from the hat's bill to the threadbare rug they'd placed over the wood flooring in the entranceway. Like Olga, she kept her hair short. Bedraggled locks hung limply at her shoulders.

Shaking loose from Tatiana's grip, Anastasia jabbed a finger in her sister's grim face. "I know you think you think you're our governess, but you've no right to force me back here. Not you, nor Olga. I'm an adult."

"You can't leave yet," Tatiana replied. Of all the sisters, she most resembled their mother: high cheekbones, delicate features, and tireless devotion to family. "Gran will let us know when the time is suitable."

"I don't care what Gran decides. She has no say in my life anymore."

Olga drew a sharp breath. It was one thing to criticize Olga and Tatiana, but now their grandmother?

Gran protected them by doing everything in her power to ensure the true enemies of Russia—the Bolsheviks—never found them. Meanwhile, her sister had nearly ruined everything. At eighteen,

Anastasia remained a stubborn girl who refused to face unpleasant truths.

Tatiana folded her thin arms over her chest and glared down at Anastasia, whose forehead came just to Tatiana's pert nose. "Even if you've a right to leave or whatever it is you were fussing about, you ran away without telling us. Like a spoiled child. Shame on you."

"M will understand." Anastasia searched the room for their other sister. She had always been closest to Maria, who was nearest to her in age. "Did you lock her in a closet?"

Olga stepped around the paneled divider and into the foyer.

"Maria is looking for you in the garden, heartbroken. She couldn't believe you would leave without saying goodbye and thought you were only pulling one of your cruel pranks."

Anastasia twirled to face Olga. Her bangs had grown so long they nearly covered her eyes.

"I found her taking the back road to the train station. As I suspected she would." Tatiana shook out her umbrella and plopped it into the brass stand by the front door. "She claims she could have made it if she hadn't stumbled on brambles and twisted her ankle."

Olga's gaze fixed on her sister's left foot. Anastasia's leather boot laces were untied, and her ankle looked puffy under a thick sock. She hopped on her good leg to maintain balance.

"I'm fine." Anastasia pushed her bangs back before placing her hands defiantly on her hips.

Olga held up the newspaper with Anastasia's hastily scribbled note. "What do we read about every day?"

Anastasia stared down repentantly, but Olga knew her too well to fall for this act. Her sister would perform regret one moment and do whatever she pleased the next.

"The Bolsheviks have agents in Paris and Berlin. They could cross the channel at any time. For all we know, they're already in England." Olga shivered. The Bolsheviks' secret police used unspeakable methods of torture on so-called enemies of the state. Chief among their enemies were those born into the House of Romanov. "If one of them recognized you, they'd snatch you off the street. If they captured you, do you think you could hold out? That you wouldn't tell them where we live and how to find us?"

"You're overreacting," Anastasia said. "Both of you. Like mother hens."

The back door creaked open. Maria slipped through the kitchen and joined them in the foyer, pulling her cloak closer around her broad shoulders. She'd clipped her wavy brunette curls with a felt bow now soaked through from the rain. While Tatiana headed to the train station, Maria had looked for Anastasia outside. She expected to find her sister sulking behind the cottage, where Anastasia had pouted and grumbled amidst fragrant sweet peas, violets, and honeysuckle many days that past summer.

"So it's true. You ran away." Maria's gentle tone made the words a statement rather than an accusation.

Anastasia poked the rug with the toe of her left boot. Now, she sounded genuinely contrite. "I'm sorry, M. I shouldn't have caused you to worry."

A flicker of sympathy softened Olga's anger. Her sister wanted more from life. Who could blame her? "Where were you going, anyway? You mentioned the United States."

"California. Los Angeles."

She may as well have said the moon. "What on earth were you thinking?"

"I was *thinking* I want to make something of my life."

"And how did you propose to get there?"

"With the pearls Mother gave us," Anastasia said. "I kept a few of mine. I sold them to the delivery driver."

Under house arrest in Ekaterinburg the summer before last, they'd sewn jewels inside their corsets. Their grandmother had arranged for those gemstones to be assessed and sold. That money paid for the boxes of food and other necessities delivered to their door. But they had not parted with their pearls because those were Mama's favorites. Olga recalled their cool silkiness against her bare skin.

"It was only a matter of getting a transfer in London to Southampton," Anastasia continued, "where I'd buy a steerage ticket on the Aquitania."

Olga scratched the back of her neck, trying to imagine Anastasia on the same type of ocean liner as the Titanic. At least these days such ships carried enough lifeboats to carry everyone to safety. "That ship docks in New York. Los Angeles is on the other side of the continent."

"I know." Anastasia was getting flustered. Perhaps she saw the folly of her scheme now that she had to explain it aloud.

"And what did you plan to do there?" Tatiana asked dryly.

"Rent a room and work in New York City for a few months. As a secretary. Once I had enough money socked away, I'd move along."

Tatiana snorted. Maria repeated "secretary" breathlessly, as though her sister had said something vulgar.

The downpour continued, hammering against the roof and filling the silence between them. If only she had the right words to make Anastasia understand. Olga hated the idea that they might remain trapped here forever, their lives getting smaller by the day.

The longer they stayed in isolation, the more often Olga caught herself mindlessly staring out the window facing the back garden. A web of branches extended from a slender birch tree, and a gray squirrel liked to scamper up the silvery trunk. Olga missed the dogs and kittens who roamed their palaces and the dashing courtiers who'd spun her around polished dance floors. She mourned the constant absence of Papa's smiles, Mama's quiet humming, and Alexei's laughter.

She still held Anastasia's note. On the other side of the newspaper, a bold headline declared *New Decade Means New Prospects for Ladies.* Below was a photograph of a young clerical worker, hair pulled under a jaunty hat, wearing a matching cardigan and skirt set with the hemline brushing her knees. Olga pictured her sister in a similar hat, taking notes for a man chomping on a cigar and barking orders in a brash American accent.

As of late, Olga sensed a greater connection between herself and Anastasia, which she didn't think Tatiana or Maria would understand. Olga and Ana longed to get out of this cottage, regardless of whether Gran gave permission. They longed for more from life than perpetual chores and needlework. While Tatiana and Maria couldn't bear their isolation forever, they wouldn't break as quickly as Anastasia. Or Olga.

"Why not stay in New York, then?" Tatiana said.

Maria answered for Anastasia: "Los Angeles is where moving pictures are produced."

"How outlandish!" Tatiana cried.

Actually, it made more sense now. Growing up, Anastasia could not remain still for more than a few minutes at a time unless she was tinkering with one of the family's box cameras. She would stand in front of a mirror with the lens pointed at her reflection, experimenting with angles for hours on end.

Moving pictures had always fascinated her sister as well. When they were children, Papa filmed his daughters while they played on the imperial yacht during summer vacations to the islands off the coast of Finland. The four sisters held hands and spun around in circles, the ribbons on their straw hats flying behind them. Papa laughed and caught it all on film.

"You're a grand duchess," Tatiana told Anastasia. "You'll get married and have children."

"She's not a grand duchess," Olga said quietly. "None of us are."

Tatiana stared at Olga as though a Bolshevik spy had snatched her and replaced her with someone who looked and sounded like Olga, but couldn't possibly be her sister. "Of course we are. Anastasia must own that responsibility. When we return to Russia—"

"What if we never return?"

Maria made a watery, gulping sound, and Anastasia was stunned into silence.

"We belong in Russia," Tatiana said firmly. "We must only remain patient."

Patience wasn't what kept them going. Fear isolated them from the rest of the world. Fear prompted Tatiana's stern admonishments and Maria's refusal, for once, to side with her little sister. They were all haunted by their memories of captivity. The sharp prod of a bayonet on the small of the back. A growling order to move faster or to get away from a window lest anyone see them. A letter from a friend torn to pieces before their eyes.

Fear kept them alive, but what a miserable way to live.

"I shouldn't have said we aren't grand duchesses," Olga amended. They were the tsar's daughters, deposed or not. "One day, we shall help restore the House of Romanov. For Mama and Papa and Alexei. Only we don't know when that day will come."

Anastasia's long bangs fluttered as she exhaled loudly, wobbling on her good foot. A part of Olga, small but insistent, wished her sister had made it across the ocean. Anastasia deserved better than a life in forced seclusion. They all did.

Olga squeezed her sister's damp shoulder. "You must express your feelings and consider how your actions impact the rest of us. We must stick together."

"I know," Anastasia said, a catch in her throat. "For Papa and Mama. For Alexei. Except Papa wouldn't want us trapped like animals in a cage."

"We're not in a cage," Olga said. "We'll determine the shape of our lives as soon as we're able. Together."

None of them looked convinced, least of all Anastasia.

"In the meantime, maybe we can venture outside a bit," Olga said. "Why don't we see a picture show in Nottingham? It's a hike, but we can walk it. Let's go. Just the two of us."

Olga scarcely believed she'd made such a suggestion. Tatiana and Maria exchanged wary looks while Anastasia's bright eyes sparkled. There she was. The mischievous *Nastasia* Olga remembered, though her sister preferred to be called *Ana* now.

"It's not safe for all of us to go out together." Olga straightened her back and clasped her hands in front of her. Her muscles moved like an automaton's, trained to appear regal. "We would be too easily recognized. But Tatiana and Maria can plan something as well."

"Have you lost your senses?" Tatiana said. "You want to take her to a cinema? Someone will notice the two of you."

Her sister made a valid point. Still, Olga pressed her case. "We will be careful. Extremely careful."

"What about the Bolsheviks? As you said, it would be easy enough for them to cross the channel. They may already be here."

"The first places they'll look are train stations and the like. I can't imagine Bolsheviks have spies lurking in every cinema, waiting for us to walk in."

"You don't know," Tatiana said. "That's the point! We will remain in hiding until we return to Russia as grand duchesses. It's what Gran wants."

Olga appreciated everything their grandmother had done for them, but Gran didn't grasp the magnitude of what had happened. She clung to the hopeless belief that Papa, Mama, and Alexei were alive, somewhere, and would be restored to power soon enough. "I'm not sure Gran understands our situation."

Tatiana shook her head. "I'm the one who found Anastasia. I say no."

"I wanted to go after her!" Olga cried, annoyed at Tatiana for trying to make a unilateral decision. "You insisted I stay behind in case she came crawling back."

"Only because you were getting emotional when we needed to focus."

"She's right. You act like our governess. I'm the eldest and responsible for the rest of you. It's my job to ensure we stay safe *and* that isolation doesn't drive us mad."

Tatiana opened her mouth, but before she replied, Maria said: "I don't know about anyone else, but I could do with tea. Earl Grey? Ana, why don't you help me put a kettle on?"

"Mary Pickford has a new picture out," Anastasia said, following her sister to the kitchen. "*Daddy-Long-Legs*. And it's playing in Nottingham! That's what I want to see."

When Maria and Ana slipped away, Tatiana hung back in the foyer, moving to the bay window. She fingered the fringe and tassels on the front drapes, braided through with metallic gold and black thread, decor Olga and Tatiana had made themselves. Olga wondered if her sister would draw the curtains and peek at the road. She'd been out in the open today. Perhaps she'd acquired a taste for it.

Instead, Tatiana dropped her hand and released an ominous sigh. "You're going to reward her for running?"

Tatiana acted like a governess because she loved them. She wanted everyone to stay safe. It was only that they all needed to regain some semblance of lives. Anastasia may have gone about it in the wrong fashion, but they couldn't stay here forever. They certainly couldn't stop their sister from trying to run again.

"She's not a little girl," Olga said. "If she wants to leave, we have no power over her. Besides, she needs a break from ... well, from all this ..."

She waved her arms uncertainly. She loved the painting on their room divider, a peacock with colorful feathers spanning the panels, but now she saw only the tiny perforations betraying its age. From the kitchen, scratchy clicks sounded as Maria struggled with the knob on the temperamental stove. The beaded trimmings on the lampshades were coming loose. Everything in the cottage needed work. Besides, the place was too small for four young women.

"Mama would want us to wait until Gran says it's all right," Tatiana insisted.

"Mama isn't alive," Olga blurted.

Hastily, Tatiana crossed herself and muttered a quick prayer. "How can you say that?"

Gran made sure newspapers were delivered to the cottage daily. When the time came for her granddaughters to re-enter society, she wanted them well-informed of current events so that they might chat charmingly with prospective husbands.

The papers kept them cognizant of the outside world. Not long after rescuing Olga and her sisters, the coalition fighting the Bolsheviks arrived to liberate Ekaterinburg. Soldiers had stormed the Ipatiev House—the House of Special Purpose—only to find the place abandoned. But in a basement room, they had discovered walls stained with blood and riddled with bullet holes.

There were no bodies, but they knew. Or should know. Only Tatiana stubbornly believed that their parents and Alexei had been relocated to parts unknown, the murder scene nothing more than Bolshevik subterfuge.

"I sense Mama sometimes," Olga whispered. "Here with us. Like a spirit."

"That's only your mind playing tricks. We mustn't lose faith. Mama walks this earth alongside Papa and Alexei." Tatiana's eyes narrowed. "I worry about you. I think back to how you were before our rescue."

Olga flinched. During their last weeks in captivity, she had deteriorated into a whisper of her former self. Since then, Tatiana constantly fretted over Olga's state of mind.

As her sister spoke, the room grew colder, and her chest heavier. And then Olga didn't just sense her mother's presence. She watched as Mama materialized next to Tatiana like an image she might fancy in a cloud: indistinct, but *there*.

Mama looked much as she had when Olga and Tatiana were little girls, her figure slim in a cream-colored day dress and her reddish-blonde hair piled high on her head. Modest lace netting covered her décolletage. She opened her mouth and then shut it abruptly, as though she wanted to speak but couldn't manage the words. She just stared at Olga, anguished.

"Olga?" Tatiana shook her shoulders. "What's wrong?"

"I'm not imagining it," Olga whispered. "Mama is here. And she's trying to tell me something."

*Our country carried England and France through the first years of war,
until revolution ripped Russia apart from the inside.*

*During those early years, we all did our bit. Tatiana and I trained
as nurses. Every morning, we accompanied our mother to the newly
established hospital ward in the Catherine Palace—sisters of mercy with
crosses hanging on long chains from our necks.*

*Despite our covered heads and full-length habits, the wounded men
recognized us.* Kak Angelie, *they'd say. Practically the same in Russian
as in English. Like angels.*

*I remember a soldier whispering that phrase as spittle drooled from
his deformed mouth. Grotesque chemical burns layered his neck and
chin. Later, I held his hand and listened closely to his slurred words, his
breath ripe with decay as he choked out a final letter to his mother.*

*Afterward, I wondered how we might avoid the same deadly chaos
that destroyed the lives of soldiers and their families.*

*As it happened, we didn't avoid it at all. Our family was destined to
rely on the whim of an English king with the power to determine who
among us would survive and who would be left to die.*

The Private Diary of Olga Romanova
December 1921

CHAPTER TWO

E lectric light streamed from crystal chandeliers above, illuminating the stairs leading to the upper level. Olga watched Anastasia sweep her hand over a faux gilded fixture atop the banister at the foot of the staircase. Though giving the illusion of grandeur, it seemed cheaply built, for the knob wobbled under her sister's gentle touch.

Olga walked unsteadily through the lower lobby. They had chosen an hour when the cinema shouldn't have been crowded. Late afternoon. Tea time.

And yet there were *people* here. Gentlemen in slim-cut suits and elegant vests who must have left their offices early to escort the women and small children, all excited to take in a picture show. Rosy-cheeked and jolly, they chattered in clusters and accidentally bumped into them with polite "sorries" before scuttling upstairs. Anastasia, unflappable under almost any circumstance, looked about anxiously.

Olga and Ana had inherited their father's distinctive blue eyes, the feature that made them most identifiable as daughters of the tsar. So Olga pulled her felt cloche hat low and pointed to her forehead to indicate Ana should do the same. The bell-shaped hats had arrived in their latest box and would soon be all the rage according to Maria, who'd ordered them and kept up on such things.

After adjusting her hat, Olga ascended the stairs. She'd reached the third step when the powerful aroma of wood varnish stopped her in her tracks.

The scent summoned thoughts of the freshly scrubbed imperial box at the Mariinsky Theatre, festooned with garlands of the two-headed eagle. She and Tatiana accompanied their father to a performance of *Sleeping Beauty*, their expensive Coty perfumes—rose for Olga and jasmine for Tatiana—subsumed under the heavy smell of lacquer. They'd worn white court gowns with crimson sashes draped diagonally over their chests. Diamond-studded tiaras encircled the tops of their heads. Hands swathed in long satin gloves, they waved to the crowded auditorium below before taking their velvet-cushioned seats.

Not minding her feet, Ana ran into her from behind. "Are you all right?"

When the war started, Anastasia had only been thirteen. By the time she turned sixteen and should have taken her place in society, Papa had already abdicated and their family was under arrest.

"I'm fine." Olga forced the memories from her mind. "Sorry about that." She continued up the staircase.

"Mary Pickford has her own production company. Did I tell you?" Ana spoke English with a posh accent she'd deployed for this occasion. "She started it with Charlie Chaplin and that foxy Douglas Fairbanks. Mary wants to control the rights to her pictures. So she hires her own writers. She helps edit her films. It's brilliant. Really."

Olga knew her sister idolized the famous actress. Ana had cut a photograph of Mary Pickford from *Picturegoer* and tacked it to the wall by her bed. In the photo, ringlets framed Mary's cheerful face and a wee kitten perched on her shoulder.

"You want to work for her one day?"

Ana gave a rollicking laugh. And then, realizing her mistake, lowered her gaze. They must never be loud and careless. They must never draw attention.

"I won't run away again," she said. "If that's what you're asking."

"I only wish you wanted to live somewhere closer. It's not like films aren't made in England. The world's best actors live in London."

"The best actors on stage," Ana said. "Pictures are silent. Images, not words."

"Still, you might find work in the industry here. You needn't go so far away."

"Shakespeare and all that is fine for you. Not for me."

Anastasia had her heart set on California's glamour and sunshine. Olga understood. If they were to make their home somewhere else, she supposed they could do worse.

For now, however, a picture would have to do. Olga pushed open the heavy doors to the screening room and stepped aside so Ana could go in first.

Quivering gray and white spots dotted the screen. The projector softly hissed as a newsreel tapered off. Voices hummed in the dark. Unfamiliar perfumes, hair pomade, and body odors clung to the warm air, and peanut shells crunched underneath their leather ankle boots.

Olga and her sisters had once been treated to picture shows in private screening rooms, usually newsreels or educational films about the far eastern regions of the Russian empire. Neither she nor Ana had stepped foot in a cinema before today. Olga wasn't sure what she had expected, but thought it would be more dignified somehow.

Ana motioned toward a pair of seats in the last row. While Ana removed her hat and shook her hair out, Olga slouched low. Last autumn, their faces had been prominent in the papers. *Grand Duchesses Feared Dead. Mystery of Russian Princesses Deepen. Young Woman*

Claims Escape from Family's Massacre. The accompanying articles related lurid tales from impostors claiming to be one Romanov sister or another. For all Olga knew, her face might appear on the screen next.

What if a fellow or lady in a center seat turned around at just the right moment, recognition lighting their eyes? One random spotting of a missing grand duchess was easily dismissed. But two of them together? In a crowded cinema with other witnesses? Olga had accepted that risk, but now it was all too real.

She glanced at Anastasia. Her sister sat stone-faced, small hands clenched in her lap. Olga was supposed to protect Ana. She should never have brought her here. When the Bolsheviks found Romanovs, they kidnapped and dragged them back to Russia. What they did to prisoners there ...

No. Olga squeezed her eyes shut. She couldn't live in perpetual fear. They had escaped. The Bolsheviks were dangerous, but they weren't *everywhere.* They couldn't be.

From the balcony, a pipe organist began hammering a popular patriotic song. She opened her eyes once more. A title card flashed: **Remembrance Day!**

This calmed Olga somewhat. Last night, from the cottage, they'd heard the *pop-pop* of fireworks in town celebrating the first anniversary of the armistice. Today, at least, the missing grand duchesses weren't news.

Flickering images appeared on the screen. The camera panned across people swarming the London streets to watch the procession, flags and hats waving and feet stomping as a carriage bearing the royal insignia passed. Soldiers raised their bayonets. Olga tensed. These soldiers may have been English, but their bayonets were identical to those of the Bolsheviks.

Another title card: **Banquet with the French President at Buckingham Palace!**

A sentry in a stiff hat helped Queen Mary alight from her carriage. King George followed. The king wore a field marshal's uniform with braided epaulets atop his shoulders and medals shining on his chest.

Papa.

The word echoed in Olga's head. Long ago, her family vacationed with the English royals on the Isle of Wight when King George was still the Prince of Wales. He and Papa had posed for photographs together. The King of England and her father were first cousins but looked like twin brothers. Same trim beards, gentle smiles, and bright eyes.

In the end, however, not the same at all. King George survived the war with his crown, palaces, and power intact. He even had a handsome playboy for a son. Once upon a time, Olga's mother thought the king's eldest son would make a suitable bridegroom. In another world, Olga could have lived in England as the Princess of Wales.

Instead, she was an impoverished ex-grand duchess. Forever in hiding. Forever afraid the Bolsheviks might find her.

Ana's fingers squeezed hers. When she turned to look at her sister, Ana was pale and her eyes looked haunted. She'd also seen Papa, the ghost of his face, in the king. Despite her confident exterior, Ana was damaged, as they all were.

Do you want to go? Ana mouthed, careful not to say the words aloud.

It felt strange enough to be out in public again. Overwhelming, really. Now, to see this simple reminder of Papa in a newsreel and know she could never escape the past, Olga wanted to leave. She was about to tell Ana as much.

Except a more powerful impulse took hold. She was tired of living in fear and allowing it to take things away from them. If they left the cinema early, it was as good as granting the Bolsheviks yet another victory, if only a small one in the grand scheme.

"I want to see Mary Pickford," Olga whispered. "We're not going anywhere."

Olga dumped a few small logs in the fireplace. Then, she opened the damper, ensuring air flowed up and out through the chimney, and struck a long match from the box on the mantel.

During their winter in captivity, Papa had taught his daughters how to chop wood for the fire. He ensured they practiced proper form: circling the ax over their shoulder, steadying their legs, and then swinging it down hard. They had all taken turns at this task, for the house in Siberia where they stayed during that harsh winter hadn't been well insulated. Those fires brought little relief from the bitter cold. Still, the process made Olga feel self-reliant in a way few other jobs could.

When they returned from the cinema, Anastasia had retired to the bedroom she shared with Maria. Her voice carried as she described the climactic scene of *Daddy-Long-Legs* when Mary Pickford's handsome benefactor reveals himself and they fall in love.

Olga had made her sister happy this afternoon. That should have been enough.

Why wasn't it enough?

As she watched the flames flicker, her thoughts wandered back to the newsreel of King George. She remembered their saviors—special agents of His Majesty's Secret Service, as Olga would later learn—who rescued them from their final imprisonment. The men had tunneled under the high wooden posts surrounding the Ipatiev House, which were meant to keep the family out of view of curious and potentially sympathetic neighbors.

Once on the grounds, the men slipped sleeping pills into the vodka the Bolshevik guards drank profusely at night. When all was silent but for rumbling snores, the agents helped the girls climb down a rope from the one window that remained unsealed. They then crept under the rear gate to a stolen motorcar that spirited them away.

Olga grabbed an iron poker and stoked the fire. She should be grateful to King George for their rescue, but she couldn't shake the sense that he should have done more. Why did he abandon her parents and Alexei? She shoved the poker deeper until embers shot back and forth.

"You've got it going well enough, don't you think?"

Olga turned to the entryway between the parlor and the hall that led to the two bedrooms, where Tatiana now stood. Her sister had changed into a dove-gray nightgown. It was too short, exposing her thin calves almost to the knee.

"I was thinking about Remembrance Day." Olga leaned the poker against the hearth and flopped into an overstuffed armchair to read the papers. She had already scanned the front page of the *Times*, comprised primarily of photographs of parades, poppies, and wreaths brought to gravesites.

Tatiana looked down at her narrow feet and wiggled her toes.

"The papers report the king's speeches in full," Olga said. "Do you suppose he had anything kind to say about Papa?"

"I read the paper already," Tatiana said quickly. "The king gave a speech about the war. That's all."

Olga's anger rose suddenly, like boiling water in a pot about to spill over. "After everything we suffered? Nothing?"

"It's the past," Tatiana said. "No one can change the past, not even a king. What more is there to discuss?"

"Papa helped England win the war!"

"Until the people welcome us back to Russia—"

"If the people want us," Olga said. "They got rid of us, after all."

Tatiana pressed her lips tight. More than anything, she wanted to return to Russia. Olga wanted it almost as badly. To set the record straight. To tell everyone the truth about what her parents had sacrificed for Russia, and the indignities they'd suffered at the hands of the Bolsheviks: the same beasts in charge of their country now. They might claim to rule on behalf of the people, but Olga didn't believe them for a second.

"I doubt the people had any say in the matter in the first place," Olga added. "They were hungry. They wanted peace, land, and bread. Isn't that what the Revolution was all about? Other than that, we don't know what they wanted. Everyone kept us at a distance from the people. That was always the problem."

Tatiana allowed a small smile to play on her lips. "Not so distant. Or have you forgotten about your dear Mitya? Your favorite soldier."

Olga felt her cheeks warm. "You know I haven't. No more than you've forgotten any of your favorites, I'm sure."

Years had passed since she last saw Mitya, but she still blushed at the memory of his earnest brown eyes and quick smiles. Even when the pain of his wounded leg afflicted him, he'd always made time for Olga.

"But flirting with soldiers at the hospital is hardly the same as understanding what our people require," she told her sister.

Tatiana grew pensive. She rarely strayed from her severe nature and never for more than a minute or two.

"Papa and Mama tried to understand and to help. Mama worked herself to exhaustion at the hospital. Don't you remember? And during the war, Papa only left Petrograd because he was needed at the front. What more could they have done?"

Mama could have stopped listening to Grigori Rasputin. Papa could have ordered him removed from the palace.

Olga didn't dare say those words aloud, even now that her parents and Grigori Rasputin were gone. The subject still upset Tatiana, so she allowed her sister's remark to pass without comment. As she had allowed Mama's starry-eyed admiration for Father Grigori to stand unquestioned.

She returned to the newspaper, scrunching the corners irritably between her fingers. "Not a word about Russia's contribution to the war? Did anyone deign to mention Papa?"

"Not Papa." Tatiana gnawed on her thumbnail and shifted her weight from foot to foot. She'd never been able to lie. She had read something.

"Mama then?" Olga flicked through the pages until she reached the back of the front section. There, she found the headline etched in bold ink.

Former Empress of Russia Denounced as Traitor

"I'm sorry," Tatiana whispered, but her voice seemed distant. The words swimming before her eyes, Olga continued to read.

> Edward Pike, 6th Earl of Hammond, has set the stage for Parliament to posthumously censure the ex-empress of Russia. Lord Hammond claims possession of letters proving Empress Alexandra, Hessian by birth, deliberately weakened the position of the formidable Russian Army.

In collusion with her much-despised personal mystic,
Grigori Rasputin, she stands accused of passing military secrets to Berlin to force a separate peace with the
Germans. Hammond will include these missives in a
forthcoming book detailing his lordship's diplomatic experiences in Russia before the war. He intends
to spend Parliament's Christmas recess at his family's country estate, Marlingham, to complete the final
draft of the manuscript.

Olga looked up from the paper, seeing not Tatiana but their mother
as she had been during the war in her plain nursing habit. Olga remembered the creases wrinkling Mama's forehead as she handed metal
instruments to a surgeon or helped stitch a wound. Their mother
worked endless hours because she loved Russia, especially Russian
soldiers. She would never betray those men.

Some view an official condemnation of the late empress—presumed to have died alongside her family at
the hands of the Bolsheviks—as a bid to end British
intervention in the Russian Civil War, ongoing in
Siberia. Such a declaration might also ease the estab-
lishment of diplomatic and trade relations with the
new government.

"How can they publish this libelous filth?" Olga cried.

Tatiana pulled up an armchair, its wooden legs tearing fibers loose from the parlor's faded Tabriz rug. "You mustn't let yourself get upset."

"This man could destroy Mama's reputation!"

Tatiana chewed at her thumbnail again. It was a bad childhood habit she had long abandoned. Until their imprisonment. "Gran probably knows more. We could ask her."

"We can't risk it. Gran disliked Mama. She might believe these lies."

Olga crumpled the newspaper. The flames in the hearth twisted and crackled. She wanted to throw the pages in the fire, to let them be consumed and burnt to ashes. Only that wouldn't make this situation any better, for the words were already seared into her mind.

"Someday we will share our side of the story," Tatiana said. "We must be patient."

"I know it's dangerous to tell our story if the Bolsheviks remain in power. This man wants to help make that so. But maybe we can set things right."

"What do you mean?"

"We tell the papers we're alive and explain how we got to England. We may not know the names of the gentlemen who helped us, but we remember important things, don't we?"

The face of the officer at Arkhangelsk remained hazy in her memory, but Olga recalled his deep voice and gentle words. *You and your sisters are safe. You survived.*

"Do you remember what it felt like to be respected after months of abuse?"

"I remember that the most," Tatiana said.

Moonlight streamed through the side window, casting a soft light on her sister's face. *Kak angelie*, just like the soldiers in the hospital said. Tatiana and Olga might now become angels of truth. Perhaps they would never need to live in hiding again.

"But that doesn't mean we can react to this," Tatiana said. "Going to the cinema is one thing. What you're suggesting? We can't risk it. Not while the Bolsheviks are still out there looking for us."

"We won't let anyone know where the information came from." Olga glanced over her shoulder to see if Ana or Maria had heard. Then, whispering, she continued. "We could compose a letter in the guise of a servant." She bit her lip. They'd never learned what became of the few members of their staff who'd remained in Ekaterinburg. Mama's devoted maid, Anna Demidova. Dr. Botkin, who was so tender with Alexei. "And not provide a name."

"What about the postmark?" Tatiana asked.

"I'll mail it from somewhere far away. If Anastasia can figure out how to sell her pearls to book passage on the *Aquitania*, I can figure this out."

"Everyone will assume it's a hoax." Tatiana worked her ragged cuticles between her lips. "Another charlatan making trouble."

Outlandish stories had made the papers. When a young Russian émigré left her English husband a large inheritance upon her untimely death, neighbors referred to her as "Princess Tatiana." They spread rumors that she was one of the missing daughters of the tsar. In a similar case, the disgraced kaiser recognized "Grand Duchess Olga," and arranged a monthly stipend for the impostor. Olga had laughed off such tales, but they'd invariably bothered Tatiana.

"If we allow this lie to stand unchallenged, we will forever be under suspicion," Olga said. "And assumed to have been complicit."

"Mama will forgive this and let it go." Tatiana refused to speak of their mother in anything but the present tense. Her gray eyes widened, just as Mama's always had when making a point. "That's what she will want us to do."

"You do not speak for her. You don't know what she would want."

"I know Mama is loyal to Russia. That is enough."

It was enough for Tatiana. She had inherited their mother's penchant for forbearance. As a result, Tatiana understood how to keep her mouth shut when the situation so demanded. In contrast, Olga had always been more like Papa, calm under most circumstances but quick to anger when challenged. Tatiana might preach patience and forgiveness, but they'd suffered long enough. They had been forced to abandon their parents and brother to a horrendous fate.

Their parents could have died in peace if only they had known the Englishmen had saved all of their children. But Alexei was so sick he couldn't walk. And so they left him behind. *Olga* had left him behind. *We will come at midnight. But only for the girls.* Perhaps she'd hadn't a choice in the matter, but that didn't diminish the sickening guilt.

And now the only remaining earthly part of her mother, her reputation, was about to be ruined. If the English Parliament branded Mama a traitor, it would haunt Olga and her sisters when they stepped back into the world. They'd have no future.

Olga had failed her brother. She vowed not to fail her sisters as well.

The Great War was an unending stand-off that resulted in mass casualties. Supply lines into the Russian cities, particularly Petrograd, were diverted to provide for troops at the front while workers grew hungrier and hungrier.

We were supposed to have been sheltered from it all. The privileged grand duchesses. Elite Romanovs oblivious to the suffering of their people. As Petrograd starved and the city fell into chaos, agonizing fevers struck each member of our family. Desperately ill from measles, we couldn't leave our beds. Our mother cared for us while gunshots and cannon fire bellowed in the distance. And yet close enough, for our palace was easy to reach from Petrograd. Especially easy for desperate workers maddened by starvation.

If it weren't for the measles, we might have escaped before the Bolsheviks rose to power. We could have left the palace together, met Papa at the front, and abandoned Russia. Except Papa would never have entertained the thought.

But had we left then, I would never have left my little brother behind later.

The Private Diary of Olga Romanova
December 1921

CHAPTER THREE

D eciding you must do something and establishing the best means to go about it are far different concerns. The first is an immediate decision made directly from the heart, while the other is a slower process and requires greater consideration. With patience, however, the right course of action will become apparent.

Papa had said this to Olga when she was a little girl. She had been crying over how to confront Tatiana after she took one of Olga's dolls without permission. When he finished, he had kissed the top of her head and allowed her to remain on his lap as he reviewed the endless stack of papers and reports from his counselors.

Olga tried to follow her father's advice from long ago. She waited, trusting the answer to come. When the weekly delivery box arrived on Friday, she sorted the groceries with her sisters, helped conjure a menu, and assigned cooks for each meal. Tatiana recorded those assignments on the chalkboard they kept near the stove. Olga swept the alcove and the kitchen and polished the wood blocks with Murphy Oil. She used a concoction of baking soda and vinegar to scrub the cast-iron bathtub, spending so long on the linoleum floor that bruises purpled her knees.

Her brain felt like two plates were constantly smashed against it, thoughts forming but not into a coherent plan. She'd tucked the newspaper away in the bottom drawer of the bureau she shared with Tatiana. No need to trouble her youngest sisters with the news. Not yet. She kept finding excuses, though, to re-read Lord Hammond's vile slander: *traitor ... military secrets to Berlin.* The words ran like a newsreel set to a continuous loop.

Whenever her mind wandered back to the article, Olga gave the spout of the porcelain teapot a vigorous rinse. Or she worked with a feather duster on the many lampshades around the cottage, waiting for the thud against the front door when the newspapers were delivered. Olga scanned the papers to see if anyone had come to her mother's defense. The king. The queen mother, who was their great-aunt. Mama's sister, Victoria, who resided on the Isle of Wight. A German relative, perhaps.

Still, she heard nothing. The British government could brand the Empress of Russia, their wartime ally, a traitor. No one seemed to care.

As the days passed in their ceaselessly dull manner, Olga went to bed too early and rose too late. She snapped at Anastasia for taking the last biscuit when she knew perfectly well that shortbread was Olga's favorite. Ana declared she knew no such thing. And when Maria tried to stop the argument by suggesting they test the old clamshell gramophone in the parlor, Olga snapped at her for no reason at all.

The following evening, after a light supper of cheddar and toast points, Maria and Tatiana cleared the table, and Ana brought out a deck of cards for bezique. Olga had no heart for the game anymore. Her parents had loved bezique, and she found it too depressing to play without them. She pleaded a headache and sprawled on the armchair in the parlor with the back pages of the *Times*.

Guilt plagued her as she recalled the harsh tone she had taken with her sisters the night before. Maria had recovered quickly enough. She always had the composure of a saint. But Ana was still scowling.

And so Olga reviewed the paper's hiring postings. She imagined young English girls eagerly reading the adverts, searching for employment as a stenographer, receptionist, typist, or bookkeeper. What skills were required for such positions? Probably nothing taught in the carefully curated language, music, and history lessons she and her sisters received from tutors brought to the palace. Then again, surely they could learn new skills.

Though she knew Ana had her heart set on Los Angeles, Olga wondered if her sister would consider a position in London were the circumstances right. There, she might enjoy independence while remaining close enough for Olga to watch over her.

Olga was about to get up to fetch a pen from the kitchen—thinking she'd circle one or two of the adverts and leave them out for Anastasia—when, among the postings for office work, she spotted a different sort altogether.

> **Maid Needed.** Seeking young woman to help clean and sundry other duties. Room, board, and reasonable uniform expenses included with compensation. The candidate will interview at Marlingham. Send correspondence to the following address …

Olga sat up straight, adrenaline coursing through her. Marlingham. Hammond's country house, as mentioned in the newspaper article, where he would finish writing his book and complete the slander against her mother.

She read through the posting twice and double-checked the listed address. It was less than an hour away by rail. She could take the train from Nottingham, from the same station Ana had been heading for when she tried to run away.

Heart pounding, Olga sat up, ready to find Tatiana and thrust the paper in her face.

But a voice in her head counseled patience. It wasn't the memory of her father's voice. Not this time.

Her mother materialized next to the hearth, slender fingers worrying a long double strand of pearls. Her features remained obscure, shimmering, a mere echo of Mama. She was gone as soon as Olga spotted her, as though she'd only needed to give her a nudge.

Their mother never tolerated discord between her girls. She wanted Olga to take care not to hurt the others, particularly not Tatiana. But Mama wanted her to act. Papa would want the same.

So Olga made her decision. First, she would purchase a local post office box to send and receive mail without revealing where they lived. Next, she was going to apply to work at Marlingham.

Olga stood before her sisters, back straight, hands clasped, and feet slightly apart in what ballet dancers called third position.

Anastasia sat cross-legged before the fire. She'd insisted on changing into the red and black checkered flannel pajamas she'd ordered from a catalog. They were tailored for men and hung too loose on her slender frame. Meanwhile, Tatiana, her dark hair gathered in a low bun, still wore her pale green cardigan sweater and skirt set. As usual, she kept her wicker sewing basket handy and had set to work darning socks.

After supper, Maria stayed behind to tidy up the kitchen, so she was the last to enter the parlor. As she took a seat on the soft footstool by Tatiana's chair, she pulled her salmon-colored kimono, a gift from the Emperor of Japan, tighter across her chest.

"I have news," Olga said.

Worry clouded Maria's enormous eyes. "They found Mama and Papa. And Alexei." She looked down. "Their bodies."

"No!" Tatiana pinched Maria's shoulder. "Don't say that. Never say that."

"Olga made such a big to-do about talking to us this evening," Ana pointed out. "What else were we supposed to think?"

Berating herself for upsetting her sisters, Olga drew a deep breath, inhaling crisp smoke and pine from the bough her sisters had placed atop the mantle on the first of December. Christmas and New Year's weren't as joyous now. Nor were any other holidays, for that matter. They'd only tried to add a bit more cheer to their surroundings.

Solemnly, Olga picked up one of the newspapers she'd placed on the end table. She handed it over.

Maria scooted the footstool closer to Anastasia. As Ana held the paper open, they read Hammond's accusations together. By the time they finished, Ana's cheeks were splotchy, and silent tears ran down Maria's cheeks.

"I'll kill this man," Ana said.

"Not you as well," Tatiana told her. "We need to forgive him. As Mama will."

"Oh, get over it! Face the facts." Ana folded the paper sharply and threw it toward the fire. Only Olga's interception saved the pages from sizzling in the flames. "You should have told us. You still treat M and me like we're little girls."

With her hair braided and in her pajamas, Ana did still seem like a little girl. Even so, Olga understood her point. She nodded. "I'm sorry."

"Olga only wanted to spare you the sorrow of it." Tatiana focused on a stocking, poking the thick material with her needle and yanking the thread.

"At any rate, now we all know." Olga grabbed the other newspaper from the end table, the advert circled in black, and passed it over to Ana and Maria. She waited for them to read it.

"You want to apply for this position?" Maria asked, eyes wide.

"Yes. Marlingham is Lord Hammond's estate. The family's country seat."

"What are you talking about?" Tatiana said, a warning note in her voice. Maria passed her the paper.

"We can't let this accusation against Mama stand unchallenged," Olga said as Tatiana read the advert. "Any so-called evidence of our mother's betrayal is a lie. Hammond will have a private study and papers. I will figure out a way to look at them. Marlingham isn't that far from here. Less than an hour by train."

"If you find anything helpful," Maria asked, "what will you do once you have it?"

"I don't know yet," Olga admitted. "But if I obtain a posting, I can try to learn more. It's our *mother*." Her fingers balled into fists as she drew one hand to her chest. "She *never* helped the Germans. I can't stand back and leave this insult unanswered."

"So you want to spy on this gentleman? Like you're Mata Hari?" Tatiana arched her delicate eyebrows. "Don't these English country squires employ their tenants' girls as maids? What chance will you have at being hired in the first place?"

"The war caused a scarcity in domestic staffing. Look." Olga leaned over and pointed to the other adverts. "All for work in offices. Mostly in London."

"But he will recognize you."

"With a bonnet on my head? In a drab skirt and shirtwaist? How many of our housemaids do you recall?"

"Maybe you can fool others, but the article said that Lord Hammond was a diplomat in Russia. He will know you at once."

"Not necessarily." Maria stared at the flames hissing and popping in the fireplace.

"How so?" Tatiana asked.

"She can change how Olga looks," Ana said. "M knows her onions on that stuff."

"Her *onions*?"

Anastasia's forehead creased. "M is clever with cosmetics. The two of you would realize that if you paid more attention."

"Come." Maria stood and patted the cushioned footstool. As Olga took a seat and faced her sister, she caught the scent of Maria's favorite lilac fragrance. It was a small luxury, like the kimono, that her sister had managed to smuggle out of Ekaterinburg in a rucksack on the night of their escape.

Maria bent over, took a lock of Olga's honey-blonde hair, and ran it between her fingers.

"This will be easier since you keep your hair short now," she said. "We can order a bottle of L'Oréal and dye it brunette."

"What about black?" Ana piped up. "Like Theda Bara."

"Theda Bara has a cool skin tone. Olga's skin is warm." Maria studied her like she was an artist staring at a fresh canvas. "We can use powder to contour your cheekbones and nose. That will alter their shape a bit."

"You want to paint her face?" Tatiana asked.

"So what? All women paint their faces now," Ana said. "If this works, then all of us can leave the house and no one will know who we are."

"What better place to hide than in plain sight?" Olga said.

"The last time one of us separated from the others, we all decided who should go," Tatiana pointed out.

She was right. Before their final relocation to Ekaterinburg, Alexei had been too sick to travel. But their captors refused to delay moving their parents. Finally, the four of them talked it out and agreed that Maria should accompany Mama and Papa while the rest stayed behind with Alexei until he was well enough to travel again.

Now, Olga cast an anxious glance at Maria, who held her head high, seemingly confident they could persuade Tatiana to change her mind.

"I understand," Olga said. "We must all agree."

"I think it's grand," Ana declared. "I say she goes."

"If we can stop this gentleman from ruining Mama's reputation, we must try," Maria added gently. "Olga should go."

"Three against one!" Ana cried.

"We *all* have to agree." Olga gathered her hands on her lap and gazed at Tatiana.

"Perhaps I should go instead," Tatiana said. "I'm organized, respectful ..."

Olga's shoulders tensed. This was *her* idea. For the first time in years, she might take control of her destiny. Tatiana couldn't take it away. But once again, Tatiana acted as though she, not Olga, was eldest.

As Tatiana went on and on, enumerating her fine qualities, Olga began to see why families couldn't remain intact forever, and why siblings parted ways to forge their own lives. In a different world, they would have been long married and raising their own families.

"... during the war, I ran a committee to raise money for soldiers. I get along with people."

"You don't get on with people," Ana said. "You keep your feelings too close to the chest. Olga is a better listener. Besides, whoever goes will need to constantly lie. Her entire time in the house will be one big lie. You can't handle that. You can't lie."

Tatiana's gaze settled on the brass hood above the hearth. Olga should have been offended by Ana's implication that *she* could lie well enough. But, desperate for Tatiana to agree, she remained silent.

"I guess if you both think it should be Olga, I shouldn't stand in the way." Withdrawing her needle from the stuffed pincushion, Tatiana returned to work on the stockings before addressing Olga directly. "But if you start feeling melancholic. Not yourself. As you did in Ekaterinburg ..."

Tatiana missed a stitch and jabbed her finger with the needle. Then, wincing, she shook her hand and tossed the work aside.

"If you feel that way, you must tell us at once. We'll figure out something else. Together. As we've always done."

Olga's lip quivered. Her sister only wanted to take her place because she was worried about her. Tatiana loved her beyond measure. She should never doubt it.

"I'm fine," Olga assured her. "I swear it. You all took care of me in Ekaterinburg. Now let me take care of the rest of you. It's my responsibility."

Tatiana moved closer and pulled Olga into a tight hug, her shoulders heaving. Tatiana never cried. This was the closest she ever came to it.

"Care for yourself as well. If anything were to happen to you, I couldn't bear the loss."

Olga cupped her sister's chin in her hand, so they were looking straight at one another.

"Nothing bad will happen to me," she told Tatiana. "I'm going to ensure no one ever hurts our family again."

After Petrograd fell to revolution, the Provisional Government took power. Reasonable men, they placed our family under house arrest but allowed us to remain in the Alexander Palace, tantalizingly close to the Finnish border.

The coming peril wasn't yet apparent. And so, we remained in Russia.

In captivity, our parents never complained. Or if they did, they were careful not to do so around their children. That is how we thought of ourselves—no longer young women with ambitions and romantic dreams, but children once more.

That winter, after being moved to Siberia, our conditions worsened. Still, we kept our heads and spirits high. Although ice cold and cramped, at least the guards in the house there treated us with kindness.

While a prisoner, Papa retained his practice of rising early and keeping a strict schedule for meals, tea, and exercise. He chopped wood and helped in the garden. He spoke up to the guards, so they would grant us time outside, decent food, and the materials Anastasia and Alexei required to continue their studies.

Papa expected us to keep a schedule as well. We cleaned in the morning and exercised by walking in the garden after lunch. When the weather was fine, Papa showed us how to split wood with axes so we would have a good supply of logs ready for winter. He encouraged us to look through books and plays, assigning parts and rehearsing to present theatricals later in the evening.

Every so often, I'd catch our guards' muffled laughter at one of Anastasia's antics. And then I dared to hope that the men who rose to power in our country were but human beings after all.

The Private Diary of Olga Romanova
December 1921

CHAPTER FOUR

Wind rustled twisted branches on the elm trees and jingled distant chimes. Clouds, fine as spun sugar, crossed the gray sky. Boxed primroses lined the pathway in shades of pale yellow, creamy ivory, and dusky purple which added color to the otherwise gloomy day.

Olga's leather boots made scratching noises against the damp gravel trail alongside the roadway. She was outside, away from the cottage, on her own at last. It was exhilarating.

And terrifying.

No. *Olga* was terrified. But Olga mustn't exist, not for the next hour or so. She had invented an English name. Olivia Bennett. *Olivia* was merely on her way to an interview for a position.

The night before, she'd calculated the precise time she needed to be at the rail station while setting aside money for a return ticket, reviewing her map, and summoning answers to questions she expected to be asked. Before she left the cottage, Olga had belted her sensible wool coat snugly over her skirt. And she remembered to glance in the mirror to check if any crumbs from the scone she'd gobbled down for breakfast had caught between her teeth.

At the sight of her reflection, she'd gasped.

She hadn't seen Grand Duchess Olga, with her blonde hair and the broad features that one of her mother's ladies-in-waiting once generously described as "pleasing." Instead, courtesy of L'Oréal, short brunette waves curled fashionably around her ears and under a rose-pink cloche. Maria had supervised while Olga applied powder to make her cheeks appear narrower. She darkened her brows to match her new hair. If hired, she would need to recreate this look on her own every day.

She'd turned slowly to one side and then the other, examining her face in profile and in full. She would never be as beautiful as Tatiana or Maria, but appeared well enough.

More importantly, she looked different.

Except for her eyes. She could never change her radiant blue eyes. Her father's eyes.

The trail forked, the winding path to the right temptingly empty. That led ... she didn't know where it led. That's what made it tempting.

But she continued on the main trail, gravel soon replaced by a paved driveway bordered by heather and shrubs and an expanse of grass, vividly green even in winter. As the morning drizzle tapered and the sun played hide and seek between clouds, she caught glimpses of balconies with parapets, glazed windows with iron bars, and a worn Union Jack hanging limp from a central tower.

Marlingham loomed ahead.

Olga and her sisters had once explored the grandest buildings in St. Petersburg, Moscow, and Livadia. Unlike those colorful palaces and churches, the two-storied, gray stone edifice before her looked somber and stolid in the manner of the English. Corinthian columns graced the front entrance. On the corners connecting the house's wings, slender turrets capped with round domes curved to pointed tops, like the fur hats worn by medieval Russian nobility. Otherwise, the manor held no promise of playfulness, only functionality.

For many a prospective maid, it might have seemed imposing, but the place seemed modest compared to the homes Olga once knew.

Perhaps Lord Hammond himself lurked behind one of the windows. For all she knew, he had been staring down at her as she dodged puddles left from last night's rain.

And so she shuddered as she proceeded down the driveway toward the manor. Olga closed her eyes, took a deep breath, and then exhaled slowly through her mouth. She shouldn't put aside Olga Romanova altogether. A grand duchess, accustomed to the most opulent palaces in the world, would never feel intimidated by the country abode of a simple English lord.

A yelp broke through the quiet. An animal. Not just any animal. A puppy.

Olga opened her eyes. A little fellow waddled out from among the flowering winter heather, panting and whipping his undocked tail back and forth, the enthusiasm at odds with his sad spaniel eyes. When she bent down to pet him, the puppy jumped up and lapped her fingers. His ears flopped to each side, too big for the rest of his body, as were his furry paws. She guessed he was three or four months old.

As Olga stroked the pup's soft fur, she thought about Alexei's cocker spaniel, Joy, a fluffy poppet, all ears and eager-to-please eyes. His coloring had been similar, chestnut and white, with brownish freckles spotting his face. Joy and Alexei liked to romp about the gardens between trees and flower beds. How old would Joy be now? Eight? Nine? Why couldn't she remember?

This puppy rolled over, offering a fat tummy for rubbing. Olga crouched to comply, and then the memories came rushing back. Like Alexei's bleeding disease, they lay dormant for months and then sprang to life at the slightest provocation.

Joy was an odd name for a male dog, but apt. He had been a friend to all, even Olga's shy cat, Vaska, but devoted to Alexei. Joy cared for his frail human companion, never bumping or bruising him.

Vaska passed away before the Revolution and was given a proper Romanov burial at their family's pet cemetery. Loyal Joy, on the other hand, accompanied the family in exile, never leaving Alexei's side. He had been there when Olga said goodbye to her brother for the last time.

No, no. Not now. The spaniel pup whined and cocked his head. Olga's stomach cramped, and she put her face in her hands. Though disguised, she was a grand duchess. She must not cry. If she started to cry, she might never stop crying. Finally, she would give up and take to bed, as she had in Ekaterinburg during those last horrible months of imprisonment.

The puppy licked her hands.

"Conall seems taken with you. Did you sneak him a dog biscuit?"

The voice was gorgeous, a rolling baritone distinguished by the effortlessly posh accent of the British upper class. The sort of voice Olga should expect to hear at Marlingham.

"I'll have you know he's tubby enough as it is," the gentleman continued, "for a fellow meant to retrieve dead pheasants soon enough. At least my father would have him do as much. I haven't the heart to take up a shotgun these days."

Olga remembered the dead pheasants, gamecocks, and, worst of all, deer, with lolling heads and vacant eyes, stacked in front of her father's hunting lodge in Spala. It was macabre, for the men always shot far more game than anyone could eat. So she was glad this gentleman, whoever he was, didn't enjoy killing animals.

Still crouched, she fumbled in her pocket for a handkerchief and dabbed her cheeks, hoping she hadn't ruined her make-up. Olga wiped her eyes. Thankfully, she hadn't used the cake mascara Maria recommended. Her face would have been a mess of wet black streaks.

The gentleman came full circle and stood in front of her, long legs in black trousers, Conall at his heels. He extended a large hand encased in a thick leather driving glove. More of a gauntlet, really, as it covered his entire forearm. The puppy gazed up adoringly, tail swinging.

"Thank you."

She slipped her handkerchief discreetly into a coat pocket and accepted his hand. His grip was firm. Olga righted herself, squaring her boots on the pavement before standing.

"Are you all right?"

This gentleman was tall and broad across the shoulders, almost excessively so. He wore no hat and had pushed a pair of driving goggles back on his head. His wavy black hair matched his long duster coat. A slate gray scarf was tucked around his neck. His features were somewhat irregular but set against a clear complexion, high cheekbones, and a nose her mother might once have described as having *character*.

He should not have been handsome. And yet he was.

Beyond the quick purchase of tickets at the cinema with Ana, and then at the train station this morning, Olga hadn't spoken to a stranger in over a year. Her gaze drifted to her feet, the pointy tips of her boots now stained with mud.

This reticence wouldn't do. Trying not to be too obvious about it, Olga drew another calming breath, subtly puckering her lips to exhale slowly through the mouth. She summoned the new brusque accent

Ana had helped her practice. It was how they imagined an English maid might sound.

"It's just that your pup reminds me of one our family had once," she said. "So this was like seeing an old friend."

"Ah! I understand." He remained jolly, so her accent must have passed muster; an Englishman would surely ask about any detected foreignness. "In my view, dogs are quite superior to humans, but then that might have more to do with my poor company than my fellow man."

When a gust of wind blew back his hair, she caught sight of a pale purple scar across his forehead, the length of a child's pinkie finger. He hunched over, trying to hide the blemish. Or perhaps he was only trying to make himself less imposing.

Either way, it didn't work, though his voice still brimmed with a happy swagger.

"What brings you to Marlingham?"

"I responded to an advert for a maid."

"Ah! And might I ask you, Miss ...?"

"Olivia Bennett."

There. Olga had said the name aloud and attached herself to it. She nodded in what she hoped was a no-nonsense manner.

He grinned when she said her name. Perhaps he hadn't expected her to share it so quickly. Maybe she should not have done.

"You worked as a housemaid before, Miss Bennett?"

"Do I seem like someone with little experience?"

"No. No. It's just ..." He shook his head awkwardly, dark waves flopping against the goggles. It had been a long time since Olga had read *Wuthering Heights*, but he reminded her of Heathcliff. Heathcliff with a posher accent. Heathcliff as an upper-class chauffeur.

The sun disappeared behind the clouds, and the sharp wind seeped through Olga's coat. Conall whined and pawed the ground. The gentleman bent down to pet him.

"It's only that I'm accustomed to seeing those applying for service postings come in through the back entrance. Nonsense, really. Shouldn't have mentioned it."

Olga clasped her hands, poised as warmth rushed to her cheeks. What a stupid mistake. Of course she should go to the back door. It was probably on an entirely different route. For all that she'd prepped her face, hair, clothes, and voice, she hadn't considered that detail. Too much of her remained Grand Duchess Olga, strutting about as though she were doing this family the honor of a visit over tea.

"I suppose I got off track." Then, to change the subject, she gestured to the spaniel rolling contentedly at the gentleman's feet. "Conall, was it? Charming, but what an unusual name. More for an Irish Wolfhound, I'd say."

"No stranger a name than Olivia. Unless you're a character in *Twelfth Night*. And if you were *that* Olivia, shouldn't you be in hiding? Seven years she kept apart from the world."

Seven years. Olga had scarcely lasted one year apart from the world. She tilted her head at a saucy angle, glad that Papa had seen fit to read and perform from the works of Shakespeare. "Do you believe I 'abjured the sight and company of men,' sir?"

His eyes lingered longer than they should have. "It seems you have not. And I wonder if you'd be better suited as a governess than a maid."

"Is one needed? Or is it just that you harbor fond memories of your governesses?"

"We do not need a governess at present," he said, straightening to his full height, dark crimson flecking his high cheekbones. "Though one never knows, I suppose. In the meantime, might I accompany you to the main house? I'm not much of a conversationalist, but Conall's good company."

A faint tingle ran across the back of her neck as she recalled the pleasure she'd once taken in harmless flirtations. Olivia Bennett should decline such a bold offer, but Olga Romanova missed spending time with tall gentlemen who blushed easily, despite their swagger.

"That's most kind. Might I ask how you arrived at the name Conall for your spaniel?"

A crease lined his forehead, odd on his otherwise youthful face. The scar had darkened. Olga noted its jagged lines.

He caught her looking and unfastened the strap from the goggles so that his hair hid the blemish.

"One of the m-men named him." The gentleman's hands dropped to his sides. "He served in my unit ... during the war. A local fellow in my section, but originally from C-County Cork."

He pressed his lips together. He'd served in the war. That probably explained the difficulty with his speech.

"He said he'd wanted a d-dog and planned to get one and n-name him Conall," the young man continued. "Once we were home. It means 'victorious,' or so he said."

Despite his best efforts, the gentleman trembled. As she had trembled when memories of Joy flooded back.

Olga wanted to take his hands and try to loosen those tense fingers. Now she was neither Olivia Bennett nor a grand duchess. She was merely Olga Nikolaevna Romanova, who once donned a habit to serve as a nurse during the war.

Her next words, though necessary, sounded hollow. "I'm sorry."

He shook his head again. Just once.

"You haven't told me your name. Are you the chauffeur? I quite like the goggles."

At first, she thought he hadn't heard. But his mouth was moving, though no sound issued forth.

Conall whimpered and flopped on the ground, placing his chin on the man's shoe.

The gentleman tried again, his lips contorting from the effort.

"P-please call me Rob ... if ... if ... y-you wish."

Rob pressed his lips together again as though somehow that might will the words to come. But he couldn't manage it this time and lowered his gaze.

"It is lovely to meet you, Rob."

Conall looked up at Olga, thumping his tail approvingly.

She might have ignored his stammer and not risked embarrassing him further. Long ago, that was precisely what her mother would have commanded her to do. But Rob may have been discharged well before the true extent of his shell shock was diagnosed. He might go months on end with no trouble at all, and then some small reminder of the war, such as she had unwittingly provided, triggered the terror. She'd risk wounding his ego if it meant giving him some degree of comfort.

"I've met other soldiers with your affliction," Olga said.

Rob remained still but stared at her with such intensity she bent down, wishing she had pulled the brim of her hat lower. She scratched Conall's floppy ears. *Please don't recognize my face, Rob.*

"You were a n-nurse? During the war, I mean?"

Soldiers who returned from the front with shell shock were treated abominably. Not that anyone knew what to call it then. They saw only bloodshot eyes and the gaunt faces of once robust young men, night-mares and terrified expressions viewed as cowardice. Some doctors and nurses refused to treat them.

Despicable. Those men suffered wounds as grave as any bodily damage, perhaps more so because it settled in their minds. Whenever she had the chance, Olga sat beside their camp beds in the hospital, reading aloud or helping them walk to the recreational room where she would play their favorite songs on the piano.

"I did, sir," she told him, struggling to maintain the accent. Her thoughts now formed in Russian, and she had to concentrate to articulate them in English.

"W-where?"

The question she'd feared. Ana may have supposed Olga could lie well enough, but manipulating the truth to secure an interview was one thing. This was a personal conversation with a vulnerable young man.

"They sent me to the Eastern Front. I don't like to talk about it."

"No, of course not." He struggled to get the next word to catch and held his hands up before him as though surrendering. "How I do run on."

"I only meant I understand what it's like to see terrible things. All our nerves shattered. For some, it just takes longer to put the pieces back together. No shame in that."

"You said that you encountered soldiers with im-impediments to their speech?"

"It was not uncommon."

His voice grew stronger, nearly fully restored. "I'm sure you saw too much during the war. Afterward, as well, I'd wager. When the new influenza strain hit. Is that why you wish to work as a maid now? To take a break from nursing?"

During their first months in England, Olga and her sisters had read about the pandemic in the papers—the churches, schools, cinemas, and shops forced to shutter their doors, and the shocking death toll. When their deliveries arrived, they heard only an abrupt knock before the courier scuttled away, as keen to be away from other people and the risk of contagion as they were grateful not to be seen.

Olga had felt helpless. Her Red Cross training could be useful, and there she was roaming about the cottage when duty called her to help the sick. She had almost—almost—broken their quarantine to volunteer at the hospital in Nottingham, but Tatiana talked her out of it.

Looking back, she wondered if her sister had worried about Olga's fragile nerves as much as she feared discovery. Not to mention the risk of bringing the deadly infection back to their cottage.

A light tap on her arm broke her reverie. Olga looked up to find Rob staring at her, brows pinched. He dropped his hand.

"It seemed you were thinking of something you didn't want to remember. I shouldn't have taken the liberty."

Olga's eyes still felt glazed, but his touch returned her to the present.

"Going forward, a position as a maid seems the better choice," she said

"Nothing more pressing than spilled red wine on a white rug and all that?"

"Something along those lines." She glanced at the tiny gold wristwatch Maria had lent her. Thankfully, the minute hand was still twenty away from the hour. Olga had given herself plenty of time and had made it to the house well before her scheduled interview.

"Anyway, I should move along to find the back entrance," she said. "It was kind of you to offer to escort me, but I should let you tend to your motor."

"Already tucked away and covered in the garage."

"You *are* the chauffeur for this family?" His accent seemed overly polished for staff, but the English were strange folk. "I suppose there's no harm in it then."

Rob made a clicking sound, and Conall came to heel as they started toward the main house.

"What is the family like?" Olga said, keeping pace with him.

The bluster returned to Rob's voice, though with a dull note. "I suppose you shall find the Pikes pleasant enough."

"The lady of the house is a kind woman, then?"

"I should say so. We live under the same roof and have done since I was a child."

"Wait." Olga stopped. "You're *not* the chauffeur?"

"One of the family, I'm afraid. However, no one refers to me as the Viscount Marling these days. Not even my father. I can't say I blame them. It's only a courtesy title. All that is rubbish, if you ask me. Rob suits well enough."

Olga's smile crumpled. Rob—his lordship, the *viscount*—didn't seem to notice. He just headed toward the manor, snapping his fingers when Conall strayed too far.

Olga continued to walk with him, slower now, remembering her lessons on the British peerage. Once she'd reached a marriageable age, they'd been drilled into her, along with those for all the aristocratic hierarchies in Europe and Asia. Though a grand duchess was meant to make a royal match, it was assumed she and her sisters would travel widely. They mustn't risk an offensive mistake in a foreign court.

So she understood the English used the title of viscount as an honorific for the eldest son of an earl.

The eldest son of Lord Hammond.

An icy shiver ran lengthwise from the tip of her head to the base of her spine. She should not have spoken with him nor accepted his offer to escort her. She should have guessed Rob was Lord Hammond's son, not the *chauffeur*, for land's sake. Who else did she suppose would stomp about the grounds with a dog?

How foolish it had been to flirt with him. And more ridiculous still to engage him in a deeper conversation, no matter how kind his eyes or how troubled his soul.

"I shan't disturb you further. Conall is lovely company, but I've taken too much of your time." She was babbling and avoiding his eyes, the fine art of flirtation abandoned. "I can manage the rest of the way."

"Oh." She detected disappointment in his voice. "Well, then ... I didn't put you off? I shouldn't have mentioned the title. It's all such nonsense, really."

"It's only that some quiet might do me good. Calm the nerves and all that."

She was walking faster now, putting space between them.

"Well, the path to the back door is just right there. Won't take you long."

That entrance was meant for servants, tradespeople, and traveling peddlers. Her place was among them now.

She gave him a little curtsy, Olivia Bennett once more. She would put this encounter out of her mind. Neither Olivia nor Olga could afford the distraction. She was here to clear her mother's reputation, which was all Olga had left of her.

Once she found the side path leading around the house to the back, she gave in to the urge to glance over her shoulder. Rob, Robert Pike, the *viscount* remained in front of the house, goggles in hand, Conall panting at his side.

And Lord Hammond's heir was still looking at her.

During the winter in Siberia, I grew to understand that my sisters and I came from a place of great privilege. Before the war, we took trips of mercy to villages, distributing food to peasants who had suffered from a poor harvest. What shelter they managed was overcrowded, small, and insufficiently insulated from the bitter cold. Our duty was to help make their lives more tolerable.

And yet I was never made aware of the plight of those in the industrialized cities and towns. Across the empire, people crowded into squalid tenements. We were never permitted to meet them.

Nor did I know how many people had a family member or close friend sent to prisons and work camps in Siberia. Sometimes for breaking the law to feed their family. Sometimes for their political sentiments. It was all the same for the tsarist police. Those who spoke against the tsar were considered criminals, the same as thieves and murderers.

I wish we'd known our people better. We might have directed our sense of duty to a finer purpose. Russia did not have to descend into the chaos of a revolution and the terror born from the Civil War. Sustaining the autocratic rule of his ancestors was Papa's fatal mistake. Our family should have enacted change. And then maybe the Bolsheviks wouldn't hunt us, for they might never have risen to power at all.

The Private Diary of Olga Romanova
December 1921

CHAPTER FIVE

A t the back entrance to Marlingham, a ginger-haired footman ushered her inside. He looked not long out of short pants, and acne speckled his chin. After a curt "good morning, miss," he offered to take her coat. Olga unbelted and wriggled out of the garment while he waited, white-gloved hand politely extended but wobbly. The boy was probably a new hire.

He hung her coat on a rack by the door and beckoned for her to follow him past the kitchen. Pans clattered and she caught the scent of frying eggs, potatoes, and mushrooms.

Olga supposed she should say something pleasant, but her disordered mind couldn't find the words. The footman directed her to a stairwell. Once they ascended, he turned to the left, leading her into the brightness of the main house.

Though they moved quickly, Olga tried to take in the gilt-framed portraits of the family's ancestors. She slowed to note the pointed beard of a stern Earl of Hammond from a century long past. The paneled walls soon gave way to pastel blue and yellow paper imprinted with curling leaves and flowers: the sort her mother might have favored for her boudoir. Only Mama would have ordered it in her favorite color, mauve.

At last, he stopped before a plain white door and rapped his knuckles on it before ushering Olga inside the sitting room. A sash window provided a view of winter cherry trees with pale pink blooms. Small animals fashioned of glass and other bric-à-brac crowded shelves on a walnut étagère. Two armchairs, cushions richly embroidered with whimsical berries and leaves, were positioned to face one another. An end table stood between them, as when she'd moved chairs for a game of backgammon or chess with Papa. But no board game was laid out, only clematis flowers wilting in a crystal vase.

The footman gestured to a chair, indicating she might sit until the lady of the house arrived. Olga would have liked to take a closer look at the glass hummingbirds and cunning little squirrels on the étagère. Instead, she chose the chair with its back to the window. The footman exited, leaving the door ajar.

With no fire lit, the room was colder than she'd expected. Olga remembered the harsh Siberian winter. Her family had bundled in overcoats and layers of stockings and mittens. The temperature never rose above freezing, even inside. If she ever regained a position of privilege, she would ensure every room of any house under her care kept a toasty fire roaring throughout the winter months.

Olga tucked her feet together and to the side. Then she noticed that someone had tied the flowers on the table with a black ribbon. That struck her as odd. She looked around again. Scraps of black crepe paper were affixed here and there on the otherwise bare walls.

The English used that type of paper when someone passed on to the next world. Mama had told her about it. Her mother's own family followed that tradition when Mama's mother—forever Queen Victoria's daughter, despite marriage to a German prince—passed away. They'd fashioned a wreath of black crepe to hang on the front door and pasted crinkly streamers of the stuff to hide the mirrors and windows.

So someone in this household had died. Judging from the bare remains of the black paper, perhaps within the past year. Olga shivered and re-crossed her ankles. Faced with familial grief, her presence felt intrusive.

From the hallway, a clack of heels on hard flooring approached. "Hello!" a feminine voice called.

Olga—*Olivia*, rather, for she must think of herself as that woman, even in the privacy of her mind—tried to remember everything she'd practiced to prepare for the interview. *I'm just a simple country girl at heart, ma'am. This position will suit if you'll have me.*

The footman reappeared, holding the door open for the lady of the house.

"Sorry to keep you waiting. It's been a dreadfully tiresome day and still another hour 'til noon." She sighed. "And I apologize. I forgot to have the fire lit."

As the lady entered the sitting room, Olga scrambled to her feet, prepared to curtsy. When they came face to face, however, she stumbled instead.

She'd been expecting Lady Hammond, a countess who would exude the stout and empty authority of a minor gentlewoman in mid-life. Instead, this woman looked to be about Olga's age. She had the same deep-set brown eyes and pale complexion as Rob. The *viscount*, rather. Olga suspected they were siblings.

This young woman wore a black satin day dress, elegantly tailored. Her long black hair was held back with sparkling pins, though the effort was haphazard. Tufts sprung out from about her ears and the crown of her head. She must have caught the trajectory of Olga's gaze because she touched her hair. "It's a fright, I know."

Olga bit her lip, stunned at her own rudeness. "It is only that the gemstones in the clips are so pretty. I didn't mean to stare, my lady. Forgive me."

"My lady! Please. I'm Celia and would be glad for you to address me as such." She extended her hand. "Unless you're uncomfortable with that."

The English certainly had embraced the modern world. Olga shook the lady's hand. "No, ma'am." She pronounced it "mum," as Ana had suggested.

"You were probably expecting my mother." Sadness shadowed Lady Celia's pretty face. "She passed away last winter. Influenza."

Mama's death must have been horrifying. A bullet in the brain, as Olga imagined it. But mercifully quick. In contrast, influenza brought a cruel death said to be akin to slow strangulation. Olga stepped back, trying not to shiver. "I am sorry."

"I daresay I wouldn't wish such a fate on anyone." Celia rolled her shoulders and gestured to the chairs. "But let's get on with this, shall we?"

Olga sat once more, spine perfectly aligned with the back of the chair. All those posture lessons, including boards strapped against her spine when she was a little girl, ensured she always carried herself like a grand duchess.

Lady Celia drew in a breath and looked to the ceiling as though trying to remember the opening lines in a stage play. "Might you tell me about yourself? What brings you here? What do you find appealing about this position?"

"During the war, I was a nurse, as I mentioned in my letter." Olga simply hadn't specified *where* she was a nurse. "The work affected me. So many souls in pain."

She remembered the effort Rob had put into each syllable when he tried to speak of the war, the agony he endured no doubt magnified by his mother's recent death.

Celia's gaze briefly moved to the glass animals on the shelves. "I served as a nurse as well. I understand. Though it surprises me you should not apply for secretarial work or such."

"I'm a country girl at heart." The answer came at once because it was the truth. "I've no desire to be trapped in a city office by day and then confined to a small flat alone at night."

"Could you not live with other young women in one of the new boarding houses?"

"That is fine for some, but an office environment wouldn't suit me. I would rather accept a position chopping wood. Then I'd spend my days out in the fresh air. I've recently turned twenty-four and know what I want."

"Twenty-four." Celia sat ramrod straight. Olga imagined they had been raised similarly. She wondered if a stern governess had subjected Celia to wooden boards to improve her posture. "I'll turn twenty-five next month. We're the same age. I must say I love that!"

Olga smiled. "As do I, Lady ... Celia."

"I'm so new at all this. My mother used to take care of everything related to the household. The housekeeper would normally conduct staff interviews, but I need practice. I've read your application letter and suppose I should now ask about your experience?"

She leaned forward expectantly. From the glowing freshness of Celia's expression, she might be play-acting. They were both doing the best they could in unfamiliar roles.

"I do have experience keeping house for my family." Olga thought it best not to mention her family consisted only of her sisters, in case something about her face suddenly seemed familiar. Celia could start putting two and two together and add it up to four missing grand duchesses. "I cannot claim training in a fine household, but I shall be eager to improve."

Celia sat taller in her chair. "I wonder, though, if you might consider a change in the terms of your employment."

The air in the room, already cold, seemed to drop in temperature. Goosebumps crept up her arms. And then Olga spotted her mother's shadowy figure in the corner.

Appearing older now than when Olga last saw her in the cottage, her mother wore a high-collared gown in fashion a decade earlier. Her jowls were pronounced, and her hair faded and threaded with gray. Yet Mama's eyes remained the same: large, lovely, and tinged with sadness.

She was but a figment of Olga's imagination, no more real than the moving picture she and Ana had watched unfold on the screen. And yet those images in the cinema meant something. They formed a story with a message about love and loyalty.

"I'm curious," Olga said. If her mother refused to disappear, she would just have to ignore her. "Change of what sort?"

"When I posted the advert, I was looking for a housemaid. And I still am. We're terribly understaffed these days. However ..." Celia patted her hair. The slight touch loosened the pins. "... as you might have guessed, it seems I am now in dire need of a personal maid to help attend to my upkeep."

Mama's hands rested on the middle shelf of the étagère, near one of the animals, head tilted quizzically at a glass bear. A Russian bear. Before she could stop herself, Olga gasped.

"I didn't mean to startle you," Celia said. "It's not a significant change. I hope you will not consider it such."

"No, no." Olga had seen similar glass bears for sale in the winter markets in St. Petersburg, which they were sometimes allowed to visit, though always under heavy guard. Lord Hammond had been a diplomat, so the bear was likely a souvenir from his time in Russia. "Only I'd never considered such a role."

"It's selfish, but I rather miss the luxury."

In the time before, Olga's toilette had been a hasty affair and one she judged a complete waste of time. But she understood what Celia would expect. Personal maids dressed hair, assisted with creams and cosmetics, prepared the lady's outfit for the day, and then a formal ensemble for dinner. They washed delicate undergarments and cleaned expensive gloves and silk scarves.

Olga had always been polite with her maids, but never intimate. She'd had her sisters. Celia had no sisters, at least none were mentioned, and she had recently lost her mother. On top of that, she'd opened up to Olga readily in the brief span of this interview.

She was offering Olga a position of trust with greater access to the family—and, therefore, a better chance to learn why Celia's father was trying to brand Olga's mother as a traitor. A *lucky break* as Ana might say.

Out of the corner of her eye, Olga watched her mother fade and dissipate.

"We might give it a go," Celia continued. "If the position doesn't appeal, you could switch. Though I daresay the allotted salary is higher. Since I'm unmarried, I would not refer to you as a lady's maid, but I would compensate you as one."

Celia didn't need a maid. She needed a friend. That Olga could provide.

She met Celia's hopeful gaze. "I accept your terms, providing you will be patient with me while I hone the proper skills."

Lady Celia smiled warmly and rose to her feet.

"As far as I'm concerned, you can begin now."

Olga's heart soared. "I should like a few days to gather my things at home. Perhaps I could start Monday of next week?"

"Absolutely. I'll manage another few days without my hair done properly, though I suspect I'll catch the scullery maid giving me the once-over. And that won't injure anything but my pride."

Olga hesitated, hoping her next question wasn't overly presumptuous. "Is there anyone else in the household I should meet today?"

Lady Celia cocked her head, a gesture not unlike the one Olga's mother had once favored. "You will meet our housekeeper straightaway. I'll have her show you to your quarters. I'm afraid the room isn't terribly large."

"I'm sure it will do." Her question about meeting others *had* been presumptuous, for she was thinking of Lord Hammond.

"Did you run into my brother on your way in?" Celia moved closer to the window and gazed outside. Olga half-expected to see Rob throwing a soggy tennis ball for Conall to fetch. But there were only pale winter cherry blossoms ruffling in the breeze.

"He was kind enough to direct me to the back entrance for my interview," Olga said. "I'm afraid I mistook his lordship for the chauffeur. I pray he wasn't offended."

"I doubt that. He adores his Daimler. It's good to see Rob out about the grounds, though. He and our father have been rather estranged as of late."

Olga's ears perked up at that.

"The war changed them both. And then our mother ..." Celia paused and straightened her shoulders. "How I do run on!"

The exact phrase Rob used earlier. "It's all right, my lady ... Celia. I understand. No families are without their dramas."

"In the meantime, I'm pleased you'll join our household." Celia reached for a plated gold bell pull next to the window. Clearly, she wasn't familiar with its placement. She clutched at the air for a few seconds before grasping the lever to summon a servant from downstairs to the room.

"I don't know how my mother did it," Celia muttered.

Olga smiled to herself. Watching her mother manage the many Romanov palaces and countless servants, she'd often wondered the same.

Footsteps pattered in the hall, and a plump woman in a long black dress and matching apron appeared at the door. She wore no bonnet. Loose gray curls frizzed out of the sides of a hasty updo.

"Mrs. Acton, would you show Miss Bennett to her room downstairs? She shall move in presently as my new maid."

The housekeeper curtsied, and Olga turned to Celia again, unsure of the protocol. She guessed enthusiasm was always appropriate.

"Thank you, my lady. I look forward to seeing you next week."

Celia was still smiling. In a different world, they could have been friends who mourned the loss of their mothers together. But that was not the world Olga now faced.

She followed Mrs. Acton out the door. Since she'd arrived, fresh flowers filled the vases lining the hallway. It smelled heady and fragrant, like a winter garden.

The woman bustled quickly ahead, her gait more that of a harried kitchen maid than a housekeeper, but Olga could keep up well enough.

"Welcome aboard and all that then," Mrs. Acton announced, her voice clear and loud as a sea captain's. "I'll be giving you the full tour soon. Past Lady Celia's morning room here, you find the library and his lordship's study." Mrs. Acton gestured to two heavy doors in succession to their right, where the portraits of Lord Hammonds past still kept stern watch. Olga craned her head to take a better look as they passed, wanting badly to enter the study and wondering if she would encounter any more glass bears from St. Petersburg.

Petrograd, she reminded herself. Papa had changed the city's name during the war since St. Petersburg sounded too German.

For now, she merely noted the study's location, and remembered that Hammond would return to Marlingham at Parliament's winter recess, a mere two weeks away. That wouldn't give her much time to snoop around.

"And then his lordship has a billiard room." Mrs. Acton waved a doughy finger to the left. "That he can't be bothered to use these days."

"Is Lord Hammond here often?" Olga asked, hoping she sounded casual about it.

"His lordship's kept busy with politicking. Works like a dog, that one, and keeps to London, though he'll be home for Christmastide. And then working on a book at that. Now his lordship expects his son to live at the same pace."

As they flew by the main entrance and closer to the stairwell leading back down to the kitchen, Olga asked, "Were you close to Lady Celia's former maid?"

"Barely knew the woman." Mrs. Acton's tone was neither gentle nor harsh, nor did she slow her step. Keys rattled against one another on a bronze hook hanging from her belt. "She moved on suddenly. Left the young lady spinning."

"Well, that's rude," Olga declared. Her servants had been honored to serve the imperial family and only retired to marry or for some other perfectly understandable reason. Or at least that is what Olga had been led to understand.

She supposed the woman who served before her might have found employment in one of London's offices. It seemed many servants had, for she'd seen far fewer staff members than she'd expected.

"Not so rude, if you ask me. She left because she thought Lady Celia made some right foolish choices. Indulging selfish whims and rot everyone else."

Olga raised her eyebrows, subconsciously imitating her mother.

"I'm just saying to be friendly, but don't get too involved in their affairs." Mrs. Acton hitched her skirt before descending the stairs. "You never know what that lot will do. And then one of us is turned out on the arse."

"I intend to focus on my work."

Mrs. Acton snorted. "That's what you say now. Wait until she chats with you and spills all her secrets."

Olga wished the staircase had a railing. She held her hands out to balance herself as they made their way downstairs, where a single electric light burned dully from its fixture on the ceiling.

"For all she is a fine lady, that girl upstairs is lonely," Mrs. Acton continued. "You might get to feeling sorry for her and think you're only helping her out of a bad spot or what have you, and *bam*! When it blows up, you'll hold the load. Though I suppose that lot has got to be careful with their airs these days. They don't have the pick of the land for servants no more, and then who will care for their grand houses? For that matter, who will care for them?"

Mrs. Acton likely meant to help, but Olga felt confident she could manage Celia and only nodded vaguely. Which didn't stop the woman's tirade.

"Can't find their trousers or skirts without a valet or maid. Look at what happened in Russia when the aristos got too uppity. Doing as they please while the rest suffer. And the German woman in charge let that demon run the show."

Olga stopped short, suddenly woozy and sure her face looked white as fresh snow.

The German woman. Her mother. And Rasputin was the demon. Everyone knew it.

Everyone except for the members of her own family.

Mrs. Acton rattled on. "Well, I say that lot can do with a little shaking up now and then. That's why I'm for the Labour Party. But I suppose his lordship doesn't have much use for other aristos, seeing as how he wants to negotiate with them Bolsheviks. That's how I heard him tell it over supper when he was here last. And he knows that land better than ... are you all right, miss?"

While the housekeeper had made it to the foot of the staircase, Olga could no longer move. But she managed a weak smile. "I didn't eat enough at breakfast."

"Take your lunch here if it pleases! We've got plenty."

"It's all right. I've planned to take lunch at home with my family. I want to share the good news as soon as possible."

"Take a few biscuits to keep you upright to the station, will you?"

"I'll do that." Though flustered, Olga filed the comments about "negotiations" with the Bolsheviks away in her mind, sure it could be of use later.

At last, she made it to the foot of the stairs and followed Mrs. Acton into the dark, narrow galley kitchen. An assortment of copper pots and cookware lined the shelves and hung on hooks from the walls.

"That's our cook." Mrs. Acton nodded at a tall, middle-aged woman with a lovely tawny complexion who was stirring a peppery-scented bean soup in an iron kettle on the stovetop. "Mrs. Dasari! This is Miss Olivia Bennett. Going to help Lady Celia, she is."

Mrs. Dasari gave Olga a friendly wave before returning to the soup.

"And this is for you." Mrs. Acton unhooked a key from her ring and unlatched a door in an alcove.

Olga expected to find rows of bunk beds. Instead, this room was just for her, with a tidy little camp bed. There was no window, but she spotted a brass candleholder on the nightstand.

"Nice and toasty!" Mrs. Acton commented. And then, showing Olga the thin mattress: "Not the coziest thing, but no bugs ... we checked!"

Olga ran her finger along a dusty oak desk in the corner, just large enough to squeeze in a chair. She'd abandoned her notebooks in Ekaterinburg, tucked deep under old blankets, thinking she might retrieve them one day. She supposed the Bolsheviks had done the dirty work of going through the diaries, scanning greedily for state secrets, and then, finding none such, burning them.

The desk might inspire her to start a new diary. She could ask for a lantern. And though humble, Olga liked the feel of the room, snug and close enough to the stove in the kitchen for her to stay warm even on the coldest nights. Not to mention that she would have the space all to herself. Before, she'd always shared with Tatiana and had expected to do so until one of them married.

At one time, the prospect of sleeping in a room alone would have scared her. Now, Olga looked forward to it. She could write without fear of one of her sisters peering over her shoulder. It felt like a good place to start anew. Olga was here to vindicate her mother's reputation. But, at night, she could escape into this room and forget the Bolsheviks for a little while.

"What do you think?" Mrs. Acton asked, grinning.

"I think I shall be happy here."

To her astonishment, Olga meant it.

When they moved my family to our final prison, the Ipatiev House in Ekaterinburg, the Bolsheviks proved they would stop at nothing to destroy us. Since I have already recorded the miseries we endured in that place, I shall not repeat them here. Suffice it to say, I came to fear the Bolsheviks as though they'd been sent directly from hell.

At first, I fought despair. I tried to rouse memories from the time before, memories that wouldn't sting. As the eldest daughters, Tatiana and I were afforded special privileges. We had our honorary regiments and trained as expert horsewomen so that we could review our troops properly. And in those days, neither of us ever tired of the soldiers' adoring gazes.

Papa was so strong when he addressed his men. I'd the honor of remaining at his side on many such occasions. With soldiers, Papa spoke in shorter sentences and clipped his words. It was meant to inspire confidence, and it worked, inspiring men as they marched off to war.

Now that the monarchy has collapsed, it is often said that Papa was a meek man. This wasn't true. He would have made an exemplary constitutional monarch had he only been given that chance. If he had only allowed more reforms to pass before our country reached the brink of destruction.

Although he was good with his soldiers, I wish Papa had never left Petrograd during the war. I try not to resent him for it. But for all his failings, if he had remained, the situation in the city might never have spiraled out of control. Our fates would not have fallen to outsiders with far more to consider than our well-being. For the English government, though sympathetic to our circumstances, had to calculate how their countrymen would receive us.

The Private Diary of Olga Romanova
December 1921

CHAPTER SIX

"When Lady Celia asked me to serve as her maid, of course, I said yes," Olga told her sisters. "But what if I make a complete mess of things? How much time should I plan to spend on her hair and clothes?"

"It depends." Maria stood next to Olga in front of the full-length mirror propped on satinwood legs with metal castors. Maria rolled it closer, bringing their reflections into sharper focus.

"I'm afraid she'll give me the sack when she sees what a poor job I make of it."

As she said the words, Olga couldn't quite picture Celia ordering anyone out for any reason. Loathe as she was to admit it, however, there was truth to Mrs. Acton's take on the "lot" upstairs. Domestic staff lived at their employers' whims. Regardless of Celia's kindness, Olga needed to hone her skills.

"I doubt Lady Celia will do any such thing," Maria reassured her. "Didn't you tell us she seemed lonely? That she might only want companionship? She doesn't sound like the sort to sack a new maid."

"Celia will still be upset if I make a rat's nest on her head."

"The lady may not require much at all. Do you remember how Mother handled her toilette?"

"She was too shy to let her ladies see her without a shift," Olga said, thinking about Mama modestly covering herself with her mauve dressing gown as the maids entered the room. "So she mostly made do without them. They helped with her corset and placed her jewels where she wanted."

"The maids didn't need to choose anything for her." Tatiana was reclining on a cinnamon-colored quilt embroidered with bright pink roses, hearts, and medallions. Wistfully, she added: "Mama understood exactly how she wished to present herself to the world."

"It sounds like your primary worry is Lady Celia's hair, so let's start with that." Maria pulled a chair in front of the mirror and took a seat. "A simple rolled bun for the day, if you please," she said primly. "No braids."

After surveying the metallic pins and silk ribbons on the end table, Olga played with a thick tendril of Maria's hair. She stole glances at her own reflection as well, still distracted by the bobbed curls, their color closer to Maria's lush brunette waves than Olga's natural blonde hue.

Olga grabbed a wooden-backed brush and ran the bushy black bristles through her sister's tresses. Maria grimaced.

"Ouch," Ana said. She had squeezed next to Tatiana on the bed, chin propped in her hand, re-reading an old copy of *Picture Play* with Gloria Swanson on the cover.

"Start with the ends and then work your way up." Maria rubbed the back of her head. "It's been a while since you wore your hair long, but remember how it tangled?"

"I'm sorry." Olga did as Maria instructed, slowly this time, taking great care with each stroke of the brush.

"And try to add volume around the face by parting and twisting it into a loose ponytail first," Maria added. "The lady will expect that."

"Twisting?"

"Around your hand and then with the hair bands." Maria hesitated. "You never did that?"

"Oh, bother all this." Tatiana rose from the bed. "Here, let me help."

Tatiana took the brush from Olga's hand, swiftly and efficiently working Maria's locks from bottom to top. She showed Olga how to gather them into a loose ponytail at the nape of the neck, and then focused on the task before her as closely as she had when rolling fresh bandages at the hospital during the war.

"Maybe you should have gone instead of me," Olga blurted. "You're so good at this."

"No. We all agreed," Tatiana said, handing the brush back. "You'll catch on soon. Besides, you're the one who wants to play Mata Hari—"

"That is *not* what I said."

"—and poke around someone else's home. I'm no use at any of that."

So Olga watched Tatiana until she felt confident enough to take over and create something resembling an acceptable bun. End pieces kept frizzing, and she reached for another pin, but Maria took her hand.

"Lady Celia will surely have pomade or gloss that will help. It's good enough. Well done."

"If only Papa could see us now!" Ana tossed the magazine aside. It landed upright on the floor, Gloria Swanson's smoky eyes staring dramatically at the ceiling. "He would take a puff on a cigarette and have a laugh. His grown-up daughter play-acting as a maid!"

"Papa might see some fun in all this, and Alexei would tease me mercilessly. Mama, on the other hand ..."

Olga, posing as a maid, would have horrified her. But then Olga remembered her mother's appearance in the morning room at Marlingham. Whether she was a figment of imagination or a spirit, nothing horrified their mother now.

"Mama would be dreadfully upset about the deception," Tatiana declared. "And petrified we're joking about Mata Hari."

"Mother wasn't always completely honest herself," Maria said.

Olga turned sharply while the mattress creaked under Ana's weight as she sat upright atop the quilt in rapt attention.

"What nonsense!" Tatiana said. "Mama was the purest soul." Her gray eyes narrowed. "*Is* the purest soul."

Maria removed the pins and shook her hair out before tying it away from her face with a pink ribbon. "I'm only saying Olga needn't feel guilty over the ruse. Given everything."

"And what do you mean by that?" Tatiana folded her arms over her chest.

"Mother always told us she supported the war with all her heart," Maria said, avoiding Tatiana's piercing gaze and focusing instead on Olga. "But when the troops mobilized, I overheard her talking to Papa. She begged him not to go to war because Father Grigori told her it would destroy the House of Romanov."

"What poppycock!" Tatiana said. "Mama may have wanted peace, but she understood what needed to happen once the war started."

"Father Grigori was right," Maria said. "The war ruined the House of Romanov."

Maria's voice echoed as Olga's thoughts drifted back to the time before the Revolution. To Petrograd during the war. When they no longer attended the ballet with Papa. When there were no more grand balls or diplomatic supper parties, but still the occasional Sunday afternoon gathering at their aunt's chic flat.

Aunt Olga, for whom her parents had named her, was Papa's youngest and most unpredictable sister. She was also the one member of their extended family who gifted them opportunities to meet people their own age who weren't flattering courtiers or exhausted soldiers. Olga always suspected their aunt pitied them. She'd convinced their mother to give Olga and Tatiana a respite from their nursing duties.

That particular Sunday, Aunt Olga was hosting an afternoon tea. Even under wartime rationing, she'd served delicious macarons, scones served with clotted Devonshire cream, and thin watercress finger sandwiches. They'd all made a great fuss over the food, though Olga had ultimately found the company somewhat stale. All the same, she appreciated her aunt's efforts and wanted to make the best of it. She had offered to play the piano so the others could sing. After Olga finished three songs, the last with an exaggerated run across the keyboard, she felt flushed and ready for a break.

A girl named Nadezhda, introduced earlier as Nadia, beckoned Olga with a dainty finger. Nadia's light blonde hair was swept back into a trio of fashionably braided buns. Jeweled pins and combs held the complex structure of it all in place. Olga would never have the patience to sit still for such an extravagant style; she wore her hair in a simple chignon with a gold-speckled headband.

When Olga approached, Nadia looped her arms in Olga's and steered her toward a corner.

"I was hoping I might speak to you alone." Lavender and lemon from a macaron clung to her breath.

Olga never forgot she was the eldest. With Papa and Alexei now living with the soldiers at the front and Mama so preoccupied with nursing and other charitable duties to support the troops, the responsibility to represent the family fell on Olga.

She suspected this girl was about to ask for a favor, and grew solemn, as she imagined her father would. "May I help you with something?"

Nadia shook her head. "It's not for me, per se."

"Your family then?"

"I meant to talk about *your* family. Your mother in particular. Does she listen to you? Would she do as you ask?"

"I must listen and do as *she* asks. What on earth would I ask of her?"

"It's only ... well, you know ..."

"No," Olga insisted, loosening her arm from the other girl's grip. "I don't know."

"People think your mother wants the Germans to win the war."

Rage flared deep inside, reddening Olga's cheeks. But her first duty was to represent the family. That meant remaining calm when tested. It was how Papa handled such things.

"Rubbish," she said stiffly. "My mother works at the hospital every day. She is devoted to our soldiers. Who told you such foolishness?" Olga searched the room as though the culprit might materialize from thin air.

"Oh, no one *here*."

"Who was it then? I should have a word with them."

"My older sister told me."

Then your sister is a fool. "She is gravely mistaken."

"She says the entire court thinks the same. They believe the empress wants our armies to fail. And all because she's under the spell of that evil man."

Grigori Rasputin. How sad that Olga didn't have to ask who Nadia meant. Before they left the palace for their aunt's flat, Olga had caught sight of Father Grigori preening before a gilded mirror, wearing one of the red and gold silk shirts Mama had sewn for him and lovingly stroking his dirty beard with dirtier hands.

Olga spotted her sister near the window, chatting with a bespectacled girl with black hair. Tatiana held a slice of strawberry cake on a china plate. With her free hand, she pointed to a pair of turtle doves perched on the ledge. She desperately wanted her sister to join them, but this girl's words would hurt her more than they stung Olga.

Rolling her shoulders, she faced the horrid Nadia on her own. "I can't imagine I heard you correctly."

Nadia paled, but her voice remained clear.

"I'm sorry to be the one to tell you, but you should know. Hypocrites surround your family. I see it today." She gestured toward Tatiana, now laughing as the doves lifted their brown stippled wings and fluttered away. "People are friendly to your faces and entirely different behind your backs. They're frustrated. While your father's away, your mother's in charge. Everyone knows it. And she keeps doing whatever that devil tells her to do. My sister met him once. Rasputin. He sat next to her at a séance. She said he kept pushing his chair closer."

At that, the color drained from Olga's cheeks. At the palace, Olga always avoided Father Grigori's vulgar gaze. But when no one else was looking, he winked at her. She guessed what Nadia was about to say.

"When the medium started to chant, my sister wanted to move away. Before she could, while everyone was distracted, he stuck his hand under her skirt. He tried to touch her *there*."

Olga's limbs froze. It was worse than she thought.

"He's a pervert," Nadia said. "Can't you do something?"

Pervert. Olga bristled at the word. Though she'd only a vague notion of what that meant, it likely applied to Rasputin. So she spoke the next words by rote, with no conviction. "Father Grigori is our friend. A friend to Russia."

"You can't believe that. People say he is a spy for the Germans and your mother shouldn't have anything to do with him. Your grandmother thinks the empress is undermining the war. I heard she's trying to send your mother to a convent."

That couldn't be true. Could it? Olga tried to speak but only ended up biting her lower lip. No one would dare, not even Gran. Papa wouldn't stand for it.

If only they all knew why her mother trusted Rasputin. If only they saw with their own eyes what the man could do.

Olga had seen it.

But she was never to breathe a word about Father Grigori's power. She was tempted because she wanted Nadia, and everyone else, to understand. Before her lips parted, however, Olga's upbringing got the better of her, as did loyalty to her family. So she said nothing. She clasped her hands together and tried to stand tall.

Nadia waited a few minutes, her heeled satin slippers tapping the woven rug beneath their feet. Then, realizing Olga would be of no further use, she shrugged.

"It's upsetting. But Grigori Rasputin is the devil and your mother lets him have the run of the palace. Someone needs to do something before matters get worse."

Watching Nadia's retreating figure, staring numbly at the blonde hair studded with sapphires, Olga realized matters must have gotten bad indeed for a young woman, a stranger no less, to dare to speak to a grand duchess in such a manner. No matter how many jewels Nadia's parents bought nor how ancient her family name, any young Russian woman was taught to revere the Romanovs.

No one ever spoke that way to Olga. Yet this Nadia seemed to have no compunctions about it. Humiliation flamed Olga's cheeks.

Then again, if Father Grigori harassed young women, didn't her family have a responsibility to stop him? That disrespect had been well earned.

A soft hand pressed against Olga's shoulder and returned her to the present. Father Grigori was dead, and she was in England with her sisters, a grand duchess no more. Not in any way that mattered.

"I didn't mean to upset you," Maria told her. "I'm sorry. But someone had to say it."

Maria's face came into focus, her features taut. As Olga looked around the room, she saw Tatiana's lips pinch and Ana casting a worried look in her direction. Olga had to be strong for her sisters. It was the only path forward.

"Father Grigori was wrong about the House of Romanov," Olga told them. "We're still here. We survived. And we will ensure our family name remains untarnished so we can hold our heads high and live in this world as we please."

Supper that night consisted of light fare, as always, but felt festive. This would be their second to last meal together before Olga left to live at Marlingham. Tatiana declared she had the right ingredients for her special leek and potato soup, to which she added a block of locally produced white Stilton cheese and served with a crusty baguette. Maria insisted they tear chunks of bread with their hands in the French manner. The savory scent clung to the cottage, making everything cozy.

After they ate, Olga lingered at the table, wanting to make the most of this time with her sisters. Though it was Olga's turn, Maria insisted on clearing the dishes. She then used a tightly folded piece of paper to wipe crumbs from the table. She would make a fine server at a fancy restaurant if ever so inclined. Meanwhile, Tatiana finished the last of a sponge cake with lemon zest.

In contrast, Anastasia had retreated to her bedroom. Olga scowled, disappointed that Ana should go off alone when they had so little time left together.

But Ana returned straightaway, holding a cardboard cylinder. Ana unscrewed the metal top of the tube and unfurled the poster inside: a world map.

"What's this?" Tatiana asked, dabbing her lips with a serviette.

"M and I ordered this from *National Geographic,*" Ana said. "It was M's idea, but I helped. I have cash socked away. After all, I never made it to the rail station to buy a train ticket."

Olga stared, transfixed, at the pastel continents and pale blue oceans. Papa had kept a giant globe in his study, but it had been years since she'd seen a proper map. This one used a newer projection to give a better sense of the spherical nature of the world and the relative size of its land masses.

Flattened, Russia dominated the left and right sides of the map, with the Americas front and center. No wonder everyone thought their country would help the allies win the Great War quickly. Other places seemed small in comparison.

Maria finished stacking the bowls neatly on the counter for washing and returned to the dining nook, her smile radiant. She held a flattened cardboard box she'd saved from their weekly deliveries, which she now set on the table.

"Maybe it will do us all good to see the world from here."

After Maria positioned the cardboard, Ana stretched the map flat on top of it and then settled tea cups and saucers at each corner to keep it in place. And then she reached into her skirt pocket. When she withdrew her hand, she'd clenched it in a fist.

"What do you have there?" Tatiana asked.

Ana opened her hand. Four silver pushpins rested on her palm. She waved the fingers of her other hand like a magician performing a trick. "Voila!"

Maria joined them at the table, and Ana placed one pin in front of each of them.

"We're going to put a pin on the city where we want to live," Maria said. "We'll go from youngest to eldest."

"We're not going anywhere," Tatiana said. "Only Olga for now. We all agreed."

"We can still dream, can't we?" Ana replied. "While waiting, we'll keep this map tacked to the wall. To remind us we have futures."

"So when the days get dreary," Maria added, "we can look at it and remember that we won't always have to hide. It will lift our spirits."

Olga scratched the back of her neck. "You feel trapped as well, Mashka?"

Maria tilted her chin. "Let's just see what happens, shall we?"

"I'll start," Ana said. Her hand hovered over the west coast of North America and then the black circle with **Los Angeles** printed next to it. No plot twist there. She ground the pin into the map and the cardboard protecting the table.

"We get it," Tatiana said drolly. "You want to run Hollywood."

"M's turn." Ana pointed to her sister.

Maria may not have been as aggressive as Ana, but she was equally determined. She found France on the map and pushed her pin into the black circle representing **Paris**.

"Mashka!" Olga said. "Really?"

"Paris is the heart of the fashion industry."

Olga's heart sank. Everyone wanted to leave. But then again, who could blame any young woman for wanting to live in Paris? "All right. *Bonne chance* and all that."

"*Merci beaucoup*," Maria said. "And now for Tatiana."

Olga watched her sister as she fiddled with her pushpin, rolling the round edge between her thumb and forefinger. And then, every bit as decisively as Ana and Maria, she stuck the pin on the map. Olga leaned in closer.

Petrograd.

Tatiana held her hands up. "I'll return to Russia. When it's safe to do so."

Olga wanted her sisters to dream, but she hadn't truly understood until now that those same dreams might push them to different parts of the world. Separated, when before they had always been together.

Besides, leaving England felt like a betrayal. Their British relations had saved them. That's why they lived in England as opposed to Paris, Berlin, or Shanghai, where other refugees formed new communities. They were their own community of four. It had always been that way. She hoped it always would be.

Frustrated, Olga grabbed her pin and let it hover over Petrograd. She changed her mind and thrust it elsewhere, satisfied with the small slice it made in the map's thick paper.

Her sisters leaned forward to see where she had placed the pin. The closest marked city was London, slightly to the south.

"I am happy exactly where we are," Olga said.

She thought they'd all made peace with her decision to work at Marlingham. Now, seeing their reactions, she wasn't so sure. Ana scowled as she turned the map to view it from a different angle. Gnawing at her nails, Tatiana wandered off to the parlor, searching for her embroidery notions.

Only Maria seemed unperturbed, excusing herself and then humming a tune popular during the last year of the war as she fetched the evening's newspaper, which waited on a stand by the door.

"I want all of us to be happy, safe, and together," Olga told Ana.

"*You* can leave the house," Ana muttered.

Maria brought the paper to the table and opened it, perusing the headlines. Olga was about to ask if she could have it once Maria finished reading when the expression on her sister's face changed. She inclined closer to the newspaper, lips parted slightly, before passing a hand over her mouth.

Dread ran down Olga's spine, stinging and cold. Tatiana must have sensed something as well. She returned to the table, stroking the silver cross around her neck.

"Is it about Mama and Papa?" Tatiana asked.

Ana got up from her chair and moved behind Maria, gently smoothing the paper so she could read over her sister's shoulder. At last, Maria found her voice.

"It's Lord Hammond," she said. "They have taken him to a hospital in London. He was poisoned. And the inspectors think the man responsible is an agent for the Bolsheviks."

PART TWO

~

SECRETS OF THE ROMANOVS

March-April 1920

CHAPTER
SEVEN

After 18 months of drifting from day to day, and another six weeks of waiting, Olga embraced purpose once more.

She woke at six every morning, almost without fail. This was a miracle of its own accord since she had always hated to rise early. By half past, she could expect a rap on the door from the kitchen maid, who woke up even earlier. The maid left a tray with a teapot and buttered toast outside her door. Though she ate porridge later, in the servants' hall with the others, she soon learned tea and toast were but one perk of accepting an assignment as Celia's maid. Since Celia took breakfast in her room—like she was already a married woman, as Mrs. Acton sometimes grumbled—*Miss Bennett* was treated the same.

With the space to herself, snug and warm, she luxuriated in the first moments of the day when she was neither Olga Romanova nor Olivia Bennett. Instead, she simply existed in the present, enjoying the early morning light and the freedom of solitude.

Once she finished her toast, she changed from her nightgown into her uniform and gave her hair a quick brush before tucking it under a lacy white bonnet. Then she applied her cosmetics, deepening the hue of her eyebrows and applying powder to contour her cheekbones, as Maria had instructed. She also added a modest lip tint, its tube being one of the little luxuries delivered in the girls' weekly boxes. Gran had always been keenly aware of her looks, and spent exorbitant amounts on facial creams and oils to maintain a youthful look. She wanted her granddaughters to always look their best, no matter the circumstances.

With her appearance changed, it was easy enough to start the day as Olivia Bennett. At a quarter past seven, she popped into the kitchen to fetch Celia's breakfast. The tray looked similar to her own but with the addition of a soft-boiled egg in a cunning china cup decorated with a paisley pattern. She always placed a fresh flower or a sprig of herbs on the corner of the tray. Once, her maids had done the same for her, and this simple gesture had never failed to brighten her morning.

Lady Celia preferred to spend the first hour of her day alone, to eat, read, and slowly awaken to the world on her terms. So, after dropping off the tray, Olga spent the next hour in the parlor and drawing room. She remembered Celia's comment about the manor being understaffed and tried to make herself useful by helping Mrs. Acton straighten and tidy.

At nine, Olga returned upstairs to draw Celia's bath, collect discarded gowns and robes for the hamper, and stoke the fire in the hearth. She then chose Celia's outfit for the day, which was never a difficult task. Every so often, Celia might mention that she felt like wearing a particular color or her ivory blouse with vertical stripes. Usually, Celia was content to leave Olga to it with no interference.

It was a fine, regimented schedule, and her father would have approved. And her mother, Olga supposed, would have seen the benefit of this structure and routine. However, Olga wondered if Mama would ever have gotten past her daughter working as a maid and taking her meals with the other servants.

But those meals comprised the most informative part of Olga's day.

Mrs. Acton and the maid who assisted in the kitchen, a sprite of a girl called Ada, both enjoyed tittle-tattle over afternoon tea in the servants' hall. While the cook, Mrs. Dasari, stayed more formal in her conversation, she also knew all about the Pike family's personal affairs. When the other staff discussed Lady Celia, Viscount Marling—Rob, except they usually referred to him as "the young lord"—and the absent Lord Hammond, they seemed content for Miss Bennett to listen and bob her head along while they shared tidbits. Breadcrumbs, really, but enough of them for Olga to piece together what happened to Hammond in London and the progress of his recovery.

In December, after Maria read the news item about Hammond's suspected poisoning, Olga had thought it wise to check on her start date. Since they didn't own a telephone, she walked to the post office in Nottingham. Sure enough, a message from the local operator awaited. Lady Celia had left for London with her brother to deal with a family emergency. As a result, her new position as a personal maid would need to be pushed past Christmas and into the following year.

Neither Rob nor Celia had understood the nature of their father's illness. Not at first. They'd received a telephone call from the hospital in London with vague allusions to stomach pains. They guessed their father needed his appendix removed. But when they arrived, inspectors from Scotland Yard stood at Hammond's bedside. When Rob pressed, they disclosed that their father appeared to have been poisoned, and the substance led them to suspect the Bolsheviks.

At any rate, the poison hadn't the desired effect. After Christmas, the doctors released him from the hospital. Since he was still weak and numb in his limbs, they ordered him to remain in London rather than risk travel. According to Mrs. Acton, it had been a harrowing experience for the young lord and lady. They'd both stayed in London with their father through the New Year, and then Rob remained longer to sort out some business or other to which none of the servants were yet privy.

At the time, Tatiana had been horrified that Olga still planned to work at Marlingham. Several heated, tearful fights ensued. If it was dangerous before, her plan was *unconscionable* now, in Tatiana's view. The Bolsheviks tried to take Lord Hammond's life. Olga shouldn't go near him or his family.

Since she had been following the story in the papers, Olga had a different perspective. Hammond was ill, but expected to survive. The Bolsheviks insisted they had nothing to do with the attempted assassination. They blamed it on a rogue agent, no less, with extreme isolationist views, who was trying to stop the new Russian government from establishing diplomatic relations with England. When they found this agent, they would deal with him accordingly.

Nevertheless, Tatiana had insisted, the Bolsheviks never spoke plainly. One could never know the truth.

On that point, Olga silently agreed, yet she wouldn't abandon her plan. This incident had merely set her timeline back. Olga still needed to salvage their mother's reputation. She couldn't worry about whether the Bolsheviks lied. Not right now. She was apprehensive but still had to stop Hammond from publishing lies about their mother. In that respect, nothing changed.

Once Celia returned from London in mid-February, Olga finally started at Marlingham—over Tatiana's objections.

Now, a month later, whenever she sat in the servants' hall at Marlingham and Lord Hammond's name popped up in conversation, it was all Olga could manage not to blurt out a hundred questions. But she imagined her mother, father, or Tatiana placing a steadying hand on her arm, telling her to be patient. "Olivia" was still new. So, for now, she needed to listen and take in all she could.

Afternoons were trickier than mornings because Celia spent much of her time alone. No callers. No volunteer work. No afternoon rides, which Olga found baffling, for Hammond likely kept a fine stable of horses. If Celia had been a social butterfly, Olga would have accompanied her on visits with a bag of toiletries, spare shoes, and the like. But Celia stayed home, dressed to receive visitors, but reading or working on puzzles instead.

To keep herself occupied, Olga organized Celia's wardrobe, housed in a mahogany armoire that took up nearly the entire bedroom wall. Celia preferred black or the rich colors of rubies, emeralds, or sapphires. Sorting the jewel-toned gowns on their wooden hangers, silk brushed her fingertips. The scent of lavender sachets enveloped her. And then Olga didn't feel at all like a maid. She was a grand duchess once more, enjoying the pleasures of a charmed life.

In the time before, Olga took her own elegant wardrobe for granted: formal and informal gowns, tiaras, sashes, gloves, stockings, ribbons, and any other adornment she desired. Her favorites had been the rounded hat crested with the imperial crown and the fitted military jacket she wore when she and Tatiana reviewed their honorary regiments.

Olga wondered how Rob, *the young lord*, would react if he glimpsed her in full uniform, expertly handling one of the finest geldings from Papa's stable. Olga may have mistaken him for the chauffeur, but how embarrassed *he* would be if he knew her true identity.

She sighed, stroking a soft velvet gown as though it were a cat curled up at the bottom of a drawer. Olga would never again review a line of soldiers, but one day, she might display her fine horsemanship again. She would choose a dappled gray mare to ride, gentle yet fearless.

Of course, she enjoyed motorcars as well. A Daimler would make for a fine drive.

Her brief moments with Rob played in Olga's mind. The quickness of his smile. The sturdiness of his gloved hand as he'd helped pull her up off the ground. His gaze on her when she headed toward the back door.

She wondered when he would return to Marlingham.

What would she say once he was here? Nothing, she supposed. For what did his smile matter when he was the heir to the estate, and she was but a maid?

And yet she thought of him still.

From the hallway came the gruff sound of a man clearing his throat. Olga shot around to find the footman hovering at the doorway. The same boy who'd escorted Olga to her interview and whom she'd since learned was named Charlie. Thankfully, he was too well-mannered to enter a lady's room. Olga returned the velvet gown to its proper slot in the wardrobe and stepped out into the hall, where Charlie explained that Lady Celia had grown bored and sent him to locate Miss Bennett, hoping she might help with a puzzle.

Olga was rubbish at puzzles. Unsurprisingly, Olivia was too. She made the best of it, though, spending an agreeable hour with Celia trying to make the tiny pieces fit to form a snowy landscape filled with ice skaters and children throwing snowballs. It made for a pleasant distraction. She hadn't liked the nostalgia of those moments alone with Celia's wardrobe. Olga's days as a grand duchess were behind her. Stroking silk wouldn't bring them back.

If she even wanted them back.

"I don't understand your hesitance," Celia said, softly touching her hair. "You seem handy enough with a brush and hairpins."

Olga summoned her English accent before responding. "I want to take care not to hurt you when I comb it out."

"Hurt me? Rather, it seems impossible I carried on so long without you."

Celia sat on a low satin stool before the gilded oval mirror propped above her dressing table, hands clasped on her lap, still in her cream-colored peignoir. Her legs were bouncing. She wasn't as calm as she wished to appear.

Olga met Celia's eyes in the mirror and gave a small smile. She wore a simple black shirtwaist with a matching skirt of three-quarters length. On her first day, Mrs. Acton had shown her how to button up the blouse to the stiff white collar at her neck. Olga was constantly tugging at the collar to get more air. At least the full white apron over the dress was feminine, as was the bonnet perched like a lacy tiara on her head.

Catching Olga assessing herself in the mirror, Celia grinned. "I'm afraid it's not the most comfortable garment. Loosen the top buttons if you wish."

Olga dropped her gaze and focused on Celia's glossy dark hair.

"I'm fortunate to have a uniform that fits well and keeps me warm. I've no reason to complain."

"Well, I won't say anything to Mrs. Acton if you won't. Were it up to me, you would wear a house dress of your choosing. Papa prefers a more formal atmosphere at home, though, and after what happened, I haven't the heart to ask Mrs. Acton to make any changes."

Papa. The back of Olga's neck tingled. She meant Hammond. Her family's enemy. Slowly, Olga rolled another section of hair around her hand and smoothed it with the boar bristle brush. Celia's hair wasn't as voluminous as Maria's, and with the unexpected delay in her start date, she'd had more time to practice. Olga could now arrange Celia's hair efficiently into a loose chignon at her nape.

"But then you understand the situation." Celia sighed and stared at the large hairpins embossed with rubies scattered across a sterling silver tray. "Perhaps I should have asked you to accompany me to London."

Olga brushed faster, imagining confronting Hammond in his hospital bed.

"It was such a shock. What happened to my father." Celia frowned at one of the puffs she used to apply her rose-scented facial cream. "Papa's back on his feet now but looked so helpless then. I shall never forget it."

Melancholy was woven like a fine thread through Celia's words. She had lost her mother and came close to dramatically losing her father. And yet for most of the day Celia kept her chin up, feigning cheer.

Olga wished she could tell Celia she needn't do that. She could cry and carry on if she wanted. Having lost her parents, Olga knew how Celia must feel underneath the polished exterior. Like her life was being squeezed out of her.

"Rob is expected back this evening," Celia added. "He'll share the latest."

Olga licked her lips, mouth suddenly dry. She was pleasantly stunned. Perhaps too pleasantly. Why should it matter? Rob's presence didn't matter. Not to her.

Celia gestured back toward her four-poster bed and the midnight-blue gown Olga had draped across the thick duvet. "I'll wear the dress at supper, but I'm not putting on a corset. I'll tell you that. I had enough of corsets in London. Forgoing them while I'm here is most appealing."

"That seems sensible." Mama wouldn't dream of letting her daughters dress without corsets, even when they had no plans for the day. In England, however, she and her sisters had abandoned corsets for the comfortable brassieres and girdles available via mail order.

Her thoughts wandered to the cottage, where her sisters probably gathered around the table for supper. Maria might have made a beef stew with dumplings. If it were Anastasia's turn, she would serve one of the spicy red or yellow curries she requested, pre-bottled and easily prepared over rice. She wondered if they looked over at the empty chair where Olga usually sat. Did Tatiana feel lonely at night without Olga asleep in the bed next to her? Or was she still angry?

"Speaking of sensible ..." Celia waved toward Olga's hair, tucked neatly under her bonnet. "... I never mentioned how much I like your bob. That is the right term?"

Maria had used the word "bob" to describe short hair. Olivia Bennett, however, had just one sister, an amalgam of Olga Romanova's four sisters. Olga reached for a hairpin to secure Celia's chignon. "I've heard my sister use that term. She said French ladies *bob* their hair."

"Are you following the lead of those fashionable mademoiselles?"

Olga wished that were so, but the reason for cutting her hair was far less inspiring. Illness felled them that last winter in Russia, just as they heard the first gunshots and cannons in the distance from Petrograd.

"After a bout with measles, I was weak for months. And losing my hair. So over the summer, I had it shaved off."

Celia gasped and made a twirling motion above her head. "You were bald?"

"Completely!" Olga remembered the tickle of a razor against her skull. "It started growing back soon enough, but I confess I enjoyed the sensation. The lightness. So after that, I kept it short."

"That sounds divine," Celia said. "The freedom of it."

"Your hair is too pretty to cut." Olga secured the chignon with one last pin and then moved back to assess her work in the low lamplight. "I'm sure yours was lovely, yet you made the leap." Celia patted the side of her head. "Anyway, you did a wondrous job with mine. I'm not sure you needed to bother since it will just be Rob and me for dinner." "No bother. I find it relaxing." Olga set the brush down. "I'm sure I'll need to dress you for formal dinner parties and balls soon enough. Perhaps once your father is back?"

Celia touched her mid-section with two fingers before quickly moving her hand away. Olga supposed she was still worried about her father and carrying on with household management in his absence.

Then again, Celia had few responsibilities that Olga could see. Mrs. Acton kept things running smoothly enough in the house, and Mrs. Dasari did the same in the kitchen. Unfortunately, that didn't leave Celia with much to occupy her time.

"Is your father to remain in London much longer?" Olga asked.

"I imagine through the spring session. The doctors said he was too sick to travel, though Papa finds his way to his office well enough."

If Hammond intended to remain in London until Easter, that gave Olga plenty of time to sneak into his study to see if he stored anything there, including any papers relating to her mother. She'd only waited because she wanted to take the time to gain the trust of the other staff. If she got caught, she would say she had stumbled into the study by accident.

"And he insists on sitting in the House of Lords when he can. Rob will know more, I expect." Celia pursed her lips. "Why do you ask?"

"I'm curious when you'll see him again," Olga said quickly.

Celia bent forward, looking over an array of glass bottles of colognes and spritzers she kept on her vanity. "There's more to it than that, isn't there?"

Pulse racing, Olga widened her eyes. "What do you mean?"

"You notice how often I stay home. You think I'm lonely."

"I'm sorry. I shouldn't presume—"

"It's touching, honestly." Celia met Olga's gaze. "It will get better soon enough. Rob has plans for this place he must share with Papa."

"Plans?"

"He won't say much about it, but then he doesn't say much of anything these days."

Despite his stammer, Rob had not seemed reticent to Olga. "I imagine it's difficult to be an heir. Uneasy is the head that wears a crown and all that."

Celia gave a tinkling laugh. "*Henry IV Part 2*! You quote Shakespeare. With such a lively mind, I fear you'll grow bored soon enough tending to me."

"It's something my father used to say. I'm not sure I realized it was Shakespeare."

"Your father seems like a wise man," Celia said. "Did he wear a crown of his own?"

She froze. Perhaps Celia had been toying with her all along, pretending to see her as a maid when she'd known the truth. Olga's white bonnet, though jolly enough, now seemed like something from a bad pantomime. And surely Celia noticed the excess of powder on her face.

How had she believed she could pull this off? Where did she get the hubris?

When she worked up the courage to look at Celia again, she saw only kind eyes and genuine curiosity. If Celia was playing games with her, she was doing a magnificent job.

"My father was a good man." Olga turned to fetch Celia's gown for the evening. "A simple man at that. But fond of reading."

"I suppose your quotation shouldn't surprise me. My brother mentioned you recited from *Twelfth Night* easily enough."

Celia rose to her feet. Olga took a minute to realize that Celia was waiting for her. Coming to her senses, Olga helped Celia finish dressing, sliding the gown over her head and shoulders, straightening it over her middle, and tugging the small hook slider for the separable fastener upward. She had trouble getting it to catch. Celia sucked her belly in, and it finally latched.

"The price of forgoing a corset." Celia smiled warmly. "You might grow bored as a maid. I like you, Olivia. I want you to stay."

"As I plan to do." Though it was an alias, she enjoyed hearing Celia call her by her first name. It was strange to remain formal with a young woman so near her age. She had to check the impulse to cry *I like you, too*, and hug Celia.

"If you're bored, please feel free to borrow books from my father's library," Celia said. "I know you have free time in the afternoon, and you needn't always spend it humoring me."

"You don't think he would mind?"

"I think he will be pleased."

"Perhaps I shall," Olga said. "Thank you."

The library was next to the study on the first floor. Olga remembered Mrs. Acton pointing it out after her interview. And now, were she to slip in there by mistake, no one could fault her. Olga hadn't been around long enough to know the ins and outs of Marlingham and could easily mistake the study for the library. She needn't wait any longer to snoop around, to spy like Mata Hari.

Olga hoped the letters between her mother and Father Grigori, which Hammond claimed to have, didn't exist. Or were forged.

If there were any doubts at all, she wasn't sure what she would do. She only prayed her mother had left nothing foolish behind.

People have always had much to say regarding our parents' supposed incompetence as rulers and the gross excesses of the Romanov lifestyle. I am no expert on the matter. I know that some of our relatives lived opulently. It must have grated at those with little in the way of sustenance, let alone material comfort

I can relay how we were raised: in a loving but strict manner. When war came, our mother did not hesitate. We older girls set to work as nurses with no corners cut. The doctors trained us properly before allowing us near patients—our status as the tsar's daughters meant nothing compared to the soldiers' health.

Something in my sister's constitution equipped her to handle her duties better than I did. Tatiana's face always looked serene as she stood next to the surgeons, handing instruments over and applying pressure on wounds, never so much as flinching. Her nerves were like steel, and she faced any horror with stoic reserve. Mama was the same.

Then again, when revolution came, Tatiana and Mama were in denial, while I suspected that the madness we witnessed at the hospital was an omen. They never believed our lives could turn upside down. Not permanently, at any rate. They viewed nursing as their duty in a crisis, and the ward as a troubled but secure sanctuary, not the harbinger of worse to come.

The Private Diary of Olga Romanova
December 1921

CHAPTER EIGHT

"What's all that then?" Mrs. Dasari angled her chin at Mrs. Acton's necklace and smiled. The two of them had worked together for years and seemed plenty chummy.

Mrs. Acton replied with an exaggerated look of shock. "I always dress for supper. It's only right. Can't we have nice things like that lot upstairs?"

Though Mrs. Acton usually changed into a long black dress for supper, nice enough though too small for her figure, this evening, she'd added a sterling silver chain around her throat to her ensemble. And while the house had been modernized with a number of electric fixtures, Mrs. Dasari made a point of lighting candles for supper. Olga found this rather touching in its simple elegance.

"Folks around here might come and go as they please," Mrs. Acton added. "But I don't see why that means I needn't bother with the nicer stuff of life."

The servants ate in shifts, and there weren't many of them, far less, as Mrs. Acton had confided to Olga, than in the manor's heyday when

Lady Hammond was still alive. So after dressing Celia, Olga found only Mrs. Acton and Mrs. Dasari waiting for her to join them for supper.

They dined at a narrow table in the servants' hall next to the kitchen. The staff's dining table stood against the wall where house bells were mounted on spiraling gold-plated knobs, a label with the corresponding room upstairs displayed below each one. During her first week at Marlingham, Olga had been anxious as she ate, expecting to hear bells pealing at any moment. But so far, she'd never actually heard one ring.

Now, this was her favorite spot in the entire house, even more so than her private bed chamber, because it always stayed warm and smelled of herbs, butter, and baking bread.

The kitchen maid, Ada, emerged from the pantry, fixing a bonnet atop her curly brown hair and smoothing her checkered dress. Ada pulled a chair back with a squeak and plopped down next to Olga. The girl had a smattering of freckles across her nose and looked fifteen if a day.

Olga sat straighter, instinctively modeling her deportment for the younger woman. The rickety wooden chairs balanced precariously and did nothing for her spine, but then Olga was taught to sit without her back touching that of a chair. Another lesson from long ago.

"You have beautiful posture, Miss Bennett," Mrs. Dasari told her amicably. She sat nearly as straight as Olga, such that her tall figure would have been imposing if her brown eyes were not so kind. "Between your elegance and Mrs. Acton's finery, we might as well dine upstairs ourselves."

Olga tried to think of something clever to say. The others welcomed her at the dining table in the servants' hall. Her bonnet and apron seemed assurance enough that she was one of "their lot," as Mrs. Acton would put it. But she felt off-key among them, as though they had all been practicing a musical performance and she was a last-minute addition who couldn't keep pace with the rest.

"Oooooh! I wish we ate upstairs!" Ada pushed her chair back, bumping the hutch behind the table. The china plates on the top shelves rattled. "Did 'ya hear? The young lord is coming this evening."

An unwelcome twinge thrummed in Olga's chest. Ada eyed her while Mrs. Acton arched an unruly eyebrow in her direction. Was she expected to comment on Rob? If so, they would be sorely disappointed, for she had nothing to say.

Mrs. Acton made a sound like a grumble in the back of her throat. Ada just frowned. Olga suspected the girl found "Miss Bennett" dull to the core.

Only Mrs. Dasari bore no sign of expectation in her expression. She was content merely to be and extended that grace to everyone else. Thank the Lord for Mrs. Dasari.

As a small wall clock ticked off the passing minutes, Olga hoped her stomach wouldn't grumble—after the poor fare during the months of captivity in Ekaterinburg, she was forever hungry. Nervous though she might be at the notion of the young lord arriving this evening, she wanted to tuck into the curried pasties before her—one of Mrs. Dasari's Indian specialties passed on from her mother and spicy enough that even Anastasia would approve. But the red-haired footman, Charlie, usually joined them for supper, and she couldn't be rude and start without him. Besides, she'd caught Ada giggling with the footman often enough. Perhaps he would provide her with a distraction from Rob.

"Where's Charles?" Olga asked mildly, keeping her face steadily neutral.

"*Charles?*" Ada said, and let out a carefree laugh. Anastasia definitely would have approved of that. If they ever met, those two girls would get on famously.

"Charlie, that is." Olga took a swallow from her glass of water.

"Gone to help serve as the young lord's valet for the evening," Mrs. Acton said. "We might as well start without him." She scooped into her pasty, steaming potatoes and peas spilling over her spoon.

"Not so young anymore," Ada said admiringly. "Fully grown, that lord is."

"I started here when he stood no higher than my knee." Mrs. Acton chewed and swallowed before continuing. "So he's still the young lord to me."

"Have you met the young lord yet, miss?" Ada asked Olga.

"I met him when I first came for an interview." Olga's stomach did a flip-flop. "I thought he was the chauffeur."

"That boy!" Mrs. Acton huffed. "What is he thinking, driving that wicked motorcar all around the countryside? He will be the death of me yet. Her ladyship never said no to him, bless her soul."

Before Olga could say anything more, the thump of feet on the wooden stairs and a hollow cry for help distracted them. She pushed her chair back, hitched her skirt, and scrambled with the others to the stairwell.

"What for the love of God?" Mrs. Acton cried.

Charlie struggled to hold another man upright, but the gentleman was taller than him and kept hunching over. The viscount's wavy dark hair was instantly familiar. His left hand aloft, she noticed a glistening blister from a burn on his palm. Olga gasped.

Rob had been injured.

"The Daimler sputtered as it approached the drive, so he looked under the hood," Charlie said. "A spark went off unexpectedly and caught him off guard. A nasty one, for sure. Got him good."

"We need cold water," Olga said, "and something to wrap it up before it erupts."

Obeying her own orders, Olga dashed into the kitchen and rummaged through cupboards crowded with cookware and utensils to find a clean bowl and pitcher. The ice chest was on the other side of the kitchen. She quickly stopped there to grab cubes of ice with iron tongs. Then Olga plopped those in the bowl and poured water from the pitcher into it. Finally, she set the pitcher down on the counter and grabbed a handful of clean tea towels.

When she turned around, Mrs. Dasari stood behind her, reaching for a basket stashed away in one of the top cupboards.

"Go ahead, Miss Bennett," she said crisply. "I shan't be far behind. Mind that you remove the ice before you put his hand in the water."

Olga recognized that no-nonsense tone: the manner of a trained nurse. She wanted to know more about Mrs. Dasari, but that would have to wait. "Of course. Thank you."

She rushed back to find Charlie guiding his lordship to an empty chair. Rob's face was pallid, and his hand too red. Ada gawked at the wound while Olga hesitated. She was no nurse. Not really. How often had she run out of the hospital ward, ready to retch from the putrid stench of gangrene? One patient had come in with sickening burns and extensive damage to his skin. At first, he'd been screaming in pain, but his will soon failed him. And then he whimpered like a little boy. When she'd seen the blistering skin and pus seeping from his blackened wounds, Olga wanted nothing more than to run as far away as possible.

But she hadn't. Not that time. She'd summoned her courage and assisted as the doctor treated the wounds with antiseptic.

"Now, don't worry," Mrs. Acton told Rob, sounding plenty worried. "Mrs. Dasari will find you some unguent or another. And here comes Miss Bennett."

As she approached Rob, Olga smiled, remembering how that seemed to help her patients from the time before. That and a note of blunt authority, such as Mrs. Dasari had demonstrated a few moments earlier. No matter how unsure she felt, a nurse did no one any good if she betrayed self-doubt.

"Bear down for a minute," Olga said in a reassuring but clipped tone. "This will be a shock. May I take your hand?"

"Please do."

His head bent. She took his hand, noting its width and how like a helpless doll her own looked as she wrapped it around his.

Except Olga was no helpless doll. She used one of the clean tea towels to sift the ice from the bowl. And then she plunged Rob's hand into the cold water.

The shock made him wince, but his trembling eased. Too focused to look at his face, Olga remained keenly aware of his masculine scent: cedar and smoke. He drew in shallow breaths and tried not to grimace at the pain.

"Ada, would you mind helping Mrs. Dasari fetch the ointments and whatnot? And maybe proper bandaging for the viscount's wound?"

She glanced up long enough to see something new in Ada's expression. Respect.

"We'll find them sure enough," Ada said with a quick curtsy.

"You'll be feeling better in a jiffy." Mrs. Acton hovered behind Olga and gave her an approving tap on the shoulder. "Miss Bennett here nursed during the war."

"So I've been told." Rob's face contorted, but he kept his voice firm. It was as sonorous as she remembered from that first day.

As she held his hand under the water in the shallow bowl, she noticed how vulnerable his large fingers seemed. They were splayed underwater, knuckles pronounced. She had held this hand before when it was swathed in a driving gauntlet. A burst of furtive energy surged through her as Olga realized how badly she wanted to hold his hand again. This time, without the thick glove shielding his skin.

When she caught Rob's eye, his brows furrowed. "I h-hope this won't bring back any terrible memories."

"No, no. Don't worry about me. I'm only sorry you're hurt." Olga's words didn't come out as steady as she'd hoped, but she kept her accent consistent and didn't lapse into Russian. "This won't give you trouble past the next day or so," she added.

His skin remained pale but closer to his normal color than the terrible pallor wrought by pain. "I'm fortunate you're here."

"Anyone could have helped. But you're stuck with me."

She lifted his hand from the bowl and let the excess water drip from his fingers before gently patting his hand with a towel. The skin around the burn looked pinkish and raised but not broken. He only needed to keep it covered until it healed.

"Prognosis?" he asked.

"You might have a scar."

Without thinking, her gaze wandered to the purple line on his forehead.

"Nothing noticeable," she added quickly, looking away.

"I've seen worse, then."

"This is what you get for taking on such chores yourself," Mrs. Acton scolded. "A motorcar's engine must be fraught with dangers. You need a chauffeur."

"I neither need nor want a chauffeur when I enjoy driving myself."

"Then get Charlie to take care of the like."

"He is busy enough and has no business under the hood of my automobile." Rob's voice was merry and presumingly familiar with Mrs. Acton's overbearing tone.

Ada lumbered back from the kitchen, bearing a basket with a red cross affixed to the front and an assortment of unguents, ointments, creams, rubbing alcohol, and gauze bandages. She held it up for inspection. Mrs. Dasari wasn't far behind her.

Olga withdrew a clean sheet of gauze and ointment, which she dabbed on the burned area of Rob's hand. She wanted to ask Mrs. Dasari to assist when she realized Ada remained at her side and seemed eager to help.

"Will you hold one end so I can roll the bandage?"

As Olga wrapped the wound, she knew Rob continued to watch her face. Privileged Olga Romanova met gentlemen on equal footing, or better, for none would have dared take advantage of her. She met his gaze and smiled.

"Good thing his lordship's not here," Mrs. Acton told Rob. "He would have plenty to say about this."

"My father has plenty to say about almost everything. I don't know if the world is any better for it."

Annoyance crept into Rob's tone when he spoke of Lord Hammond. How curious. And potentially useful.

Olga scrambled to her feet. The bandage appeared secure but not too tight. So the wound would have plenty of air to breathe. She gave Ada an approving smile, and the girl positively beamed.

"Good as new!" Ada declared. Charlie looked at her and grinned. Olga was sure she had caught a hint of color in Ada's cheeks when he did so.

"I'll get things in order and settle you in then, sir," Charlie said, retreating up the stairs. "And I'm happy to assist with your engine as you need. It's no trouble."

"Don't want to deal with another mess, is that it?"

"He's only trying to keep you from harm!" Mrs. Acton said.

Ignoring her, Rob held his bandaged hand up in front of his face. "You did a fine job, Miss Bennett...and you....m-miss."

He shook his head, clearly embarrassed at not remembering Ada's name.

"Miss Tully is doing a fine job, too." Unlike Mrs. Acton, Mrs. Dasari seemed shy around Rob. More carefully formal.

"Thanks to you as well, Miss Tully," Rob said, nodding to Ada.

When he stood, Olga stepped back, still intimidated by his height and the breadth of his shoulders. Intimidated and fascinated.

"I suppose I should join my sister if there's any supper left," he said.

"Lady Celia will be glad enough to see you," Mrs. Acton told him, "though I'm sure she'll agree with me on the notion of you sticking your head under the hood of your motor."

Rob strode over to Mrs. Acton, bent down, and kissed her forehead.

"You needn't worry, but thank you. To everyone." He held up his bandaged hand before placing a foot on the first step of the stairs. "I'll take greater care in the future."

It might have been her imagination, but Olga thought he gave her a smile before heading back upstairs.

"Chauffeur!" Mrs. Acton harrumphed once more, sitting heavily in her chair. "That's as fine a gentleman as comes from that lot. Too bad he'll be wasted in the House of Lords."

"If only he were destined for the House of Commons," Mrs. Dasari agreed. "Where things get done."

Still hungry but too agitated to return to the table just yet, Olga busied herself setting the bowl in the dish basin and the soiled towels in the kitchen hamper. Mrs. Acton and Mrs. Dasari were political women and liberals at that, proudly exclaiming their allegiance to the Labour Party whenever they had the chance. It was a novel experience to listen to ladies speak so openly of their opinions on political matters and not an unwelcome one.

"The young lord has ambitions to serve the public, then?" she called over her shoulder.

"Only if we can see to it his father gets out of his way," Mrs. Acton declared.

"I don't know he'd accomplish much as Lord nor MP when his speech gives him trouble," Ada groused. It was a mean-spirited comment, but Olga supposed Rob hurt Ada's feelings when he didn't remember her name.

"How unkind," Mrs. Dasari said mildly.

"It's only the truth."

"And who are you to point it out? Nothing's wrong with him." Mrs. Acton cut into her vegetable pasty, a good deal colder now. "A bit of shell shock, that's all. He'll sort it soon enough." Then, under her breath, she added, "If his lordship would let him be about it."

Appetite returning, Olga took her seat. "Does his lordship not have sympathy for his son's condition? Many young men returned from war with such impediments."

"His lordship could stand to be a sight gentler with the young lord," Mrs. Acton said.

"Now his lordship is a good father. Let's not forget that," Mrs. Dasari countered. "They are honorable men. Only they can't seem to find much to agree on these days."

A smile tugged at her lips. Olga shouldn't have been glad to hear of the quarrels, but this was welcome news.

If Rob and his father were at odds, then perhaps she and Rob were not.

While my mother and Tatiana had their blind spots, I also found it easy enough to fool myself when it suited me. For example, I assumed that as a grand duchess, when I married, it would be to a husband from a family with whom the House of Romanov could forge a powerful alliance. And yet I still dreamed of romance and love to match that I had witnessed in my parents' marriage.

Before the Bolsheviks brought all my dreams to a halt.

The Private Diary of Olga Romanova
December 1921

CHAPTER NINE

With Mrs. Dasari's blessing, Ada did the honors, slicing the delectable sponge cake with double cream and raspberries set aside for the staff. When she placed the dessert—their "pudding"—before them, Olga kept imagining Maria and Ana's eyes glowing. It would have been wrong to pass on something so delicious.

But though Olga ate with gusto, she had difficulty focusing on the conversation, even when it revolved around her. Ada was running on about how well they'd handled the situation. How she, Ada, might consider going into nursing one day herself.

Olga only managed a weak smile as she pressed her fork into her cake.

When Ada paused, staring at her expectantly, Olga realized she was supposed to say something. She lost the main thrust of the conversation, for she'd been wondering how quickly she might excuse herself and make her way upstairs to the study.

"I'm sorry." Olga looked at Ada.

"I said you served as a nurse in the war. Isn't that right?"

"Yes." Olga remembered how many times she complained of the itchiness and stiff wool of the habit they'd worn to the ward.

"I'm sure you were marvelous," Ada said wistfully.

The girl's eyes may have been green, not blue, and her hair more brown than blonde, but at the moment, she was the absolute picture of Anastasia. As she spoke, however, Tatiana came to Olga's mind.

"I was fine, but you should see my sister ... Tess ... in action." Olga used the name she'd invented for her imaginary sister—an amalgam of her three actual sisters and christened in honor of *Tess of the d'Urbervilles*. She'd loved the novel but had never confessed to reading it. Mama would have been too shocked.

"She had a true talent for that work," Olga added.

Mrs. Acton noticed Olga's eyes misting over. "Missing her, are you?"

Olga folded her hands in her lap, threading her fingers nervously. "I confess I am."

"Oh, dear." Mrs. Dasari reached across the table and gently pressed Olga's arm. Through the wool fabric of her blouse, Olga could feel the cook's calluses and small hard scars, no doubt from kitchen accidents past.

"It doesn't mean I'm unhappy here." Olga regarded the smashed sponge cake and raspberries on her porcelain plate. "This is lovely. Just a long day, I suppose."

"And ended by tending to the young lord. Who would have thought?"

Mrs. Acton cupped her hands around her mug of coffee. Olga had no clue how she drank it so late into the evening and yet rose with the sun every morning. The others raised their water. Olga smiled and clinked her glass against theirs.

"I shall retire early after all the excitement," Olga said. She ate the last bite of cake and then pushed her empty plate away, sensing the opportunity to exit gracefully. "Lady Celia mentioned I might borrow a book from his lordship's library."

She hadn't seen her mother's apparition in weeks. Perhaps, after finding her way here, Olga no longer needed her. Regardless, with any luck, she might find something in his lordship's study that she could use to help redeem her poor mother's reputation.

With Rob in the house, her senses grew more alert, as though her body was attuned to his presence. Standing before Lord Hammond's study, Olga detected the rhythmic ticking of a grandfather clock, the distant clatter of spoons against plates, and the vague murmur of Celia and Rob's voices traveling down the hallway from the formal dining room.

She wondered how Rob got on with his meal, his hand bandaged and still throbbing, no doubt. But Olga only had about fifteen or twenty minutes, she guessed, before Celia would be ready for bed. She had no time to waste.

The brass knob squeaked when she applied pressure, but she found it unlocked. Olga slipped into the room, carefully shutting the door behind her.

Inside, it was nearly pitch black. Stale remnants of tobacco clung to the air, like in Papa's study. Her father had smoked incessantly, sometimes two packs a day. As her eyes adjusted to the darkness, the scent made Olga feel like a little girl again, sneaking up behind her father as he hunched over the papers on his desk.

But she needed to remember that she wasn't in Papa's study. Rather, she'd entered enemy terrain.

With only the light from beneath the door to guide her, Olga crossed to the window. Fumbling in the dark, she found a drawstring and tugged the curtains apart. The chill from outside seeped through cracks between the panes, but the nearly full moon illuminated the room. By moonlight, Olga noted the walnut paneling and bookcases lining the walls, shelves filled with leather-bound volumes. On the desk, a globe tilted on its axis, alongside a pair of binoculars and a mini bronze pendulum that swung back and forth, making a whooshing sound—the sort of pieces Papa kept as well. Items a gentleman collected to demonstrate refinement and class, whether he actually used them being far less important than the mere fact of possession.

The desk itself was immense and crafted of walnut that matched the wall panels, with a low hutch on top. An expensive swivel chair upholstered in leather had been pushed in neatly alongside a filing cabinet with three drawers. On top of the desk, a small ledger book lay flat next to a photograph of a young woman in an oval frame.

Olga leaned in closer. The photo showed about three-fourths of the woman's figure, trim at the waist and curvaceous elsewhere. Unruly hair was swept into a full up-do, making her the ideal Gibson Girl of a decade earlier. Her face bore an open, sorrowful expression, and she had Rob and Celia's dark eyes.

This was the late countess, their mother. His lordship had positioned the picture so the young woman would have been gazing at him while he worked at the desk. Hammond must have loved her.

Staring at the countess, Olga's thoughts grew frantic and disordered. Apart from his affection for his wife, Hammond had two children who had shown Olga nothing but kindness. Could Hammond be such a villain? How was he connected to her family? Why had a Bolshevik tried to poison him?

Why did he hate her mother?

Traitor ... at the behest of her personal mystic, the much-despised Rasputin.

When Olga remembered those words, all sympathetic thoughts fled from her mind. Olga recalled Ana unfolding the map and spreading it out before them on the table. The pushpins in the cities. Her sisters wanted to move about the world freely. Someday.

If Hammond tarnished their mother's legacy, they could be stuck in that cottage forever, traitors in the world's eyes. Olga decided that Rob and Celia must have inherited their pleasant natures from the maternal side. Lady Hammond might have been entirely different from her husband. She may not have loved him. Families pushed women into marriages for various reasons, especially when property and titles were involved.

Behind the picture, Olga spotted the corner of what looked like a wooden frame. She nudged the photo to the side and found a small icon. The tempera painted on the wood depicted Mary holding Christ as a baby.

An icon of the Russian Orthodox Church.

Hammond could have easily acquired the Russian bear in Celia's sitting room on one of his diplomatic trips. But this? An icon might also serve as a souvenir, she thought with some distaste, but to place it next to the picture of his dead wife? It must have more significant meaning for him.

Heart racing, Olga explored once more. Two small drawers attached to the desk, filled with blank note papers, fountain pens, and loose envelopes and stamps. She crouched to investigate the filing cabinet and grappled for a cold metal handle. Then she tested the drawer.

When the knob rattled, the sound echoed, drowning out the soft whoosh of the pendulum.

Olga wiggled her fingers around the handle once more to still it. With a lighter touch, she tugged at the others. All locked. She needed to determine where Hammond kept the key. Celia might know and be persuaded to share.

She released the last of the handles and flexed her fingers, gaze running over the hutch. There, several more ledger books were propped between two wooden bookends carved to resemble owls. These ledgers were larger than the one on the desk and bound in leather, peeling at the edges. She tipped one apart from the others and opened it.

On the first page, neatly written in black ink, she read: *Estate Accounts 1905-1908.*

That did her no good. She returned the ledger to its rightful place and selected another. The other rosters proved equally tedious: accounts kept in order every three years. As Olga thumbed through the pages, she found only endless strings of numbers. By the time she reached *1912-1915,* her vision was spinning.

Olga was about to shut the ledger, ready to leave the study and take a quick turn in the library before retiring for the night, when she noticed something on the next page. The numbers suddenly stopped. The page was nearly blank except for what looked like a book title transcribed in indigo ink.

Complicity in the House of Romanov

Olga's breath hitched. Slowly, she traced the words with her index finger.

The doorknob screeched. Olga slapped the ledger shut and returned it to what she hoped was its rightful place. When the door opened, the light from the hallway was just bright enough for her to make out Rob's tall figure.

He ducked to avoid hitting his head in the doorway and leaned over to pull the chain on a nearby lamp.

"Oh!" Rob blinked twice, startled. "Hello again."

Gray spots danced before her eyes as she reacted to the lamplight. Once she'd regained her vision, Olga curtsied and took a moment to summon Olivia Bennett's voice, the one she must always use in his presence.

"I am sorry, but I'm quite lost. Lady Celia said I might borrow a book. I thought I was in his lordship's library."

"Why didn't you didn't turn on a lamp?"

"I made do with ..." Olga gestured to the window.

"So you made your way by the light of the moon. Like a sprite in the forest."

"Not quite like that." Olga's cheeks flushed pink, but at least he didn't seem angry. Only distracted. Maybe he shouldn't be in his father's study either.

"What did you wish to borrow in the library? I can tell you if my father has the book or not. I've been through them more times than I can count."

She couldn't think straight or summon the name of any book except for *Wuthering Heights,* and she didn't want to tell him she was looking for a romantic novel. So instead, she switched topics. "How's your hand? I'd be happy to take another look."

"Why not? My father's correspondence can wait a few more minutes."

"Do you track his correspondence while he's away?"

"Yes, but I expect nothing of interest. Everyone knows he's still in London. Still, I told him I would review mail from the post, and I should peek at the ledgers as well."

Complicity in the House of Romanov. The terrible words rang in her head like someone swung a mallet to a dinner bell. Olga fought to maintain her neutral smile. She extended her hand. "If I may?"

He held his left hand up for inspection. Olga hesitated, realizing she felt shy about touching him again. Downstairs, there had been an urgency to it. But this seemed deliberate and almost calculated, too much like a maid trying to seduce the lord of the manor.

"I'm sorry," she exclaimed, withdrawing. Even wearing a maid's white apron and bonnet, Olga tried to keep her hands clasped as a grand duchess should. She felt more than a little silly. "I spoke too informally in your presence. When we first met, I mean. I can't believe I thought you were the family's chauffeur."

He met her gaze, hand still raised like a priest about to offer a blessing. "No need for an apology. It took me long enough to introduce myself properly."

"Why didn't you set me straight right away?" She winced. That sounded too forward, entitled Olga pushing Olivia's common sense aside. "I'm sorry."

"Stop apologizing. Please." Some playful swagger had returned to his voice, though a pensive smile softened his features. "It's a good question. Honestly, a part of me liked the idea of being a chauffeur. I see now that this put you in an uncomfortable spot. So *I'm* sorry."

"No, no. As you said, no need to apologize."

The moonlight suited his black hair and dark eyes. He may have called her a forest sprite, but he looked far closer to a supernatural being. Not a sprite, of course, nor a satyr, despite the promise of mischief on his full lips. More like a prince enchanted by a sorcerer, cast out to make his way in the forest until recognized by his own family once more.

And yet Rob had seemed more comfortable in the role of a chauffeur than heir apparent. At the very least, he enjoyed the masquerade. Olga heard Tatiana, a voice so unmistakable her sister may as well have been standing next to her. *What nonsense. Focus. Please.*

Despite that voice, Olga had a strange urge to confess the truth. She wanted to tell Rob she wasn't a maid. Not really. She could explain how much freer she felt in her black dress and white lace cap than in any formal gown she'd worn as a grand duchess, how this version of herself moved about with a natural sense of grace more exhilarating than the carefully curated manners expected of her imperial highness, Olga Romanova. She wanted to tell him because she sensed he would understand.

Perhaps Olga could communicate that she understood, even if she couldn't express everything. "I suppose much responsibility must come with being an heir."

Rob's eyes scrunched as he shrugged. "All nonsense. I'm the heir to land and title because I happen to be my father's son. It's outdated. Medieval."

"It's the way of the world, my lord."

She hesitated. Hopefully, Rob wouldn't ask her to address him by his first name, as Celia had done. She could not maintain an appropriate distance were she to freely call him *Rob*. Nor did she suppose Mrs. Acton would care for it, no matter how much she might talk about the Labour Party and greater equality between classes.

"Your birthright is not by choice and certainly not your fault," Olga continued. "Only your responsibility."

"That's one way of looking at it. But perhaps it doesn't always have to be so. Maybe we can find new ways of going f-forward."

Rob pressed his lips tight and closed his eyes. When he opened them again, the casual aristocratic tone was restored. "But then I shan't be capable of much if I'm trying to make my way through life with one hand tied behind my back, as it were." He wiggled his fingers.

She took his hand once more. Her skin tingled when they touched. He felt warmer than she'd expected, though not so heated as to suggest a fever or anything alarming. Olga told herself that she only missed talking to gentlemen and the thrilling brush of her soft skin against theirs.

With great care, she unwrapped the bandage and guided his palm toward the lamplight for closer inspection. "Looks good."

She turned his hand over. It wasn't rough or calloused nor smooth as she might expect from a pampered young lord of the manor. It seemed just right.

"No swelling," she continued, trying to steady her voice. "No excessive redness. Healthy and pink and ready to heal. You can remove the linen while you sleep so the wound can breathe. Perhaps Charlie might re-wrap it in the morning with a clean bandage."

"You would not do the honors? I should find it more pleasurable."

He looked away, clearly ashamed at flirting with the staff. He wasn't supposed to do that. Once again, Olga longed to reveal her secret. She was no maid. They could flirt on equal terms.

Only she was a maid, as far as he knew, anyway. She must always seem to be such.

"Again, I'm sorry," he told her. "My mother will turn in her grave."

She decided it was best to ignore his comment. *Least said, soonest mended*—one of her mother's expressions, borrowed from Mama's grandmother, Queen Victoria. Olga focused on re-wrapping the bandage.

"I was sorry to hear of your mother's passing. And then to deal with his lordship's grave illness on top of it all."

"Celia and I will manage. We always have done. I intend to spend more time here to keep her company, what with Mother gone and Father in London constantly."

He grimaced. At first, Olga thought she had inadvertently hurt his hand, but then realized he only believed he'd said too much about his family.

Good common sense dictated she say something nice about Lord Hammond. "I imagine your father's responsibilities to the House of Lords keep him well occupied." She hesitated. But then the next bit was public information as well. After all, she had read about it in the newspaper. "And I understand he will publish a book soon. I saw something like that in the papers."

"Well occupied is putting too fine a point on it, I think. As for the book, I don't know why he has focused attention on the empress, dead and gone. I suppose he has his reasons. But he hasn't confided them to me."

Olga kept her head bowed, frowning and tightening the bandage. Rob sounded hurt, as though accustomed to his father sharing confidences. She wondered if Rob might know enough to divulge more information. Something that would hint at why Hammond would keep notes on *Complicity in the House of Romanov* among his household accounts. But she couldn't muster an innocent question to lead him to disclose such.

At any rate, now Rob seemed eager to change the subject. He flexed the fingers of his left hand. "I feel the fool that I can't check an automobile's engine without injury."

"You wish to understand your motorcar and fix it. Nothing foolish in that."

"Kind of you," he laughed.

"Only the truth."

They smiled at one another, and then she was the one to look away. *Olivia's* cue to leave had long since come and gone. "I should get along to the library. Might you point me in the right direction?"

"Next door down. Simple mistake."

His deep voice was like cozying up to a warm fire at night. She longed to stay, but that would never do. She gave a quick curtsy in his general direction and headed for the door.

"Oh, and Miss Bennett ... might I make a suggestion?"

Hand on the doorknob, she turned around. Robert withdrew a key from his pocket.

The key for the file cabinet! It must have been. She licked her lips.

"Suggestion?"

"Alexander Pushkin," Rob said. "My father owns an excellent translation of *Eugene Onegin*. Pushkin's not well known in England, but he is a literary god in Russia."

Olga exhaled too loudly. She adored Pushkin. Papa had read *Onegin* aloud one Christmas as they'd all gathered before a blazing fire in the hearth. She tilted her head in what she hoped was a thoughtful manner. "I shall consider it."

Rob did not move toward the file cabinet. Instead, he eyed his father's desk. Though she tried to tell herself it was only her imagination, Olga thought his stare landed on the ledger she had been looking at before he came in.

If he suspected she'd been poking around, he said nothing. Olga hoped she had left everything as she found it. She needed to remember why she was at Marlingham in the first place and couldn't risk letting down her guard. No matter how much she enjoyed Rob's company.

When I was at my lowest in Ekaterinburg, the guards would peek in. Some of them bore sympathetic expressions. They knew I hadn't left bed for a week. They knew I refused to eat. I had never flirted with the guards as Maria had. Never been friendly with them. Deep down, I understood it wasn't their fault. They were pawns, the same as we were, only on the opposite side of the board. Still, the guards had no reason to like me but only felt sorry for me. I figured they would leave me to wither and die in peace. I prayed for such a death.

I was no longer the eldest daughter of the tsar. Not really. I was no longer living at all. I had no purpose and no hope, and without either, how can one embrace life? I'd taken to my bed, melancholy overwhelming me. I had no desire to do anything, not even to eat.

Tatiana tried to help. When I cried, she held my hand. She saved the sweets smuggled in from the local convent and brought them to me, trying to tempt me to eat something. My sister found books in the abandoned house and read aloud from Pushkin, Dumas, and Shakespeare. I listened dutifully but didn't rise from bed.

During the war, Tatiana had been a talented nurse, but she couldn't treat this affliction.

Two weeks before our rescue, the Bolsheviks replaced our guards with men who were rougher, harder, and hated the tsar and empress with a passion. They hated our parents, and so they hated us.

They tried to force me out of bed. One of them forced me to eat. He'd done so by whispering threats to my sisters when no one else was in earshot. I remember the foul odor of his body, unwashed for days in the heat of summer. That one didn't want to give me the satisfaction of wasting away on my terms.

I once overheard a group of guards placing bets on which of us would die first. Two of them said Alexei, but overall I had been the favorite. Except they hadn't used my name. They called me "the little empress" and then laughed as though the very idea was the most foolish notion they'd ever heard.

After we were rescued, living was the only option, and surviving was the first step toward truly living. Independence would have to come as well. Life without freedom is no life at all.

The Private Diary of Olga Romanova
December 1921

CHAPTER TEN

S taring at the cracks zig-zagging across one another on the ceiling, Olga stretched her arms wide and arched her back. Overnight, she'd tossed off the blanket, which now lay in a heap on the floor. Fresh rosemary and thyme scented the air. Every morning at five, Mrs. Dasari lit the stove and got straight to work.

This was all familiar. And yet Olga felt different.

When she woke, there'd been no moment of disorientation nor startled confusion when she didn't hear Tatiana's light snores. She hadn't experienced that limbo between sleeping and wakefulness when she couldn't distinguish dreams from reality.

Olga's room in Marlingham had become home. Not her permanent home, perhaps. Not without her sisters. But a place where she felt safe and somehow right: a sensation she'd never expected in Lord Hammond's house.

She blinked and spotted the book she'd tossed on her writing table the night before—an ostentatious volume of *Eugene Onegin* bound in red leather with gilt English lettering. Hard to miss. Last night, Olga discovered that Hammond kept an impressive collection of Russian literature in his library.

Russian bear, Russian icon, and now Russian literature. Hammond had served as a diplomat, but there was more to it than that.

Complicity in the House of Romanov

The horrible words rang in her mind again. Olga forced down her anger. Hammond may have known her country, but he didn't understand her family. And this may have been a warm space to land, but it wasn't her home.

Regardless, *Miss Bennett* was expected upstairs soon enough. Olga needed to focus on the day ahead. And then she'd figure out a way to sneak back into Hammond's study without anyone noticing.

After Olga had drawn a bath for Celia and spent her usual time tidying the parlor, she returned to the washroom, ready to help Celia dress. She gathered two fluffy white towels from the linen closet. They were made of Egyptian cotton and soft, though not quite as soft as those Olga had once luxuriated in after her baths.

As she walked to the washroom, Olga drew the towels closer, taking in the spicy-sweet scent of potpourri. She rapped on the door. "Ready?"

Celia wasn't fond of pleasantries first thing in the morning, but by the time she'd finished her bath, she usually seemed in a better mood and would respond with *ready as I'll ever be*.

Olga waited, tapping her foot. This morning, she received no response.

"Celia?" She tried again. Still no answer. Olga cocked her head closer to the door. "Are you all right?"

She heard sniffling. Was Celia crying? Olga wondered if that consti-
tuted enough of an emergency to force the lock. If Celia didn't come
out soon, perhaps she should ask Charlie for help. But while he was
handy with locks and such, the footman would die of humiliation if
he caught a glimpse of Lady Celia in a state of undress.

Before Olga determined what to do next, the lock clicked and unlatched. Celia opened the door. Except she didn't stand before Olga
but crawled on her hands and knees on the tile floor. She'd grabbed
her peignoir and wrapped it loosely around her.

After she opened the door, Celia scooted back and leaned against
the wall by the claw-footed tub—her hair a mess of wet black tangles
and her cheeks pink and streaked with tears. Olga moved the towels up
to her face again, hoping the potpourri would counteract the foulness
in the air. Celia used citrus salts and sometimes lit candles when she
took her bath. Olga detected those scents in the room, but a more
pungent smell overlaid them.

She glanced at a tin bucket in the corner.

"I'm sorry, my lady," Olga said. She'd no right to be on a first-name
basis with Celia when she'd violated her privacy so terribly.

"I don't feel well," Celia whispered.

The nurse in Olga took charge. She set the towels down on the stand
below a potted fern. "I'd like to see if you're running a temperature,
then. If I may?"

"Very well," Celia said miserably.

Olga pressed the flat of her hand gently against Celia's forehead.
Thankfully, her skin was not hot. Only her cheeks were flushed. Celia
must have been out of the tub for some time because she felt cool to the
touch. She couldn't sit here nearly naked and still wet from her bath.
Olga pressed the soft towels against Celia to dry her off and draped
one over her shoulders.

Celia tried to push her away, but all the strength seemed to have drained from her body. The pressure felt light as a feather. "Please. No. I'm so embarrassed."

"There is not a thing to be embarrassed about." Olga tried to knot the towel around Celia's shoulders and chest so she couldn't dislodge it. "If you caught a stomach bug, you belong in bed. Perhaps something you ate for breakfast didn't agree with you?" Olga wracked her brain, but she had brought only Celia's usual tea, toast, and egg.

Celia drew her slender legs closer to her chest and then wrapped her arms around them, rocking back and forth.

Olga should look in the bucket to see what had emptied from Celia's stomach, but she felt squeamish. She had once been asked to assist with an emergency tracheotomy on a soldier shot in the neck by a German sniper. Olga had fetched the right scalpel, but then she'd heard the suction and caught a glimpse of the incision and the man's exposed larynx. She hadn't fainted, but it was the closest she had ever come. She shuddered at the memory.

And now, a world away, similar waves of revulsion turned her stomach. She hated to listen to anyone vomit. It always made her want to do the same. If she saw the source of the stench, she might kneel before the bucket and add to its contents.

But Olga needed to know if she should ask Mrs. Acton to place a call to a doctor. She couldn't quite see into the bucket, so she scuttled closer.

"No," Celia protested weakly. "You needn't do that."

"I think I do."

Taking a quick breath, Olga peeked. What she found was not nearly as bad as the smell would suggest, though the yellow-brown sludge made her gag. Nevertheless, she didn't believe they needed to call a doctor.

When she turned back, Celia had her head in her hand, and her shoulders were heaving. Then she started to cry again.

"No, no, no," Olga told her. "It's all right."

Celia shook her head furiously, fingers splayed. Her other hand went to her belly.

"Should I ask Mrs. Dasari to make you ginger ale? Sometimes I like it mixed with orange juice." Olga blinked back a memory of her mother handing her such a drink when she was unwell before placing a gentle hand on her forehead.

"No, thank you," Celia whispered.

Olga crouched before Celia and gave her elbows a tentative pat. "It's nothing. You'll feel better soon enough. We'll take it easy today."

"It's not nothing." Celia wiped her face with her hand and then looked at Olga, her eyes red. "You worked as a nurse. I daresay you understand female anatomy. You must know."

"Know what?"

"You are too polite to say."

Without thinking, Olga glanced at Celia's midsection. And then she gasped. "Oh!"

No wonder Celia assumed she already knew. She should have known. Olga washed Celia's delicate, intimate items. There had been no cloth pads, no menstrual blood spotting the under things. When she thought no one was looking, Celia touched her belly protectively, and now her breakfast had made her sick.

Celia had fallen pregnant.

"I didn't know," Olga said quickly. "I mean, maybe I should have known, but I wouldn't have said anything. But I didn't know."

Celia tightened the towel around her shoulders like a blanket. "I'm the one who should explain."

"You don't owe me an explanation."

"I should have told you when I first hired you. I was afraid if I did, you would never accept the position. And I liked you. I didn't want you to leave. It's frightfully lonely here."

Olga nodded absently. She'd never come close to this situation herself, though she once worried about Maria. Her sister was an incorrigible flirt—even with the guards who watched over them in captivity—and overly fond of romantic novels.

"I've been afraid to call on friends or visit anyone. Thank goodness for Rob."

Olga hesitated. "Your brother knows?"

"I told him. Yes."

"And his lordship? Your father?"

She snorted and looked up at the ceiling. "Heavens, no."

Olga lowered herself to sit on the tile floor. She knew little about what was involved in raising a child. Yes, she had four younger siblings, but royal babies were a different matter. She'd been allowed nowhere near her little sisters or Alexei when they were infants. And none of them had been illegitimate.

If the child's father remained in the picture, Celia would have less of a problem. They could get married. If the baby came a few months early, so what? Olga had done the math on a few hasty marriages and subsequent births in St. Petersburg. As long as the couple wed before the child was born, society politely ignored the timeline.

"Can the child's father help?"

Celia wouldn't look at her.

In the time before, Olga and her sisters had the most stringent chaperones in the empire. In the world, for all she knew. With less supervision, this predicament could have happened to any one of them. She recalled the afternoons she'd spent laughing and joking with her favorite patient, Mitya, while he recovered in her hospital ward.

Under different circumstances, she might have given in to liberties beyond the already intense pleasure of their all-too-brief kisses.

How would she then break the news to her sisters? Maria would cry, hug her, and try to think out how it would be all right. Ana might also accept the situation. But Tatiana? She didn't know how she would share such news with Tatiana.

"This will remain between us," Olga said.

Celia stared at her. "Are you going to leave?"

"Of course not!"

Celia remained on the ground, legs still drawn up. "Aren't you afraid of scandal?"

"It would be horrible to quit because of this." Olga recalled how her father would modulate his voice to motivate a regiment of soldiers. So she tried to do the same. "Why would I let this stop me from living here? I like it here. I've no plans to leave."

Celia blinked slowly, reminding Olga of Maria with her saucer eyes. And then, as though a spell had been broken, she jumped to her feet, adjusted her peignoir around her chest, and offered her hand. She pulled Olga upright and then enveloped her in a tight hug.

"Thank you," she said. "I don't deserve you, but thank you."

Olga's hands hovered awkwardly at her sides. Tentatively, she returned the hug.

"What am I going to do?" Celia whispered.

"What comes will come. We shall handle this. Together. I promise."

Relief washed over Celia's features. "I am blessed. Truly. I cannot tell you what it means to me."

Guilt wormed its way into Olga's stomach, twisting it into a knot. She'd earned Celia's trust only with great deception. The least she could do was help her now.

Olga lugged the bucket from Celia's washroom across the grounds and tossed the contents far from the main house into a neglected side garden festering with weeds. Hopefully, no one would see.

As she approached a spigot to rinse the bucket, a goose and gander passed by haughtily. The first set of fuzzy goslings for the season waddled behind them.

Before heading outside, she had grabbed a sweater to throw over her uniform to shield her chest from the snap in the air. But it was spring all the same. The thought cheered her. Olga smiled as the water ran.

When she returned to the main house, she found Mrs. Acton in the kitchen, helping Mrs. Dasari with the menus. Despite a new pair of spectacles, Mrs. Dasari struggled with her near vision. Though the cook never ate meat, Mrs. Acton asked if they might serve Toad in the Hole for supper. This made no sense on any level and sounded vile to Olga, though she suspected Olivia Bennett should be familiar with the dish. She didn't dare inquire.

Instead, she said: "Do you know where I can find Rob this morning?"

Mrs. Acton turned to face Olga, eyebrows raised. And Mrs. Dasari looked put off by Olga's use of Rob's given name.

"I'm sorry." She shook her head, wondering why, after six weeks at Marlingham, Olga supplanted Olivia so often. It was only that she heard Celia refer to him as Rob this morning. And then she'd been distracted, speculating about what on earth Mrs. Acton had in mind with the toad dish.

"I meant his lordship, of course. The young lord."

Mrs. Acton planted her hands on her ample hips and eyed the bucket in Olga's hand. Olga believed the housekeeper liked her well

enough, but she maintained an air of suspicion whenever they interacted. Olga sensed the woman didn't understand why someone who'd
trained as a nurse would prefer to work as a maid.

Olga lifted the bucket. "I was just out cleaning this up. Lady Celia
isn't feeling well. I'm to tell his lordship that she won't join him for
lunch today."

"What?" Mrs. Dasari looked over her spectacles at Olga. She and
Mrs. Acton exchanged concerned glances, perhaps remembering Lady
Hammond's bout with influenza.

"Should I ring the doctor?"

"The one in Lincoln can come straight away," Mrs. Acton added.

"No. No. I checked her temperature. She doesn't have a fever. Lady
Celia's doing better now and resting. I've no reason to think it's anything contagious. Something she ate didn't agree with her."

"Something she ate?" Mrs. Dasari turned a plaintive eye to the
pantry.

"I mean, I don't know," Olga said quickly. "That was but a guess.
Nothing to worry about. Just one of those things."

These women were no fools and would figure out Celia's condition
soon enough. Still, Olga needn't make that time come faster.

"Well, the young lord is in his father's study," Mrs. Dasari said,
calmer now.

"Oh." She'd rather hoped they'd say Rob was playing with Conall
at the nearby creek.

"And he's been asking after *you*, believe it or not," Mrs. Acton said.
"When I went upstairs to dust, he asked when you were due down."

A nervous lump lodged in Olga's throat. "You mean he asked after
Lady Celia."

"He asked for you." Mrs. Acton narrowed her eyes. "Something
wrong?"

"No, no." Olga heard the strange, high timbre of her voice.

"You seem jumpy."

"I'm fine. I remember what you mentioned about the quarrels with his lordship. How they haven't been on the best terms."

Olga looked down at the linoleum kitchen tiles, scrubbed so clean she felt terrible about tracking in mud from outside, despite her effort to wipe her boots before re-entering the house. She hadn't planned to bring up this topic, but the idea sprang to mind.

"Have they always been at odds?" She made a little circle with the toe of her boot. Then, from the corner of her eye, she saw Mrs. Dasari had turned back to the menu, forehead creased.

"His lordship needs to learn to appreciate his boy now that he's a grown man. That's all," Mrs. Dasari said.

"They must share a love of Russian culture," Olga said carefully. She was taking a risk, but would rather do so with Mrs. Acton and Mrs. Dasari than with Rob or Celia. "The young lord recommended a Russian book, and I thought I spotted a knick-knack or two from that land. And what with his lordship's interest in the empress and all ...."

"Their mother was originally from Russia," Mrs. Dasari said. "The late countess."

Of course! Olga should have guessed.

"You probably know that his lordship served as a diplomat to that country in his youth," Mrs. Acton said. "That's how they met. Why is it any concern of yours?"

"I was only curious," Olga said quickly. She turned to head upstairs for the study when Mrs. Acton took her arm.

"Take care around the young lord," she whispered. Her voice was kind but tinted with a note of pity Olga didn't like. "It makes little sense for a maid to get any notions the likes of him would show an interest. No matter how good at heart, that lot is that lot. They'll just hurt you."

When our true fate is known, there will be those who say the tsar's daughters haven't the strength to protect our family's legacy. We were believed to be weak and overprotected. Barely distinguishable as separate personalities, we were only seen together posing in identical white dresses. That is how Papa and his advisors presented us to the world. Over and over, my sisters and I sat for photographs, carefully posed for the camera to look both regal and endearing. With such sweet-faced, innocent daughters, how could anyone believe Papa to be anything but a loving and kind tsar and a father to the Russian people?

We four may have been cloistered before the Revolution, but we weren't as innocent as everyone presumed. Before everything came crashing down, we had some taste of life outside the family's palaces.

And I fell in love.

Dmitri Shakh-Bagov. Mitya. He was a member of the Erevan Regiment from Georgia and twice wounded in the war. The first injury was minor, but the second required an extended stay at our recovery ward.

He shared my feelings. I'm sure of it. When Mitya returned to the hospital, he sought me out. I remember the moment our gazes met. When I rushed to his side, he told me it wasn't so bad to be back; otherwise, how would he talk to me? How would he see me again?

Mitya spoke of life in the villages near his home and how the people there struggled. So even before revolution upended our lives, I had some sense of our family's complicity in their misery. I may not have appreciated it as much as I should have, but I understood my life consisted of privileges out of reach for most Russians. If our lives had not been so thoroughly overturned, my sisters and I could have done more about it.

My love for Mitya was never destined to last. I was intended for a royal bridegroom. If Mitya and I wanted to be together, we would've had to run away, deeply wounding my family. And Mitya would never ask me to betray my parents.

But Tatiana noticed how Mitya and I behaved around one another. Tatiana saw everything when she spent time with her own favorites in the recovery ward. My sister once asked if I meant to pursue a gentleman I could not marry. I sighed and collapsed on a satin pillow in our bedroom. I looked dreamily at the borders of our walls, stenciled with morning glories, acting as though the unfairness of it all was the worst fate imaginable.

At the time, it played like such a grand tragedy in my head. How little I'd known of tragedy back then. And how far away it all seems now.

The Private Diary of Olga Romanova
December 1921

CHAPTER ELEVEN

O nce Olga made her way up the narrow staircase from the kitchen, past the portrait gallery of the grim Lord Hammonds of the past, she paused and placed a hand lightly on the wallpaper, giving in to her urge to chuckle. It wasn't funny, exactly, what Mrs. Acton had said. Only Olga didn't know how else to react. Mrs. Acton was probably trying to do Olivia Bennett—the poor, overeducated maid—a favor.

But Olga was no stranger to the nuances of love. In the time before, she and her sisters mingled with courtiers, dancing and flirting and choosing favorites. In the hospital recovery ward, Olga flirted with handsome soldiers who hadn't been terribly injured. Under those circumstances, she might have sought Rob's company.

The irony, what Mrs. Acton couldn't possibly know, was that nothing would have come of it. Though titled, Rob would never have been considered sufficiently highborn for the daughter of a tsar.

Sobered, Olga smoothed her hands on her white apron. Such rubbish, these false barriers between people. Neither Olivia Bennett nor

Olga Romanova could risk thinking about Rob in any terms other than that of an employer. And her employer had asked to speak to her.

Continuing down the hall, she stopped in front of the study and took a moment to gather herself. She stared at the metallic detail edging the closed door, a pattern of curlicues and flora that reminded her of winter berries and holly leaves. And then she knocked.

"Come in!"

When she opened the door, she spotted Conall on a pillow on the window seat, keeping a careful eye on the birds outside. Then, turning his attention to Olga, he wagged his tail and bounded across the room, slipping on the smooth hardwood floor before scrambling over and pawing her leg. She curtsied and then bent down to give him a proper scratch behind the ears. Conall flopped on his back, whimpering, and she proceeded to rub his fat little belly.

"I swear he knows you from somewhere," Rob said, looking up from a sheet of paper. "It's the only explanation."

"Puppies love everyone."

"I'm not sure that's true. Conall has no use for my father, for instance. He gives him a wide berth whenever he's round."

Conall stared up at her adoringly. Olga couldn't help but think the pup had excellent taste.

"I came from the kitchen. I probably smell good."

Olga winced. That had sounded dangerously close to a flirtatious remark.

Rob arched an eyebrow but only said, "Are you sure you didn't bring him a biscuit? Perhaps that's it."

Something in his mock seriousness compelled her to smile. Then again, the earthy and comforting puppy scent may have prompted it.

"If I had thought ahead, I would have brought him a treat," she said. "I didn't realize you allowed him in the house."

"There are some benefits to being the heir apparent, you know."

That might be true, but Olga wasn't sure the benefits outweighed the responsibilities. She gave Conall one last pat, and the pup trotted to the desk and lay down at Rob's feet.

"I take it you're not here just to see Conall?" Rob said. "I told Mrs. Acton I was looking for you."

"Is it about Lady Celia?"

Rob frowned. "Is Celia all right?"

"Nothing serious. Your sister was sick this morning but feels better now, though moving slower than normal. I'm afraid she won't join you for lunch."

"I see." He hesitated, eying her curiously. Celia had told Rob her secret, but he wasn't sure that she, Miss Bennett, knew. Already, the situation was overly complicated. This might have been what Mrs. Acton meant when she'd warned Olga not to get too close to *that lot* upstairs. Not that the housekeeper seemed to follow her own advice regarding Rob.

"She only needs to rest, I'm sure," Olga said. "Was there something else?"

Rob rolled his shoulders, the sort of gesture Olga herself would make when gathering her courage. Surely Rob wasn't nervous about talking to a maid.

"I wanted to ask what book you chose," he said.

"Book?"

"From the library."

"Oh! I took your advice and selected the book by Mr. Pushkin."

Rob angled his hands together, long fingers forming a steeple, left hand bandaged. His posture made him look like a stern schoolteacher about to discipline a pupil. Except he was smiling warmly and his dark eyes positively twinkled.

"What do you make of *Eugene Onegin*?"

Olga fought to retain a neutral expression, remembering Papa reading the story by the fire. How fluidly he switched from Russian to English whenever Mama entered the room to listen for a bit. English had always been the language her parents preferred in conversation, for Mama never grasped Russian as well as she might have.

But Pushkin was meant to be read in Russian, and when Papa did so, losing himself in the melodic verse, it delighted her. So when Olga read it last night, she heard Papa's voice in her head.

"You look as though it made an impression. Though if I remember correctly, the title character's something of a boor at the beginning."

"I don't know about that."

"You don't know about the impression the book made or that Onegin is a boor?"

"Well, I'm only getting to know him," she said, trying to keep her tone light, "but I suppose I shall like him well enough."

"Perhaps we can discuss the nature of his character further once you've finished."

His hopeful gaze betrayed him. Rob was lonely, too. Like his sister. Anyone could see it. Olga was already picturing how pleasant it would be to sit with him in the garden as the days grew warmer and how her arm might brush against his. "I should like that."

Rob smiled, but she had taken up enough of his time. Olga was curtsying when she realized he was compressing his lips, as he had before, when his impediment threatened to stifle his words. She waited to see if he had more to say.

At last, he found his voice, melodic and soothing. "I don't believe there is a way to translate and retain the flow of the language properly."

"Exactly right. None can touch Pushkin's work when recited in Russian."

Olga clamped her mouth shut. Caught in the moment, she failed to realize Rob had spoken in Russian.

She had responded in kind.

By speaking in Russian, had he been trying to trick her? He must have done. He wouldn't have slipped into the language by accident.

His voice remained pleasing to her ears, but no longer playful. "Why were you here last night?"

Her cheeks warmed. "Pardon?"

Rob gestured behind him. "You want to see my father's files, don't you?"

Clasping her hands in front of her apron, Olga tried to steady her feet and stand tall before him. As tall as she could manage, given that she had made a foolish mistake. She gave her steeliest stare.

"I don't know what you mean."

Rob stood. At his full height, he was imposing. Sensing the tension in the room, Conall whined.

"When my father is away, I attend to his correspondence and accounts. I started reading the ledgers before I left for London. I remember the order in which I placed them back precisely. It was the last thing I saw before receiving word my father was in hospital. When I reviewed them again last night, after *you'd* been in here, they were out of order. You were looking at the one where he was jotting down titles for his other work. The book about the Romanovs."

Olga's thoughts darted about. Were the house fully staffed, she might have claimed innocence and declared she didn't know what he meant. Perhaps a parlor maid had been in here dusting and misplaced them. She did help Mrs. Acton tidy the house, except she should have said as much last night. Instead, Olga had told him she was lost. She had just doubled down on that lie by backing it up with the truth that she had been searching for a book. And then topped it all off by speaking in Russian.

Olga's gaze dropped to the tips of her leather boots, now scuffed. Mud clung to them despite her best efforts to wipe them clean before.

"Please look at me, Miss Bennett."

It took all her will, but Olga tilted her head up. His scar seemed more pronounced than before, even if his black hair mostly hid it. Still, she didn't think Rob was angry. Or not as angry as he might have been, given that she had lied. But the initial pleasantries were undoubtedly meant to lull her into a false sense of security. How silly of her to think about reading in the garden.

"My father was poisoned. He almost died. So when I re-examined the ledgers and saw this one out of place, I worried. Now I know you speak Russian fluently."

He showed her the ledger at the very place she had stopped last night.

Complicity in the House of Romanov.

The corners of his lips twitched. "I need the truth of it. Right now, I can't help but wonder if you are meant to spy on my father. If you might be connected to the Bolshevik government in Russia."

"Dear God, no!" Olga cried. "I despise the Bolsheviks."

Rob's brows lifted, and he drew his head back in genuine shock. "Despise them?"

Olga had not thought out her words before she spoke. "I didn't mean to be so bold."

"Why do you hate the Bolsheviks?"

Now, she would need to explain. Why would an English girl feel such vitriol?

"Might I sit down, my lord?" she said weakly.

Conall was still whining. Rob bent down to pet him. "Of course."

A wooden chair faced the desk. Olga imagined Lord Hammond placing it there for such an occasion as this: reprimanding a servant. She moved the chair and sat opposite Rob.

But she could not speak and stared out the window, trying to get her thoughts in order. A trio of tiny sparrows fluttered from the branch of a slender poplar tree outside. Rob knew now that she was no simple English girl. Or, at the very least, she was a bilingual English girl. She kept as close to the truth as she dared.

"My family is Russian. As you might have guessed."

Only the slightest movement of his hands betrayed his surprise. He looked down at the ledger. Olga imagined it was so she could not see his expression as he processed what she said.

"Recently arrived?" he asked. "And is it because of the Bolsheviks?"

"Yes. We've been here a year and some odd months."

"And yet your English is impeccable."

"I should have said my father's family is Russian. My mother's family is English." That was accurate enough. Her mother may have been vilified as the German woman during the war, but *her* mother had been English. Olga herself was a great-granddaughter of Queen Victoria. She wished she could share that bit with Rob. "We spoke both languages at home."

He drummed his fingers on the desk with his uninjured hand. "You and your parents live in England now?"

"My sister and I settled here thanks to the generosity of my mother's family." Again, partly true. Her mother's sister, their Aunt Victoria, was one of their benefactors. She didn't tell him about the jewels they'd smuggled from Russia or their grandmother's help. "I sought this position because I wanted to repay their kindness. Help pay our way if you will."

"And your parents? Do they work?"

"They didn't make it out of Russia," she said sharply. "The Bolsheviks murdered my parents."

His hand froze abruptly. "I'm sorry."

Olga shook her head. "I wasn't upfront when Lady Celia hired me. Please understand that the Bolsheviks taught me to be afraid. To hide who I am."

He was still frowning. "Forgive me, but it seems strange you would want to work here in the first place given that my father has made a point of seeking relations with the Bolsheviks."

Olga dared not look away, hating what she was about to say but not seeing another option.

"Your father claims our empress was a traitor. If so, she is to blame for what happened to my parents, at least partly. I knew she was an incompetent ruler and wanted to see the evidence with my own eyes. I have to know if she betrayed us to the Germans."

"That is why you sought employment at Marlingham?"

"It is," Olga admitted. "Not that I could have found a better woman to work for than Lady Celia."

"And why not simply wait until his book is published? It won't be that long."

Olga folded her hands in her lap. Once it was published, it would be too late.

"Curiosity got the best of me. I hate to think I endangered my position, but you asked for the truth."

Rob would now order her to pack her bags and leave. He might keep his tone pleasant. He might apologize. But he would send her away all the same.

Olga Romanova had failed again. She could not save her brother and her parents when she left them behind at the Ipatiev House. The House of Special Purpose. The house where the Bolsheviks murdered them. Now, she could not salvage their legacies. Besides that, she would be forced to abandon Celia right after she had promised to stay. Papa would have been ashamed of Olga for breaking a promise to someone who needed her. Olga scrunched her hands into fists and placed them before her on Hammond's desk as though presiding over a court of law rather than begging a young lord for forgiveness.

"Before you decide whether to send me away, consider Lady Celia's welfare," Olga said quickly. "She is lonely. I hope to be a friend to her."

It was a great liberty for a maid to say, but Olga was desperate. Her jaw tightened as her teeth clamped together. She could only imagine what she must look like, the incongruity of her determined face with her bonnet and apron and grubby ankle boots. She feared he would laugh at her. Not with her, which was delightful, but *at* her.

Then again, she knew he wouldn't. No matter what Rob did next, he wasn't the type to take his power over others lightly, no more so than Olga had been when she held a lofty position in the world.

His gaze shifted. He was looking at her lips.

Olga felt the blush coming, for she was now gazing at his lips as well. They appeared soft and inviting. She wondered what they would feel like on hers.

It seemed impossible, but was he thinking the same?

Stop it! That was Tatiana's voice in her head. Olga ignored her sister as she imagined bending forward slightly, offering herself to him.

Before she could consider anything further, Rob let out a substantial sigh. It was almost comic, and she suppressed a smile. It snapped the spell between them. And that was for the best.

He was not sending her away. Not today. Which meant she could stay with Celia. And she still had a chance to find something to help prove Hammond was wrong about her mother.

"I'm sorry about your parents," Rob said. "We should have done more. The English government, I mean. We could have helped additional people escape."

Olga couldn't have agreed more. The English agents had saved Olga and her sisters, but abandoned the rest of her family and the staff members who remained at their side until the bitter end. She may never learn exactly what happened to her family in Ekaterinburg, but the English government had allowed them to be murdered and for Olga to bear the guilt.

But she appreciated the sentiment and felt touched by the sincerity in Rob's voice. Besides, she knew her father might have done more to prevent what had happened. If Papa had instituted the reforms his people had been calling for, revolutionary passion would have had less space to breathe. The Bolsheviks would never have risen to power.

As a constitutional monarch, Papa could have thrived. He would have been like his cousin King George, safe after the war.

Olga couldn't share this with Rob, so she merely said. "Thank you." And then, feeling that response insufficient, she added: "Your Russian is most impressive if you don't mind me saying so."

"I don't mind you saying so. Why would I begrudge a compliment? My mother was from Russia and taught me the language. My father wasn't thrilled about that. He didn't see the need for it, but I'm glad she did."

"It was a part of her. She wanted you to understand her fully."

"Yes!" Rob said. "That's precisely it. When I speak Russian, I feel closer to her. Perhaps more so now."

"She must have been proud of how you handle the language. I can tell you that."

He looked away, sorrow pronounced. Olga wanted to rest her hand on his cheek and tell him it was all right to feel sad. He needed to mourn.

This was not the way of the English. Rather, Rob and Celia were raised to push their true feelings as deep down inside as they could and put on a brave face. Something akin to how Olga was forced to navigate the world now.

Rob forced a stiff smile and spoke once more in a casual tone.

"I have two requests. First, please tell my sister what you told me. It wouldn't do for me to know when she doesn't. If she sacks you, it's her business. Though I can't imagine she will."

Olga didn't think so, either. "I shall do so as soon as I return to her room."

"Secondly ..." He flashed a crooked grin. "What is your real name?"

She tried not to wince. She should have reversed it and told Rob her father was English, so she could claim Bennett as her own. Perhaps he would be satisfied with her given name alone, common enough. Yet could she dare say it aloud?

That beguiling smile convinced her. In an alternate life, he might have gifted her such while visiting the Russian court. It wasn't so fanciful, his father being a diplomat and all. She could have chatted with Rob as he pulled her close in a waltz. Or met him in a side alcove, distant from the prying eyes of the court. She could have flirted with him, told jokes, and maybe been bold enough to touch his arm before shyly pulling her hand away.

She wanted that so badly she thought her heart might break apart.

No matter how snug her room here at Marlingham, Olga was lonely, too. Desperately lonely. Perhaps that was why she recognized the same quality in Celia and Rob. She wanted someone like Rob to ask delightful questions, tease her, and let her slowly reveal herself to him as he revealed himself to her. She wanted him to know her actual name.

"Olga."

His eyes lit with interest. "That's pretty. What does it mean?"

"Blessed."

She didn't feel blessed in the slightest. And she had said too much. Olga felt especially self-conscious when he tried to look into her eyes, which were similar to her father's. She was growing as reckless as Anastasia.

Olga lowered her gaze and forced a more formal tone. "During my time here, I prefer to remain Olivia Bennett. If I might be excused? I want to check on Lady Celia."

The sound of his sister's name broke his concentration, and Rob gave a quick nod before glancing down again. "Of course. And thank you for taking such good care of her. You can understand why I worry, given her condition."

Olga was looking at her lap when she realized he'd just assumed she knew of Celia's pregnancy. Her head shot back up.

"I can't imagine you wouldn't have figured it out by now," he said. "No matter how clever Celia is with her gowns. I heard the sympathy in your voice when you asked to stay with her. I assume she has confided in you. Otherwise, I would never betray her secret. If our mother were here, maybe it would be different. She wouldn't be in this predicament at all."

Rob gave another hefty sigh, but there was no humor this time. He pressed his lips together. She wondered how much he knew about the baby's father.

Olga waited. When he said nothing further, she met his gaze.

"We will make the best of it," she told him. "Lady Celia has been good to me."

"Thank you," he said softly. "But I wish Celia would tell our father. He is a kind man. Despite our disagreements, I know him to be honorable. He might be angry at first, but ultimately, he will ensure Celia and the child are cared for. We must make that the priority now."

Olga tried not to betray her disappointment when he spoke well of his father. It was selfish, but she had hoped they were so irrevocably estranged that Rob would take her side against Hammond's. He might not know he was doing so, but somehow she longed for it all the same.

Rob tilted his head. She thought he was examining her eyes. If he had recognized a grand duchess, he would have said something. Surely he would. Even so, Olga kept her head bowed as she curtsied and left the study.

Though my relationship with Mitya was doomed, I drew to him like a flower to the sun. We could not touch one another, not in those days when I was still a grand duchess and he a soldier. So I would gaze longingly at his beautiful face, tanned from his days in the field. The black beard he was growing and which I so yearned to stroke. The soft lips from which I had stolen a kiss. The tenderness in his gentle brown eyes when he took the leather-bound photograph albums I'd brought to pass the time, pictures of my family taken with the box cameras Anastasia adored.

He turned the pages thoughtfully, smiling when he came upon a picture of me. And then his expression changed. I looked down and saw that Mama had pasted a photograph of Grigori Rasputin in the album. He wasn't posing with us. Instead, he stood with the ladies of Petrograd encircling him, admirers who flocked to him for what he called spiritual advice.

Mama thought his picture belonged among those of our family. No matter what others might say about him, she saw nothing but holiness in Grigori Rasputin.

"How can your mother trust that man?" Mitya had said.

I'd fingered the oval locket I wore on a chain around my neck, an expensive piece made of gold and edged with diamonds. Of course, I didn't think twice about such luxuries in those days. Inside lurked a few greasy strands of Father Grigori's hair. Each of us had one. Father Grigori had told Mama to have us hold this simple part of him close to our hearts. It would grant us all protection.

I know it sounds ridiculous. It sounded ridiculous to me at the time. However, I was not about to question my mother, certainly not about Father Grigori. I was the eldest daughter meant to set an example for the rest. My duty was to obey. Even when her instructions were outlandish.

Mitya could never know why Father Grigori remained close to our family nor why our mother placed so much faith in his words. So I kept silent until Mitya awkwardly changed the subject. And not for the first time, I wondered if I would have been better off not being born a royal. Despite our mutual desire, the gulf between us had never seemed so vast.

The Private Diary of Olga Romanova
December 1921

CHAPTER TWELVE

C elia appraised a collection of perfumes, holding each one up to her nose. She was expecting visitors. More accurately, Rob was expecting visitors, a couple who owned a small plot on their father's land, and he had asked his sister to join them. They were the first callers to come to Marlingham since Olga had arrived.

Olga braided Celia's hair along the crown of her head, twisting the band around the ends. While waiting for Celia to choose a scent, she took a moment to admire her work and reflect on how well she'd progressed since first practicing on Maria.

Still, Olga chewed her bottom lip, worried. They'd had drawn-out moments of silence before, for they were both quiet by nature. They sat comfortably together in silent contemplation, enjoying the comfort of one another's presence without needing to say a word.

However, Olga sensed the tension in the quiet, where none had existed before. Things were different between them, strained somehow.

As promised, she had shared with Celia what she'd told Rob, letting the story unfold in a burst of frantic exposition. She was Russian.

After the tsar abdicated, she and her sister were sent out of the country. Her parents remained and were killed. She hated the Bolsheviks.

When Olga got to that part, Celia had sat up in bed, her peignoir falling around her shoulders, wide-eyed as the maid previously known to her as Olivia Bennett apologized for the deception. Olga said she would leave if that's what Celia wanted.

"Absolutely not," Celia had declared. "It seems we both have our secrets. You had your reasons for not sharing. And you've lost your mother, as I lost mine."

Olga had exhaled, relieved. After that, she considered matters settled. Now she wondered if Celia had mulled over what she had shared. After all, Olga thought about Celia's secret all the time. Was the baby a boy or a girl? How would their lives change once the sprout arrived? Should they build a nursery in secret? That seemed nearly impossible, but perhaps there were hidden rooms in the house.

"You mentioned your callers are tenants—"

Just as Olga got the words out, Celia exclaimed, "I'm not sure what—"

They both paused.

"I'm sorry," Olga said. "Please. You first."

"No, you."

Olga gave Celia a skeptical look. They could play the "you first" game all evening.

"Fine. I'll talk," Celia said. "I don't mean to pry, but I am curious about your time in Russia. Did you live there all your life? And I am so sorry about your parents. It must be painful."

"It happened after I left."

Celia drummed her fingers against the vanity, reminding Olga of Rob making the same gesture in Hammond's study.

"Your English is flawless. Though, I confess, I always detected an accent."

Olga bowed her head. She and her sisters may have spoken fluent English, but were prone to odd inflections inspired by the array of tutors and governesses they'd had growing up, some from Scotland and others from Ireland. They also spent many pleasant afternoons chatting in English with Jim Hercules, one of Papa's guards. He wore the uniform of Abyssinia but hailed from the American south, the grandson of a gentleman once enslaved. Jim's charming drawl influenced their speech patterns as well.

Only Anastasia had perfected an English accent. Olga imagined her sister could speak in a perfect American accent as well, if she desired. Ana had once been a talented actress in their home-produced plays and skits. Unfortunately, Olga was not as skilled.

"My parents preferred to speak English," she said.

Celia met Olga's gaze in the mirror. "Is it hard not to speak Russian, though? Mother taught Rob, but I hadn't the opportunity. My mother read fairy tales in that language sometimes. I caught on to the story from the pictures. How wonderful it would be to learn."

Olga looked down at her ankle boots. For her, Russian was now forever the language of pain and captivity, a dull thud in her head. It might have been the language of Pushkin, but it was also the shouts of Petrograd workers approaching their palace while Olga and her sisters remained ill and helpless in bed. It was the slurred taunting of the drunken red guards assigned to their family, and the terrible graffiti about her mother scrawled on the lavatory walls.

"I prefer not to speak it. Right now, I have no desire but to be thoroughly English." She hesitated. "If that suits."

Celia reached back and clasped Olga's forearm gently.

"I was silenced when my mother died. It took me ages to speak of her. And that was a natural death, not ... not what happened to your parents. So I want you to find peace here."

Olga smiled, but peace seemed a distant dream.

Celia started fingering the glass bottles once more. "What do you think? What should I spritz on?"

"Perhaps the rose water?"

"A fine choice." Celia chose her rose water bottle and tapped it on her wrists with her finger. The heady scent reminded Olga of the rose Coty perfume, ordered directly from Paris, which she used to dab liberally about her neck.

"You were going to ask me something," Celia said. "About our callers?"

"Nothing important." Olga withdrew a wooden box filled with pendants from one of the bottom drawers of Celia's armoire. "I only wondered if you were looking forward to their visit."

"Rob has business with them, though I'm not sure how I shall be involved."

"To charm them?" Olga asked cheekily. She sorted through Celia's pendants, a variety of finely crafted and jeweled pins alongside quirkier costume jewelry.

"More like it would be too strange to exclude me." Celia selected another bottle on the vanity and rubbed lotion into her hands. Her eyes sparkled. "Rob asked me to listen and ensure everything sounds on the level. They're the last of Papa's tenants, and Rob wants to purchase a part of their land that has gone fallow. He wishes to build an infirmary for veterans of the war. Or, rather, a rehabilitation center. It's in the early stages but terribly intriguing."

From listening to Mrs. Acton and Mrs. Dasari, Olga understood Rob was keen to do something unconventional with Marlingham once it passed to him. They were always going on about how different he was from his father. Still, Olga hadn't expected this. She tried to keep her response muted, even as she felt impressed. "Noble work, indeed."

"I think so, though I'm not sure we can get everyone to agree. I don't believe this couple is as sold on the idea as Rob hoped."

"Why not?" Olga remembered the soldiers at the hospital with haunted eyes, and how they would cry out for their mothers. "It's the least anyone can do. We owe these men our world."

"Would everyone felt the same," Celia said. "Only this is not meant for the wounded as such. Not physically wounded. Rather, the soldiers Rob wishes to provide for endure afflictions of the mind. He intends to give them a temporary space where they can be properly evaluated and set up with the right long-term care."

Olga remembered the pain in Rob's features when he tried to control his stammer. What had he seen during the war? She'd assumed rank granted privilege. And yet, with a title, Rob had experienced the heat of battle.

"It scares them." Celia frowned, working the lotion deeper into her skin. "I suppose I understand on some level. We're taught to fear the mentally unbalanced, taught they might hurt us, but many soldiers returned with such wounds. Those we cannot see. They deserve care, the same as the others."

"I whole-heartedly agree," Olga said. "Does his lordship view it that way as well?"

"Rob has mentioned it to him. I believe Papa supports the idea in theory. Only he turned his attention back to Russia, rather suddenly, I might add, and never seems to have time for anything else these days. Anyway, I want to help Rob."

Olga settled on a pendant shaped like a butterfly with emeralds studding the delicate glass wings. She thought it would add a measure of whimsy to Celia's violet day gown. Not that Olga knew whether whimsy was something the visitors would notice, but Celia appreciated it. She beckoned for Celia to come nearer and pinned the butterfly on her short jacket.

"Now you're ready to seize the world!" Olga declared.

"You don't think—"

Celia turned again to take stock of herself in the mirror, smoothing the folds of her dress and straightening a thin gold chain around her neck. She touched her stomach. It wasn't difficult to read her thoughts.

Thankfully, the fashions were looser fitting than they had been a few years prior, with skirts cut generously around the middle and higher waists. Still, Olga had cheated somewhat. She tied the skirt sash above Celia's natural waist to better disguise her tummy. Maria would have been proud of her for creating the illusion.

"Not noticeable," Olga assured her. "You only see a bump because you know."

"I didn't have you put me in a corset."

"Which only makes you a modern woman."

"What if the neighbors don't like modern women?"

"Then they're perfect *rotters,*" Olga said, repeating one of Ada's salty expressions.

Celia laughed. "You always know what to say to make me feel better. You make me wish I'd had a sister. Not instead of Rob, of course, but in addition."

Sadness pinched Celia's features. Olga wished she could have invited her to supper or tea with her sisters. Celia would have loved that.

"I want to make a good impression," Celia said.

"I've every confidence you will," Olga replied. And then, hesitating for a moment: "If you don't mind ... may I ask how far along you are?"

Celia twisted one of her rings. "It is obvious, then."

"No! If it were, I would have found something looser for you to wear." When Olga had first discovered Celia in the bathroom, she'd hardly noticed the bump, but it was growing and would eventually be impossible to hide. "I was only curious, so we might better prepare for when ... well ..."

"When I have to tell people. I should come up on the fourth month soon."

Calculating the time in her head, Olga realized this had likely happened when Celia was in London. The child's father must live there. Celia reached out and took Olga's hand, which Olga squeezed in return.

But then her expression changed. She released Olga's hands and snapped her fingers.

"Oh! I forgot. Rob told me Mrs. Pendleton is allergic to nuts. Will you check that the others haven't included any in the tea service?" She turned back to her mirror. "I'll be down soon."

"Of course." Olga tried to hide her disappointment, but it hurt when Celia moved so quickly from confidante to the lady of the house. Had she been raised differently, Olga might have taken it in stride. As it stood, Olga felt diminished.

But what else could she expect? Much as she wanted to be friends with Celia, it wasn't possible. She needed to remember her place.

Olga gathered a few things to toss in the laundry, as she was accustomed to doing when she left Celia's room. Even if Rob and Celia knew more about her now, she would remain Olivia Bennett for the duration of her time at Marlingham.

Thoughts of Celia's baby and Rob's plans for a rehabilitation center distracted Olga. As a grand duchess, she might have provided patronage for both. Now, she could only offer encouragement. Anyway, Olga suspected that emotional support was more important than money for Rob and Celia.

Engrossed in thought, she stumbled on the last step of the central staircase and into the hallway, bumping into a heavy frame around a former Earl of Hammond. It made a terrible scratching sound against the wall, and she wondered how much damage she'd wrought. Thankfully, neither Mrs. Acton nor anyone else was in sight.

As she shifted Celia's laundry, two dirty towels she had grabbed before leaving the room, under her arm, she tried to right the frame. A knob squeaked. So much for no one noticing. If only she had a feather duster or some such in her hands, she could pretend to be cleaning.

The door to Hammond's study opened.

"Are you okay?" Rob said. "I heard a clatter."

He wore a gray morning coat and matching trousers that Charlie, who sometimes acted as valet, must have pressed to achieve the sharp crease down the front of each leg. Rob's usually disarrayed hair had been slicked back with a pomade that smelled of the same cedar and musk as his cologne. She supposed he wanted to make a good impression on their callers, just as Celia did, but Olga decided she preferred his black hair to run wild, like when they first met. Like Heathcliff in *Wuthering Heights*.

Still, in his stiff coat and with his hair tamed, she could more easily imagine him a little older, perhaps a streak or two of silver threading his hair, when he took his place as the new earl with a seat in the House of Lords. And then she tried to place herself in that picture, watching him from the viewing gallery and bursting into applause whenever he made a salient point before Parliament.

If only her mind weren't given to such foolish flights. As though she could ever accompany Rob to Westminster Hall. Or anywhere else.

"Clumsy of me," she told him. "I jostled the frame. I'm sorry."

Rob shrugged and gave her a cheeky smile, his expression at odds with his solemn attire. "These good fellows could use some shaking up. Their portraits have been here too long."

Olga used to wander the gallery in the Hermitage adjacent to the Winter Palace in St. Petersburg. The museum housed portraits of her father's Romanov predecessors back to the first: Tsar Mikhail, who took the throne in 1613. Three hundred years and then some before the Bolsheviks crushed the dynasty under their simple workers' boots.

"Might I ask how far back these date?" she said.

Rob raked his hand through his hair. He wasn't wearing a bandage on his left hand any longer, and the skin was healing with a rosy hue.

When Rob stepped out of the study and stood next to her, Olga took in the good puppy smell still clinging to his clothes. Perhaps he'd tussled with Conall before cleaning up for his guests.

"The first Earl of Hammond was awarded the title after serving as a cavalier and pledging fealty to the monarchy during the Civil War." Rob indicated a Lord Hammond in red and gold court garb and curly black locks hanging past his shoulders, as was the fashion of that time.

"Mid-seventeenth century, then." Olga appraised the portrait, the gentleman's long nose and the steely glint in his dark eyes. She thought she saw something of Rob in him, though that might only have been a fancy.

Either way, his family's claim to a noble title dated almost as far back as her family's claim to a throne. And his family still held their titles, whereas the Bolsheviks had unceremoniously stripped Olga and her sisters of theirs.

"Right," he said. "Father will insist the family tree stretches farther back, all long-lived and hale gentlemen, naturally."

"Naturally." Rob's more formal look was growing on her. The single-breasted waistcoat drew attention to the width of his chest. Olga had little experience with the opposite sex, but she knew how fine those muscles would appear if he removed the layers of clothing covering them. She was confident they would *feel* fine as well, though she'd never had the pleasure of such a touch.

Her cheeks flamed. Wasn't she just telling herself she should accept her new lot in life as a maid?

"I believe my father would claim King Arthur as an ancestor if he could," Rob added. "Which makes his backing of the Bolshevik government all the more baffling."

"Indeed. His ancestor was a cavalier, yet he supports the beasts who now run my country. Who murdered their monarch in cold blood."

That comment would probably push Rob's goodwill too far. But Olga's outrage at Hammond—and, by extension, all his glorious and inglorious ancestors—always simmered beneath her stoic surface.

"One can be a monarchist and a forward thinker," Rob said. "We've done an adequate job of that in this country, though some would like to transition to republicanism."

"The Bolsheviks are not forward thinkers," she said evenly. "They are monsters who took advantage of a terrible situation." Her English accent crumbled, and she thought she'd used a Russian word, *izvergi*, instead of the English term.

"Quite so. You would know that better than anyone."

Olga didn't respond or dare look at Rob, but felt the intense curiosity in his gaze. If he expected she would break down and share more with him in the hallway, staring at pictures of old Englishmen and holding Celia's soiled towels, he was wrong.

"And you are still determined to learn if the Empress of Russia had anything to do with the downfall of your country in the war?" he asked.

"I owe it to my parents."

"I can't blame you. Alexandra's reputation was awful. All of that business with Rasputin."

Olga squeezed the towels tighter. Rob didn't understand, and she couldn't say what she wanted to say. Her parents had trained her not to say it. Even now, when it no longer mattered, she had to hold her tongue.

Father Grigori helped my brother.

And because she couldn't stop herself: "Perhaps your father is wrong. The empress might have had nothing at all to do with the Germans. Maybe she was maligned because the Kaiser was her kin. That's hardly her fault."

"What a change in tune!" Rob said. "Now, you accuse my father of lying?"

"I didn't say that," she amended. "But what proof does your father have?"

"You sound sure he has no substantiation for these allegations."

"I did not claim to be sure."

"My father is an honorable man," Rob said, too emphatically, as though he were trying to convince himself. "He must have his reasons for accusing the empress. He wouldn't do so without evidence of her wrongdoing."

More than ever, Olga wished she could reveal who she was and why she was here. Rob would then understand why she needed to ask these questions. "I'm only considering the possibility that his reasons may have more to do with political expediency than truth."

Anger edged Rob's voice. "You might think differently if you'd seen ..."

Olga grew cold. "Seen what?"

He shoved his right hand deep into his pocket, ruining the creases on his trousers. The other hand fell to his side.

"Sometimes it's best to let these things be. You're starting a new life. What good does it do to dredge up the past?"

"No," she said weakly. "I don't believe in forgetting the past but confronting it."

"What if you find something you don't want to know?"

"I must face it. Otherwise, I'll never truly start over. I would only be running away."

"Is that what you think you did?" he asked her. "By leaving Russia?"

"The Bolsheviks forced the situation. My parents had to send me abroad. I had no choice but to leave."

With a scowl, Rob motioned for her to join him in the study. He turned the lamp on and moved behind the desk.

Olga stifled a gasp as Rob withdrew the same ledger he had been looking at the other night.

"If this is so important to you, why don't you take another look? See for yourself."

He opened the ledger to where she had left off and pushed it toward her. Olga hesitated, placing Celia's towels on the floor before picking up the journal and reading.

Complicity in the House of Romanov
The Tsar, the Empress, and the Mad Monk

Betrayal: Alexandra, Rasputin, and the Fall of the Russian Empire

After those phrases, she saw only a continuation of the dry household accounts. Olga slumped.

"He was testing out titles for his book." Rob reached behind and lifted a bookend, producing a small brass key. After unlocking and pulling open the top drawer, he withdrew several manila file folders. "I guess he decided his first title was the strongest. Go on. Take them."

Olga didn't dare. Rob's shift of tone scared her. Suddenly, she was afraid of what she would see.

"If you want to look at them so badly," Rob insisted. "You may do so."

She could hardly turn away now, not after everything she'd risked. Olga snatched the folders from his hands. There were four in all, each filled with neatly typed papers clipped at the top. It would take some time to get through them.

"Your father—"

"Still in London. Anyway, he plans on publishing these notes. All of his readers will see them. All the same, I'm not sure I want him to know I let you see them in advance. Return here to read them this evening. I'll steer clear, so you have privacy."

"Thank you." Her voice cracked. She set the files back on the desk and gathered the towels again. "I only need to learn the truth. That's all."

"So be it," he said, his tone formal. Perhaps she'd grown too accustomed to the warmth in his voice. She'd read more into it than she should have done.

Something occurred to her as she proceeded down the hall, clutching the towels. If Rob allowed her to read in the study on her own, then she could leave, sneak away, steal the files, and review them with her sisters. Although she didn't think those were the only copies. She doubted she'd stop Hammond by taking them, but she might slow him down some.

She would have done that except she remembered Celia on the cold tile floor of her bathroom, confessing the truth of her condition. Olga had promised to stay with her. She'd made the same promise to Rob.

Olga wasn't going anywhere. Not yet. They still needed her at Marlingham.

Mama may have mistakenly trusted Grigori Rasputin, but her love for Russia—its people, church, customs, and culture—was absolute.

As devoted as she was to Russia, my mother sometimes spoke of her childhood in the German land of Hesse. On those occasions, she would sigh and stare dreamily out a window. Who could blame her? She left home as a young woman because she'd fallen in love with the then-heir to the Russian throne. My father, Nicholas.

Though born a princess, Mama came from a humble court and was never comfortable around the glamorous Romanovs and their gossipy tittle-tattle. That discomfort was only part and parcel of her shy personality.

She hated the Kaiser for what he had done to her adopted homeland, and though he was a cousin, she stopped considering him kin. She was loyal to the people, even when they whispered and mocked her accent behind her back. When they called her the German woman and drew vulgar cartoons. And when the red guards made her life an unbearable hell.

When she drew her last breath on Russian soil, I can only imagine it was with a silent prayer to forgive all who had caused her suffering in her new home.

The Private Diary of Olga Romanova
December 1921

CHAPTER THIRTEEN

Olga looked twice over each shoulder before pressing her ear closer to the wall. She heard only the click of spoons against saucers. While Olga couldn't risk returning to the study to review Hammond's papers—not yet, anyway, with company here and Mrs. Acton prowling about—she strained to hear what was being said inside the parlor.

A few minutes earlier, Ada had brought the tea service: a teapot on a cloth cosy, milk and sugar in silver serving dishes, and delicate puff pastries stuffed with Mrs. Dasari's curried salad. Ada expertly balanced the heavy platter in her thin arms.

Once she delivered the tray, Ada scurried off, leaving the hallway to Olga alone.

When the visitors first arrived, Olga had lingered near the entrance hall. With no butler at Marlingham, she'd helped Charlie collect their coats and then pretended to give them a thorough cleaning with a valet's brush. As she did so, she heard their names. Mr. and Mrs. Pendleton—an older gentleman with a closely clipped silver mustache and his soberly dressed wife whose smile was exceedingly tight. She would have appeared significantly younger than her husband but for the lines at the corners of her eyes and fine gray hairs in her sparse brows.

Olga wondered what they would make of Rob's plan once he put it before them. She sensed he could be wonderfully persuasive when he set his mind to it. If they were stuck in their ways, as so many of her Romanov relatives had been, he might not convince them. Still, she hoped for the best.

At least she had helped in a small way by adjusting Celia's outfit to disguise her stomach. Celia looked well enough in her violet day gown and jacket, though Olga suspected someone could guess her condition were they paying close enough attention. Hopefully, neither Pendleton had a keen eye for such matters.

From the parlor now, murmurs of subdued chit-chat between Celia and Mrs. Pendleton reached Olga's ears. And then Mr. Pendleton cut in, his voice a healthy tenor. "I imagine this is more than a neighborly call."

She couldn't make out Rob's exact response. His voice was so low she knew he was talking, but the words scattered. *Best I can manage ... consider it ... in need of a different sort of service.*

"Different sort?" the other man asked.

Celia answered, her voice high and distinct. "It's difficult to find mental health services even in the largest hospitals in London. So my brother proposes a centralized space where the lads can locate that help more easily."

Further mumbling ensued. Olga leaned in closer, her fingers spread against the wall.

"Well, it is something to consider, for sure," Mr. Pendleton said. "Though I admit I have more pressing matters on my mind at present."

This time, Olga heard Rob clear as a bell. "Pressing matters?"

"His lordship's health. Your father that is. How does he fare? We thought we'd see him here for Eastertide, but it seems he's in London still."

"His trip back was delayed," Rob said. Olga couldn't tell if he was happy or upset with this.

"But his health is much improved," Celia said. "Thank you for asking."

"Does Lord Hammond plan to return soon?" Mrs. Pendleton asked.

"My father shall return soon enough. He still wants to work on his book here. Only his doctor said he's not quite ready for travel."

His book. Olga hissed in a sharp breath. Soon enough, she would read what Hammond intended to include in this book: his so-called evidence of her mother's betrayal of Russia and the Allies. And then she would make sure that the book never saw the light of day.

"I must say, I wouldn't be surprised if the incident changed his lordship's politics," Mrs. Pendleton said slowly. "His attitude toward Russia, that is. He wanted to work with the Bolsheviks?"

"Yes, hasn't his last encounter with those devils changed his mind?" her husband added. "Doesn't seem like you can trust them even when you're on their side."

Olga smiled. Mr. Pendleton sounded like a sensible man.

"Hey! What are you doing there, then?"

The female voice came from behind, startling her. Peeking over her shoulder once more, she saw Ada holding a tray bearing a plate of fresh scones with small bowls of jam and clotted cream. Olga backed away from the wall.

"Begging your pardon." She turned to face Ada. "I only wanted to make sure Lady Celia was all right."

"Why wouldn't she be?" Ada's features scrunched into a frown. Her bonnet could not contain her curly brown hair. Mrs. Dasari and Mrs. Acton had her running to and fro all morning to prepare for the visit.

"I thought I heard coughing." Olga shrugged helplessly.

"Hmm." Ada didn't look fooled. She knew Olga was snooping. But she didn't care, not really. "I thought maybe you were peeking in on our young lord. I feared this visit was to do with setting him up with some lady."

A fit of ridiculous prickling jealousy settled in Olga's chest. It occurred to her then that she didn't know if Rob had his eye on a lady or not. Celia might have mentioned it, but then *she* might not know. And then how would Olga ever find out? Her heart flip-flopped, and she felt suddenly woozy.

"From the looks of that lot, I should say no," Ada added.

"I shouldn't have tried to listen in," Olga said. "I must look silly."

"Oh, I don't care about that. I thought you might want to join us downstairs for a cuppa. Take a load off and all now that we settled the guests."

Olga glanced at the parlor door. Rob was rumbling a response to the question about his father and the Bolsheviks, but she missed it. "That's kind, but Lady Celia may need me."

"We're not some grand castle! You'll be right below the stairs. The lady can call with the bell if you're needed."

Olga had run out of excuses. "I suppose you're right."

"Mind getting the door?" Ada nodded to her tray.

Olga opened the door, and Ada stepped inside the parlor to deliver the treats. Olga saw Celia passing her frilled handkerchief from hand to hand while Rob leaned forward with his mouth open as though about to speak.

Unfortunately, before she could hear what he said, Ada pushed the door back with her foot, and it shut in Olga's face. There was nothing left to do but join the other servants downstairs.

Sipping her black tea with milk and nibbling on a scone, nothing was wrong, per se. And yet Olga found her chair too wobbly and the heat from the kitchen so excessive she needed to fan herself with a napkin. Upstairs, she hadn't heard—or overheard, she supposed—anything she didn't already know.

Part of her discomfort had to do with recounting her background with Rob and Celia while leaving those gathered around the table in the servants' hall in the dark. Particularly now that Marlingham felt like home.

She stopped herself mid-bite. How could she think that way? Home was with her sisters. This place wasn't her home.

Still, it felt jolly to be included at tea time below stairs, and it was considerate of Ada to make a point of inviting her. Ever since the evening when Olga had bandaged Rob's wound, Ada tried to loop her into more chats and tittle-tattle.

This afternoon, Mrs. Dasari had taken off for one of her brisk walks around the grounds, and Mrs. Acton was still cleaning rooms upstairs. The footman, Charlie, had joined them. He was trying his best not to stare at Ada, but anyone could tell he was mad for her. With Olga,

Charlie was personable, a far different young man than the stiff and nervous boy who'd first greeted her at Marlingham when she came to interview. Ada and Charlie were trying to make *Miss Bennett* feel welcome in their world, even if they teased her whenever she glanced at the bellpull, worrying over Celia.

"She's fine," Ada said with a dainty wave of her hand.

Olga made a mock-serious face. "You don't believe she requires twenty-four-hour care?"

Ada wrinkled her nose. But then, realizing it had been a joke, she let out a snort of a laugh and reached for another scone.

Charlie beamed and watched Ada's fingers as she tore off small pieces of the pastry and popped them into her mouth. Olga wondered if Ada and Charlie were accustomed to holding hands during their free time in the afternoons. She almost told them they should go ahead and do so, never minding her presence, but she wasn't that comfortable with them. Not yet.

While Ada munched on her scone, mouth full, the conversation lagged. The silence was companionable enough but awkward. Charlie cleared his throat and Olga looked all around the kitchen, wondering what Rob was saying upstairs. To fill the quiet space, she was about to make a random comment about the gazebo Celia had identified for a paint job once the weather warmed, but Charlie spoke before she had the chance.

"Seems like a long time since callers last came round. Makes me wonder what they're talking about, you know."

He licked his lips. Ada took another sip of tea. Olga could practically see the wheels turning in Charlie's head as he tried to sort out something interesting to say to her.

"It's been a while." He scratched his head and left it at that.

"That it has, as Mrs. Dasari would say." Ada had lowered her voice into a pitch-perfect impersonation of the cook but with no malice. And then, in her usual tone, she said: "It seems strange though, don't it? Mrs. Acton said there used to be visitors here all the time."

"I wonder if the rumors might have anything to do with it," Charlie said.

Olga stilled, fingers curled around the teacup. She had been trying to warm her hands, but now the rest of her body went cold. Perhaps she hadn't done a fine enough job concealing Celia's condition earlier when she'd helped her dress.

"Not that such rumors are fair or that anyone should spread them," he added quickly.

"Oh, come out with it," Ada said. She looked so flirtatious when her eyes met Charlie's that Olga knew he would say something. *No. Please. Don't do it, Charlie.*

"It's only old gossip about Lady Hammond."

Olga's heart started pumping. How could Charlie possibly know Celia had fallen pregnant? But then he was shy, and such people often took in the most information. Maria was like that—sweet and quiet. And then, seemingly out of nowhere, she'd drop a bombshell.

"What gossip?" Ada leaned in closer, eyes wide.

Charlie's chest puffed out. "Only about her pregnancy. The birth father. All that."

"No, no, no!" Olga couldn't bear to hear him talk about Celia.

"What's gotten into you?" Ada exclaimed.

Though Charlie meant no harm, his loose lips could endanger Celia's reputation. He might be discreet, but Ada certainly wasn't.

"I only think we should keep to our own business." She sounded more like her mother than ever, prim and proper, with subtle judgment in her tone.

"Ordinarily, I'd agree, miss," Charlie said. "Idle chatter, yes. But this could impact us."

"Even so, we can't speculate." Olga tried.

"Out with it then." Ada's eyes were shining at Charlie.

He leaned in and whispered, "His lordship? He may not be our young lord's father."

Olga took a moment to let that sink in, for the comment made no sense. And then, with a strange mingling of relief and horror, she realized she'd made a mistake. Charlie had said Lady *Hammond*, not Lady *Celia*. So Charlie was talking about Rob and Celia's late mother.

"I heard whisperings of it when I let the callers in," Charlie continued. "Heard them talking whilst waiting for the young lord and lady. Could be nonsense."

"Most such rumors are. Nonsense, that is," Olga said.

"Not that I knew her well, but I met Lady Hammond briefly before she passed. The countess was a kind woman, and I've no wish to soil her reputation. I should have made that clear." Charlie flashed Ada a small, apologetic grin.

As he spoke, Olga tried to think this through. If Rob were not Hammond's son, but the earl and countess were married when he was born, Rob would remain the heir.

"I still don't see how this should matter to us," she said.

"If word were to get out and cause more problems between the young lord and his lordship. And we're short-staffed as it is." Charlie gestured vaguely around the servants' hall. "Who knows what could happen to our situations here? That's all."

Now she understood Charlie's concern. The house was not well staffed, which indicated the family might not be interested in keeping it up as they once had, particularly now that the countess had passed away.

At one time, letting go of such a property, one that had been in the family for generations, would have been unthinkable. No longer. Times were changing rapidly, and these old houses were more and more like relics of the past with no place in the post-war world. Suppose the divide between Rob and his father were to deepen. Perhaps to where their differences became irreconcilable. In that case, Hammond might decide the manor wasn't worth the trouble. He might lease or sell the place.

"Do you think he knows?" she asked. "Lord Hammond?"

"I've overheard feuds between them," Charlie said, "but nothing to make me think his lordship knew he wasn't raising his biological son."

"That makes it worse, doesn't it?" Ada said. "The news could break his heart."

Olga frowned. "Why would the Pendletons bother to discuss the young lord's parentage at this late date?"

"He wants them to agree to this convalescence center or whatever," Charlie said. "They aren't keen to do so, I'd wager. Trying to find a way out of it. Perhaps his father might have better luck convincing them."

"Are the Pendletons on good terms with Hammond?"

Olga bit her lip. He wasn't "Hammond" with no Lord before the title, not to the likes of her. Not outside of her private thoughts, anyway.

Fortunately, Ada and Charlie were too preoccupied to notice her mistake. "I don't know," Charlie said. "I only hope they don't ruin this for the young lord. It would be nice to have this place thriving again, even if that means filling it with nut jobs."

"Charlie!" Ada cried.

The footman blushed, cheeks bright pink. "I didn't mean it like that. It just came out wrong. It's well and good what the young lord has planned."

"I should say so," Ada declared. "I plan to ask about nursing if it all works out."

"You will?" Olga was happy for Ada but found it hard to smile. "That's wonderful."

"That it is," Charlie agreed, looking down at his hands.

"You should consider the same, miss," Ada said.

"Perhaps." A single thought kept running through Olga's mind, distracting her so she couldn't manage a better answer for Ada. *Poor Rob.*

Another thought crept into her mind, unbidden. If there was truth to this rumor, and if it resurfaced after all these years, it could create a powerful distraction. She wondered if she might use it against Hammond, perhaps affect his plans to publish his book. At the very least, it might get him to stop talking about this public censure of her mother.

With shame, Olga wondered if she was capable of revealing this secret, should it come to that, if it meant saving Mama's reputation.

She tried not to think about Rob's words. *My father is a good man. Despite our disagreements, I know my him to be honorable.*

Olga hated that he was wrong. Worse yet, once she reviewed this so-called evidence his father kept against her mother, she would be responsible for making him see his father as he was. A liar. A man with no honor at all. How could an honorable man persist in hurting Mama, particularly now that she was gone?

She didn't want to hurt Rob, but it couldn't be helped. Truth always came to light, no matter how much one might want to keep it in the dark. No matter what secrets it might hold.

Despite my faith in our mother, I admit to moments of doubt.

"Quickly, quickly!" Mama's voice. Forever in my head.

At one point, while we were still under house arrest at the Alexander Palace, my parents hadn't been allowed to see one another for weeks, not even to dine together. The guards kept them separated because Mother was officially under suspicion. The Provisional Government, the liberal party in power before the Bolsheviks, was determined to find the evidence they needed to prove "the German woman" was a traitor.

So they spilled the contents of drawers onto the palace's parquet floors and richly woven carpets: the stray papers, ledgers, and files one would expect to find in Papa's study, as well as delicate undergarments and lavender sachets from Mother's boudoir. They searched our rooms, which were in the wing of the palace still known as the nursery, though all of us were well past our toddling years. Our cats crouched under our beds while the spaniel, Joy, followed the men around, barking. I prayed he would not nip at one of their ankles.

The men found nothing. I like to think it was because there was nothing to find. In retrospect, it was only a brief respite. The Provisional Government was honorable enough to require evidence before pursuing allegations. The Bolsheviks merely concocted whatever evidence they desired, such that they shot my parents with little preamble, or so I've been made to understand.

Dramatic as it was, the search might have slipped to the back of my mind, for afterward, my parents could dine and sleep together once more. The men issued apologies and even helped us straighten our things, a minor inconvenience compared to the humiliations we would suffer later.

Still, at the time, I'd made a silent vow that someday I would make things right. No one would ever treat my parents this way ever again.

Amidst the search, I remember sidling up to the door of my mother's boudoir, teary-eyed and exhausted, hoping for a moment away from my sisters. I caught the smell of smoke in the air, thicker than that which emanated from my parents' cigarettes. When I tilted my head to the door, I heard the frantic patter of footsteps and a murmur from my mother's maid.

"No!" my mother exclaimed. "All of them. Even the ones from Father Grigori. Especially those. No one must ever know. Quickly, quickly!"

I did not have it in me to open that door and ask her what she was doing. Deep down, I was afraid to know.

The Private Diary of Olga Romanova
December 1921

CHAPTER
FOURTEEN

Nothing came easy in this life. By now, Olga should have understood as much. She checked Maria's wristwatch, which her sister had allowed her to borrow for the duration of Olga's time at Marlingham. It was nearly midnight, and she still had several files to read. The ones she had reviewed thus far were filled with dreary statistics and Hammond's long-winded observations about his time "in country." He meant Russia. Her country.

Before the monsters took over.

Olga set the watch down and took a quick sip from a glass of water on the night table near her camp bed. She hadn't followed Rob's instructions as precisely as she might have. Rather than reading in Hammond's study, Olga spirited the files away to her room by the kitchen to avoid the nighttime chill. Besides, while Rob might have allowed her in the study alone, she didn't want to deal with questions from Mrs. Acton, should the housekeeper catch her in there or, worse yet, need to summon some plausible explanation for Ada. If she told them the young lord gave her permission, it would only create more questions.

She would return the files later tonight while everyone was asleep. Rob would be none the wiser.

But spreading out as best she could on the narrow mattress, Olga had no desire to move or even to think. She'd neatly stacked the files on her nightstand. Now, she scarcely found the strength to look at them, let alone grab another one. Her eyes hurt from squinting, and her limbs were stiff. Reading in bed now seemed like a miscalculation.

She draped an arm over her eyes, but her mind ran rampant. Perhaps the best-case scenario had unfolded, and Hammond could produce no evidence of any betrayal on the part of her mother. Maybe this entire matter was a ruse to boost his book's sales.

Though her body was fatigued, as usual, from the day's work, Olga needed to finish going through every file Rob had given her, and two remained. She grabbed the top one from the night table. It felt light in her hands, perhaps ten pages inside.

When she turned the file, her breath caught in her throat. A photograph was clipped neatly to the front.

And she was staring once again into the eyes of Grigori Rasputin.

In the picture, Father Grigori wore his customary black habit. A wooden cross hung from a beaded lanyard down his neck, peeping out from under the scraggly black beard that nearly reached his waist. One hand pressed the cross to his chest, and his other hand raised as though to offer a holy man's absolution. Those eyes—even in the sepia-toned picture, and knowing Rasputin met his end before Olga's parents had—were as penetrating as they'd been when he was still alive.

Olga shivered, but her paralysis broke. She had to face whatever was in this file. She flipped it open.

The thin, white piece of paper inside looked different from those in the previous folders. Olga didn't see Hammond's neat script, easily recognizable to her now. Rather, this paper contained correspondence dated 1916. The writing blurred slightly, making it evident that this was a mimeographed copy, not the original.

Still, Olga knew Mama's handwriting.

Words floated, ghost-like, before Olga's eyes. Clearly, her mother was responding to a previous message from Rasputin.

I know what you think of this cursed war, my friend. I know you wish it would end.

Father Grigori had always pleaded with her to end the war. Olga had overheard those pleas often enough in person, in the palace, though they happened behind her mother's closed boudoir door. Father Grigori's booming voice shouted like a cannon in her ears. *"Talk to him."*

He wasn't referencing Papa, but Mama's cousin Kaiser Wilhelm.

"I can't," Mama had cried, her voice high-pitched and strained. *"You must understand."*

"The empire is in peril. You must put a stop to this madness."

Olga knew that what Father Grigori asked of her mother was dangerous. Bad enough that people sneered at her and called her the German woman behind her back. Were she to speak with Kaiser Wilhelm or entertain that idea, no one could help her, not even Papa. Hadn't that girl at Aunt Olga's flat suggested Gran wanted to send Mama to a convent? Olga hoped that was a lie but couldn't know for sure.

But Father Grigori refused to acknowledge that Mama's hands were tied.

Though she dreaded what was to come, Olga forced herself to read the rest of the letter in the file, the copy of her mother's correspondence that had somehow landed in Hammond's possession.

I confess your words have had a profound impact on me. To my soul, I agree. This war must end. I understand and kiss your dear hands as I confess it. You were right all along, my friend. Russia can no longer bear the burden for our allies.

Let us try to negotiate with Willy. I can get a message to him without Nicky knowing.

Nicky. Her pet name for Papa. Fingers trembling, Olga continued to read her mother's devastating words.

My brother might help with this matter as well. He plans to come to Petrograd in secret. Have faith, my friend. I've no wish to leave my son an empire in shambles.

Olga's vision blurred. She tried to focus on her mother's signature. The first A in Alexandra was bold, and the last bore a curling tail.

She didn't cry. She was too numb for that. Olga only considered how the empire had ended up in shambles, regardless, because her mother followed all of Father Grigori's terrible advice. And Papa never intervened.

On top of that, Olga couldn't imagine why Mama thought Alexei could ever be tsar. He was too fragile. They had been ordered to keep his illness a secret, but she'd assumed her parents understood the truth.

She turned the page, hating every small motion required to do so. The next paper was also a letter, another mimeographed copy, but this one was from Father Grigori. His childish scrawl looked sloppier in reproduction.

He began with his usual praise for Mama. Olga read through this part quickly because she'd heard it all before. Repulsive as he might have acted otherwise, Father Grigori was always on his best behavior around her mother. Deferential and lavish with compliments. This was but one way in which he manipulated her. He made her feel like a true empress and convinced her she was the savior of Russia. The people loved her as they did their own mothers, for she was *matushka* for the entire empire.

Once the tribute ended, the heart of the letter began.

I am glad you have come to see the light, little mother. You speak of a message passed to your cousin, the Kaiser, without your husband's knowledge. But I need further reassurance, for your sake. Now that our little father is with the troops, you are charged with governance. You have access to secrets that could shift the tide of this war.

If you hand over the military codes I requested, I will take them to Berlin without involving your brother. That will convince the top brass of the German military that you mean to see this through and that any message from you is no trick. You will negotiate for peace before the German armies can destroy our poor Russian boys who've already suffered too long. This is the only way the German military officers will deem negotiation a viable option.

Already, I hear the protests from your sweet lips. Understand you do this because it is the holy course of action to preserve the empire and the House of Romanov. You have no choice. You must betray Russia for only a moment to save her forever.

Olga dropped the file, papers spilling around her, and pressed her skull between her hands. Now that the tears were coming on, she mustn't let them flow. She mustn't cry. She had to be strong.

Could her mother have betrayed the army? Or considered it? Olga assumed Mama would do anything Rasputin asked, but this? Never this.

Olga had once told her sisters that Rasputin had been wrong, that the House of Romanov wasn't destroyed because they lived. If her mother had been a traitor, the Romanovs would never be more than a sad footnote in history books. Once Gran sold the remaining jewels they'd smuggled out of Russia, Olga and her sisters would be destitute, relying on charity and what odd jobs they could manage. They would never return to Russia as grand duchesses, even if the Bolsheviks lost power. Instead, they would always be part of a treacherous family that had destroyed an empire—pitied at best and reviled at worst.

She beat at her ears, first softly and then in a harsher rhythm, forcing her mind to focus not on the past but on how to handle the present moment. *Think, think.*

Mama's consideration of a negotiated peace looked terrible on paper. Her brother had indeed visited Russia in secret. Olga knew they had spoken of a separate piece, but nothing moved forward. At least as far as she knew. Vile as they were, Father Grigori's words made sense. No one had taken negotiations seriously because neither army took the slightest step toward standing down.

Unless Father Grigori convinced Mama to pass the codes to Berlin. Those would give the German officers access to troop locations, mobilizations, and countless other factors that would grant every advantage to the German army.

And yet there was no proof she had done so. Privately, she *considered* direct negotiations with her German relatives. And then Father Grigori sent his request.

If, as Hammond claimed, her mother was a traitor, there should have been a third letter from her with an answer. Something indicating whether she would or would not comply.

Slowly, Olga began collecting the papers from the file again, re-ordering them by page number. Only the letters had no page numbers. She drew in a deep breath, hoping against hope Hammond lacked that one vital piece of evidence. The letter to prove her mother had not only been complicit in Russia's troubles but actively contributed to the defeat of its armies.

Methodically, Olga went back through the papers, ensuring she checked every one. Still, she found no response from her mother to Father Grigori's terrible demand.

Olga jumped off the bed and retrieved her travel satchel—once fine leather, now worn and splitting at the seams—from under the camp bed. Without thinking, more like an automaton than a human being, she removed the copies of the letters from Hammond's file and placed them at the bottom of her bag. Hopefully, Rob didn't know they existed because these two letters were not returning to the study with the rest of the papers. They might not have proven treachery nor provided evidence Mama had passed military secrets to Berlin, but they were bad enough. Olga would make sure they never saw the light of day.

Except the originals were likely either with Hammond in London or with the Bolsheviks in Russia ...

She couldn't think about that now. Right now, she had to get back to her sisters. She needed to discuss the letters with Tatiana, and then she could return them to the study before Hammond realized they were missing.

A competing idea snaked through her mind. She could destroy them. The original letters were *probably* somewhere safe, but she didn't know that with any certainty. In the chaos, the letters may have been destroyed. Perhaps they had been mimeographed and sent to Hammond precisely because the originals were in jeopardy.

The thought of burning them gave her great satisfaction.

Ultimately, though, Olga couldn't bring herself to do it. If her mother had been a traitor, she couldn't live with this knowledge alone. She needed Tatiana's counsel.

Olga's gaze shifted to the last file. She imagined Hammond would group all the letters between her mother and Father Grigori together, but she had to be sure. There could still be a letter that damned her mother yet.

Don't do it. Please. Read nothing else.

Her mother's voice rang shrill in her head but had no effect. From now on, her mother's spirit had no power over her, not after what Olga had just seen.

What came next was far worse than what had come before.

In this last file, the papers still dealt with Grigori Rasputin, but they were transcriptions rather than letters. They comprised a dossier collected and certified by agents of the English government and her father's secret police. First-hand accounts of Rasputin's deplorable behavior toward women. Women in Siberia, St. Petersburg, Moscow, and all points between.

Guilt soured her stomach. Rasputin once wandered the land, claiming to seek holy revelations. Now she saw the truth. He had forced himself into private flats and homes. Forced himself on women. She read five statements from women he victimized written by hand. Olga saw the tear stains on the paper as they recounted their assaults and rapes. One of them, occurring in Petrograd during the war, was so brutal Olga could hardly bring herself to finish reading the statement. She wondered if it had happened on one of the same days Grigori Rasputin had visited the palace, held her mother's hands in his, and prayed for Alexei.

Perhaps it had happened on a day he'd winked at Olga. What had been running through his mind?

Now she understood Hammond's title: *Complicity in the House of Romanov.*

Had it been complicit when they ate full dinners while the rest of the country struggled through food shortages and deprivations?

Yes, a voice she didn't recognize whispered.

Had it been complicit when her mother permitted Father Grigori behind closed doors?

Yes, the voice whispered again. It wasn't her mother. Who was in her head?

Had she been complicit when she didn't follow the advice of that girl, Nadia, who'd approached her at Aunt Olga's flat and told her the other Romanovs wanted her mother banished?

The voice hesitated.

Was it complicit of Olga to ignore what Nadia had said, that Rasputin had put his hand between her sister's legs?

Yes.

Now she recognized the voice as Nadia's. Olga remembered the jewels in her elaborate hairpins. Olga should have done something when she confided the story about her sister. It was only that this had been during the war, when she had a million other things filling her mind, primarily her duties at the hospital. Besides, Mama would never have listened. Her mother had been so in the thrall of Father Grigori that she likely would have slapped Olga's cheeks for such disrespect.

Olga could have told Papa, though. She didn't know if he would have done anything, but he would have listened.

Instead, she'd told herself Papa was too busy, preoccupied with the war, prematurely graying and worrying about the troubling reports of German gains on the Eastern Front. He had been living at a camp with his soldiers. She couldn't imagine disturbing him during his brief respites at home.

She might have told Aunt Olga, who loathed Rasputin. But she allowed the information to slip from her consciousness.

All of her excuses seemed weak and duplicitous. There had been complicity in the House of Romanov. Olga had been a part of it.

Even so, the letters would remain hidden in her satchel. For her sisters' sakes. She would figure out a way to get back to them quickly, and together, they would decide what to do.

The dossier on Rasputin was a different matter. Olga shuffled the papers and neatly returned them to the last file. That was Hammond's business, and she would leave him to it. The truth about Rasputin would injure her mother's reputation, though not as much as being proven a traitor. But Olga would not protect Father Grigori. Not this time. It was true he could save her brother, but at what cost? Her parents had allowed a rapist to have run of the palace.

Back in Petrograd, she may have failed Nadia and her sister. Now, the truth would come out at last.

Rasputin was "Father Grigori" to our parents or sometimes, more simply, "our friend." I'd always been frightened of him, even when I pretended trust. For my mother's sake. After Papa left Petrograd for the front, Rasputin's influence over her only gained strength.

Whenever she saw Father Grigori, Mama's face lit up, no matter how greasy his black beard or grimy his coat. When he visited the palace, we were all expected to rush to greet him. He was overly familiar with his too-long hugs and kisses on our cheeks.

I was the eldest and supposed to set an example for my sisters. I had to be respectful, for he was Mama's friend.

Secretly, I loathed his touch. His fingers were callused, his lips dry, and his unwashed body smelled of a neglected barnyard. Father Grigori used to pat Alexei on the head like a dog, as Alexei's actual dog, the otherwise friendly Joy, growled at this supposed holy man.

Once he'd finished with us, he always asked to speak to our mother behind closed doors. First, he would turn, direct his penetrating gaze in my direction, and wink at me just before those doors shut. And then Grigori Rasputin was alone with the Empress of Russia to say and do as he pleased.

The Private Diary of Olga Romanova
December 1921

CHAPTER
FIFTEEN

The next day passed as though in a bland dream, neither pleasant nor nightmarish—simple existence. Olga knew the truth now—about her mother, about Father Grigori—and wanted nothing more than to disappear. In her worst days at the cottage, she never felt so low. This sensation was closer to what she'd experienced in Ekaterinburg during those final hopeless weeks of imprisonment. Melancholy had circled, a hovering dark form whose vicious tendrils wrapped around her, squeezing her spirit until it seemed the Bolsheviks had stolen her very soul, and only a dull shell remained.

Olga fared better this time around for one reason alone. She wasn't Olga, but Olivia Bennett, or she could pretend to be. After returning the file on Rasputin to the study, Olga avoided everyone. She just wanted to get on with her day and sink into a deep sleep at night.

When Olga opened the door to her room later that evening, ready to crawl into bed, she spotted a small envelope waiting on her night table. Every day, Mrs. Acton sorted through the mail and personally delivered it to the staff. Olga must have been out for a walk when

Mrs. Acton did so today. After all, Olga never expected anything, for how could her sisters risk communicating with her? She'd noticed the pitying glances Mrs. Dasari and Ada sometimes exchanged as they looked through their correspondence. Olga did her best to keep her chin up. Miss Bennett did well enough on her own, or at least it must appear so.

Tatiana had addressed the envelope to Olivia Bennett in her lovely, curving script. Ana or Maria might write a casual letter, thinking it worth the risk, but Tatiana? Something must be wrong. Olga tore into the envelope.

As it turned out, everything was fine. Better than fine, actually.

Tatiana, writing as *Tess*, asked if *Olivia* could come home for Easter, perhaps stay a day or two, as Mrs. K would be there on a visit and very much wanted to see her.

For the first time since she'd read Hammond's files, a smile tugged at her lips. *Mrs. K* referenced their Aunt Olga, recently rescued from the Crimea, as their grandmother had been before her. A few years earlier, Papa had granted Aunt Olga permission to marry her true love, a soldier named Nikolai Kulikovsky. Hence Mrs. K. Their entire family, which included children now, planned to live in Denmark near Gran.

The Bolsheviks were desperate to arrest her aunt, Olga was sure. After all, she was the sister of the late tsar. But her lively aunt would never agree to live in hiding, as Olga and her sisters had. So they'd agreed on a secret name for her. A code.

Olga pressed the thin paper to her chest. If anyone could help her now, it was Mrs. K. She would show her the letters between Mama and Rasputin, and perhaps her aunt would have thoughts on what to do next. Regardless, Olga decided to request an extra day off over

Easter, which was a week away by the Orthodox calendar; in England, the holiday had already passed.

The following morning, when Olga worked up the courage to ask Celia if she might take an extra day to see her sister and a visiting relative, Celia assured her it would be fine. She then suggested Olga take not only all of Sunday, but Saturday and Monday morning as well.

Three days! Olga felt a flicker of something resembling happiness once more. After everything they had endured together, she knew she could handle anything as long as her sisters were at her side.

The sun peeked over the horizon, a pale blue sky promising a fine day. After a night of rain, the cleansing scent of it clung to the air. Other than the birds twittering and calling to one another, the world remained in peaceful silence.

If only it could always be so.

Olga had risen earlier than she did when working. Perhaps she hadn't needed to get up so early, strictly speaking, but she wanted to catch the first train. She longed to get back to her sisters as quickly as possible.

She looked forward to the train ride ahead, when she could sit in a cushioned seat and stare at the sparkling green countryside as it rolled past her outside the window. In transit, not connected to Marlingham or her sisters, she'd empty her mind.

That was probably too much to hope for, no matter how content she felt at the moment.

Olga clutched the handle of her worn leather satchel. She couldn't stop thinking about the letters she'd stolen from Hammond's file, the exchange between her mother and Father Grigori now tucked away and hidden beneath her change of clothes and nightgown. The secrets inside could not remain hers to bear alone.

As for the revelations about Father Grigori, she hadn't yet determined whether to share them. The accusations would come as no shock to her aunt, but she wasn't sure how her younger sisters would react.

When Olga crossed the expanse of lawn outside Marlingham, her boots became wet. She'd worn thick stockings but didn't want to ruin her shoes. So she stepped onto the long paved driveway. She'd nearly made it to the end of the driveway and to the winding path adjacent to the road that led to the rail station, when Olga heard the hum of a motorcar's engine behind her. Even before she looked, she knew who she would see. She glanced over her shoulder anyway.

Rob's Daimler approached, slowed, and pulled up alongside her.

Olga knew little about cars, so she couldn't place the exact production year for the Daimler. Based on the style, she suspected it was several years out-of-date. Rob must have had it freshly painted and refurbished. The dark red paint shone on the metal, and the brass and gold fixtures and headlights gleamed in the morning sun. The black leather roof looked in good shape, as did the tires, with a spare attached to the driver's side door.

Her gaze wandered from the details of the motorcar to Rob. He wore driving goggles and gloves as he had when she first came to Marlingham and mistaken him for the family's chauffeur. She wished he had been the chauffeur. How much simpler things might be now.

As matters stood, she didn't know what to say. Why was Rob up and about so early? Had he followed her? Should she address their previous conversation? She didn't want to discuss what she'd found—the letters hidden in her satchel. Rob hadn't explicitly told her not to take them out of the house, but surely he'd implied as much. She decided it might be best to put the entire topic behind them. A playful demeanor felt easiest.

"You're up with the chickens," Olga declared, wondering where she'd picked up such a strange expression. Likely from Ana. "Are you trying to taunt me?"

"How am I taunting you?"

"Pulling up to show off your motor as I walk to the train station."

Rob removed the goggles and shook his black hair free from their band. And there he was. Heathcliff in a Daimler. When viewed through that lens, it was easy not to think of him as Hammond's son or the man who had led her to discover the truth about Grigori Rasputin. She could simply enjoy his company.

Rob tilted his head, a hint of confusion clouding his eyes. "Is that any way to greet a fellow after you requested a ride?"

Now it was Olga's turn to be confused. "I was joking about walking. I don't mind. And I made no such request."

"My sister said differently. At the very least, she implied you would appreciate a ride."

The realization dawned on her exactly when it did for Rob, given his sudden intake of breath. Of course Celia would ask her brother to give Olga a ride. She could guess what Celia had said. *Poor thing hasn't seen her sister in ages, and after what they've been through, the least we can do is ensure she gets to spend as much time with her as possible. The train takes nearly an hour.*

"I suppose she wants us to be friends," he said sheepishly.

For a fleeting moment, as the Daimler's engine purred beside her, she wondered if Celia hoped Olga and Rob would become more than friends. Then she and Celia would be sisters.

The thought wasn't unpleasant at all. Still, Olga found it hard to believe that Celia, for all her lack of pretense and airs, imagined anything could happen between her maid and her brother.

"And I can't say I like how we left things last time we spoke," Rob said.

Olga leaned over so she could look into his eyes.

"I returned your father's papers." Most of them, anyway. "I saw what he said about the empress and that vile man, Rasputin. I learned what I needed to know, and now I can let it rest. I would rather not speak of it further." She hesitated. "As you said, sometimes it's better to keep the past in the past and all that."

"All right." Rob's lower lip twitched, but he said nothing more.

"Thank you," she said.

"I want us to be friends as well, you know. As my sister does." He lowered his voice. "Celia told me you took an interest in my idea for the rehabilitation center. She suggested I might speak to you about it if I offered you a ride. This is terribly important to me, and I would value your opinion."

Olga felt an irresistible pull: to be near him, hear his voice, learn his secrets. Much as she enjoyed the swagger and flirtatiousness he affected, this serious version of Rob was closer to his authentic self. That he would share this aspect of his personality made Olga feel special in a way she'd never previously experienced. Not even with Mitya, who, by necessity, had never disclosed his deepest thoughts. He'd known it was hopeless to imagine a future with a grand duchess. He'd needed to protect his heart.

If Olga had any sense, she would have followed Mitya's lead in this situation. But she craved Rob's company, more so than she'd realized now that she was near him once more. She wanted to accept a ride, but couldn't let him know where she lived or let him come anywhere near her sisters. "I appreciate the offer, but I'll take the train. My sister will be waiting for me at the station."

When his features crumpled, a fresh idea popped into Olga's mind. She just had to summon a plausible reason for it.

"So I'd have you take me home, only my sister will expect me on the other end of the line, and I hate for her to worry," Olga said. "But I wouldn't mind a ride to the station in Lincoln."

"I'll take any time you can spare!"

Rob hopped out of the motorcar and came around to open the passenger side door for her. Then he took her satchel and placed it in the back seat. On the one hand, she didn't like being separated from the bag but wanted to keep it in her line of vision. At the same time, she got some sense of relief from putting distance between herself and the mimeographs of those letters. She could use a break from the restless guilt that settled into her mind whenever she thought about them.

Since he was driving, Rob sat up front. Usually, Olga would take a seat in the back compartment, luxuriously upholstered with thick, corded, dark gray fabric. However, in this situation, that didn't seem right. Despite her fanciful notions, Rob was no chauffeur. And yet, joining him in front seemed presumptuous and overly intimate. Moreover, the space was smaller than that in the back; the motorcar had been designed to be driven by a chauffeur who would escort family members wherever they pleased.

Perhaps sensing her quandary, Rob said: "I always prefer to sit in the front seat myself when a passenger. You feel the breeze that way." He waved his arm through the windowless open gap between the front door and the roof. "Not so pleasant when it's raining, but since it's nice today, it might be a treat. Entirely your choice."

She slid onto the black leather bench seat up front. Rob shut the door after her and walked back round to the driver's side, placing his goggles back over his eyes. The engine was still idling, and he pressed his foot down on the central pedal to accelerate.

With a bump and a grunt from the engine, they were on their way.

As the Daimler got going, Olga pressed her body into the passenger's side door, carefully keeping distance between them. She removed her scarf from her neck and wound it around her head to keep her bobbed hair in place. Then she ran her hands along the upholstery. This Daimler seemed less sleek than the motorcars that once comprised her father's fleet. But Olga liked the sensation of machinery rumbling beneath her, though she would probably suffer from a sore tailbone by tomorrow.

"Are you sure you won't let me take you directly home? See you to the front door and all that?" Rob turned briefly, his eyes shadowed by a tint in the goggles. "It's no trouble. You'd have more time with your sister that way."

"Just the station." Olga folded her hands in her lap. "I've plenty of time."

"I'll get you home well before your sister leaves to fetch you, surely," Rob said.

Her sister. The imaginary sister she'd concocted so as not to betray that she actually had three of them.

"You don't know her. She's the sort to consider five minutes early far too late."

Olga flicked her tongue over her bottom lip. She intended to walk from the train station to the cottage. She would not risk her sisters' safety by asking them to meet her.

Little fibs were the best Olga could manage under pressure, as she found it increasingly difficult to lie to Rob. Even about seemingly inconsequential matters. Rather, Olga longed to tell him the truth. Her truth.

This must not happen.

She remembered what Ana had said when they were deciding who should apply for the position at Marlingham. *Tatiana can't lie.* And then she thought of the unspoken part of the sentence. *But Olga can.* It gave her no pleasure, but Ana was right. Olga lied well enough. She'd proven that over and over.

"You don't think I can beat her in this beauty?" Rob tapped the steering wheel fondly.

"She'll get there well ahead of us. I assure you. No offense meant."

"All right then." He turned onto the road. "I guess that's what I get for not upgrading to the newest model. But I've a fondness for this one."

A cool wind ruffled her scarf and caressed her bare cheeks. Olga smoothed the scarf around her head. Wispy tendrils kept escaping, but her hair was so short now that it hardly mattered. She had little trouble brushing out tangles at night. She imagined what would happen when she got home, though. Tatiana would fuss, and Maria would immediately grab a brush to help Olga de-tangle as soon as possible. Ana would probably laugh and make a sarcastic comment.

Without thinking about it, Olga pressed her own feet against the floorboard as though she might find a throttle there and help the motorcar gain speed. She couldn't wait to hug her sisters and take in the familiar scents of their snug cottage.

And then, a hard shock jolted her spine as her side of the motorcar sank and stopped. Olga looked outside, craning her neck to the road below to see what was wrong.

One of the front tires had stuck in a pothole. They'd barely started and already stalled.

Rob grumbled something she couldn't make out and thrust the gear shifter into reverse. The motorcar shook, and the engine wheezed. The Daimler was a beautiful vehicle, but definitely a few years past its prime. She wondered if Rob took too much pride in keeping it up himself.

"Come on, gorgeous," he muttered under his breath as the gears were grinding. "You can do it."

Olga couldn't help but laugh. Rob reminded her of Papa trying to coax one of the imperial geldings through muddy riverbeds. Not that those fine steeds ever needed encouragement. They were fearless.

Her laughter died as she remembered how happy Papa had been around horses. How full of life. Had he been born into a situation similar to Lord Hammond's or Rob's, a peer of the realm in a democratic monarchy, he would have thrived.

Instead, he'd been destined to become an autocratic tsar. And it killed him.

Rob released the shifter to rest the gears. He looked at her and then did a double take, sensing her change in mood.

"I'll have us out of here in a jiff. I promise."

Olga tried to maintain a casual tone. "It's only that you speak to a machine as though it's a horse."

"As though *she's* a horse," Rob insisted.

It was pretty adorable how attached he was to this motorcar. Again, Olga wished he *had* been a chauffeur. What a shame, indeed. Olga looked at her hands.

"I daresay I would have greater faith in a clever young gelding or mare right now." She twisted her fingers together, trying to resist the urge to look back at the satchel. There was no way anything could have happened to the letters, and yet she longed to check on them. "Though I suppose I'd rather a hunk of metal fail than a horse fracture an ankle."

"You have so little faith, my lady."

At those words, Olga felt a private space in her heart melt. *My lady.* Celia always treated her with affection, but also always as the maid. In Rob's voice, however, she sensed both affection and respect, undergirding his playfulness. She far preferred "my lady" from Rob's lips than "your imperial highness," her formal title from long ago.

Rob shifted the gears into reverse once more, his face screwed up in concentration. For a passing moment, Olga wondered if there was any truth to the rumor that Lord Hammond wasn't Rob's birth father. She'd yet to see Hammond and so had no basis for comparison. But she saw the resemblance between Rob and his mother, the late countess from the picture in the study. They shared the same beautifully unruly hair and expressive brown eyes.

At last, with a loud and frustrated exhalation, the Daimler deigned to grind backward, loosening the tire from the pothole in the road. The exertion was evident in the muscles of Rob's arm, which now strained against the thick, dark fabric of his coat. He shifted once more and twisted the wheel. And then they rumbled toward the train station once more.

"See?" he said proudly. "I told you she could do it."

"I stand corrected. Though I think you had something to do with it as well. You handle this motor well."

"Well, I ...." He fumbled with his words. "It is a well-designed vehicle."

A quirk of pleasure made Olga return his smile. But she glanced away, suddenly shy. Her gaze wandered to the impossibly green field to the side of the road opposite the creek, the blessing of so many gray skies and rain storms.

"Your infirmary seems like an appropriate venue for those suffering from injuries of the mind."

"You have thoughts about it? Any ideas?"

"I don't know that I'd go so far as to say I have ideas. Perhaps I might read more about the impact of war on the mind if you have books to suggest. As a nurse, I saw how those who had suffered such afflictions were shunned. How extraordinary to have a place fit for them. A place where a doctor can determine the best course of care."

Rob's hands tightened over the wheel. For several minutes, he didn't speak. Faced with his silence, Olga couldn't talk either, afraid she had unwittingly offended him, though, for her life, she couldn't imagine how. Not when earlier he'd asked to discuss his plans.

"My sister told you about what happened to me after the war?" he said.

"Only that you had a hard time."

Rob pumped the brake pedal as he slowed the car and pulled over to the side of the road.

Olga looked about, confused, for she had heard nothing to indicate further trouble after the incident with the pothole. And he left the engine running. How much petrol was left?

"I need a moment," he said. "I'm sorry. I know it's unchivalrous, but I think it would be more unchivalrous to ... to...t-t-to ..."

He loosened his grip on the wheel as his fingers flexed, stilling the trembling long enough to remove his goggles and let them fall to his neck. Olga felt the pain emanating from him as though in waves.

If he was remembering the war and whatever had caused his stammer in the first place, the slightest stimulation could cause him to panic or lash out. As a nurse, she'd watched a soldier wake from a terror-filled night, his fists swinging and accidentally hitting one of the other nurses flush in the jaw.

The best thing she could do now was to sit quietly with Rob. She tried not to worry about the petrol. Eager as she was to see her sisters, it felt right to sit in silence with him.

"I'm s-sorry for delaying you." His face was immovable as marble, and he stared straight ahead. He pressed his lips together and then shut off the engine. "I shouldn't have offered you a ride if I couldn't get you there on time."

Olga tucked her hair tighter under her scarf and re-adjusted it, smiling, trying to show she meant what she was about to say.

"We may stay here as long as you wish. And you may share or not share as you wish. There are several trains today. For now, we can enjoy the countryside."

Rob squeezed his eyes shut. "One of my men. James. I think I mentioned him to you before, though not by name. A German sniper shot him."

Rob's voice was barely audible. He hadn't stammered, despite what must have been terrifying words to utter, but he shuddered. Olga reached out and touched his arm. She feared he would flinch or pull away, but he did neither. Regardless, Olga removed her hand. She must allow him space to work through what he was about to say.

"He hadn't a gun on him. James was opening a tin with his knife and making jokes about our rations. One minute talking about that.

And then the n-next." Rob inhaled sharply. "The sniper was trying to shoot me: the officer in charge. I leaned down to remove a pebble from my boots. They got him instead."

A shiver pulsed down her spine. "It was not your fault," Olga said.

"It *was* my fault. I was supposed to ensure our intelligence was up-to-date. I should have known there were snipers in the area. James should never have been in such a vulnerable position. I failed him. I failed my men."

Rob and his soldiers may have been sent to the front lines, to the nightmare of the endless trenches at the front, but they hadn't yet been men. She was sure of that. The soldiers Olga met at the hospital ward were but boys. Boys who were subjected to more horror than she could imagine; more than she could have imagined before the so-called House of Special Purpose in Ekaterinburg, at any rate. The constant fear of death. And then the guilt of surviving when her parents and brother had not.

So she understood why Rob thought James's death his fault and believed it deep in his heart. Somewhere in the rational parts of his mind, he must have recognized that he couldn't have known about the sniper. He may have been charged with intelligence, but the German boys on the other side of the battlefield, trapped in their trenches, countered his intelligence. Snipers were notoriously unpredictable and lethal. The allied forces used them as well. Papa had personally approved dozens of Russian snipers, boys clever with rifles.

"It was not your fault," Olga repeated. She didn't think Rob could hear those words often enough. "James wouldn't want you to bear guilt over his death."

Olga twisted her fingers together, grateful for the chill of the breeze against her now blazing cheeks. Papa and Mama wouldn't want her to bear guilt over their deaths, either. Nor would Alexei. And yet, how many times had she turned it over in her head? What would have happened had Olga stayed at Ekaterinburg? She could have sent her sisters off and remained with the others. Perhaps she could have determined a way for everyone to escape.

At the very least, couldn't she have carried Alexei out of the house? Helped him? She'd tortured herself over that decision, just as Rob was doing. Olga stared at the tall grass rippling in the wind, wondering if she would ever be free.

"James isn't dead," Rob said at last. "He survived the wound. But half of his face is gone. He lives in agony. He will never leave his parents' house nor see me. Not that I can blame him for that."

She turned to Rob, wanting to make this better, though she knew anything said would be woefully inadequate.

"It is a tragedy, but you aren't responsible. Those who drove us to war are responsible. Men like ..."

Men like Papa. She forced the disloyal thought from her head.

"I think about it all the same." Rob pushed his hair back, hands trembling. His scar stood out, purple and bleak, on his pale forehead. "James would never have suffered had I not bent down."

"Then you would be dead or gravely injured. You cannot think that way. And you bear your own wounds."

Olga gestured clumsily to his forehead and then immediately regretted the words. She hadn't intended to make him feel self-conscious. "I shouldn't have said anything. I'm sorry."

"It's all right. But this isn't a battle scar."

Rob's gaze focused intently on hers. People used to say Father Grigori had the power to mesmerize with his stare. She had never found that to be so. Rasputin only wanted others to see him and nothing else until they forgot themselves. Rob's expression was the opposite. He tried to assure Olga that he truly saw her. And that he trusted her.

"It happened after the war." Rob lifted two fingers and tapped the scar. "I came home nearly unable to talk. I mean, I c-could talk, but my words were so jumbled I soon gave up. It was inexplicable. Sentences formed in my head, but I could not force them out of my mouth."

"Perhaps your mind was protecting you somehow," Olga said. "You were healing."

"Yes. I think it was something like that. But Father grew frustrated. He wanted me back to normal, or rather what he considered normal."

Yet another reason to detest Lord Hammond. Olga didn't dare interrupt, but inside, she screamed: *What did they do to you?*

"At that point, I was nearly mute. Apparently, others suffered in the same manner, and there was a place ... in the n-north ... that was known for treating these men. I'm sure Father m-meant well."

Rob pressed his lips together abruptly.

"They used electric shocks," he said.

Terror rippled through her. Olga had heard of shock treatments. Patients strapped to a cot with leather bands tightened around their arms and legs and their heads secured. A bit in their mouth, like that used with horses, so they would not swallow or choke on their tongues. When the electricity shot down the patients' limbs, the convulsions started. She couldn't wrap her head around the agony of it.

"Evidence suggested such shock was an effective therapy," Rob said. "So Father wanted me to try it. I suppose I've never really forgiven him."

Doctors also used such treatments for afflictions like depression: the illness of the mind that bore down on Olga when the Bolsheviks held her captive with her family. Had things unfolded differently, a doctor might have administered the barbaric treatment on her.

Surely Mama and Papa would never allow it. And yet, she recalled their anguish when Olga took to her bed in Ekaterinburg, overcome by depression. Perhaps her family would try anything to rid Olga of her mind's demons.

Olga hated Hammond, but he'd likely done what he thought best for his son.

"I recovered," Rob said. "I don't know why. Perhaps the terror of the treatments worked in the end. Or perhaps I would have recovered, regardless. Anyway, the convulsions were intense." He gestured to his forehead. "I lashed furiously against the restraints and cut myself so badly I needed stitches. So this is a reminder of it all. I s-see it every day. I hope the experience of others might be better. If I can make that happen, I must."

"You should never have had to experience it yourself," Olga said.

He bowed his head. Once again, Olga rested her hand on his arm, testing his reaction. When he did not shake her hand away, she moved her hand upward. Then, she tilted his chin toward her with the softest pressure possible.

His expression broke her heart. It was not merely the memory of the physical agony that haunted him. He was ashamed.

"You are a strong and honorable man."

Rob's eyes brightened. When he looked at Olga, she saw more in his gaze than hope. There was joy in hearing her utter those words. Her opinion was vital to him. Their connection transcended her station and his, whether he knew her as Miss Bennett, the maid, or Olga, a refugee from the Russian Revolution.

Surely that connection could withstand anything, including knowing her as Grand Duchess Olga.

Olga's fingers moved cautiously toward his cheek. Rob's skin was smooth and warm under her touch. She inhaled the leather of his gloves and the cedar and musk of his cologne. When he bent closer, their foreheads touched. She wanted him to kiss her. His lips were so close. So lush and inviting.

And then Olga remembered the documents she had packed away in her satchel, the letters she had taken, stolen. All the reasons she'd come to Marlingham in the first place tumbled in her mind like a barrage of hail in a storm. But she couldn't bring herself to move her hand away from Rob's face, even as she could tell from his sudden frown that he'd sensed something had changed.

"I'm sorry." He pulled back, but his hand rested lightly on her knee.

"It's fine." This had been a bad idea. By accepting this ride and being alone with Rob in the motorcar, Olga had behaved like a foolish girl.

"It was presumptuous of me to be alone with you," he said. "I'm sorry."

"I agreed to come," she blurted. "It's not that."

Olga was so tantalized by the idea of a new life and identity that she hadn't stopped long enough to consider the consequences. Her true self must remain concealed.

Slowly, she moved to face forward again. His hand dropped from her knee.

"Perhaps we should get going. If you're feeling well enough to drive, that is."

Rob was gentlemanly enough to manage a small smile. "Of course. I'll get you to the station straightaway. And then you can enjoy Easter with your sister."

Father Grigori was no man of God, even if he claimed to be such. Our faith was of a far higher order. In exile, both in Russia and England, we maintained that faith.

After our world changed, Easter celebrations were not as glamorous as before. I miss those magical services of the past. We girls stood in a row at church, scarves wrapped around our heads, eyes fixed on the priest in long silver vestments, fragrant puffs of incense swirling around us.

I remember one year in particular when a frail woman fainted right in front of us during the service. In the weeks leading to Easter, she'd abided by the strictest rules of the Lenten fast. Though never as rigorous in my observation, my stomach always rumbled loudly on Easter Eve, as I thought only of the feast our family would enjoy upon returning to the palace.

At midnight, bells rang as the priest declared, "Christ is risen." We lit candles, sang, and held banners and icons of the savior aloft, joining a procession outside the church to celebrate rebirth and new life. Alexei, dressed in one of his best sailor's suits, couldn't walk, so he rode on Papa's shoulders.

I took it all for granted because I assumed life would continue. First with my family and then with a husband and children of my own. Many glorious Easters were ahead of me, for I never imagined fate could steer me on an entirely different course.

The Private Diary of Olga Romanova
December 1921

CHAPTER
SIXTEEN

Tatiana tugged Olga's arm. "I know we didn't get to bed until well after midnight, but surely you won't fall asleep at the breakfast table."

The previous day, Olga's sisters had greeted her with a flurry of hugs and tearful kisses on her cheek. After sunset, Tatiana and Maria created an altar on a side table using a freshly washed white cotton cloth embroidered with an orthodox cross, cut flowers, and candles. Olga and Ana collected prayer books and icons from where they had been hidden away, and ensured all the electric lighting was off.

The four of them recited the liturgy by candlelight. It wasn't the same as Easter night services from the time before, yet a sense of peace had settled over Olga. She and her sisters were together to greet Easter.

And now their aunt had joined them.

Olga forced herself back to the present. Maria and Ana chattered and praised their aunt for bringing everything needed for a proper Easter supper. Aunt Olga had arrived earlier with the necessary items nestled in a wicker basket: a side of ham, kielbasa sausage, horseradish, salt, soft cheeses, and tapered yellow candles sticking out from freshly baked, braided sweet bread which would be complimented by the butter Maria had fashioned into the shape of a lamb.

The mere sight of it all made Olga squirm with hunger. She was sure her sisters felt the same way. Their appreciation for good food had heightened since the last time they'd gathered with their aunt. Before everything fell apart.

For breakfast, platters of scrambled eggs with chives and the English bread pudding Ana insisted on making graced the table. She'd burned the edges of the bread, but Olga appreciated her sister's effort.

While Tatiana and Ana scooped food onto everyone's plates, Maria distributed hard-boiled eggs. Her sisters spent the previous afternoon tinting the eggs to a deep reddish gold using onion skins and juices from beets. While they were all pretty, Maria's were the best. She used flowers and herbs as stencils, patiently wrapping them around the eggs before placing them in dye.

It occurred to Olga that everyone had contributed to this meal—even their aunt, who was their guest and traveled so far to see them—except her. She chided herself for not thinking of purchasing a bouquet at the train station, but she'd been so eager to get to her sisters that she had winded herself walking so quickly to the cottage.

Now she was allowing them to wait on her as though they were her maids. However, when Olga tried to help, Maria placed a calming hand on her shoulder.

"This is your holiday. Remember?" Her sister selected an egg with the delicate lines of a sprig of mint wrapped around it and placed the egg next to Olga's plate. "Just eat and rest."

"And perhaps taste the *Paskha* to make sure it's sweet enough," Tatiana said. "I hope I added enough honey and sugar."

"I've no doubt you did," Olga told her. And then, noticing the taut nervousness in Tatiana's smile and feeling the stare, she turned to the other side of the table, where her aunt sat.

She was staring at Olga's hands, dry and chapped from the time spent laundering Celia's delicate items. Embarrassed, Olga hid them under the table.

Tatiana had assured Olga that she would convey to their aunt why Olga was at Marlingham and her position as a maid there, emphasizing the pains they'd taken to hide Olga's identity. However, Olga wasn't sure how much her sister had revealed about Olga's plan to help vindicate their mother. She knew her sister well enough to tell Tatiana was upset, despite her gentle manners. For all Olga knew, Tatiana's frustration may have led her to spill everything.

"So," Aunt Olga began. "You're a lady's maid now."

"Not precisely," Olga said. "My lady is not married."

Though she would be a mother soon. But Aunt Olga needn't know that.

Olga stared at the steam rising from her scrambled eggs, thinking of Celia. And Rob.

"What's wrong with you?" Ana said. "You look like you're in the middle of a daydream. Is being a maid that big of a privilege?"

Ana's sarcasm stung. Her sister was still jealous of Olga for working outside the home, even if Ana had agreed that she was the best choice for this job. But that didn't mean Olga had to put up with her sass. Since she didn't want her aunt to give reports of any tension between the girls to their grandmother, she said nothing.

"Do you ever wonder what your parents would have thought of such a thing?" Aunt Olga said. "Your father ..." She smiled sadly at the memory of her beloved brother. "... I suppose he could grow accustomed. He always had such a pure heart. As long as you were happy and well."

Olga met her aunt's gaze. "I think Papa would have been proud. He never shirked from an honest day's work. We saw that well enough in Siberia."

Aunt Olga fiddled with the egg Maria had placed at her table setting. Her aunt's features looked much like those of her father, the hearty and bear-like Tsar Alexander. Like Olga, she tended not to pay much mind to her appearance, anyway. Still, Olga was only thirteen years younger than her aunt, and she remembered her as youthful and merry, always with a bright expression. She appeared much older now, with shadows under her eyes and a constellation of age spots on one side of her throat.

"What of your mother?" Aunt Olga asked. "She always had a particular fondness for the ways of the English. I think she would have liked to have seen you embedded in such a household, but as the lady of the manor, of course."

"This isn't what she might have wished for me, but I think Mama would have accepted the situation. She accepted most things with grace when it came down to it."

"I suppose you saw that in Siberia as well?"

Aunt Olga gave a tired smile. Her entire family, husband and children, had made it out of their palace in Crimea courtesy of the British Navy. They were waiting for her in Copenhagen. Despite her good intentions, she may have lost her brother, but she couldn't possibly understand what Olga and her sisters had lost.

"I am satisfied with my work," Olga said. "Honestly, I am."

"Let's talk further after we've eaten." Aunt Olga shifted her napkin on her lap and closed her eyes for a moment. When she opened them

again, her quick smile returned, the cheerful aunt Olga remembered.
"And then you can tell me all about your new life."

After breakfast, they sat together in the parlor. Olga's sisters had
cleaned until the cottage was spotless, and decorated the parlor
with more eggs, the insides blown free. Painted eggshells hung from
pine-bough garlands around the corners of each wall, both inside and
outside their front door. The entire place smelled of honey and vanilla
from the *Paskha* Tatiana had prepared, mingled with the lingering
savory scents from breakfast.

Aunt Olga had come bearing gifts: a pink silk capelet for Maria, and
Olga and Tatiana's favorite Coty colognes. Rose for Olga and jasmine
for Tatiana. As they admired the pretty glass bottles and took delicate
sniffs of the perfume, Ana rattled a medium-sized box wrapped in blue
and green tissue paper.

"Oh! Don't shake it too hard," their aunt laughed. "Your gift is the
best, *shvybzik*. That's why I made you wait."

It felt strange to hear the old endearment for her sister, a German
expression that meant something like *troublemaker*. And though that
description still applied, Olga thought Anastasia would correct their
aunt, asking her to call her Ana now.

But nostalgia had gotten the best of their youngest sister, for Anastasia didn't say a word.

"Though it's something you can all enjoy," Aunt Olga added. "Go
ahead."

Ana tore the paper and opened the box's lid before flinging it aside.
She withdrew a new camera similar to the old Kodak Brownie box

cameras they'd had in Russia. This was a smaller and more sophisti-
cated model. Ana fiddled with it, folding the box to reveal the black
and gold lens with the embossed *Eastman Kodak* logo.

"Thank you!" Ana ran to hug Aunt Olga and then immediately
returned to the camera.

It would likely take some time for Ana to acquire the proper chemicals and set up a dark room so she could develop the pictures. But Olga
knew her sister would take photos of them soon enough, even if the
images could never leave this house.

Watching Ana, bittersweet memories burned in Olga's heart. She
thought back to the dark green leather-bound photo albums her family once kept. All of them were long gone, in the hands of the Bolsheviks in Russia. Destroyed, no doubt.

When imagining those photographs in flames, Olga thought she
might collapse, just like that woman at the Easter service long ago. Olga
might crumple onto the rug, crying until no tears were left.

Their aunt eased back in her armchair and sipped Earl Grey tea
from a chipped cup. She was trying not to be obvious about it, but
was clearly appraising the parlor. Not in a judgmental way, but with a
wistful frown. Olga assumed her aunt would report the condition of
their home to Gran in Denmark. Then, if Gran thought their cottage
needed work, she'd either send someone she trusted to help or shrug
and say the girls would have to make do. But if Aunt Olga reported
her eldest niece displayed signs of melancholy, Gran would demand to
know more. She might prevent Olga from returning to Marlingham.
Gran always found a way to get what she wanted.

Olga gritted her teeth and clenched her hands into tight fists, stuff-
ing the emotions back inside. She couldn't let her aunt see her break
down. It was bad enough that Tatiana and Maria kept exchanging

worried looks. And Ana, normally insensible to such things, cocked an eyebrow in her direction.

She thought of Rob's suffering when his father tried to cure him of the stammer. The electric shock treatment. Olga wondered again if her own family wouldn't fall under the spell of some charlatan who claimed he could ease Olga's ever-shifting moods. Her grandmother loved her, as Hammond likely loved Rob, but could be convinced that radical therapies were in Olga's best interest should it come to that.

So she needed to convince her aunt that she, Olga, was fine. Perhaps this was the right time to share what she had found in Hammond's files.

"Aunt Olga," she began slowly. "I have something I'd like you to see. I want everyone to see, actually."

Her aunt looked her over. "Oh?"

"It is to do with where I work," Olga said. "I wanted to tell you face to face."

Her aunt set the cup down abruptly.

"Marlingham is the country home of Lord Hammond." Olga paused, hoping recognition would light her aunt's face so she wouldn't have to explain further. When it didn't, she continued. "He was a diplomat to Russia. Now, he has accused our mother of being a traitor to Russia during the war. Lord Hammond plans to write a book and claims to have evidence of her betrayal."

"Olga!" her aunt cried. "What were you thinking?"

So Tatiana hadn't shared that part with their aunt. Olga glanced at her sister, who was now seemingly fascinated by Ana's new camera.

"I was thinking I might find something of use," Olga said. "And I did. I can't say it gives me any satisfaction."

Biting her lip, she remembered the accounts of Rasputin's crimes, the splotches of tears on the page.

"I read through the files he kept."

"Olga, not now," Tatiana said, making those simple words a warning.

"I feel like I am always sharing bad news. Still, I must hear what you make of it."

Olga's satchel was in her bedroom, the mimeographed copies of the letters still tucked away. Reluctantly, Olga went into the room to fetch them.

"I'm sorry," she blurted once she'd returned to the parlor. "Only I can no longer bear to deal with this alone."

While Ana remained on the floor, scuttling close enough to peek, hands gripping the new camera, Maria and Tatiana sat on each side of the armchair to read the letters.

Olga couldn't bear to watch them. Still standing, she focused on a reddish egg dangling over the hearth.

"Forgeries," Tatiana said confidently, though her eyes telegraphed her anxiety. "It is only a likeness to our mother's writing, and as for Father Grigori ... who can say?"

"Nothing proves Mother wrote back and gave him those codes," Maria said.

"Even so ..." Olga leaned over and tapped the section where Rasputin had asked their mother for military codes. "Once he crossed that line, she should have banished him or had him stand trial for treason. She may not have directly betrayed the army, but this communication implies her complicity."

"You can't believe these letters are genuine," Tatiana said. "The Bolsheviks must have forged them. It is precisely the sort of trick they would pull."

"It doesn't matter what I think, or any of us think. It is about what Hammond can claim and what others will believe."

Aunt Olga sat silent, working her lips between her teeth, frowning.

"Please, Auntie," Tatiana implored. "Tell her Mama couldn't possibly have written this."

"I don't know," Aunt Olga said. "I'm not familiar with his handwriting, nor your mother's. Truly. I wish I could say differently. But I don't know if they're real or not."

Tatiana's voice turned on a dime, her tone ice cold. "You believe our mother is a traitor?"

"Now, Tanuchka, I said nothing of the sort. Let me consider this a moment."

Their aunt stroked Tatiana's hand, a condescension inherent to the gesture even if she intended kindness. Olga wanted their aunt's opinion, but as part of a group discussion, not to make a unilateral decision. They weren't young girls anymore, desperate for guidance, but women who had gone through hell and survived.

Aunt Olga lifted a finger to tap her lips. "Do any of you have letters from the empress?"

Olga shook her head. She wished she had a letter from her parents or a watercolor Alexei had painted. Any memento. Anything. But they had left Ekaterinburg so quickly. And she had been sure they would reunite.

Back straight and head high, Tatiana rose grandly from her armchair and walked to their bedroom. She emerged holding a tattered piece of paper, torn on the edges, which she handed to Aunt Olga.

They all rushed to look. Tatiana's letter was from their mother.

Olga shivered and looked about, sure she would see her mother's spirit in the cottage, vague but present. She imagined Mama sitting on one of her impossibly delicate French chairs before her writing desk in the mauve boudoir, faithfully composing her daily letters. Whenever the girls were away, she wrote to them as well. Mama always wanted to stay close to them.

A lump caught in Olga's throat. She looked over her shoulder in case her mother's figure stood by the window. There was nothing, not so much as an echo of Mama's voice. For a horrifying minute, she couldn't remember how it had sounded. Perhaps she had scared her mother away for good. Olga felt abandoned. And alone.

"You see here," Tatiana pointed to her letter and then to the mimeograph, oblivious to Olga's distress. "The way she crosses her t. In my letter, it's curved, while in this one, it's straight. This isn't her handwriting!"

Olga peered closer. She saw the difference, but it was minuscule. She glanced at her other sisters. Maria looked unconvinced. Even Ana had paled. Much as they didn't want to believe it, they wondered if the letters were authentic. And just because Hammond didn't have the third letter in his possession, that didn't prove their mother *hadn't* betrayed the Russian soldiers by relaying codes to the Germans. She might have done.

She hated herself for it, but Olga thought it all the same.

"We need an impartial source," Aunt Olga said, "to study the letters more closely. I'll find someone who can examine and compare. An expert in the field."

Olga panicked. "I need to return these. I can't let anyone know I took them."

"Leave that to me."

Ana held up her new camera. Aunt Olga set their mother's letters side by side on the end table, and Ana snapped pictures, taking care to capture them from different angles and at a close enough range to see everything. Olga took a moment to admire how her sister handled the camera, but her thoughts spun again. She stared at Tatiana's letter, the neatly curving hand of her mother, and the letter she'd taken from Marlingham. Other than the tiny difference in the t, they looked like the same handwriting. Despite Tatiana's unwavering optimism, Aunt Olga's "expert" might determine the letters were written by the same person.

For all her insistence that she needed to learn the truth, Olga wondered if she had made a mistake.

Perhaps it's not surprising that only the tsar's daughters escaped the horrors of the revolution. After all, Alexei had always been fragile. Death stalked him from the time he was a toddler.

Once, while we were away from the palace on a royal tour, Alexei nearly died. He had been playing too rowdily, as he was prone to do when not supervised, and tried to dive off the side of a deep bathtub. His injuries were internal: unseen and unknown at first. The bleeding disease was insidious that way. Our family moved on to Spala, in Poland, to Papa's hunting lodge there, and Alexei got injured again, this time from a rough carriage ride. They took him to bed, and it seemed he would never rise again. His fever rose. His wails increased as he suffered until he begged for death. Father's advisors prepared for a grim announcement: the tsarevich had passed from this world.

Until Father Grigori caught word of it.

The Private Diary of Olga Romanova
December 1921

CHAPTER SEVENTEEN

After supper, Aunt Olga and Tatiana worked on embroidery projects in the parlor, stitching delicate sprigs of leaves and flowers that would eventually adorn tea towels or pillowcases. Olga didn't see how they could remain so calm. She supposed Tatiana wouldn't even consider the letter might be genuine. And Aunt Olga... well, she never had liked Mama, anyway. Neither her nor Gran. They thought Mama was stiff, prim, and standoffish.

They never understood that Mama had been none of those things. Olga's mother had only been shy.

Ana was fiddling with her camera and telling Aunt Olga what chemicals she'd need to set up a dark room at the back of the cottage. That left only Maria and Olga at the table. While Maria enjoyed a second piece from the *Paskha*, Olga stared at her hot tea. An intricate floral design rimmed the cup, but a large chip was missing near the handle. She had to take such care whenever she sipped that it hardly felt worth the trouble. Mindlessly, she ran her fingertip around the saucer.

Once Maria had finished the last of her cake, she dabbed her lips and beckoned for Olga to follow her into the washroom. There, she kept scissors and a bottle of L'Oréal in the same color Olga had used before. Maria gestured for Olga to sit on a stool and then examined her hair, fluffing it and running strands through her fingers.

"Your color stayed well," she said, "but some blonde is growing out at the roots. So a touch-up couldn't hurt. And I can give you a quick trim if you like."

"Thanks, Mashka," Olga squeezed her sister's hand before turning the faucet on and dunking her hair into the basin of the pedestal sink. She let the water swirl around her head, thinking how nice it was to wash her hair quickly. In the time before, cleaning all the girls' long hair had been a major production, and it took forever to dry.

When she finished, Maria handed her a gray towel, hardly as luxurious as one of Celia's but soft enough. Olga pressed the excess water from her hair, and Maria tied another towel around Olga's neck.

"Won't my hair look too dark now?" Olga said.

"I won't put in as much as before. It should blend well. And you wear a bonnet most of the time, right? It will cover the roots when they grow out. Trust me, unless someone is looking closely, they won't notice."

Olga thought of Rob's gaze, the steady intensity of it. She swallowed hard as Maria tilted the bottle toward her head and worked the dye through Olga's hair. The pungent smell reminded her of disinfectants used in the hospital and she took shallower breaths.

"How are the cosmetics working out?" Maria asked. "I can help you tomorrow before you leave if you like. But it seems you do a fine job yourself."

"Sure. I wouldn't mind the company." Olga hesitated, watching her sister's reflection in the mirror. "Mashka, what do you think of the letter from Mama to Father Grigori?"

Maria tried to keep her expression neutral, but Olga caught a hint of a frown. "I don't think it proves anything one way or another."

"Do you believe Mama *could* have written it?"

Tatiana would have shamed Olga for suggesting such a thing. Anastasia would say the Bolsheviks could do anything, including forging an empress's handwriting. Olga trusted Maria to give a straight answer.

"Mama was extremely loyal to Father Grigori," Maria said carefully.

"Loyal enough to do anything he asked?"

Maria smoothed the color to the ends of Olga's hair and then wrapped her head in an older towel, where the stain wouldn't matter. The slick wetness in the chilly air made Olga shiver.

"Do you think she was more loyal to Father Grigori than to Russia?" Olga asked.

"I don't think she saw a difference between the two."

"I never liked him," Olga told her sister. "Father Grigori. I never trusted him. He always spoke to Mama behind closed doors. Why? What didn't he want the rest of us to hear?"

"He helped Alexei."

"That doesn't mean he was good for the rest of us."

"No, I suppose not."

Her sister leaned against the wall and looked at Olga with the enormous eyes their parents used to call "Maria's saucers."

"I saw other documents as well," Olga blurted. "I didn't bring those with me but returned them to Hammond's study. Papers that show Father Grigori hurt women."

Maria's gaze was steady, but Olga couldn't bear to share any more with her.

"What good does it do to bring any of this up now? Anything about Father Grigori." Disdain shadowed Maria's words as she spat out his name.

"I guess I want closure," Olga said. "If Father Grigori convinced Mama to betray her country, we must make amends somehow."

"You're not thinking of letting this man publish Mama's letters?" Maria closed her eyes for a moment. "Letters allegedly written by Mama."

"No. We still don't know if they're real or not. And I don't want them published either way." Olga straightened her back and looked toward the doorway. She didn't think Tatiana could hear her, but she lowered her voice.

"Still, I think we owe something to the Russian people. We need to atone for Rasputin's sins. We were complicit in them."

"You mean well. I know that." Maria bent down and looked Olga straight in the eye. "But what can we possibly do? They threw us out. If we hadn't been rescued, the Bolsheviks would have killed us. And what happened to Mama and Papa and Alexei ... isn't that atonement enough for any sin?"

"The Bolsheviks killed them. Not the people. We still owe our people."

"They're not our people anymore," Maria said. "There is nothing we can do for Russia. Father Grigori is dead. We're not. You told us that. Remember? The House of Romanov survived because we survived. We can't return to Russia, but we can make something of ourselves here. Or elsewhere."

"Tatiana wants to return to Petrograd." Olga didn't mention that she had also wanted to return to Russia someday. Now, she wasn't so sure. England seemed safe, but perhaps they would all leave one another as the map on the wall had predicted. Those four pushpins glinting in the sun represented the end of their time together.

"Tatiana will come around and understand she is no longer a grand duchess," Maria said. "Not really. Not in the ways that count. It's all well and good to dream of Russia, but she needs another purpose in life. She may only need longer than the rest of us to find hers."

Before leaving the cottage the next morning, Olga stowed the letters in her satchel. Then, following several rounds of tearful goodbyes, she set out for the train station.

But she got no further than the front path when she spotted a Daimler idling on the street. The driver wore gloves, a scarf, a duster coat, and goggles.

Olga dropped her bag. A heavy weight pressed against her chest, and her breathing nearly stopped. *No.* The cottage's location was a closely guarded secret. At least, she thought so. Had one of the delivery drivers betrayed them? Of course not. Why should they? No one was supposed to tell them who lived in the cottage, anyway.

When the driver removed his goggles and stepped out of the motorcar, she recognized his beaming face at once.

"I hope you don't mind," Rob said.

Seeing him was surreal, like something from a dream or one of her mother's now infrequent ghostly appearances. Olga lived life in two separate spheres, one at Marlingham with Rob and Celia and the staff downstairs, and the other with her sisters in this cottage. Somehow, Rob had figured out where she lived. The two spheres of her life came crashing together, and she wasn't close to being prepared because it was never supposed to happen.

She must have given the location away, but though she wracked her brain to determine how exactly, she couldn't summon an answer. Olga had failed her family in many ways, but not this one. No rule was more important than keeping her sisters hidden and safe. She had been exceedingly careful.

You are the eldest daughter of the tsar.

Olga remembered to take a deep, calming breath. In through the nose and out through the mouth. She clasped her hands before her. She didn't move toward Rob, only angled her head to meet his gaze. Despite her impulse to run to him. For all her worry over seeing him here, she longed to be close to him even as she held her ground.

"How did you find me?" she asked.

"You were easy enough to find."

She was not easy to find. And Olga detected a note of uncertainty in his voice. "I don't think we are."

"Well ... Celia mentioned you lived near Nottingham and something about your home being on the outskirts. I saw the street name in my father's notes, though no number was attached. Celia suggested I give it a go. She seemed quite keen, actually."

Olga's head spun. Lord Hammond knew she worked at Marlingham. Of course he did. She'd always known that would be the case. How else did she expect to be paid but through the family's accounts? Hammond's accounts. He must have known about Olivia Bennett, his daughter's new maid.

How had he learned the name of their street, though? Olga had rented a postal box when she first applied for the position. That was in Nottingham and should have been the address in Hammond's records, not the name of their street. Olga wracked her brain to think of something she might have said that would lead Celia to believe she specifically lived on the outskirts of town. And how had Rob found the correct place on the street? They had been placed on a long and winding road for a reason.

This wasn't right. Rob wasn't telling her everything. Often enough, she'd felt guilty for not sharing everything about her background with Rob. She'd never considered that he might not share everything with her. His father had been a diplomat to imperial Russia. His mother had *been* Russian.

Had Rob guessed her identity? Or, worse yet, known it all along?

Olga dropped her hands to her sides, fingers curling into her palms. "How did you know the precise location of this house?"

"I didn't but hoped to get lucky. And then I saw that."

He gestured toward the door, where Anastasia had placed a garland of dyed eggs. Olga should have told her not to put any decorations outside. She should have asked Ana to take them down, only they looked charming, and she'd been so focused on the letters. She'd let her guard down, being with her sisters and aunt.

"For most everyone else, Easter has come and gone, so chances were good that this was your house," Rob continued. He tilted his head, not in curiosity, but to try to win her over. She understood the difference by now. "I hope I haven't overstepped."

Rob was holding something out to her: a small package wrapped in pale pink paper and tied with a rose-colored ribbon.

"Oh, yes!" he said, following her gaze. He placed the package in her hand. "This is for you. In honor of Easter. I confess I couldn't wait for you to see it."

Though she didn't know all the English etiquette dictating a relationship between a maid and a young lord, showing up unexpectedly at her door with a gift must have been frowned upon. Then again, their connection was hardly typical. She thought back to the conversation in his motorcar when she had come close to kissing him. Before common sense had reared its head at last.

When Olga was with Rob, her common sense had a rough go of it. As she tried to determine how to get Rob away from the cottage, she was also considering how long it had been since she'd received a gift from a gentleman. Aside from Aunt Olga's gift of perfume—now tucked in a kerchief at the bottom of her satchel—it had been a long time since she'd received any gift at all.

Olga examined the package, enjoying its slight heaviness in her hand. The delicate wrapping paper had been neatly closed on each side.

"Mrs. Dasari helped me wrap the box. Pretty, isn't it?"

It was pretty, yet she recoiled because she doubted Mrs. Dasari knew the young lord's package was intended for a maid. "I'm not sure I should accept."

"Why don't you take a look first? And then you can decide if it's appropriate."

No matter how Rob had learned where she lived, Olga had to get him away from the house. Away from her sisters. It might be best to accept the ride without further questions and not fuss over the gift. Once she had put a safe distance between Rob and the cottage, she could try to learn more.

"Might I open it once we're back at Marlingham?" Olga tried to smile.

"Please open it now," he said. "The suspense is killing me."

"Surely you need to get back."

"I do not. And you have the rest of the day as a holiday, yes?"

He was right. Olga had no reason to rush away.

She glanced back at the cottage with the drapes shut tight over the front bay window.

In for a penny, in for a pound.

Olga jumped, sure she had heard someone say that aloud. But no, it was only in her head. Mama's voice. Her mother liked that expression, one she claimed her grandmother, Queen Victoria, had taught her. Whenever Papa heard it, he would smile, take a puff on his cigarette, and mutter something good-natured about the English always making life about pence and pounds. Before, Olga never understood the phrase, but now thought she had some sense of it.

Fingers trembling, she unwrapped the pink paper covering the package.

"Here." Once she had the paper torn off, Rob took it, so her hands remained free. She held a velvety indigo box with *Selfridges* embossed in curving gold letters.

After she opened it, Olga gasped.

An enameled pendant charm rested against blue padding. It was only the size of the top of her pinkie finger and shaped like an egg. She recognized the design at once. Based on Fabergé, this was a miniature likeness of the egg Papa had commissioned as a gift for Mama not long after Tatiana's birth: the pink "Lilies of the Valley" with white blossoms and green leaves scattered over it, and beaded chains of diamonds encased in gold.

"Though you are intent on becoming an Englishwoman," Rob told her, "I hope you won't lose sight of where you came from. I'm sure you're familiar with Mr. Fabergé's designs."

The original egg was more ornate, and the colors more vibrant, topped with a gold reproduction of the imperial crown. When one twisted a little button, the dome rose to reveal three portraits: her father, baby Tatiana, and Olga, hardly more than a toddler at the time.

Her family as they had been over twenty years before. This replica captured much of the original's magic.

Olga had been too young to recall her mother's reaction when she received the egg. She only knew how fondly Mama had regarded it whenever she passed by. Seeing it again, in likeness, proved that their world from the time before wasn't completely lost.

"I couldn't help myself," Rob said. "When I was last in London, I saw it and bought it on a whim. It reminded me of my mother. But when you told me of your past, I figured it belonged to you."

He bent down, searching Olga's face to determine what she made of the gift. "I hope you will keep it."

Olga wiped a stray tear from her eyes. She didn't know what to say. She felt like there had been a lock over her heart, perhaps keeping her safe but also serving as another prison. She recalled something Ana had said after she'd tried to run away. *Papa wouldn't want us trapped like animals in a cage.*

At the time, Olga denied that was true. Their lives were isolated but hardly caged. She wondered if she'd been fooling herself. She was tired of waiting, tired of holding herself back. Life was in the here and now, and they must all—what had Maria said? Find their purpose?

Surely they were meant to find joy as well.

Olga moved closer to Rob and stood on her tiptoes. She touched his cheek tentatively, closed her eyes, and pressed her lips against his.

There was a slight hesitation, his lips barely responding as though caught off guard. Then, after a moment, he understood what was happening and returned the kiss, gently probing her lips. Olga surrendered to the exquisite pulses of energy in her chest and stomach, the delicious melting thrill of it.

Reluctantly, and probably too slowly, she pulled away.

Her eyes were still closed, and she felt her breath move through her lungs. Their foreheads touched as he explored the lines of her face. The sensation was perfect. She didn't dare open her eyes for fear she'd ruin the moment.

"So you do like your gift, then?"

His voice was low and alluring, sweeping over her as a caress. She savored the moment, pushing worries to the back of her mind. Olga wasn't sure where she had summoned the courage to kiss him, but she couldn't take it back now.

"I love it."

At last, she opened her eyes. Rob's gaze had shifted. He looked confused. Something behind her was distracting him. He frowned, and then his mouth dropped open in utter shock.

No, no, no.

Olga turned in time to spot her sisters at the front window before they scuttled backward and closed the drapes. She didn't have a chance to wave them away.

Not that it mattered. Rob had already seen them.

She was too astonished to think straight, only knew that yet again she had failed and given away their secret. She could fool Rob on her own, but when all four of them were together, their identities were clear.

"Your imperial highness?" he whispered.

She saw it in his eyes. Rob knew he had seen the missing grand duchesses.

When our little brother was closest to death, I prayed for Alexei, as did we all. I cried, as did all those around us.

We tried to visit Alexei, but he was in such pain that he didn't recognize his sisters. We were all helpless in the face of this mysterious illness, even the doctors. Finally, our mother sent word to Father Grigori, begging for help. Soon a telegram arrived in response:

The illness will not harm him. Keep the doctors from making him tired.

Grigori Rasputin's simple words worked when all the doctors' treatments failed. Alexei felt better. It convinced our mother of his power once and for all. Father Grigori had prayed for Alexei, but then we all had done the same. God answered Rasputin's prayers alone.

If, by some miracle of fate, I became heiress to an empire, an empress like my mother, would I do the same for a son? After all, I carry the lethal gene. I could have a son who might suffer as Alexei suffered. Would I have the strength to resist anyone who could cure him, no matter their crimes?

The Private Diary of Olga Romanova
December 1921

CHAPTER EIGHTEEN

"You can't tell anyone!" Olga blurted. "Not Celia. Not your father."

Rob's gaze shifted from the cottage's front bay window to her face.

She snapped the jewelry box closed, shuttering the enameled pendant, for now, the Lilies of the Valley. She deposited the gem in her coat pocket and grabbed Rob's wrist.

"No one. Do you hear me?"

He took a step back, appraising her with fresh eyes.

"It is you then," he whispered at last.

She shook him gently, fingers tight around his wrist.

"You know what happened to your father. The poison. Imagine what would happen if the Bolsheviks found *us*. Please. You must promise."

"There were rumors, of course. That you were rescued. That you were here. In England."

"Rumors? About us?"

"That someone smuggled you from Russia. It wasn't c-clear if it was just the children or the whole family or perhaps only one daughter ... that is ... one of you. It was said to be a covert operation."

The memory remained hazy, coming so soon after the trauma of the House of Special Purpose. The men involved in their rescue were sworn to secrecy, but how many English soldiers had seen them afterward? Ten? More?

She released Rob's hand. What was she thinking by risking a trip to the cinema with Ana, let alone working as a maid? Had she thought her dyed hair and contoured cheekbones sufficient disguise? She was the eldest daughter of the tsar—a symbol of the Romanovs. For many people, the Romanov family remained a dangerous symbol of an oppressive old order.

Deep in her heart, Olga had been sure they could convince those same people otherwise. That she and her sisters belonged in this newer, freer world.

Inevitably, word might escape. No matter how careful they were, she and her sisters couldn't remain hidden forever.

Staying in England would be a mistake. Olga saw that now. Settling here had not been her choice but a miscalculation on her grandmother's part.

Either way, Olga should have determined how to take her sisters farther away from their old lives to the Americas or Japan. The Bolsheviks could easily guess they were in England. *If* they didn't know already. Olga's mother and father both had close ties to the English royal family. It was only a matter of time before the Bolsheviks came after them, possibly disguised as Englishmen.

And now she had kissed this Englishman. She had *kissed* him. Olga allowed herself to get swept away, and now Rob knew her secret. And how much did she know about him? Gran shouldered some blame for sending them to England in the first place, but giving away their location? That was all Olga's fault.

Rob must have known who she was all along. Or suspected. "Did you know before?" she asked.

"Know you were a grand duchess?"

"If you heard those rumors, you must have wondered. Especially after I told you I was from Russia." Olga thought of something worse and suppressed a shudder. "Does your father know?"

"No one knows," Rob said, more assured this time.

"Even if you didn't *know*, you must have guessed."

"As I said, the rumors were just that. Though sometimes when I looked at you—I don't know. It must have jogged some part of my memory. But it's not as though I had her ... your ... face committed to memory. I'd seen your picture in the papers. Your sisters' pictures." He gestured toward the cottage, hand trembling.

Of course he had. Their pictures were all over the papers after the anti-Bolshevik forces captured the House of Special Purpose. Well before that, too. Papa never considered the potential dangers inherent in his daughters' fame. He never imagined half-starved workers might seize Petrograd, nor that the tsar and his family could ever be arrested as enemies of the state. Who would have thought the tsar's daughters could remain in danger even after a revolution?

"That first day we met, I thought you looked familiar," Rob said. "But I couldn't place from where. In all truth, I thought perhaps I had met you at a party and forgotten."

"You never asked me. Not directly."

"You were bent over Conall and so upset. I thought I knew you somehow, but it seemed foolish to mention it since I couldn't offer any details. Deep down, perhaps a part of me always wondered. But it seemed so outlandish. Why would you be at my home? A maid? I looked at you, though. Often. Perhaps more often than I ought."

Olga's cheeks flamed, anger and pleasure at war with one another. Though she supposed most lords looked at maids. In the same manner that Grigori Rasputin looked at women. As though they were his for the taking. As though they had no will of their own.

But not Rob. He wasn't the type. So, though it horrified Olga to think he might have guessed her identity, it also helped to think he knew, on some level, that she was no maid.

"The way you carried yourself was odd," he added.

"How I carried myself?"

"Your posture. Your confidence. More than that. I can't explain, but I thought something was off."

Olga was about to interrogate him further when she heard her aunt's voice, higher in pitch than usual. Not snappish, exactly, but firm and focused, as she used to speak to Olga and Tatiana after they attended one of the parties at her flat and then were reluctant to go home.

"What are you doing?"

Her aunt hobbled down the cottage's front steps as fast as possible in her long, narrow skirt. This made her seem older as well. The aunt she remembered would have worn the latest fashions, which allowed for greater freedom of movement.

Once her aunt was close enough for them to hear her without the need to shout, she said: "Niece, please introduce me to your friend. But only after we are inside and the door shut. Sir, I must insist you either leave or follow us in."

"He knows," Olga said flatly. "If you had my sisters hide or something, it doesn't matter. He already saw them. You needn't bother to deny it."

Her aunt's kind expression crumpled, but she held her smile—the sister of the tsar trained to be gracious under the most trying circumstances. She put a hand on Olga's shoulder but addressed Rob.

"Then it is imperative you come inside."

Olga bent down to fetch her satchel.

"No, please. Allow me."

Rob grabbed it for her, a new glint of wonder in his voice. Maybe he only picked up her bag because he knew her identity now. But, no. He probably would have done so regardless. Either way, Olga had no desire to keep up the charade. Rob knew she was a grand duchess. Olga might as well behave like one. She straightened her back.

"If you would be so kind as to follow me."

With that, she pivoted and turned to the cottage, trusting Rob would obey her command.

Aunt Olga ushered Rob inside and to the parlor while Olga's sisters gaped. She heard a wolf whistle and spun around. Sure enough, Ana grinned and shrugged. The cheek of that girl.

"May I present Robert Pike, Viscount Marling." Olga turned to Rob. "I suppose you know my sisters well enough. The grand duchesses."

Olga's blunt revelation of their identities landed like a slap. She could see it in the sudden pallor on her sisters' faces. This must have come as a total shock, a strange man entering the cottage, no matter his title. Still, Tatiana and Maria retained their composure and curtsied.

"He should bow to us!" Ana angled her jaw toward Rob.

"Oh, what does it matter now?" Olga snapped, still irritated at Ana for whistling at Rob like some street urchin from a Dickens novel.

"Maria already put the kettle on for tea. Why don't we get settled?" Aunt Olga offered Rob the armchair nearest the window. He stood near it uncertainly, waiting for the rest to sit. Always the gentleman. While he waited, however, he took in every detail of their humble surroundings, the worn furniture and discolored wallpaper. The cottage didn't look as shabby as Olga once considered it, particularly not with the colored eggs hanging about. Her sisters didn't have laundry scattered about, hanging from clothespins to dry. The place had never looked better, really, though Olga still berated herself for not making Ana take the garland outside the front door down.

The situation was so odd that Olga might have found it comical if she weren't so anxious. The secret of their escape, survival, and path toward a new life had been contained for so long between the four of them. That their grandmother, rescuers, and a few relatives also knew remained hypothetical. It had been a secret bubble sealed to ensure their survival.

Now the bubble had popped, but at least Olga could stop pretending to be someone else.

The kettle screeched, startling Rob. Maria went to fetch it from the kitchen. Ana sat on the rug before the hearth while Olga and Tatiana sat on the sofa. Olga felt glad for the reassuring pressure of her sister's legs against hers and the quiet rhythm of her breathing. It had a calming effect as her nerves frayed.

Maria returned to the parlor and carefully placed a cup of tea and a saucer on the side table nearest Rob, blushing deeply. She then sat next to Ana, though the floor couldn't have been more comfortable than squeezing in to join Olga and Tatiana on the sofa.

At last, Rob sat, though Aunt Olga remained standing and then paced back and forth across the parlor.

Rob's hand shook as he brought the cup of tea to his lips. He let his gaze fall on each of them in turn, finally resting on Olga. She looked down at her hands. If she looked at him, she would think about how it felt to kiss him.

"Your imperial highnesses." Rob took a deep breath before exhaling slowly. Then, giving up on keeping his hands steady enough for tea, he set the cup down with a clatter against the saucer. "I am so sorry for everything you and your family went through. The murder of your parents and brother will always ..."

Tatiana's legs tensed. Olga looked up at Rob and shook her head. No point in testing Tatiana's patience. With a nod, Rob dropped the subject and continued:

"Grand Duchess Tatiana. I'd read a story in the paper about you possibly surviving and marrying an Englishman. The journalist re-ferred to you as Princess Tatiana. I knew that title was incorrect, so I didn't give it much credence. That wasn't you, I take it?"

Anastasia snorted and answered for her sister. "One of the phonies. Not the real thing like *Miss Bennett* over there."

"I'm sure the viscount understands why Olga used an assumed name," her aunt said.

"And changed her appearance," Maria added, with a note of pride.

"But h-how?" Rob pressed his lips together. "How did they save all four of you? I thought it was impossible. That's what we were told."

Olga's heart fluttered. Not in a good way. "Who told you? Why did anyone tell you anything?"

"My father mentioned that your family was placed under house arrest." Rob shot her an apologetic look. "I'm sorry I didn't mention it outside. I was still gathering my senses. But he said it was impossible to get you all out of Russia."

Hammond was apprised of their rescue plans? If he hated her mother so much, why did he care? "How did he know?"

"At the time, he still held his army commission from the war, and apparently, there had been some talk of a rescue, even after you were transported from your palace near Petrograd to Siberia. I'm sorry I forget the name of the town."

"Tobolsk," Tatiana said quietly.

"Right. But then you moved again to Ekaterinburg, and the Bolsheviks held that city tight. My father said the king's men were advised it was all but impossible to attempt a rescue at that point."

Olga glanced sideways at Tatiana while their aunt said, "I'm sure you respect the secrecy surrounding that mission, and why it must remain sacrosanct. I suspect the king's men, as you call them, were misdirecting your father."

"I suppose so."

"You must not disclose the girls' location now," Aunt Olga said firmly. "No matter what."

Rob held his hands up as though in surrender. "I will say nothing. You have my word. But this is astonishing."

"Astonishing," Olga repeated under her breath, fidgeting and nudging the satchel at her feet. She still had her coat on. Olga wondered if she might run for the door and keep running. Find another place of employment now that she'd proven she could get on well enough as a maid. Find a country home where she was not yet known and where she might disappear in utter anonymity.

She could never do that. Olga was too much Papa's daughter. Papa had his faults, but he never ran away. After her father abdicated, he remained in Russia when, amidst the confusion, he and Alexei could easily have slipped out of the country. In retrospect, he probably should have. It would have made it easier for their mother to flee from the Alexander Palace with her children before Petrograd fell, regardless of their illnesses.

That wasn't how Papa conducted himself, though. He saw things through, even when they became unbearable.

Olga reached into her pocket and withdrew the jewelry box Rob had given her earlier, cradling it in her hands. Though a childish fancy, she longed to return to the time when Rob hadn't known her identity. Even if it had been unseemly for him to pay attention to a maid, the relief she'd felt at having her secret out was now displaced by fear. She should return the pendant to Rob, for how could she accept this gift? This blatant reminder of her failure to keep the secret that protected her sisters?

Shocks of heat blazed Olga's cheeks before migrating to her neck and stomach. And yet she couldn't bear to part with the gift. Olga slipped the box back into her pocket.

"Now I understand why you were peeking around my father's study," Rob told Olga. "You don't hate the empress. Rather, you wanted to vindicate her. You wanted to see what evidence he had on your mother, didn't you? You must hate my father."

Rob hesitated, and Olga waited for him to finish. She knew what he was thinking. *And so you must hate me.* The resignation in his tone said it for him.

She looked into Rob's sorrowful eyes. "Can you blame me?"

He dropped his gaze.

"Only because he hates my mother so much that he would forever destroy her reputation and that of my family," Olga added. "The war is over. Revolution shook our country to the core. And then the Bolsheviks destroyed what was left. So what's the point?"

Rob remained silent. She took a deep breath.

"Why does your father hate us, Rob? What did we ever do to him?"

Tatiana tensed. And then Olga realized she had said "Rob." Her sister knew Olga would never use such a familiar name had she not interacted with him in a manner that suggested a relationship beyond maid and lord.

"He doesn't hate you," Rob said. "He doesn't hate any of you."

"He hates our mother. Our father too, I should think, though Mama always was the easier target." Olga heard the anger rise in her throat. "The German woman. That's what they called her on the streets—that and far worse. And the guards in Ekaterinburg? In that filthy house where they kept us the last few months? They drew terrible pictures of her. Vulgar and hateful. They thought she was a German spy. The Bolsheviks did. As your father believes she was a spy."

"I'm sorry," he whispered.

Now that she'd started, Olga couldn't stop. All the rage and frustration she'd buried for months finally emerged and broke through. "Where did that idea come from, anyway? It couldn't be enough that she was born in Hesse. Not that alone. Perhaps someone put the idea in the Bolsheviks' collective head. Perhaps your father did."

"Olga!" her aunt cried.

Though Rob was shaking, he looked at Olga once more, eyes pleading. "I know you went through a painful experience," he said. "Things no one should have to endure. But my father knows Russia well, and he is not cruel. He is a good man. I know it. He must have his reasons for wanting the letters between Rasputin and the empress published."

Complicity in the House of Romanov.

Olga remembered something Father Grigori had told her mother after he'd helped Alexei recover from one of his bleeding spells. *The little one is meant to suffer, but he will survive.*

What nonsense. Rasputin was far from the prophet his legend has made him out to be. He was only half right. Alexei had suffered but not survived.

Why did Alexei have to die? How could he possibly have been *complicit* in anything?

"Our brother was only thirteen. Completely innocent. He never harmed another soul in his entire short, agonizing life. No matter what your father might say."

"I don't believe my father said—"

"Perhaps your father made our lives hell and poisoned our people against us. Perhaps he helped murder our parents and our little brother."

"Olga Nikolaevna, that is enough!" Aunt Olga roared.

The room was silent, as though Olga had spewed toxins in the air. Maria closed her eyes. Ana looked at the floor. Olga couldn't bear to face Tatiana's reaction.

"Those wild accusations are completely unfair, and you know it." Aunt Olga frowned at her and then regarded Rob with the same gentle expression Olga remembered gracing her aunt's features in Russia. War and revolution may have aged her, but they failed to steal her compassion. "I'm sorry. You know Olga is not herself right now. It is just the shock of the memories rushing back. Surely you can see."

"I can see," Rob said quietly.

He would not look at her. Olga felt a deep, curdling shame. Rob had been through as much as she had, and he had not once raised his voice nor taken anything out on her. She may have ruined everything special between them.

"May I ask after your father?" her aunt said. "I hear he has an issue with the girls' late mother. Perhaps we should start there."

"He was a diplomat in Russia before the war," Rob said.

Aunt Olga paused. "Did he have contact with the tsar? The empress?"

"I don't believe so. My father would have spent most of his time there at the beginning of their reign. That's when he met my mother. In St. Petersburg."

"Wait. Is your mother Russian?"

"She was. She passed away. The influenza pandemic."

"Oh no," Maria said. "I'm sorry."

"We all are," Aunt Olga added.

Rob swept his hair away from his face, but a lock fell back over his scar. Olga could still make out its edges, redder than she remembered.

"My father wants Parliament to censure the late empress," he said. "He believes she was a traitor to her country. He wants to restore diplomatic relations with Russia, for the sake of peace and stability, but he is no friend to the Bolsheviks. They tried to kill him. I do not think it was a rogue agent out of their control."

"You don't believe them?" her aunt asked.

"I have come to see there is little reason to take the Bolsheviks at their word."

Rob glanced around the room again. Olga realized he was referencing her survival. She and her sisters. The Bolsheviks still wanted people to believe the tsar's daughters were dead despite the rumors and impostors.

Aunt Olga leaned against the wall, running her tongue over her bottom lip. And then she regarded Rob again, eyes wide.

"Wait. Pike. Olga introduced you as Robert Pike. And you said your father was a diplomat. What is his name? Apart from his title, I mean. His family name."

"Edward Pike." Rob's expression brightened somewhat. "You know him? You know then that he's an honorable sort overall."

"I do not know him. Not personally."

Tatiana piped in at last. "Does Gran know him?"

She answered Tatiana with a wary glance. Olga knew her aunt well enough to see that something about that name had resonated. Whatever she knew about Rob's father must have been too awful to say in front of the man's son.

"Do you know why I asked for your father's name? Do you know what he did?"

Olga's heart skipped a beat. Rob only shook his head uncertainly.

"Edward Pike is one of the gentlemen who helped arrange the girls' rescue."

When at long last the English king decided which Romanovs to save, my sisters and I escaped the horrors of the House of Special Purpose in Ekaterinburg.

My brother did not.

He was the heir. In the old world, that put him in a position of privilege. In the new world wrought of a revolution, it made him a liability.

That was not what they told us, of course. The English claimed my brother was too weak to travel: a plausible excuse. When I hugged Alexei for the last time, his body felt so fragile I feared he'd break apart in my arms. He was thirteen years old but had the frame of a far younger boy.

After I released him, he buried his face in the fur of his faithful little spaniel, Joy. I remember turning back for one last look, seeing only the pale back of Alexei's head, his once abundant hair reduced to straggly patches, and his dog's sad eyes.

Leaving Alexei made the night of our rescue the worst of my life. Even if it was the same night my life was saved.

The Private Diary of Olga Romanova
December 1921

CHAPTER NINETEEN

As though watching a moving picture on the screen, Olga returned to that morning in August 1918 when she'd emerged from the gloom of the rickety field ambulance in which they had escaped to a bright sky and the clean salty scent of the sea. She remembered the wind ruffling her hair and the indistinct sound of men's voices in English as her eyes adjusted to the light. The short-lived exhilaration of freedom.

And then she'd asked the officer in charge, the one who'd addressed her as *imperial highness,* if they were going back to save the rest of her family. That was the moment she understood the English would never rescue them.

Lord Hammond had saved Olga and her sisters but left their parents and brother to die.

"My father never spoke of a rescue," Rob exclaimed. "He was gone from the country for a while around that time, but that wasn't unusual. He said rescue was impossible."

"It was almost two years ago now," Aunt Olga said. "But he must have pledged to continue to keep it secret. Even from his son."

Dragging herself away from the memories, Olga looked at Tatiana. Her sister had been strangely silent, but her lips moved as though she wanted to say something.

"If it's all so secretive, how do *you* know our rescuer's name?" Ana asked.

Aunt Olga sighed. "Your grandmother is experiencing the ill effects of old age. She wasn't supposed to say anything but mentioned a few names, Edward Pike among them. She kept saying, 'my nephew has done it. He has ordered his men to save them. My son will live. My grandson and the girls will live.'"

Except they hadn't all lived. Gran's nephew, the King of England, allowed the tsar, his wife, and their son to be left behind. And it seemed Gran hadn't bothered to mention Mama when she gave thanks for the rescue.

"They could not save the others?"

It was as though Olga had spoken her thoughts aloud, except it wasn't her voice. Instead, Tatiana had aired what all of them must have been thinking.

"That couldn't be helped," Aunt Olga said. "At least that is my understanding."

"But if Lord Hammond, or Edward Pike, I suppose, helped us, why is he so upset with Mother now?" Maria asked.

"Maybe he's always hated our parents." Tatiana's tone was as tart as Olga had ever heard. Sometimes it startled her all over again how embittered her sister had become. "After all, the English rescued us but left them behind. Along with Alexei. They never sent anyone else back. Perhaps they never planned to do so at all. Maybe they *purposely* left our parents and Alexei behind. "

"That is quite harsh. Shame on you." Despite her words, Aunt Olga scratched her head in a way that made Olga think she was also considering this possibility. "There simply wasn't time. Everything moved so fast. And Alexei was too ill to make the journey."

Aunt Olga squeezed her eyes shut. Olga had spent so much time mourning her parents that she didn't consider the suffering of others in her family. Her aunt had lost a brother. Her grandmother had lost a son. The least Olga could do was help them find some resolution to help ease that pain.

Rob sat in his armchair, pale as a ghost, saying nothing. There wasn't anything more to say. Now that the truth had come out, she didn't have to lie to Rob.

But she knew that the distance between them had grown too far.

"I think you should go," Olga said softly. "I'll see you to your motorcar."

Rob stood. What else could he do? As he approached the doorway, Aunt Olga grasped his arm and looked up at him.

"You say nothing," she told him. "Understand?"

He nodded, and they stepped outside to a glorious spring day. Was it always like that? The weather so fine when her life was in the most turmoil? The sunny day seemed deliberately at odds with her mood.

Olga walked Rob to his Daimler, fearing that with each step, she was closer and closer to letting him go completely.

"Drive back with me," Rob said once they reached his motor. "Please. Let's talk this through."

Olga had missed the train back to Marlingham, yet she didn't agree to join him.

"Don't you see?" she said in a dull voice, refusing to meet his eyes. "Everything has changed."

"Nothing has changed."

"You know my secret! And now I know your father's."

"None of this should matter. Not for us."

If it were only herself, perhaps she could believe it didn't matter, but Olga had her sisters' welfare to consider. Rob might give away some clue inadvertently. Eventually, the Bolsheviks could learn where they were hiding.

Worst of all, the more Olga considered it, the more she thought Tatiana was right. The English never intended to go back for their parents and Alexei. Lord Hammond, Edward Pike, must have had something to do with that. How could she consider a relationship with the son of a man who had left her family to die?

Even if Rob was a good man. Even if Olga did care for him. Deeply.

In allowing herself to trust Rob, she had betrayed her sisters' location and put them in danger. She would always regret it.

Olga took Rob's hands in hers, minding the tender skin healing around the scar from his burn.

"Tell Celia I'm sorry," Olga told him. "I need to stay here and determine what my sisters and I should do next. We can't stay in England. And I can't return to Marlingham."

The bedroom she and Tatiana shared was too cold, but as the first signs of morning light filtered through the lemon yellow curtains they'd hand-stitched for the window, Olga could not will herself to leave it. Neither the prospect of spending time with her sisters nor the first trill of the birds outside motivated her to rise from bed.

Olga sighed and turned over on her side, propping a thin pillow against her lower back to ease the pain of remaining in bed too long.

She'd learned that trick from her mother. In Ekaterinburg, Mama slept for days at a time, as Olga had.

She heard rustling as Tatiana stirred in the bed across from Olga's. Olga waited, eyes open, to see if her sister was getting up. It wouldn't be long before Maria and Ana woke as well. Then the pleas would begin. Tatiana would list off all the chores for the day that they absolutely could not accomplish without Olga's help. Olga wished her sister had a better understanding of exactly how little desire she had to do anything right now, let alone housework. The endless upkeep of the cottage, of any place she might live, was but one of the many daunting tasks that kept her in bed.

Maria and Ana took different approaches. Maria sang the old songs they'd loved, trying not to cry. She brought Olga tea. She mentioned that Olga's favorite biscuits were expected in their next delivery package. Meanwhile, Anastasia had taken to bringing magazines into Olga's room and reading the latest gossip about starlets and handsome actors aloud, periodically shaking Olga's shoulder and asking if she was still awake.

Strangely, Ana's strategy was the most comforting. Olga almost enjoyed listening to the dramas of starlets she didn't know, the intricacies of their love lives. It took her mind off her own troubles for a while. And their stories reminded her of a world outside her increasingly morbid thoughts.

If Tatiana woke now and started reciting the daily chores, Olga couldn't handle it. She held her breath, but Tatiana didn't rise. Olga closed her eyes and kept still, feigning sleep.

A few minutes later, a firm shake jolted her body. Olga opened her eyes to find her aunt hovering over her. She was smiling but with a nervous tremor at the corner of her lips.

After Olga announced she wasn't returning to Marlingham, and after a whispered discussion with Tatiana that neither of them thought she'd heard, Aunt Olga changed her travel plans and announced she would stay a few more days. Olga couldn't find it in her to care. Thankfully, her aunt steered clear of Olga's room, though her worried voice carried through the thin walls. Had Olga fallen into such a depression before? What had worked? What hadn't? Should she leave her alone?

After three days, it seemed her aunt's patience had run short.

"I thought I'd give you some space, but I can't encourage you to remain this way forever. You'll need to face life eventually."

Olga blinked rapidly, trying to rid the grainy sleep from her eyes. She was far beyond shedding more tears at this point. "Isn't Gran expecting you?" she whispered, the most she'd uttered in days.

"She can wait a while longer. Frankly, I have no problem with delaying our reunion."

Olga almost smiled. Aunt Olga had a similar relationship with her mother as Olga had with hers: loving but tense. She understood completely.

"That's my girl," her aunt whispered. "We must figure out a way to get you up for a little while today."

"I don't want to wash the dishes," Olga whispered back.

"No, no. We don't have to worry about your sister's list. Let's take it one step at a time. Would you like to sit in the garden?"

Olga turned her head, facing the wall so she wouldn't have to see the disappointment on her aunt's face when she declined the invitation. Every movement felt like forcing her way through mud. "No, thank you."

"Just a little sun on your face," her aunt insisted. "It will make you feel better. And it will certainly make me feel better."

"Why should I bother?"

"It was what your father would have wanted. And your mother." She hesitated. "And Alexei."

Olga thought of her brother romping in the garden with Joy at his ankles. And then she recalled his devastated expression when she left him for the last time.

"Alexei should be here," she whispered. "I should have carried him out."

Her aunt touched her shoulder gently and rolled her back over to face her.

"Listen to me," Aunt Olga said. "Your brother couldn't have gone with you girls."

"I could have found a way."

"He was too sick. He would never have made it."

"It doesn't matter. I failed Alexei. And now I failed my sisters."

"You did not fail your sisters," Aunt Olga said. "One gentleman knows your secret. And I like that young gentleman. Rob, you called him?"

"I called him Rob by mistake," Olga said. "He's Viscount Marley. Someday, he'll be the new earl. And I'm only the maid."

"Either way, he seems to have sense in his brain and respect for you." Her aunt arched her eyebrows and wiggled them, as she used to do when Olga was a little girl, and her aunt was still a teenager. A smile played on Olga's lips.

"Perhaps there is more than respect between the two of you?"

"It would never work," Olga said. "Our families are completely at odds. It's impossible."

"Nothing in this world is impossible. The last few years should have taught you that."

"The last few years have taught me pain."

"Pain makes happiness all the sweeter."

Aunt Olga extended her hand. She couldn't deny the goodwill on her aunt's face. Besides, it was clear she wasn't planning to withdraw her hand until Olga accepted it.

"Thirty minutes in the garden," her aunt said. "You and me. That's all you have to do today. Nothing else. Is it a deal?"

With great effort, Olga slipped her hand out from under the blankets to clasp her aunt's and shake it. Perhaps she wasn't too far gone after all.

"Deal," she whispered.

Olga kept her word and spent thirty minutes in the garden with her aunt. She found the sun's warmth on her face and the sound of chipmunks chittering and birds twittering agreeable. After thirty minutes passed, however, she was exhausted and crawled back into bed soon afterward.

By the following day, she felt well enough to rise for breakfast, though much later than the others. Her aunt had already gone outside to help Maria and Anastasia tend to the weeds. Olga didn't know what Tatiana was doing. She had the nook to herself and summoned enough energy to prepare a pot of strong black tea, stirring in generous amounts of milk and sugar.

Ravenous, she searched for a scone or bread for toasting. Strange how depression alone could drive her hunger away and how that hunger returned with a vengeance once the melancholy dissipated.

Finally settling on a pair of shortbread biscuits she wrangled from the bottom of a tin, Olga tried to imagine what her life would look like if she stayed here, indefinitely, with her sisters.

On the bright side, she could spend more time in the garden. It was a pleasant enough space, and she feared she hadn't appreciated it properly. Perhaps Ana would spend time out there with her, reading rather than moping. Or they could all paint with watercolors, as they used to back home. The supplies were one of the first things they'd ordered, though none had the heart to start a project. It reminded them too much of the time before. Ana seemed to enjoy working with her camera as much as ever, but the rest of them needed to find new hobbies which didn't call to mind the past.

Olga could never change what had happened. Rob knew who she was. He knew where her sisters lived. As long as they remained here, they weren't safe. But where could they go? Aunt Victoria lived on the Isle of Wight and would surely take them in. Olga frowned as she munched on a biscuit and took a tentative sip of tea. They'd never been close to Aunt Victoria, and the Isle of Wight was still on English soil.

They could move to Copenhagen and live with Gran, she supposed. Aunt Olga and her family would be nearby. But that wouldn't work either. Given Gran's ties to the country, Denmark might be the first place the Bolsheviks would look for them, an even more obvious choice than England.

Nibbling on the shortbread, Olga was still wondering where they could go when Tatiana walked into the dining nook with an envelope in hand.

"So you are up and about," Tatiana said. "Ana told me as much, but I needed to see it with my own eyes."

"I'm up, but I'd hardly call this about." She took a bigger bite of the shortbread, savoring the sweetness on her tongue.

"You seem better, though." Tatiana took a seat across from Olga and placed the envelope on the table. "It's for you. Aunt Olga went into town earlier this morning to check your post office box. She asked me to give it to you once you were awake."

Seeing the neatly curving penmanship on the thin beige envelope, Olga knew this was from Celia. She wasn't sure she should open it. Celia might be angry. She might be hurt. Olga didn't want to face it, but curiosity got the better of her, as did Tatiana's probing stare. She pushed her cup and saucer aside and then slit the envelope with the flat edge of her teaspoon.

O,

Rob said you would not return because you're needed at your sister's home for an extended period. I am sorry to hear it. I hope everything is well with you and yours, or will be soon enough. I am imploring you to consider returning to work as quickly as possible.

I believe word has gotten out regarding my condition. I see how the staff members look at me now. Has the rumor mill done its ghastly work? Maybe I am so far along that it's impossible to hide. Either way, I am miserable. But I must stay strong for the child to come and make good decisions for the future.

Your family comes first, and I would never ask you to turn away from them. Please know I need you as well. I could bear anything were you at my side. Please come back when you can.

I miss you,
Celia

Olga stared straight ahead, not really seeing anything. She felt terrible for Celia and missed her as well. It seemed clear Rob had said nothing to his sister, as he'd promised. But Olga's place was here.

After another minute, she realized Tatiana was still staring at her.

"May I read the letter? I take it this is from your employer."

Olga had promised not to share Celia's secret, but it sounded like it was out, regardless. Besides, if she refused, Tatiana would grow suspicious and probably read the letter anyway when Olga wasn't looking. Tatiana might not have been able to lie, but she was better than she liked to admit at snooping.

So Olga pushed the letter toward her. Tatiana read quickly, her lips moving slightly as her eyes scanned the note. Her only reaction was a slight raising of her brows. "Oh."

"Aren't you scandalized?"

Tatiana placed her elbows on the table, something she wouldn't have dreamed of doing in the time before. Her long fingers touched and slanted downward. She rested her chin between them while gazing thoughtfully at Olga.

"There may have been a time when I would have been scandalized, but I think we're all past that now. What if something had happened to one of us? You know what I mean. The guards. They were so forceful toward the end. I admit I was worried. Any of us might have found ourselves in the same situation as Lady Celia. We would have asked for compassion for ourselves and our baby."

Olga was shocked at Tatiana's bluntness. They had all been worried about the guards. The young man had free access to their rooms and leered often enough, especially after drinking. And yet something had stopped them from pushing things too far. Perhaps strict orders from their officers to leave the young women alone. They'd been saved from that much.

But Tatiana's point was well taken. Their vulnerability to the guards' whims opened their eyes to the realities of the world outside their sheltered lives, the dangers to women. But she didn't want Tatiana to get the wrong impression.

"I don't think it's that sort of situation. She wants the child."

Thankfully, Tatiana remained serene. "The father won't marry her?"

"I don't think so. Celia is in trouble. There's no doubt about that."

Tatiana nodded calmly. "She lost her mother. No sisters. I can only imagine how isolated she must feel. Of course she wants you back. She needs you. And I've never known you to turn your back on someone in need."

"I wish I could be there for Celia, but they know too much," Olga said. "Rob does, at any rate. And his father as well. Hammond will return from London soon. He must be nearly well enough to travel by now."

"We can't change what they already know."

"You were right, though. Once he's back, he'll know me in an instant. It was a mistake to go there. It was a mistake to stay as long as I did." Olga hesitated, staring at the cracks in the tabletop. "And it would be a bigger mistake for us to remain nearby now."

Tatiana frowned and lowered her hands. "What are you saying?"

"It's too dangerous to stay in England. Let's move. We can ask Aunt Olga if it's possible for us to relocate. Farther away from Russia this time."

Rather than the cry of protest she'd expected, her sister only looked at her. Tatiana had gained some weight back since imprisonment. She remained slender, her cheekbones pronounced, but less so. "Would you have us all go to Hollywood, then? I'm sure Anastasia could take care of all the details."

Despite everything, Olga laughed. It felt good to talk, really talk, to Tatiana again. "I suppose she would. I thought Gran should sort those details, but who knows? Maybe Los Angeles makes sense. Ana might have had our best interests at heart after all."

"That would be a world away from the young lord at Marlingham. Your Rob."

"*My* Rob?"

"I doubt you want to live so far from him."

Olga blushed but couldn't deny the truth of what Tatiana said. There was no point in denial. Her sister always knew Olga better than anyone else. She was sitting comfortably with Tatiana, but something felt off. Something had changed. Olga kept insisting she should remain here with her sisters. Now, she realized she'd never asked them what they wanted.

Not that this changed the complications between Olga and Rob, a missing grand duchess in hiding and the heir to an earldom. Rob would have a public life one day. That was the way of the English. He may have been able to duck some of those responsibilities now, but eventually, he would be the new Lord Hammond. He would solicit contributions for his rehabilitation center. He would take his place in the House of Lords. And that didn't account for social expectations: dinner parties, balls, and weekend visits to other country manors.

Rob needed someone at his side who could show her true self to the world.

"He is a good man," Olga said, "but it's impossible."

"I think you're happy at Marlingham," Tatiana said. "Maybe Anastasia will find her happiness in Hollywood, but that doesn't mean we all need to follow her. We should find and follow our own paths."

"Returning to Marlingham isn't an option," Olga said.

Isn't it?

A voice again, one that sounded eerily like Mama's, trapped inside her head. Olga's shoulders tightened, and she looked all around but didn't see her mother. Still, she couldn't shake the sensation. Her mother was watching over Olga. Listening.

"You must go back there. Don't you see? You took those letters from that man's study intending to return them. They're forgeries. I know it. The one supposedly from Mama is, at the very least. I'm sure Aunt Olga will find someone who can prove it. In the meantime, Lord Hammond mustn't suspect anything is amiss."

"Even if his son knows who we are?" Olga heard her voice rise to meet Tatiana's. After days of saying next to nothing, it felt good to get this out. She wanted to go. Truly. And yet her sisters' safety must always come first. No matter what voice she heard in her head. "How can I go back? I revealed our secret. I've been a disappointment to you all. We can't stay in England because of me."

Tatiana slammed her fist on the table. "Stop that! You mustn't speak that way."

Olga hesitated, stunned.

"I understand what you've been through. We all do. It doesn't mean you get to give up. I know you suffer. Believe me, I do." Tatiana pulled a fist to her heart. "I wish there was something I could do to ease your suffering. Rest and recuperation will have to be sufficient at this point. Yet you can't spend the rest of your life in recovery. You're our best hope. You've always been. You're the eldest. Don't you remember? Don't you remember how people treated you before Alexei was born?"

She had been quite young, so the memories of that time were faint. Olga recalled maids in the nursery curtsying to her when they only greeted her sisters with laughing nods.

"You do remember, don't you? They always taught us Alexei would inherit the throne because he was a boy. I remember the time before he was born, when you had a chance of being the chosen one. You were a girl, but Papa could have changed the law."

Their aunt came in through the back door. When she realized her nieces were in the middle of a passionate conversation, she hesitated. Like Tatiana, she knew a time when Olga might have ruled after Papa. Olga beckoned for her aunt to join them in the nook.

"Papa tried to change the rules of succession which barred women from the throne," Tatiana said. "He looked into it, anyway. Did you know that? Mama told me."

"That's right," their aunt said, slipping into a chair next to Tatiana.

"I remember some," Olga said. "I was only a little girl. In the end, none of that mattered. Alexei was born and it became a moot point."

"It's not a moot point now," Aunt Olga said. "The Lord bless and keep Alexei."

Olga gave her sister a questioning look, but Tatiana's face remained bowed. Maybe she had finally accepted the death of their brother.

"Except there is no throne," Olga said. "It's more of a moot point now."

"So you don't wish to go back?" Aunt Olga asked.

"Nonsense. You still have a responsibility to our family." Tatiana turned to their aunt. "The letters from Mama are forgeries. I looked at mine again. I'm sure the writing is different. Olga should monitor Lord Hammond until we can prove it."

"I promise to hire someone to confirm the writing has been forged," Aunt Olga said, "and then everyone will know of the deception. You needn't worry."

Tatiana gnawed on her thumbnail, glum once more. Olga suspected her sister had heard the same note in her aunt's voice as she did. A mixture of placation and condescension, as though her aunt were only saying what she thought Tatiana wanted to hear.

"We can't return to Russia," Olga said. "And we shouldn't stay in England."

Aunt Olga startled, her shoulders rolling back. "What?"

"It isn't safe here anymore. If Rob can find us, anyone can find us."

"His sister's in trouble," Tatiana said. "Lady Celia. Olga's employer."

Olga studied the tiny blue flowers dotting the rim of her teacup, trying not to think about Celia splayed on the tiled floor of her washroom, her blotchy face and all the tears. Did she think about her mother? Cry at night, wishing she was there? Olga had done so often enough for her own mother, and she'd heard Tatiana do the same.

"Lady Celia is with child," Tatiana said.

"How far along?"

Her aunt looked no more put out by the news than Tatiana had been. She'd been far more concerned with Olga's comment about leaving England. Then again, her aunt had also successfully pushed to dissolve her first marriage, one she never wanted, so that she could wed her true love. Of all their close relations, she had always been the most worldly.

Olga calculated the time in her head based on what Celia had told her at the end of March when she was going into her fourth month. "September."

"She's probably showing then," Aunt Olga said. "Or will be soon enough."

"She can't abandon her," Tatiana said. "It isn't the honorable thing to do."

Olga felt the words like a flick of a knife against her skin. Not deep enough to wound, but only enough to show the assailant knew her weak spots. She had promised Celia she would be there for her. Olga imagined how disappointed Papa would have been if he knew she'd broken a promise.

She'd help Celia through the next few months until the baby came. She'd made a promise, and Tatiana was right: Olga wouldn't abandon someone who needed her. At the same time, she couldn't let herself get attached to Marlingham. Not anymore. Papa would also expect her to protect her sisters. Olga turned to her aunt.

"I'll go back if you promise me something."

Aunt Olga lifted her hands. "Anything within reason. You know that."

Olga wasn't sure it was within reason, but she was determined to ask.

"Help us move. Ana will try to talk you into taking us to California. I trust your judgment. Do what's best."

Tatiana bit her cuticles. "We're safe here."

"As you've told me many times, we don't know that."

"Your grandmother may have something to say about the matter," Aunt Olga said. "I know you want what's best, but she won't like the idea of you and your sisters living so far away."

"I trust your judgment, not Gran's. She thinks we'll return to Russia as grand duchesses or marry into royal families. I love her, but she is living in the past. You will do what is best for us in the present and the future. You always have. Convince Gran that we must live farther from the Bolsheviks. Will you promise?"

Her aunt reached out to lay a gentle hand on Olga's wrist.

"You have my word. You are truly your father's daughter, and I trust you completely."

PART THREE

~

THE SURVIVORS

April 1920

CHAPTER TWENTY

Not a fortnight had passed since Olga had last been at Marlingham, but she couldn't deny the change in Celia. Her once modest bump had developed into a bulge far more difficult to hide under clothing, though Olga could help disguise it somewhat. This little bud, evidence of her indiscretion, was ready to sprout and make its presence known.

Worse still, she noticed the furtive glances directed at Celia's mid-section when the others thought she didn't notice. The confusion on Ada's face, the distress on Mrs. Dasari's, and, most heartbreaking, the disappointment etched into Mrs. Acton's brow. It was all Olga could do not to call them all aside, summon her mother's most indignant tone, and say shame on them. *We all make mistakes. Lady Celia only made a mistake, and the consequences are clear to all. Who is to say any of us couldn't find ourselves in the same situation were the circumstances right?*

At any rate, they owed Celia compassion, particularly considering how well she treated her staff.

On Olga's third day back, Celia asked if she wanted to take a leisurely walk around the grounds after lunch. Her tone was different, and she smiled shyly. She was asking Olga as a friend, not as her maid.

That meant Olga could say no. She could make excuses or claim Mrs. Acton had given her extra cleaning duties.

But Olga didn't want to refuse her. She'd returned to Marlingham because Celia needed her, even if a sympathetic ear and kind words were the only help Olga could offer.

For this casual afternoon walk, Celia wore a simple jade-green frock and matching hat with a big bow on one side. The wide brim shielded her face from the sun, which shone brilliantly in a cloudless blue sky. Before they left the house, Olga traded her bonnet for a simple straw hat with a black ribbon around the crown. She wished she had a uniform made from lighter material. Olga felt plain and overly warm in her black shirtwaist, skirt, and sturdy leather boots. Still, it was good to be outside, and she drew in the fragrance of freshly clipped hedges and flowers in bloom.

As they strolled through the back gardens, they passed rows of parterres bordered with boxes of lavender and heath aster. And then they walked by the neglected gazebo, which Celia had hoped they would paint and refurbish together. The weather was fine enough for it, but Olga didn't dare suggest an activity that required exertion on Celia's part.

A line of goslings crossed their path, a goose and gander flanking their young and hissing at Olga and Celia. That made Olga laugh as she remembered the first brave goslings of the season she'd seen in late March. The laughter made her neck strain against her stiff white collar. Back with her sisters, she'd grown accustomed to doing without the collar. It was easy to abandon the trappings of femininity that had once seemed important: first, long hair, then corsets and tight necklines. How difficult to return to such constraints once free of them.

Olga was glad to hear Celia's tinkling laughter join her own. Over the past few days, she hadn't seen her employer so much as smile.

"That shall be me soon enough." Rubbing her belly, she added, "I'll hiss at anyone who dares come near my child."

"Plenty of people in this household will join you in defending the sprout."

"They shall as likely leave once the child is born."

"Now, you know that's not true," Olga said, realizing she sounded like her aunt. She had tried to be comforting but sounded condescending. So she modulated her voice before continuing. "They shall grow accustomed to the situation. Do you really think Mrs. Acton or Mrs. Dasari would ever leave Marlingham willingly?"

Celia punted a rock aside with the toe of her shoe, a stylish leather creation with straps around the ankle. This was as close to an expression of frustration as Olga had ever seen from her. "No, I suppose not."

"And they shall adore the child as I will. As your brother will."

Rob. Olga hadn't been avoiding him, exactly, but neither had she sought him out. Her lips tingled when she remembered their kiss. Before everything was ruined. Eventually, she would find herself alone with Rob. What would happen then?

Nothing. The memory of the kiss needed to remain just that. A memory.

Mindlessly, Olga's hand fumbled through her apron pocket. For a moment, she panicked, expecting to find the jewelry box but grasping nothing. And then she realized she wasn't wearing her coat. Why should she in the heat of the afternoon? The Lilies of the Valley pendant remained in her room, tucked away in that coat pocket. She couldn't wear it, nor did she wish to return it to Rob. She wanted to keep something to remember him by, a reminder of his favor.

For soon enough Olga would be far away.

Aunt Olga had already made the arrangements quietly by telephone. Her aunt had shared everything with Olga before leaving the cottage for Copenhagen and Gran.

At the end of September, Olga and her sisters were moving to San Francisco. Olga could scarcely wrap her head around it. She knew nothing of the city, only that it was in California, which should make Ana happy, and that a massive earthquake nearly leveled the place in 1906. However, Aunt Olga had found a connection there: a family who fled Russia, hated the Bolsheviks, and could be trusted to help the Romanovs. Russia once had imperial designs in the northern part of California. That all may have been in the distant past, but there was an established Russian community in San Francisco.

And so their destiny had been determined. Olga and her sisters would move to a city still being rebuilt fourteen years after a catastrophe. Given their situation, Olga found it fitting.

"You all will adore the child, perhaps." If Celia noticed Olga's thoughts had wandered, she said nothing. Olga supposed that she had too many other matters on her mind to bother. "I wonder if I shall say the same about my father. Will he love my child?"

Olga's boot grazed a rock on the path. She stumbled but remained upright. "You haven't told him yet?"

"How could I? I can't bear the thought of sharing such a thing in a letter. Can you imagine if someone else were to see it?"

"By telephone then?"

"That doesn't seem right, either. No, I must disclose this news in person, no matter how difficult."

"Does that mean you'll go to London to see him?"

"No need. He's been waiting for his doctor's permission to travel, but it sounds like that's been granted at last. So he should be here any day."

Any day. Olga hadn't yet returned the letters her mother and Father Grigori exchanged to the dossier in Hammond's study. She'd thought she'd have more time and kept delaying, always summoning some excuse or another. Ada was sweeping in the hall near the study, or Mrs. Acton was making her rounds with a feather duster.

Perhaps she simply wasn't willing to part with the letters yet.

"I just hoped I wouldn't be quite so round when I told him." Celia gestured toward her stomach. "I confess that's the reason I wanted you back here. I can't face him alone."

"What about the viscount? Your brother, that is. He's here for you."

"Yes. Rob has vowed to help me figure out how to handle the next steps. If need be, he will stand up to Papa. I hope that's not necessary. It's not the same as having you at my side, though. A woman. I am grateful you agreed to return."

The entire situation continued to strike Olga as unfortunate and unfair. She had hoped the gentleman responsible for the babe would finally see the light of day and propose marriage. "What of the child's father?"

Celia kicked at a stray weed in a clump of dirt. By the time they'd ended their walk, her dainty shoes were sure to be ruined. "You must think him a cad and total devil."

Olga had been thinking something along those lines. "It's not for me to say."

"Oh, you can say it," Celia told her. "Except that isn't the entire story. You see, I met him in London shortly after my father fell ill. When I lost my mother, I felt like my world had ended. I was facing losing Papa as well. I was an absolute mess. He stayed with me during that cruel time."

Olga licked her lips. She didn't know how far she could test her relationship with Celia, but she needed to help her see she had built up a delusion regarding the fellow, a stranger to her at that.

"Is it possible this gentleman took advantage of your emotional state?" Olga asked. "He knew you were at your weakest, after all."

"I understand why it might seem that way, but no. I knew exactly what I was doing. He did not take advantage. We were equally responsible for our indiscretion."

"That's just it, though," Olga said. "Why should you have to bear this alone?"

"Not quite alone."

Celia laced her arm around Olga's and gently steered her back toward Marlingham, gray and stolid against the blue sky.

"I'm glad to help," Olga said, "but the child's father should be involved."

"In most cases, you'd be right. But this is a different sort of situation. In London, Rob was busy attending to Papa's business. We left for the city in haste, and I had no other chaperone. I shared marvelous evenings with this gentleman. *I* invited *him* to my father's townhouse. I admit it. I expected only a few nights of pleasure. Nothing more."

Olga felt her face turn crimson. She did not judge Celia. How could she? But Olga had never spoken of relations between men and women so plainly, not even with her sisters.

"I hope I haven't shocked you," Celia said, touching her stomach with her free hand.

"I shall grow accustomed to it. Please continue."

Celia looked to the side of the path at a sadly neglected rose garden, her expression now somber.

"It wasn't that I didn't know better. I didn't take the right precautions on purpose. You might think it foolish. But I've always wanted a baby. Always wanted to be a mother. Ever since the war, the opportunities have been slim. You know how many men were lost."

"Too many," Olga agreed.

"Rob is nearly the only unmarried man around here. It's the same in London. It's the same everywhere. War and then influenza. We lost a generation of young men."

Olga thought she understood, even if Celia had an unconventional approach to becoming a mother.

"So when the opportunity presented itself, I decided to take the risk. If something happened, I would be shunned, but I would also become a mother."

"Does the baby's father know?" Olga asked.

"When I missed my courses, I wrote to him. By then, he had left London. I never received a reply. I suppose I should try to find him, but haven't the foggiest notion where to start, nor if I want to try."

"Your father will want to go after him," Olga said. "Your brother as well, I'm sure."

"I hope they don't. You see, I was attracted to this man but never loved him. How can I find happiness by starting a family with a man I don't love?"

"If you marry, you might grow to love him. Over time."

"People always say that. I've seen little evidence to believe it's true."

Nor did Olga. Not really. Her parents had been a love match, rare for royals, but she couldn't name another marriage like theirs. Aunt Olga despised her first husband, and it took forever to annul that marriage so she could be with the man she truly loved, who had the supposed misfortune of not being of royal blood. Another aunt, one of her mother's sisters, Ella, came to Russia before Mama to marry a stern and cold grand duke. Aunt Ella bore it well, though anyone could see her husband didn't love her. After he was assassinated, she had entered a convent.

Olga's flicker of understanding blossomed into admiration as she realized Celia was brave enough to resist a life that didn't suit her.

"I can picture a life for myself and my child here," Celia continued. "Working for Rob. My due date is still a few months away. That will give me proper time to retrain in nursing."

"You wish to return to nursing? With a child?"

"And why not? Once I can find someone to help care for her."

Olga raised an eyebrow. "Her?"

"Or him. I think she's a she, but I suppose that's but a fancy. Anyway, when the time comes, Rob says he will have a place for me."

The goslings had found shade under a tree and sat with their parents, quiet and content except for one who kept waddling away. Like Ana.

The serenity of the scene struck her. All living creatures felt compelled to find the right place for their needs. If Celia found hers here, with a child, who was Olga to object? Who was anyone to object?

"I wish you all the best," Olga said.

"You will stay on, of course?" The question in her voice indicated she wasn't sure. "I will need a nanny. Would that interest you?"

If this were anything resembling a normal situation, Olga would have agreed at once. She loved babies. She knew little about caring for one, but felt confident she could learn.

Yet she couldn't accept. After the baby came, Olga was moving to San Francisco.

When Olga didn't respond, worry creased Celia's brow. "Mind you, I've no intention of being one of those mothers who leave their child in the care of nannies. I will be on hand with the child, as my mother was with me. I would not overwork you, I promise. Only it would be lovely to have someone I know and trust with the little one."

"I understand, but —"

"I shouldn't presume," Celia said. "I thought I would ask with the hope you might consider it. If I am to stay and help Rob, I will need someone." Celia exhaled a quick puff of air as a thought occurred to her. "Would you consider staying on and working at Rob's rehabilitation center as well? We'll need all the help we can get. Did he tell you of his plans? When you were in the motor with him?"

Olga fought the blush creeping up her cheeks.

"Rob went through the hell of war and then returned to the same," Celia said. "He won't talk about it much. I don't think he wants to upset me. Papa sent him for treatment up in the north. Something new, innovative. Electric shocks were a part of it, supposedly to treat his mutism. As you probably heard, he still stammers some, but the impediment was far worse when he first came home. Our father was desperate. But how could anyone do that to him?"

"It sounds terrible." Olga stepped over a cluster of daisies straggling on the path, remembering the pain in Rob's face when he'd described the therapy.

"There are better ways to achieve the same results. Rob will need nurses to help with the patients and keep the records in order so we might help move them to an appropriate treatment facility."

Against all better judgment, Olga imagined working alongside Rob and Celia, wondering how it would feel to have a purpose in life not connected directly to her family. One that looked forward rather than back.

Perhaps she didn't need to move halfway around the world to make that happen.

Olga smiled solicitously but knew she couldn't commit to this idea. However, she wasn't willing to dismiss it outright either.

"I'll consider it," she told Celia. "I promise."

After they returned to the manor, Olga parted ways with Celia upstairs, excusing herself to collect fresh biscuits from Mrs. Dasari and refill the bowl Celia kept filled in the parlor.

She felt uncomfortable leaving Celia alone, given all they'd discussed on their walk, but Celia assured her she'd be fine; the walk had worn her out, and she planned to nap for an hour or so before tea. So Olga grabbed towels from the washroom floor to deposit in the laundry hamper.

Before she could worry about the biscuits, Olga needed to get to her room and fetch the copies of the letters between her mother and Rasputin. She would return them to Hammond's study at once. Her fingers trailed along the smooth banister as she hurried down the central staircase.

She did not reach the bottom stair but froze in place.

Rob's tall frame leaned against the newel post at the foot of the stairs. Their eyes locked.

Over the past few days, he'd been on her mind constantly. Olga thought about what she might say to him when they finally ran into one another, how she might smooth things out and try to make matters right. Except she never found those words. Now, the moment had come, and she found no words at all.

Olga drew the towels closer to her chest. She must talk to him. More than that, Olga needed to fetch the letters from the satchel in her room. She couldn't delay any longer. Hammond was returning to Marlingham.

"Your lordship." Olga curtsied. It made for a poor pantomime now that Rob knew she was a grand duchess.

"Your lordship, is it? After everything." His features remained stoic, though his gaze was as powerful as ever, as though he recognized some greater truth she hid right beneath the surface. Well, now he knew that truth.

Olga glanced over her shoulder to ensure no one was around the corner, listening. She wouldn't put it past Ada, who would then spend days trying to determine why *Miss Bennett* was alone in the stairwell with the young lord. While Olga could live with Rob knowing she was one of the missing grand duchesses, she couldn't let gossip spread downstairs. She remembered how easily they all theorized Lord Hammond might not be Rob's biological father based only on the word of the Pendletons' valet. She could only imagine what they might dream up about her and how those rumors would circulate and take on lives of their own.

Olga's next words tumbled out. "I'm sorry we left things as we did. I've spent nearly two years hiding. The idea that someone outside our family had learned about us was a shock. I struggled to make sense of it."

Now Rob looked around, apparently also wary of eavesdroppers, before saying, "He knows."

She paled. Furtively and in a half whisper, Olga said, "Who knows?"

Rob stepped forward while maintaining an appropriate distance. But she took in his cologne and the lingering oil and leather scents.

He lowered his voice. "My father says the letters are missing. I wish I had known."

The back of Olga's neck bristled. "So he is here?"

"He returned while you and Celia were out."

Hammond. Now that he was at Marlingham, at long last, she felt unreasonably territorial, as though he were an intruder in her space rather than the reverse. Strangely, she first thought not of his slander against Mama but of Celia, who had been dreading the moment when she disclosed that she'd fallen pregnant. Olga needed to warn her and help her prepare. "I imagine he wants to see Celia. Should I fetch her?"

Rob's gaze never wavered. "As soon as Father arrived, he looked at the dossier and saw that the letters between the empress and Rasputin were missing. He is livid and honestly ..." Rob threw his hands up. "I can't say that I blame him. I told him I took them, but now he wants them back. Please tell me you have them."

"I'm sorry."

"When you returned the files, I assumed everything was in place."

She inched closer. Olga came only to Rob's chest and he had to look down to see her. He blinked rapidly. She didn't know if that was from nerves or shock or, God forbid, revulsion. Her arms trembled, and she dropped the towels she'd been carrying. Neither one of them bent to pick them up.

"I intended to return the letters. I swear it. But surely you can understand why it's hard to part with them. It's directly injuring my mother. Besides, I thought I had more time to return the letters before your father returned."

"You could have been honest with me from the start. You could have told me everything. Have I not earned your trust?"

"If I had told you who I am, would you have let me look at those files? I should think, rather, you'd have kept them under lock and key."

"We might have reviewed them together." Rob pointed toward Lord Hammond's study. "You put me in a terrible spot."

Her heart fell. "I meant to prevent that."

"It's more than that," he said, voice breaking. "You lied to me. Even when I thought we were growing close. When I thought p-perhaps ..." He tightened his lips.

"Thought what?"

"Never mind. It doesn't matter now."

Olga felt hot and cold at once. He couldn't possibly believe they could be together. Despite everything. Despite all the women that must have been clamoring after him. And yet the thought persisted. "I couldn't tell you. Please understand. Don't despise me for this secret. I didn't know you."

"You know me now. At least, I thought you did."

Somehow she'd forgotten how deep his voice was and the effect it had on her. How he made her wish to share every truth in her heart. Without thinking, Olga placed her hands flat against Rob's chest.

"I know you now," she whispered. "Of course I do, Robert."

Olga hadn't called him by his given name before. Not out loud. She liked the sound of it on her tongue.

Her fingers, of their own volition, moved ever so slightly, thrilling at the sensation of his muscles through his linen shirt. It was one thing for them to kiss impulsively on the road outside her cottage. That had been a space in-between, literally and figuratively. Here, she was the maid, and he was lord. To think differently, only invited—

Rob wrapped his arms around her lower back and their lips met. She pushed him back against the wall, luxuriating in the entire length of his body against hers. Waves of pleasure overcame her. All that mattered was their bodies melding together over the thick fabric of her dress and his trousers. Olga cradled her hands behind his neck and pulled him down into a deeper, more intimate kiss, craving the sensation. She felt attuned to her body and floating above it at once.

They were dangerously close to a point where they wouldn't stop. Olga knew that much. He could lead her into a secluded room and satisfy her desire. Olga was long past the age when she should have been married. She could not find any sin in wanting what she should have, by all rights, already experienced.

But the practical side of her mind fought through the haze of lust, warning her to stop. She could end up in the same situation as Celia, with none of the resources.

So she moved her hands back down Rob's chest, but this time to gently pull away. He understood and lifted his head, but his hands locked around her waist. Their foreheads touched.

"Robert," she said, solely for the pleasure of it.

He slid his finger over her lips. "Your imperial highness."

He wasn't the lord to her, nor was she grand duchess to him. It was both simpler and more complicated than that. "Olga."

"Olga," he agreed.

And just like that, she sensed her mother's presence. Abruptly, Olga released Rob and spun around. Her mother's figure appeared clearly enough, though her features remained fuzzy. Her mother's hands were clasped before her in the same manner Olga placed her own hands when she wanted to feel confident and in control.

How much did you see?

Even as a spirit, her mother would have too much decorum to say. Anyway, Olga didn't think that was why her mother had appeared. She didn't believe Mama was disappointed, not about anything to do with Rob. Rather, she'd felt neglected. Olga had not finished what she'd come here to accomplish. She'd never proven her mother's innocence.

She had one last option at her disposal.

"What's the matter?" Rob asked. "What did you see?"

She owed him the truth. Hopefully, he wouldn't think she was insane. *In for a penny, in for a pound.* "Only my mother's ghost, though she'd fading away now."

"Oh." He took a step back.

"You think I'm seeing things."

"I think none such. I only wonder if she will accept my apologies." Olga pressed her palm against Rob's cheek. "You do not need to apologize. You aren't put off that I saw a ghost?"

"I lost a mother as well, you know," he said softly. "And others who are now gone from this world. I understand ghosts better than anyone."

"Of course." Olga lowered his hand slowly. "Of course you do."

Her breath hitched. She had to ask Rob for this last favor. If she didn't, there was little hope for a future with him.

"Your father rescued us," Olga told Rob. "I didn't realize that when I first came to work here. You said you didn't know either?"

Rob grew somber again. "I knew of his time as a diplomat in Russia, but his part in the rescue? No."

"Does it bother you? That he lied?"

"I trust my father had his reasons." He wavered. "Do you still hate my father? Now that you know he helped you?"

"I'm confused," Olga admitted. "I don't know why he would go from rescuing us to turning against my mother and supporting ..." She had trouble spitting out the next word. "... the Bolsheviks."

Rob sighed and looked toward his father's study. "He inherited an earldom but feels the divide between classes can't stand."

"The Bolsheviks are not the Labour Party like you have here in England. They're not trying to make the world better. They aren't who they claim to be at all. Their leaders are cruel. They murder at will and bring nothing but pain to this world. What good does that do anyone, no matter their class?"

"That's how my father saw it as well," Rob said. "So I don't know what changed his mind. And he won't tell me."

Olga took Rob's hands and pressed them tight, marveling again at how small hers felt in his.

"We might ask him," she said. "Together. When I return the letters to his study."

"I don't want to put you through that. I can make excuses. Just give me the letters, and I'll return them."

"I want to talk to him—as Grand Duchess Olga."

"You don't have to do that."

Olga knew she didn't *have* to do it. But Hammond knew that she and her sisters were alive. She could reveal herself on her terms. Perhaps when Celia came to him with her big secret, Olga's revelation would soften that blow somewhat.

"He needs to hear what I have to say. I'll beg him not to publish those letters."

Rob cocked his head to the side, tensing but not withdrawing her hands from his. Olga remembered Charlie sharing the rumor that Hammond wasn't his biological father. Did Rob know of the whispers? He gave no sign he did, but that could be because the story was already well-circulated, and he'd long since dismissed it. Either way, it was slander.

"Would you let such a vicious story about your mother stand?" she asked him. "I know you wouldn't."

"Of course not."

"Then let me see your father. Come with me."

"Do you only wish to save your mother's legacy? Do you still believe he left the rest of your family behind on purpose?"

Olga inhaled sharply, letting the air fill her lungs. "Before I do anything else, I will thank your father for his part in our rescue."

"That's not an answer."

"I don't know," she blurted. "But I want the opportunity to ask. Regardless, I owe him my life. No matter what has happened since. And I must own this, face the past. Otherwise, how will I ever move forward? How will my sisters?"

In Rob's eyes, she saw everything she wanted from a gentleman. Adoration. Respect. Love.

"You were a grand duchess just then," he said. "Your father's daughter, for sure."

Olga indicated her bonnet and humble maid's attire. "And dressed for the part."

He touched her hand. "None of that matters."

Her heart hammered in her chest, but his comment inspired her and made her think she could tackle most anything.

"Together then?" she said.

Rob clasped his fingers around hers. United, they walked to Hammond's study.

By the time my sisters and I settled in our new home in England, my dreams of romance had long since evaporated. I focused only on survival.

Mornings were agony. I awoke expecting to hear Mama and Papa in quiet conversation or Alexei running down the hall, as he'd done before his final sickness confined him to bed, and the happy yelps as Joy followed my brother. Perhaps the gentle mewing of the latest litter of palace kittens.

In those first precious moments when I woke, I believed our family was whole and together.

And then, like a bolt of lightning, I felt sure my sisters were in danger. I would sit straight up, exhaling hard, often long before dawn.

Still in darkness, my breathing heavy and ragged, I'd hear Tatiana's gentle voice. "We're here. We're safe. You can go back to sleep."

Every morning, along with that safety, came the crushing realization, as though for the first time, that our parents and Alexei were forever lost. All we have left are our memories. All they have left are their reputations. It is our responsibility now to protect their legacies.

The Private Diary of Olga Romanova
December 1921

CHAPTER
TWENTY-ONE

O lga couldn't make out Hammond's face. As she and Rob entered the room, he stood hunched behind his desk, facing the window. One hand remained in the warmth of Rob's, but the fingers on her other hand tightened into a fist. She was about to meet the man who was both her enemy and savior.

"Where are the letters?"

His voice differed from Rob's, or at least from Rob's authentic voice. The one he used when not playing the viscount. Rather than a rolling baritone, Hammond spoke in a polished tenor, with a posh English accent that made the harshest words seem flippant. She knew he had been frantic, despite his calm manner now. Sundry notebooks, loose papers, and metal pens were strewn about the top of his desk. Before they came in, Hammond must have been tearing his study apart trying to find those letters.

"I've brought someone with me." Rob glanced at Olga, and she squeezed his hand reassuringly. "We would like a word. Let me turn the light on so we can see you."

Rob reached for the cord on a lamp. Before he could pull it, Hammond raised a hand, his back still to them. "No."

"Then let me draw the shades."

A note of irritability crept into Rob's voice. She'd heard it in her own voice often enough when speaking to her mother. When tensions between them had flared—over what she would wear, time spent with Mitya, the next party at her aunt's flat—Olga could hardly manage three sentences without snapping. Mama always sighed and looked martyred when her adolescent daughter dared anything other than perfect obedience.

"I wish you wouldn't," Hammond said. "I get migraines from that terrible mixture the Bolshevik snuck in my drink. Keep the light dim."

"The light can remain dim without conversing in total darkness," Rob muttered.

He released Olga's hand and moved to the window, dragging the curtain to one side so they could see one another, though not well. As her eyes adjusted, Olga noted more details of Hammond's figure. He wore a plain gray jacket and trousers. Strands of silver wound through his fading black hair. He was balding at the crown, as Papa had been when he reached middle age. The scent in the study reminded her of Papa as well, that of the herbal cigarettes her father smoked later in life.

This man was trying to ruin her mother's legacy. And yet he was also a simple papa.

He looked over his shoulder so she could make out some of his profile but not his entire face. Spectacles perched low on his nose and he sported a full beard.

"Who have you brought, Rob? Are you going to pawn this off on some maid or another? I thought you said you took my papers."

Olga straightened her back and tried to channel the authority in her father's voice when he addressed his troops.

"I took them, your lordship. I am here to sort things between us."

"Then tell me who you are and why you sought work in this house."

"Must you start in on her straightaway?" Rob asked peevishly.

Olga held up her hand and gave Rob a look to let him know it was all right. She could handle this. He nodded. How comforting it felt to communicate with Rob without saying a word. He just seemed to understand. She didn't think she could say that about anyone she'd ever known except Tatiana.

"Other than this single transgression, I've done nothing wrong," Olga said. "I've been a pleasant companion to Lady Celia."

"And to my son as well, it would seem."

Lord Hammond turned on another lamp nearer to him on the desk. It emitted a rosy glow. On instinct, she bowed her head. To calm herself, she focused on her breathing.

For a long moment, Hammond said nothing. She'd planned to assume a regal stance and ask if he knew her. In this dreadful silence, however, Olga kept her head low so he could not see her face nor notice the color of her eyes. The tsar's eyes.

Another moment of unbearable quiet passed. Olga stared at the hardwood floor, poking the toe of her boot into the crevices between the walnut floorboards like a child.

She heard the air exit his lungs.

"Still hiding?" Hammond said at last. "Surely we're past all that, your imperial highness."

When Lord Hammond said her title, something in his voice struck a chord in her memory.

"Let me see you," Hammond said.

Olga might have come here specifically to reveal herself, but he'd beat her to it. And though she'd planned to show him her true self, it was disheartening how he saw right through her changed appearance. She had expected Hammond to recognize her, but the apparent ease with which he did so, with her head down, reinforced the fact that anyone else might also identify her. And if the Bolsheviks were so bold as to poison an English peer of the realm, they would have no compunctions about doing the same to the fugitive Romanov sisters.

She only hoped San Francisco would be far enough away.

And so she fought to keep her expression neutral. Olga had come here to confront Hammond. To do so properly, she must meet his gaze and appear confident. She must not allow her face to betray her apprehension.

Slowly, Olga raised her head, carefully keeping her focus above his shoulder. She could not find it in her to meet Hammond's eyes directly. Not yet. But she could tell that his gaze was as intense as his son's. Only when Rob looked at her he sought to understand her better. With this man, the stare felt more like the beginning of an interrogation.

When he spoke next, however, his tone softened. "I would know you anywhere. A daughter of the tsar."

Finally, she found the courage to look at him. When she did, she couldn't stifle her cry. Olga now understood why his voice sounded familiar. She recognized the long, placid face she associated with the English aristocracy, at odds with the warm brown eyes and thick, unruly brows. Since she'd seen him last, his beard had turned to salt and pepper.

Not only had this gentleman arranged their rescue, but he had been there to greet them. That summer morning in 1918, after she and her sisters had endured their perilous journey to Arkhangelsk. The first time she'd felt human in months, let alone like a daughter of the tsar.

I know you're in pain. Remember that you and your sisters are safe. You survived.

A tear threatened to slip down her cheek. She mustn't cry. She stood taller and tried to infuse her voice with authority.

"I meant what I said, Lord Hammond. I am in your debt, as are my sisters."

"Ah," he said. "You remember me then?"

"How could I not? You saved me. You and your men."

"They were the king's men," he said crisply.

"You were waiting for us in Arkhangelsk. Wearing the uniform of an officer. You are Edward Pike, who assisted in our rescue."

He sat down in his swivel chair. Perhaps his opinion toward royalty had flipped since they first met. Or, since Olga looked so far from who she once was in her black dress and white apron, it was possible he could no longer perceive her as a member of a royal family. If he did, he wouldn't sit while she still stood.

"Which is why I don't understand ..."

Olga glanced at Rob, who gave another subtle nod to ensure she maintained her courage.

"You know who I am," Olga said. "You can probably guess why I'm here and took those letters. I can't let your accusations against my mother stand."

Hammond let out a sarcastic laugh, bereft of joy. "Too late."

"But your accusations are malicious and false. My mother would never betray our soldiers to the Germans."

"Even if her corrupt monk told her it was the only way to save Russia?"

He knew her mother well. And that meant he could wound Olga in the most vulnerable spot: the space in her mind that suspected her mother *had* written that letter and perhaps agreed to betray the troops by passing codes to Berlin. It was heartbreaking how easily someone like Hammond believed her mother a traitor because she was in Rasputin's thrall.

"What can you possibly hope to gain by saying something so foul about a woman who can no longer defend herself?"

"You wouldn't understand. Nor would I expect you to understand. The German woman was your mother."

The German woman. The exact phrase cruelly employed during the war and after whenever people grew desperate to blame someone for their country's ruin. Olga's anger flared. "Her father was German, but she loved Russia as she loved my father."

"Her cousin was the Kaiser."

"Your king is also kin to the man. So what?"

"You stole the letters." Hammond pointed an accusing finger at Olga. Rob stepped forward, but she motioned for him to stay put. "This makes me think you understand the magnitude of your mother's treachery."

"They're only copies. I know you must have the originals in a safe place. Anyway, I don't need them any longer." Olga gave him a fierce smile. "We took photographs of them. My aunt is out of Russia and free. An expert will compare the handwriting to my mother's. Are you certain the letters are genuine?"

Hammond's posture crumpled, as though she had fired a gun and planted a bullet in his chest.

"Father?" Rob asked, his voice cracking. "Are the letters forged?"

From the slump in his shoulders and the regret in his eyes, Olga could see how much Hammond loved Rob. She almost wished she had said nothing.

"It doesn't matter," Hammond told his son.

"How can it not matter? This could ruin Olga's life."

"Tell me why," Olga said. "Why did you want to humiliate her? And us?"

"I understand this hurts, but the accusation is only against the empress. Not you girls. Still, I wish you weren't present for this conversation. I have some things I need to say to my son. Better you do not hear them."

"I prefer to stay."

"Then you will hear the worst of it," Hammond said tersely. "It doesn't matter if those letters are real or not. They might as well be real. Everyone knows the empress was a traitor. She destroyed your country from the inside."

Rob moved closer to Olga. "Don't say such things to her."

"She wanted to stay. Besides, we are all caught in this new world now. Best to know the truth of the old world and learn from its mistakes, even when we don't like what we hear. Especially then. Otherwise, what hope is there to move on?"

Olga's hands trembled as she considered how closely Hammond's words reflected her thoughts. That one couldn't move on without facing the truth of the past.

What had she done?

"My mother was a nurse during the war," Olga said slowly. "She loved Russia. She loved the soldiers."

"I've no doubt the empress loved some Russians," Hammond replied bitterly. "Such as Rasputin."

Father Grigori. Why must he continually return to haunt her, to hurt her family? Before she could compose herself, Olga shivered.

"So you know his true nature," Lord Hammond said. "I see it in your reaction."

"I don't know anything."

"Then why shudder at his name?"

Olga struggled to articulate what she felt about Father Grigori. The old loyalty to her family, and the need to present a unified front to the world, still prevented her from speaking her mind fully. "I think of him as unhelpful."

"Unhelpful? He manipulated your mother. He got away with doing anything to anyone. She gave him free rein to do so. That is intolerable. I take it you saw the dossier? I noticed you didn't steal that. Maybe you didn't bother to read the documents in that file?"

"I read them." She'd read every word—the accusations of rape, the tearful testimony of the victims documented in Hammond's files. "I left those papers here because *his* reputation means nothing to me. My mother could not possibly have known the extent of Rasputin's crimes."

"People tried to tell her. No one could convince her he was a demon. You girls were blameless. But your father needed to stand up to his wife and banish the man."

Olga remembered her aunt's party in Petrograd and the desperate look on Nadia's face when she'd described what had happened to her sister. How Rasputin molested her.

"The tsar abdicated responsibility long before he abdicated his throne," Hammond said. "His own family wanted him to get rid of his wife."

Your grandmother thinks the empress is undermining the war. I heard she's trying to have your mother sent to a convent.

"You blame my parents for Russia's troubles as though you are judge and jury," Olga said slowly. "But what of Alexei?"

"Your brother was innocent. I wish we could have saved him." Hammond raised both hands. "That poor boy. But he could hardly move from his bed toward the end, from what I understand."

Olga's breaths grew ragged and uneven. She thought of her brother, withdrawn and defeated when she told him goodbye, and Joy resting his chin on Alexei's thin chest.

"But the tsar and his consort? The tsar who allowed his wife to let Rasputin rule the palace as Petrograd starved? They deserved what they got."

She heard Rob's voice, but it seemed distant. "Take that back."

"The Romanovs let the country slip from their hands. Little wonder the Bolsheviks took advantage of the situation. And the people let them."

"Our people had no choice," Olga said weakly, a sinking sensation crushing her chest. "The Bolsheviks are beasts."

"For many, the Romanovs were the beasts."

Olga stood in stunned silence, thinking of her family. Not her father, necessarily, but her uncles, Gran, and her dear Aunt Olga. Romanovs were proud, arrogant, and a study in contrasts. Emotional one moment and ruthless the next. And yet she had thought them honorable, regardless of their careless tittle-tattle, and glamorous, but ultimately empty. They inhabited an enclosed world of private supper clubs, opera seats, and salons. But she believed that deep in their hearts, they wanted what was best for Russia.

And yet, no one had truly known what the people wanted. They never asked. The grand ladies and gents of her family and the aristocracy of the court empathized with those who had less but never adjusted their point of view sufficiently to see the world through the eyes of another. They always thought they knew what was best for everyone when, in reality, they hadn't a clue.

"*Your* people wanted land, peace, and bread. The Bolsheviks gave them that. They are ruthless in their methods, but keep promises. The people will remember." Hammond leaned forward. "If the tsar had instituted reforms earlier in his reign, they would have nothing."

At times, Olga had thought the same, but she wasn't about to admit as much now. She felt her strength return. "He tried! My father created a Duma. A Parliament."

"Only under extreme duress. And even then, it had no power. Which left his country vulnerable to that devil."

"Papa was at the front commanding his troops."

"He rode off to play soldier at the very moment his country needed leadership most. That did nothing to change the tide of the war in the allies' favor. The tsar should have remained in Petrograd."

Olga glanced at Rob, whose cheeks splotched with rage. He might lose his temper and lunge at his father. Still, he must agree with much of what Hammond was saying, if not how he said it. She remembered Papa as a doting father but understood he'd failed Russia.

And paid the ultimate price for it. So she didn't need to hear Hammond enumerate her father's faults.

"The tsar wouldn't act decisively in the war, and he left the country to fend for itself," Hammond said. "Is it any wonder the most rabid internal forces were victorious?"

Rob's brows furrowed. "Wh-what is truly going on here? You've gone on and on about mistakes of the past. What do you have to say for yourself? You've made m-mistakes."

He closed his eyes and pressed his lips tightly together. When Rob opened his eyes again, his voice changed and became softer, with a stronger undercurrent of love than anger.

"This isn't like you, Father. The man I know is honorable and would never stoop so low as to pass off a forged letter as evidence to his peers. Something doesn't add up."

Olga looked curiously at Rob, wondering where he was going with this.

"What are the Bolsheviks holding over you?" Rob asked.

Of course. It may not explain his anger at Olga's parents, but blackmail *would* explain Hammond's willingness to work with the Bolsheviks.

But he only waved a hand dismissively.

"It must be something," Rob insisted.

Hammond rose to his feet, straightened his back, and looked sadly at his son. "I don't think we should explore this line of inquiry."

"We're well beyond what we should and shouldn't explore."

"I am warning you to tread lightly. You won't like what I have to say."

"If you won't apologize and own up to your deception with these letters, at least have the decency to explain why you put Olga through all this."

"Olga, is it? Her given name, not her title?"

Olga and Rob exchanged glances but said nothing.

"I see. Then I take it there are no secrets between the two of you."

"Not anymore," Olga offered, more to Rob than his father.

"Even so ..." Hammond looked at Rob. "All right then. I did this for *your* mother."

"How?" Rob sputtered. "How could this p-p-possibly ..."

Try as he might, he could not get out the next word. His lips only pressed against one another uselessly. Hammond stared at his son while Olga gently rubbed Rob's arm.

"Never mind," Hammond said. "Nod if you want me to continue."

Rob gave a fierce nod, black hair falling over his scar

"But I warn you, son. What I say next will hurt you."

Olga's thoughts returned to the visiting neighbors and the talk in the kitchen. Lady Hammond. The late countess was originally from Russia.

Suddenly, she very much wanted Hammond to stop. They could rush out of there before Rob's father told him everything. She could pull him out of this room.

Before she could move, Rob nodded again. "Tell me."

"Your mother was already pregnant with you when we married," Hammond said flatly.

"Hardly a scandal," Rob said.

"You don't understand. Something happened to her in Russia. She was assaulted. Another man." Hammond closed his eyes, visibly in agony. "Not a man. A demon."

Rob could speak. Barely. "Who did it to her?"

"Do you know?" Olga was so focused on Rob's ashen features that it took her a moment to realize Hammond had addressed her. "Do you know who assaulted her?"

"How could I—"

She stopped mid-sentence. She knew. Deep in her heart. Before Hammond said the name aloud.

"Rasputin. The devil himself is my son's natural father."

Father Grigori's voice used to reverberate throughout the palace at all hours. None who heard it will ever forget the sound.

"Remember what I said. Prayers on the hour."

He closed Alexei's door softly and with exaggerated effort. Alexei had bumped against the banister of the elegant Jordan Staircase in the Winter Palace. My brother's fragile skin hit marble, awakening the bleeding disease.

Our mother was so afraid for Alexei that she'd commanded us all to continue wearing the unique locket with Father Grigori's hair tucked safely therein. I hated the thing, but I would reject nothing that might help Alexei, no matter how outlandish or superstitious it seemed.

Father Grigori turned and saw me. This time, I wasn't quick enough to avoid his smirking gaze.

"Olechka." His words slurred, likely from drink, the endearment morbid on his lips. "You have been waiting to see me."

It was not a question but an assumption. I tapped my foot against the mosaicked tiles in the hallway, patterned with curling flourishes. "I wish to see my brother."

"The little one will be fine."

As Father Grigori moved closer, I caught the pungent odors of earth, barley, and animals that always seemed to cling to him. Mama said his lack of bathing was a sign of holiness. I never understood how one connected to the other.

When he stepped forward, I moved back until my body pressed flat against the cold wall.

"You are a brave girl and care about your brother," he said in a hoarse whisper.

He was so near to me, as Mitya was in the hospital ward when he stole a kiss, a quick press of his soft lips against mine. I desired none such from Father Grigori.

He lifted his arm to my right side, trapping me. My limbs were motionless, petrified.

"Father Grigori?"

He dropped his hand. Without thinking, I silently prayed in grati-tude as my Aunt Olga strode down the hall. She was only thirteen years older than me, our father's youngest sister, and never a great beauty. And yet, for all she might have lacked the regal good looks of the other Romanovs, Aunt Olga always more than made up for with her pleasant nature, optimistic outlook, and what our grandmother used to describe as joie de vivre.

Only when she saw Father Grigori did her features twist with concern.

"I just learned that Alexei shall recover," I told her quickly. "Praise the Lord."

My aunt stopped in front of us, hands on her hips. I'd witnessed Father Grigori cast spells on my mother and other ladies of the court with those ridiculous eyes of his, but my aunt was impervious to Grigori Rasputin's so-called charms.

"What joyous news," my aunt said. "Shall we go to see Alexei?" She linked her arm around mine.

Father Grigori did not dare follow us. Instead, he scampered down the hall in the opposite direction. He would not fight my aunt.

So I understand why people hated Father Grigori, for I hated him too.

The Private Diary of Olga Romanova
December 1921

CHAPTER
TWENTY-TWO

"That's impossible." Rob gripped the back of the chair opposite his father's desk. "You're lying."

"It's the truth," Hammond said. "Though I wish to God it wasn't."

"Why didn't you tell me before?"

"I hoped never to tell you."

"I don't believe it."

Still in shock, Olga stared at Rob. She now recognized the features of her mother's mystic, though softer and far more handsome on him. Rob could choose to disbelieve it if he wished, but that wouldn't make it any less true.

Father Grigori. Back to haunt her again. The man must still exist in some spirit realm, trying to take down the House of Romanov for going against his advice. For going to war.

"If it is true, how could you keep it from me?" Rob could barely stand upright. Olga wanted to comfort him but found she could hardly move.

She saw Rasputin. Even if Rob hadn't inherited Father Grigori's blue eyes. Thank the Lord for that. His eyes were a warm brown, as Hammond's were. No. As his mother's had been. And yet those eyes still held the same ferocity as his biological father's.

"Your mother and I agreed to keep it a secret," Hammond said. "We didn't see a reason anyone should know. Particularly not you."

Rob's breath grew hoarse. Anger smoldered in his eyes and anguish tightened his features, which made him suddenly resemble Rasputin. The man who had terrified her when she had to pretend he didn't.

Though she knew it was but a trick of her mind, Olga moved away from Rob. Father Grigori had indeed reached out from the grave. No matter where Olga might go or what she might do, he would always be there. No matter how far she and her sisters ran to distance themselves from their past, he would always be right behind them, ready to cause havoc in their lives.

"What happened to Rob's mother?" Olga said shakily.

Hammond seemed to have forgotten she was there. "Perhaps you could go?"

"No," Rob said. "She stays."

Hammond raised a finger but let it hover in the air. He didn't object.

"Take a seat then, grand duchess."

Trembling, Olga did so.

"My wife was not in any relationship with the devil if that's what you were going to ask. Nor did she seek his company. She was assaulted. It happened not long after we were married in St. Petersburg. As a diplomat, I had been tasked with accompanying a mapping expedition to Siberia. It was my first diplomatic mission for the crown. Your mother stayed with friends near his village. She encountered him there. Long before he made his way to you Romanovs."

Olga had imagined the late countess as a woman of means in her own right. A member of the Russian aristocracy. Father Grigori hailed from Pokrovskoye, near Tobolsk. When she and her family were transported through Siberia, they'd passed the ramshackle huts. Her mother sighed loudly and commented on the sanctity of the place.

Now, Olga thought it odd that a noblewoman would have friends in rural Siberia. The Russians were snobs about marrying those in one's social class and keeping friendships confined to those same circles. The English were much the same in such matters, or so she had been led to understand.

"She was not of rank?" Olga asked.

"My wife was not of noble birth, but neither was she of humble means. Her great-grandfather made his fortune in Catherine the Great's time, providing munitions for the army in the Crimean Peninsula. She didn't care to speak of the fact that her family's wealth was built on war and weapons. She was far too gentle a soul to find anything but shame in that."

Olga understood. She felt guilty about her own family often enough. But surely a woman couldn't be held responsible for the actions of their family—at least not actions from so long ago.

Lord Hammond moved the icon on his desk closer to him, along with the picture of his late wife. He stared at her photograph, lip quivering.

It was just as Olga had suspected when she first snuck into this room and saw the picture. He loved her still. Hammond looked as though he couldn't believe she was really gone. Perhaps he saw her as Olga saw her mother: in the form of a memory or a ghost or a figment of imagination.

"Keep going, Father," Rob said quietly.

"While in school, your mother had befriended a daughter of one of the local landowners," Hammond said, still staring at the countess's photograph. "She stayed near Pokrovskoye while I continued on with the expedition. My wife was a city girl and still young. Eighteen when I married her and hardly more than that when it happened. When she encountered him."

Olga remembered Rasputin leaning toward her outside Alexei's room. His arm on the wall and the feral scent of him. Trapped until Aunt Olga saved her.

"She told me later that she'd done her best to avoid him. But he was persistent and always found her. Finally, he was alone with her. Through no fault of her own."

Rob looked ready to collapse. "He raped her."

The word sent shock waves down her spine. "That is hardly your fault, Rob," Olga said shakily.

"Nor did she love you any less for it," Hammond told his son. "As you well know."

"She hated *him*, though."

"We both did. From the moment I saw her in St. Petersburg, I loved your mother. Then, when the expedition ended and we were reunited, she didn't tell me. Not at first. But she was sad, withdrawn."

"She was afraid to say anything," Olga said, thinking of Celia. Perhaps this experience would make Hammond sympathetic to his daughter's condition, even if the circumstances were entirely different.

"When she told me what happened, I wanted to kill him. I would have given anything to kill him."

If he had succeeded, what a different world she might have inherited. Grigori Rasputin would never have crossed her mother's path.

"You didn't kill him *then*," Rob said slowly. "But you did so later, didn't you? Using your connections in Russia?"

Hammond looked older now. Too old to be Rob's father.

"Did you take part in Rasputin's murder?"

"You're a clever boy to suspect as much, Rob. I wish I had been there. When I heard about it, I relished every detail. To kill the devil, the assassins poisoned, shot, and drowned him. I would have liked to watch him suffer. Unfortunately, my help in the matter was strictly diplomatic. I encouraged the tsar's police to investigate the man's crimes against women as best I could from a distance here in England. Memos and such. When that didn't work ..."

He looked at Olga, fury restored.

"... when your parents would do nothing in the face of overwhelming evidence. When Rasputin still ruled in your father's stead and had his run of the palace. I convinced the king to send a message to Rasputin's enemies, assuring them of immunity in England should they decide to take matters into their own hands. Yes. I wanted that man dead. I used all of my influence to make it so."

Rob winced. Olga supposed it was hard to hear someone wish your father dead, even if you had never known the man. Even if you learned your birth resulted from an assault.

"That's when everything fell apart," she said. "I understand why you want this man dead, but he'd cursed us. He'd cursed our country. First, he said the House of Romanov couldn't survive the war. Then he said that we depended on him. If he died at the hands of the tsar's relations, the House would fall. And he was right."

"Did he hurt you?" Hammond asked suddenly, eyes pinched. "You and your sisters? Did he force himself on you?"

Hammond must have assumed Rasputin took advantage of his proximity to them. Given everything he'd said, she understood why he thought Father Grigori had hurt them. Perhaps it was part of what compelled Hammond to help with their escape.

At that moment, she hated Grigori Rasputin every bit as much as Hammond did.

"He did not hurt us," she said. "My parents wanted us to revere Father Grigori, though I suspected his true nature. Once I was old enough."

"His true nature." Hammond scoffed. "Apparent to all except your family. Truthfully, I always blamed the empress. She could have stopped him if she wished. She betrayed her country. If not to the Germans, per se, she certainly betrayed her people's trust."

"It was all because of my little brother." After years of silence, the last of her family's secrets slipped from her tongue more easily than Olga would have supposed. "He was sick. When he bled, no one could staunch it. Rasputin was the only one who made him better. You must understand. You must have some empathy for my mother. Alexei had hemophilia. If it weren't for Father Grigori, he would have died."

Hammond maintained what Ana would have described as a *poker face*. Olga couldn't tell if he'd known of her brother's illness.

"How could he help him?" Hammond said. "How is that possible?"

"I don't know." Olga shook her head, trying to push out the memories as they worried their way into her brain. Alexei crying out in agony, calling for Mama. Her mother would have died for Alexei if only that were possible. As matters stood, she could only rock him helplessly. He was a little boy and already done with this life.

"I only know that I saw it with my own eyes," Olga said. "Alexei was my mother's world, and he was hurting. He was always in danger. Rasputin could stop the bleeding inside Alexei. She believed God sent Father Grigori to us."

"What did it mean if the man sent by God to help was a deviant? A demon?"

"I don't know. Perhaps we were cursed."

Olga had said it in Russian, aloud but under her breath.

"I can't say I hold much account in a curse," Hammond replied in English, "but the country went to pieces under the Bolsheviks. Saving you girls was the least we could do."

"All of this is long past. Terrible, but long past. Rasputin is dead. My mother is dead. Why speak of it now?"

"During the trip to Russia to help with your rescue, I made a mistake."

Hammond moved toward Rob. He placed his hands on his son's shoulders awkwardly. Rob flinched but didn't shake his father's hands away.

"I let the truth about what happened to your mother slip to another officer," Hammond told Rob. "The Bolsheviks got wind of it. They have agents everywhere. I should have known better. I shouldn't have spoken freely."

"Why would they care?" Olga looked steadily at Lord Hammond, Edward Pike, without dropping her gaze at once. And now she saw the dark circles underneath his eyes and the unkempt beard.

"They wanted to know where we'd sent you girls," Hammond told her.

Olga's blood turned to ice.

"I told them I didn't know because we were all kept in the dark on everything except our piece of the operation. But that wasn't good enough. I needed to offer something else instead."

"My mother," she whispered.

"Your mother's reputation. The empress is gone, grand duchess. You and your sisters are alive. What should I have done instead? I considered what Lenin wanted."

She recoiled. Lenin. The Bolsheviks' leader. She never uttered his name, nor did any of her sisters. The man who had ordered her family's execution. He could deny it all he wanted, but she knew he'd been responsible.

"Say what you will about Vladimir Ilyich, but he is no fool," Hammond continued. "Lenin believes Alexandra's denunciation will help smooth relations between his government and their former allies. Destroying your mother's reputation abroad retroactively justifies her execution. With the tsarist regime thoroughly disgraced, the Bolsheviks can reach a new accord with England."

"The Bolsheviks tried to poison you!" Rob said. "Your plan didn't work."

"The poisoning was a miscommunication between agents. That's all. Thankfully, they did a sloppy job of it. Lenin would never risk killing an English diplomat on English soil. He's far too shrewd for such nonsense."

"Then why would you agree to any of this?"

"They threatened to tell you about your birth father."

"So you're hurting Olga because of me? For my sake? I'm not your son. Not truly."

Hammond's gaze softened, the tenderness overpowering Rob's anger.

"You are and always will be my son. I'm proud of you. I don't want any public embarrassment to stand in the way of the great things I know you will accomplish."

Olga looked down at her hands, fingers twisting. Once he established his rehabilitation center, Rob would assist ex-servicemen who couldn't find help elsewhere. This situation couldn't stop him. She wouldn't let it.

"You were married to Rob's mother at the time he was born," she said to Hammond. "That means he's still the legal heir, correct?"

"Yes. The Bolsheviks didn't realize that. They're ruthless fellows but sloppy at the edges. The men in contact with me assumed Rob would lose his inheritance if the truth came to light. As it stands, they could still embarrass him. I never wanted Rob to know. Besides, they claimed they had evidence against your mother. I had no reason to disbelieve it and had already started my book. They wanted the letters made public."

"Are the letters forgeries?" Olga asked.

Hammond dropped his hands to his sides and shrugged miserably. "I can't say for certain."

Everything he had was crumbling around him. Olga knew how that felt. She'd never imagined she could be sympathetic to this man, but she understood him. At least, she thought she did. He was no monster. Rather, he was a man haunted by demons: Rasputin and the Bolsheviks. The very same demons who haunted Olga.

Her presence was only causing pain. Olga had borne so much pain over the past few years she had no desire to burden anyone with more of it. Not even Hammond.

Back stiff, she rose to her feet, clasped her hands together, and placed her feet in third position, as she had been taught. The past may haunt her, but she could also use it to her advantage. Olga needed no royal status to carry herself with dignity and behave with honor. Papa had shown her as much during their time in captivity. Stripped of his title and all the privileges that came with it, he carried on, held his head high, and tried to find purpose amidst his reduced circumstances.

"As you reflect on your options, I only ask you to remember that you hold my sisters' fates in your hands."

When Hammond heard the note of authority in her voice, he narrowed his eyes. And then, perhaps sensing she would not budge, he
dipped his head.

"I would like to take the night to think about this," he told her. "You
and I can speak again in the morning."

"Yes, your lordship."

Hammond gave her a curt nod. She couldn't tell if it was trying to
get rid of her more quickly or if he had as little taste for titles as Rob.

"Let my daughter know I wish to see her. If you will."

"Of course."

Before she left the study, Olga squeezed Rob's hand. He had been
staring at the floor but looked up at her then.

All she saw was Grigori Rasputin. The man who hurt women and
got away with it. Not sent from heaven, nor a demon, but an evil
man who manipulated her mother and contributed to the chaos and
tragedy that shattered Olga's world.

If only Rob's father had been anyone else.

She told herself Rob needed time alone with Hammond. How
could she possibly admit that she couldn't look at him without seeing
Father Grigori?

"I'll leave the two of you to talk now," she whispered. "If I may."

Hammond gestured vaguely at the door, distracted. Out of pure
habit, she curtsied and then exited the room without another word.

Rasputin and the Bolsheviks had tried to crush her, but her family
still bore a great measure of responsibility for what had happened to
Russia. They were no beasts, but they had contributed to the misery.
And Olga was left to consider how much damage the Romanovs had
wrought and exactly what she needed to do to make it right.

Time and time again, Father Grigori saved my little brother. After such, how could my mother not have faith in everything Rasputin advised? I want to think my mother could not possibly have thought any differently, that no one could see the truth beneath his seductive shell.

Except the rest of Petrograd came to hate the man. Eventually, two gentlemen took matters into their own hands and murdered him. Behind closed doors, perhaps sensing their hatred, Rasputin warned my mother that if he were to die, the entire House of Romanov would fall. After he was killed, this came to pass. When they seized power, the Bolsheviks hunted the Romanov family and tried to execute every last one of us.

That was all in the future. When we first heard of Father Grigori's murder, my mother was devastated. The rest of us had to pretend to be as well. She buried him on the palace grounds, where we would soon be held under house arrest.

But Rasputin found no peace there. After the revolutionary forces took control of our palace, the guards discovered his grave, dug him up, and tossed his body up from the depths of the earth so they might abuse it.

Grigori Rasputin was Russian to the core, but the people did not love him. They saw him for who he was when my mother could not.

The Private Diary of Olga Romanova
December 1921

CHAPTER TWENTY-THREE

O lga tried not to betray her impatience. She had already taken tea and breakfast upstairs to Celia's room. For once, she wished her employer was a morning person.

Celia had faced her father last night, and it seemed to have gone well. Or as well as could be expected, given the circumstances. Celia hadn't shared many details with Olga, which was odd on the face of it, so she wanted to check up on her. But per her custom, Celia was still eating breakfast upstairs and slowly waking to the world.

Not that Olga could offer much comfort at the moment. Awaiting Hammond's decision, she could barely focus on nibbling the plain piece of toast before her, finding that for once she wasn't hungry. Her feet refused to remain still, the toe of her ankle boot tapping the floor with a rat-a-tat, like the sound of keys striking on a mechanical typewriter.

"No butter with your toast this morning, Miss Bennett?"

Mrs. Dasari sat across from Olga in the servants' hall. Mrs. Acton and Ada were off on a quick run to the garden to gather fresh flowers for the vases in the hallway, while Mrs. Dasari read the morning paper and waited for a pie to finish in the oven. Every few minutes, she looked up from the paper and gave Olga a sidelong glance. Evidently, she'd noticed something was amiss. But until she caught a glimpse of the plain toast, she hadn't said anything.

It was too odd to pass without comment, Olga supposed. Every morning, she helped herself to a second round of toast and heaped butter on top of the bread, always remembering the days of stale black bread and bitter tea during the last months in captivity. "Not much of an appetite this morning, I guess."

Olga managed a small smile. She didn't have it in her to make up a story to explain away her nerves. If she said anything so much as skirting the truth, she was bound to break down right there.

Deep as her concern for Celia was, she felt more anxious about Rob and his reaction to what he'd learned yesterday. Everything he'd thought about himself wasn't true. Or perhaps true, in a sense, but stripped away in an instant with one simple revelation. Olga couldn't stand to think of him enduring this alone. Should she try to find him? Did she dare ask Mrs. Acton? She always seemed to know his whereabouts. To secure the information, however, Olga would need to endure the spectacle of Mrs. Acton peppering her with questions and disapproving looks. Ordinarily, she could deal with such, but not this morning.

Olga was half-way through her tea, and thinking she should go back up to Celia earlier than normal, when Mrs. Acton and Ada returned from the garden, arms full of fragrant flowers and herbs. After such morning walks, they were usually full of chatter and laughter. Today, they were silent and tense.

Behind them, looking as though he hadn't slept a wink the night before, stood Hammond.

Mrs. Dasari's chair scraped against the floor as she pushed it back and rose to curtsy. Mrs. Acton and Ada might have already been standing, but they moved to either side of Mrs. Dasari, to keep a respectable distance between themselves and his lordship. That left Olga on her own on the other side of the table and slow to her feet.

"No, no, none of that. Please sit." Hammond rubbed his beard, as though that might make his face appear less haggard, before motioning for them to return to their seats. "I only wanted to see .... Miss Bennett." He stumbled on the name.

Olga wiped her mouth slowly with her linen. Ada made a face, barely perceptible, but Olga understood the silent question. Why would his lordship travel downstairs to see a maid?

Well, Ada would just have to wonder about that.

"This will only take a minute. Perhaps we could speak in the kitchen? Mrs. Dasari, I take it you won't mind?"

"Of course, your lordship," she said.

Olga followed Hammond into the kitchen, wondering how a once welcoming space could seem so ominous now. She stared at the copper teakettle on the stove, and tried to focus on the smell of baking bread.

Hammond fished in his pocket for a handkerchief. He cleaned his thin-rimmed spectacles before replacing them on his nose. Though she couldn't swear to it, she thought he was wearing the same gray waistcoat and trousers, significantly more rumpled, he'd worn the day before.

"Then I'll get right to it. I have decided not to go forward with what the Bolsheviks asked me to do. I will not publish the letters and shall retract the statement I made before the House of Lords."

She closed her eyes, relief washing over her like fresh water. Her sisters were safe. Their secret was safe. For now. Olga felt the burden lift from her shoulders, the weight of the last few months, of her mother's worried presence, dissipating at last. If Olga never had to think about Grigori Rasputin again, she would thank her lucky stars every night.

Except that she now saw Father Grigori in Rob's features.

Olga opened her eyes. "Robert agreed to this? What if the Bolsheviks share the truth about what happened to your wife in Russia?"

"Regardless of the consequences, my son supports this course of action." Hammond's chest puffed slightly like a proud papa. "He told me he'd rather live with the truth about his parentage in the public eye than protect a falsehood. He is an honorable gentleman."

"Yes, he is," Olga said quietly.

"It would be different if his mother was still alive, of course, for the decision would be hers alone to make. As it stands, we will defend her reputation. As you defended your mother's. So I will hold Grigori Rasputin accountable for his crimes. Posthumously. I will make sure the reports in his dossier are published. His victims will have a voice, even as they remain anonymous."

Olga tugged at the stiff collar on her blouse. Her parents should have atoned for Father Grigori, for they had empowered him in the first place. Then again, they'd paid the worst price of all for their shortcomings and could do nothing more. That left Hammond to expose Rasputin's crimes.

She swallowed hard and met his gaze. "And what of your daughter? Lady Celia?"

Hammond folded his arms in front of his chest. "I take it you know?"

Olga bobbed her head, impatient to hear more.

"Apparently, she has no desire to marry anyone, least of all the baby's father. She made that abundantly clear. I wish she'd made different choices in London, but she's a strong young woman. Like her mother. And if she wants to work with Rob, I see no reason she shouldn't."

"That is generous, your lordship. I'm sure she was delighted to hear you support her choices."

"If people wish to gossip, that is their affair. We've always had thick skins in this family."

Olga thought of the portraits in the hallway. She wondered if their ghosts haunted the present Lord Hammond. Not in a fiendish way, but in a manner that granted him strength. She liked Hammond despite herself. She almost smiled at him.

Still, there was one hanging thread ...

"The Bolsheviks tried to poison you," she said. "I know you were told it was a mistake, but are you sure? You know what they are capable of doing. How can you ignore such a thing?"

"I'm not ignoring it. I have requested protection from His Majesty's service. I've enough sway there to be granted that much. Neither the crown nor parliament want further trouble with the Bolsheviks. We may not like it, but they are in charge of Russia now. Too big to ignore. England must remain at peace with Russia. The consequences of not doing so would be far worse."

"I understand, your lordship." She didn't want to understand, but she did. If the Bolsheviks remained in power, other nations could not provoke or ignore them.

"What I said about the empress, your mother."

He removed his glasses again, blinking rapidly.

"My wife used to wake up in the middle of the night, screaming, perspiring, and thrashing. She never lost her fear of the world. Maybe it shouldn't matter. That man hurt my wife long before he made it to court. And yet it does. It matters because he did the same to other women once he was in your mother's inner circle and she did nothing. How can I let that go?"

The countess needed justice of some sort, even if she was no longer in this world. She could only imagine the woman's pain. She must have been reminded of Rasputin whenever she saw Rob. And yet, from all Olga could see, the woman loved her son with all her heart.

"I know," she told Hammond. "Revealing his crimes is the right thing to do."

"My responsibility now is to my children. It's what my wife would want. To help Celia get through the next few months and set her up properly for the years ahead. And to support Rob as best I can. He is a fine young man and will find his way."

"He is that."

Hammond hesitated. "But what of you?"

It took Olga a moment to realize he genuinely wanted to know if she would be all right.

"We are moving to San Francisco," she said. "Far away. It's for the best.

"So you and ... Rob?"

Olga dipped her head. Anyone looking at her would know the extent of her feelings for Rob. Hammond laughed softly.

"I always dreamed of a good match for my son. What parent doesn't? But a grand duchess? Who would have thought?"

"My sisters and I can't remain this close to the Bolsheviks," she told him, looking up again. "They must remain safe."

Hammond pinched the bridge of his nose and then put his spectacles back on. "I see."

Her heart was thudding. She thought she detected a hint of dis-appointment in his voice. Surely that was only her imagination. This situation was impossible.

"How will you make your way then?" he asked. "Still as Olivia Bennett? Still a maid? Will your sisters have false identities as well? They'll need them."

Olga had thought none of that out yet. She'd been too distracted. She supposed her sisters would need alternative names. She didn't know if she would keep hers.

"If life has taught me anything, it's that we can't know what the future holds," she said. "If I am to be Olivia Bennett, and a maid, so be it." There were worse fates. Far worse.

"Should circumstance dictate, you always have a place here. It must be difficult. Once a grand duchess and now working as a servant."

Olga was sorry as well, but not for the reasons Hammond might think. She need never be a grand duchess again. She was fine with that, and happy to simply exist as Olga Nikolaevna.

What pained her was the realization that after all this time, after everything she'd been through, and after meeting a man she cared for—even might love—she still lacked purpose. Perhaps she would find that purpose in San Francisco, but right now she couldn't envi-sion how. She only knew it would hurt to leave Marlingham.

"I'll manage," she told Hammond.

He stepped closer. His hand hovered awkwardly near her shoulder. She could tell he wanted to comfort her, but wouldn't presume to touch a grand duchess.

Still alone, when it came down to it. Olga and her sisters. Their own community.

"You are a strong young woman." Hammond lowered his voice. "You and your sisters survived. Do you remember when I said that to you? We assisted you, but the four of you are survivors. You will always be so and forever thrive. I know it."

He bowed, just as he had when he first greeted her, back in Arkhangelsk, before leaving the kitchen. When he opened the door, Olga glimpsed Ada scuttling backward before disappearing back into the servants' hall.

She'd been eavesdropping. What did she hear?

If Ada had learned Olga's secret, she would tell others. She wouldn't be able to help herself. And yet, the intensity of that secret had become too much for Olga to bear. She felt no jolt in her stomach, no stab of terror. The fatigue of her disguise had finally settled.

Besides, Hammond hadn't said anything directly. If Ada knew, Olga would figure out how to handle it. That Ada could learn Olga's identity so easily only reinforced why she needed to move away. Her sisters' safety must always come first.

Even above Olga's happiness.

"Grand duchess is what he said. I know what I heard."

Ada's voice carried to the kitchen. Olga wondered if Ada realized she was still in there. Olga wiped her face with the handkerchief she kept in her apron, having ruined the cosmetics she'd applied that morning. What did it matter now?

After Hammond left the room, she'd finally cried. Olga didn't find any shame in it. Now, she leaned over the basin and turned the spigot on so she could splash water on her face. As she dabbed her forehead, she checked her reflection in the window to ensure her cheeks weren't too splotchy.

When Olga returned to the servants' hall, Ada was still exclaiming: "It makes sense, you know! The new miss was always an odd duck." And then, sensing Olga's presence, she clamped her mouth shut.

Mrs. Acton planted her plump hands on her waist. "Is it true then? What Ada said?"

It was one of those situations where the least said the better. That's what Tatiana would have told her anyway, parroting their mother. In this case, Olga agreed.

With a shrug, Olga took a seat and reached for a pat of butter for her toast. Mrs. Dasari eyed her, likely noting her resurgent appetite.

"I think Lord Hammond did not sleep well last night," Olga said. "Perhaps that's why he's been saying strange things."

"No matter who you are, Miss Bennett," Mrs. Dasari said, "and no matter what you can and can't say, I hope you decide to stay. We've grown accustomed to having you around."

"I figured you'd work with the young lord and his sister when they open the rehabilitation center," Ada piped up. "You being a nurse and all. I want to do the same, and working together wouldn't be so bad."

Olga swallowed a bite of toast and grinned, proud of Ada for thinking ahead and wanting to pursue nursing. She still seemed like another sister for Olga to watch over, and she would have liked to continue working with her if possible.

She didn't say anything. Not yet. Olga would only make the most of the time she had left at Marlingham.

Though I wasn't a true heiress to the throne, my parents raised me as a grand duchess—a life devoted to our empire, to Russia, to the preser-

vation of the House of Romanov. In the time before, I never questioned whether that was good or bad.

I remain a Romanov heiress, if not destined for a throne, then certainly in my heart. I am the heir to the name. And I shall ensure that when my sisters and I are finally free to reveal the truth, we shall redeem that name. We may not be able to atone for the past, but we can help create a better future.

The Private Diary of Olga Romanova
December 1921

CHAPTER TWENTY-FOUR

As it turned out, she didn't talk to Rob. After learning the truth about his birth father, Grigori Rasputin, he took off in his Daimler. Without a word, according to Mrs. Acton.

That he should leave suddenly, without saying goodbye, cut her deeply. Olga imagined it was now as hard for Rob to look at her—a living reminder of the family who had empowered his mother's assailant—as it was for her to look at him.

An oddly hopeful expression swept over Celia's features when Olga asked after Rob. Though her brother seemed shaken, Celia assured Olga he was all right. Rob had been known to depart alone for a day or two to gather his thoughts. He'd told Celia he only needed space to come to terms with what his father had revealed.

She could tell Celia wanted to chat further about Olga and Rob. To distract her from that topic, Olga asked if Celia and her father had discussed plans for a nursery. Her heart might have been in pieces, but the sprout would soon join the world. Somehow, she'd already grown attached. Life went on.

Olga's temporary duty was to Celia and her baby. Her permanent allegiance was to Tatiana, Maria, and Ana.

That Saturday, she went to visit her sisters at the cottage. Since Celia needed her on Sunday night to help her dress for a dinner Lord Hammond was hosting, she suggested Olga take all of Saturday as a holiday rather than Sunday as was customary. She could stay overnight before returning in the afternoon.

Olga was curious about the dinner, as the guests were to include the Pendletons, the neighbors who had previously called and still hadn't given an answer to Rob about his plans for the rehabilitation center. Apparently, Hammond was confident he could convince them to let Rob use their land; he would ensure he appropriately compensated them. And though Olga hadn't asked, Celia assured her Rob would return in time for that event.

As she sat down for an early supper with her sisters, Olga tried to stop thinking about Rob, about Marlingham. As midsummer approached, the days had grown exceedingly lovely, and they decided to eat outside. Olga's sisters must have tended to the unruly shrubs and plants, for the cottage now boasted a thriving garden. Purple foxglove edged the fence, bordering clusters of pale pink hollyhock. Matching peonies grew near the honeysuckle, sweet peas, and violets. Their perfume filled the air.

"This is gorgeous!" Olga exclaimed, kneeling to examine a clump of blossoming white flowers whose petals made them look like snowflakes. "You three have kept busy."

"It was mostly Ana's doing," Maria told her.

Olga must have looked confused because Tatiana added, "It's true."

Little had Olga suspected that when Anastasia was hiding out in the garden, she hadn't spent the entire time moping and fretting over how to get to Hollywood. Or, at the very least, she kept her hands occupied while moping. She'd cultivated an English garden that would have made their mother proud.

"What a shame we won't have much longer to enjoy it properly," Olga murmured as she rose to her feet again.

"We may not have much time left in England," Ana told Olga sheepishly, "but that doesn't mean we shouldn't leave this place better than we found it."

Olga made a mental note to learn which flowers were best suited to San Francisco's climate. They could start a new garden. After all, perpetually starting over was their destiny now.

In addition to her contributions to the garden, Ana had transformed an old workbench in the shed. After much scraping and sanding of wood, it served as a low table now. They draped a blanket over the top and sat on the ground as they ate, like a picnic. Nibbling at delicate watercress and cucumber sandwiches, anyone would think them four English ladies. Nothing more.

As they ate, her sisters' voices grew distant. The thought bothered her: this notion that they were English now. The Russian parts of themselves remained in hiding. They hardly spoke the language anymore. In the time before, on a warm evening such as this, they might have feasted on cold bowls of borscht with sour cream and flaky pastries filled with salmon and hard-boiled eggs. Fresh mushrooms. Black caviar on toast. And yet, it didn't occur to any of them to supplement their English food with Russian dishes.

"Do you think we'll forget?" she asked suddenly.

All three of her sisters set their teacups back on their saucers, centering them as they were taught. Maria had been gesticulating with one hand. She dropped it slowly to her side.

"M was telling us about a couturière in Paris," Ana said. "Mademoiselle Chanel. She designs outfits with not a thought given to a corset."

"I'm sorry," Olga said, shaking her head. "I interrupted. How rude of me."

"It's fine," Maria replied. "There wasn't much more to tell. You're worried we'll forget something?"

"Yes, do tell." Tatiana gave Olga an appraising look. "What do you mean we'll forget?"

Olga sighed and took another sip of tea, trying to collect her thoughts as a fat bumblebee buzzed around the foxglove.

"We'll forget the Russian language," she said. "But more than that. What it felt like to live that life. To be in Russia. To be the daughters of the tsar."

When Olga spoke, Maria and Tatiana looked furtively toward the fences on either side of the yard, well away from where they'd situated on the table.

"Oh, bother that!" Ana declared. "No one is listening on the other side of the fence. We're quite alone."

Self-consciously, Tatiana and Maria turned back, almost as though they'd been caught doing something wrong. Maybe it was a good sign. They needed to take proper measures to protect themselves, but they shouldn't live in constant fear.

"I don't think we'll ever forget," Maria said. "How could we?"

"Our lives are different now," Olga told her.

"Sometimes I forget," Ana said. "Not the language. But I forget what someone looked like. Our tutors, cousins, guards."

"As long as you don't forget Mama, Papa, and Alexei," Tatiana replied.

Ana scowled. "I will never forget them. You know that."

Olga looked down at her plate, picking at the thin sandwich and letting the bread crumble between her fingers. She wasn't as confident as Anastasia. Not in the way she wished. Familiar faces from the time before grew less distinct in her memories. And while it felt good to support herself and live on her own, it scared her to think she would become an entirely different person than the one her sisters had grown up with in Russia. It wasn't about the palaces, the trappings of wealth, or any of that, but their shared history. The bond between them.

"I wonder if there isn't something we might do to help remember them," Maria mused. "Surely that wouldn't hurt."

"We don't have pictures," Olga said. "We had no time to pack them before we left."

"We can draw," Maria said. "We can look through the papers. Mama and Papa still appear now and again. Alexei, too. Sometimes."

Olga reached out and squeezed Maria's hand across the table. "I like that idea. "We'll make sure they remain a part of us."

"Even in San Francisco?" Tatiana said wistfully.

"Even there," Olga said. "We will be together and happy. That's all that matters."

She wished she could summon more conviction in her words. Only she mustn't let her sisters know how she truly felt. That happiness had been in her grasp, and she'd let it slip through her fingers like water in a sieve.

Olga rose from bed early the following day to fetch a glass of water. She'd had trouble sleeping, still troubled by thoughts of Rob. Besides, Olga had grown accustomed to having a room to herself. She used to sleep through Tatiana's tossing and light snoring, but no longer.

After she walked from the kitchen into the dining nook with the water, she looked for a pen. She wanted to record her memories of Russia. She'd intended to do so at Marlingham, but never found the time. After discussing her fear of forgetting their past life in Russia, Olga felt an increased urgency to commit her thoughts to paper.

As she approached, she heard a quick intake of breath. Anastasia sat at the table, still in her red and black checkered men's flannel pajamas. A letter lay in front of her sister, along with an envelope too small to contain it. The paper creased along the diagonals from excessive folding.

The last time Ana had left a note on the dining table, she was running away.

"What are you doing?" Olga cried.

She lunged toward the table, water splashing from the glass as it fell to the floor, and tried to grab the letter. Ana was too quick. Before Olga could reach them, her sister snatched both the letter and the envelope.

"Can't a girl have a little privacy?" Ana said.

Olga took a deep breath and counted silently to ten.

"What are you up to this time?"

"So nothing has changed?" Ana cried. "Even though you spent time away from us, you play the mother hen. You still think we should stay captives for the rest of our lives. Will you move us to San Francisco and then hold us prisoners there? Well, maybe that's dandy for you, Olga, but not me."

"No one is a captive," Olga said. "You know that. But we can't keep secrets from one another. We went over all of this. Why won't you show me what you wrote?"

Ana pulled the letter closer to her. "I knew you would get mad. Why are you up so early, anyway?"

From behind them, Tatiana cleared her throat. It was an unmistakable sound, and one her sister had often employed growing up whenever she'd caught Ana or Maria doing something naughty. Olga turned to find Tatiana in her nightdress, a long braid over her shoulder. Maria stood next to Tatiana. Overnight, her hair had loosened from its customary ribbons and spilled down her back in disarray.

"You're trying to leave us again?" Tatiana said to Ana.

Maria pushed her hair back over her ear, sensing the fight ahead. "I'll fetch a towel to clean up the water."

Though her chin jutted out defiantly, Ana looked close to tears. "This is my business alone."

"We agreed," Olga said. "No more secrets."

"You'll all be mad again."

"We won't be mad," Olga said. "I promise. Let us see what you're doing."

Reluctantly, Ana handed Olga the envelope, but kept the letter clutched tight to her chest. Maria re-entered the room but dropped the towel carelessly on the floor, over the water, so she could join Tatiana and peer over Olga's shoulders to read the words on the envelope.

Amherst Productions

It was addressed to a film company in California. "You still want to go to Hollywood?" Olga said.

"Once I have a job secured, yes. This studio doesn't know what positions might be available yet, but I want to get my foot in the door."

She shrugged. "San Francisco is not exactly next to Los Angeles, but much closer than here. So I can visit you all."

"You should have let us know you were still trying to find work at a picture studio," Olga said. "Don't you trust us?"

"It's not that." Ana looked down at the floor.

Tatiana moved a chair near Ana and took a seat. Her voice was exceedingly gentle, particularly given how angry she must have been. "What then?"

"I have no idea if I'll get an offer," Ana blurted.

"It's true," Maria said. "She's mentioned this to me."

"I mean, why should this Amherst character hire a girl with no experience? I was afraid if I said anything ... I don't know. I'd curse it somehow. If anything came of it, I planned to tell you all."

Ana had learned from her past mistakes. She'd put more thought into it this time around. Olga had been wrong. This wasn't like before at all.

Olga wanted her sister to be happy. If Hollywood would make her happy, then Olga wanted her to receive a job offer.

The room remained quiet until Maria said, "Once we get to San Francisco, I intend to look for work as well. Maybe at a boarding house or hotel. I could wait tables or clean rooms."

"What about Paris, M?" Ana asked.

"I still want to go to Paris. Someday. Maybe to work for someone like Mademoiselle Chanel. But I don't want to wait for that to make something of my life."

Olga squeezed her sister's arm and then turned to Tatiana. "Do you have plans as well?"

Her sister shivered and pulled her thin nightgown closer to her chest. Even in summer, the early morning air carried a chill in it.

"I plan to go back to Russia," Tatiana said. "I don't expect it will happen soon. In the meantime, I will learn to make the best of it in San Francisco. I may not have mapped my future, as the rest of you have, but I understand there are other Russian émigrés there and a church or two of our faith. I shall figure something out."

They needed to be strong for one another, as always. Olga stretched her arms, and they bundled together in one giant hug.

"We will take on the world," Olga said. "Each in our own way. I'm sure of it."

When she heard the knock on the door, Olga thought one of Gran's regular men must have been out sick. They were low on supplies, but never received boxes on Sunday morning. And no one ever knocked. That was part of the arrangement.

With her sisters out in the garden, she was alone in the cottage. Olga had only run inside to fetch a watering pot. She waited, not quite daring to approach the door, assuming the delivery man would soon be on his way. But no motorcar engine roared to life outside.

More thudding. Olga didn't understand. A delivery man wouldn't expect someone to come to the door and sign for the package. A terrifying thought occurred to her: Bolsheviks.

Then again, if they ever learned where the missing daughters of the tsar lived, they wouldn't bother to knock.

She supposed she could open the door just a sliver, not enough for anyone to see her face, and peek. Before she had a chance, a familiar voice called out.

"Hello? Olga, are you in there?"

The rolling baritone that made her want to listen for sheer pleasure. The voice that made Olga feel like he was already caressing her.

Rob's voice.

Pulse quickening, Olga opened the door.

"Ah!" A broad smile filled his face, but his feet shuffled awkwardly. "I was hoping you'd still be home."

"You left without a word." She tried to keep the hurt out of her tone. "I didn't get to talk to you about what your father said."

"When you see why I left, you'll think it worthwhile."

He gestured toward his Daimler parked on the street. She spotted Conall in the back seat, happily panting.

"I don't suppose you would fancy a drive? Conall is always up for such. I want to show you something."

Slowly, she drew her gaze away from Conall and back to Rob. The eager look on his face broke her heart. She wondered if Lord Hammond had mentioned anything about Olga and her sisters leaving the country. "I'm supposed to return to Marlingham this afternoon."

"Celia said as much. But I understand we may not have you there for much longer. San Francisco, is it?"

So Hammond had told him. Her shoulders dropped, the joy of seeing him obliterated by the knowledge that their reunion would be short-lived.

"It can't be helped."

"I can return you to Marlingham with time to spare," Rob said. "And I know you won't want to miss this."

Olga hesitated, but not for long. No matter how difficult it might be, she couldn't *not* take advantage of any time she might steal alone with Rob. At least then she would have memories to hold and treasure.

"Let me gather my things," she told him. "And tell my sisters."

As they drove, the wind ruffled her short hair. Olga tried to think of something innocuous to say, something which wouldn't bring up the past and the circumstances under which she'd leave Marlingham. She ran through several topics in her head, but having none more intriguing than simple comments about the weather, soon gave up. Finally, she found the nerve to ask one question fretting in her mind.

"How are things between you and Lord Hammond?"

Rob's gloved hands gripped the wheel tighter. "Father knows he made mistakes."

"He only wanted what was best for you. He wanted to protect you."

"We are talking things out as best we can. It will be sorted in the end. We will focus on Celia's well-being and that of her child. They must always come first. And he supports my plan to help veterans of the war, the walking wounded. But ..."

"What?"

"After everything that happened, he still wants to work with the Bolsheviks." Rob exhaled sharply. "Lenin is intent on establishing relations with the British government."

"He thinks the Bolsheviks are rational?" Olga said. "I can't say I agree with him."

"He thinks they are here to stay, and we must learn to live with them."

Olga looked out the window. Her family's killers. She'd already acknowledged Lord Hammond was right in terms of pragmatic diplomacy, but how could she ever live in a world that treated these murderers with respect?

After a few minutes, Olga felt the light press of Rob's hand on her wrist.

"I'm sorry," he said.

She stared at his hand, remembering other times when they'd touched. Electricity shot through her. She'd tried not to stare at his lips and remember how it felt to kiss him.

He withdrew. At first, Olga thought he was afraid he'd overstepped. But he only needed both hands to guide the steering wheel into a right turn along the country lane they'd traversed. He then pulled in front of a modest beige cottage on the corner.

"Will you accompany me inside?"

While Conall panted expectantly behind her, Olga regarded the cottage, wondering what exactly Rob had in mind here. The place wasn't so different from the one where she and her sisters lived, right down to the bay windows in front.

"Please. I have a surprise."

"A surprise?"

The word sounded frivolous, even if it once would have made her squeal with delight. A surprise. It held a different meaning for Olga now. She'd always wondered if the Bolsheviks had told her parents and Alexei they were in for a surprise when they marched them down the stairs to the room where they would be shot.

It had been a long time since her mother had made her presence known. But as soon as Olga imagined those last terrible moments in Ekaterinburg, she sensed Mama again. Not as a corporeal figure but more of a presence. Despite Olga's gruesome thoughts a moment ago, she detected neither anxiety nor fear. Rather, her mother seemed content, as she had been when Olga was a little girl. Before multiple pregnancies, the pressure to produce an heir, and Alexei's sickness took their toll.

Her heart raced. Olga knew she shouldn't dare to hope, yet she did just that. Was it possible her parents and Alexei were alive? Perhaps

Tatiana was right after all: the Bolsheviks faked the murders to hide their incompetence.

No. She couldn't let herself think that. Hammond had made it clear enough. Her parents and Alexei were gone. Regardless, Mama's presence calmed her. The prospect of a surprise was tantalizing once more. She wouldn't let false hope ruin it.

"All right," she said.

Rob smiled and opened his door. Conall jumped off the back seat and outside after him. When Rob came round to get her door, Olga remained still. She needed to gather herself.

After taking in the clean, sweet scent of the air, Olga followed Rob and Conall up a pathway edged with boxed primroses. When the breeze picked up again, she bundled deeper into her coat, glad she'd remembered to bring it. As they approached this cottage, Conall grew more excited, yelping happily and then bounding ahead.

A young man with curly blonde hair and a scruffy beard appeared at the doorway and waved. "Pike!" he shouted to Rob.

When the man saw Olga, he tilted his head. Olga stopped short, frozen on her feet. She hadn't realized they were meeting anyone else. Rob should have told her. She would have taken greater care to ensure she looked nothing like Grand Duchess Olga.

Before she could say anything, the young man addressed her: "Imperial highness."

He lowered into a bow. Olga remembered arriving at Arkhangelsk, terrified after the ordeal, and then seeing the men bow. The all-too-brief sense that everything would be well.

"Tom served with the British forces in Russia during the Civil War," Rob explained. "He's one of the few who know."

"And you trust him?" she whispered.

"Absolutely."

She nodded in Tom's direction as Conall raced through the man's legs and into the house, yapping his head off.

Inside, the cottage looked much as she'd expected, though it was clearly a bachelor's residence. While the layout was similar to the cottage she shared with her sisters, the drapes over the windows were plain, and the furniture serviceable rather than decorative. Still, everything was tidy, and it smelled fresh but for a faint undercurrent of dog which she didn't mind at all.

She spotted Conall in the drawing room's corner, near a cushioned footrest, his undocked tail whipping to and fro. And then another dog emitted a squeaking yawn. A second tail emerged from behind the footrest. Conall moved aside to give his canine friend room to get to his feet.

The resident dog rose unsteadily. He was older and also a spaniel. Once he regained his balance, he ran forward, headed straight for Olga.

"Joy!" she cried.

Olga kneeled to meet Joy's nose with her own and hugged him, taking in the familiar comfort of his fur.

"I was part of the expedition to Ekaterinburg, grand duchess," Tom explained. "After the Red Army abandoned the city, we found your friend."

"He escaped?" Olga said, clutching Joy tighter and trying to hold back tears.

"We found him wandering near the house where you and your family lived in Ekaterinburg, still searching for you all, poor fellow."

"Searching for Alexei," Olga whispered. Joy would never have left his side. The Bolsheviks must have put him out of the house before the murders.

"He couldn't stay there," Tom said. "We didn't know how long we could hold the city. The Reds would regroup soon enough. So I took him home with me, and he's been in England since, living near Windsor. Rob was kind enough to suggest I bring him here."

"Thank you." Wriggling, Joy lapped at her cheek, happy as a puppy again. "With all my heart, thank you."

"He belongs with you and your sisters now," Tom said.

"Oh, I couldn't," Olga replied. "You saved him. I wouldn't want to take him from you after all you've been through."

Joy let his chin rest on Olga's leg. He hadn't taken his sad brown eyes off of her.

"He's a good boy, but we've had our time together," Tom said. "He belongs with his family now."

Tom suggested Olga take Joy out for a walk so the two of them could get reacquainted. And he insisted on staying behind. Olga thought she caught him winking at Rob as they set out together with Conall and Joy.

They followed a path along the creek near Tom's house, Conall bounding ahead while Joy came to heel at Olga's side. They were quiet, Olga content to savor the moment, the triumph in re-capturing this small part of her family. Somewhere, she was sure, Alexei sensed Joy's happiness and found peace in it.

At last, Conall pestered Joy long enough that the older dog chased the younger through the creek bed, barking happily. A breeze rippled through Olga's hair, for while she had taken her coat, in her haste to walk with Joy, she had forgotten to grab her hat.

Rob stopped and shoved his hands in his pockets. She felt keenly aware of his tall body and the enticing scent of his skin, even as he kept a gentlemanly distance.

"I missed you," he said at last. "When I returned, I thought I was too late. That you had already fled the country with your sisters."

Olga saw the same intensity she remembered. The same longing in his eyes.

There was a time when she would have been coy and let him wonder if she felt the same. She would have flirted with him, but kept her emotions on a tight leash. She would have done so because that was expected. As the eldest daughter, Grand Duchess Olga did what was expected of her. It was the only way.

Such nonsense no longer mattered. It had probably never mattered. Life would take dips and turns. She could only muddle her way through as best she could.

Now, with fate taking a turn for the better, she'd be a fool not to accept happiness.

"I missed you, too," she whispered and then glanced away. After speaking the truth of her heart, she felt vulnerable.

"When you look at me, though," Rob asked, "do you see *him*?"

He couldn't bear to utter the man's name. She stood her ground and indicated Rob should do the same. She summoned every memory of the man she'd once tried to forget. The only way to know for sure was to stare at Rob to see if Grigori Rasputin haunted her still.

Olga only saw Rob. Handsome, awkward, smart, sweet Rob. She touched his cheek.

"I admit, the news was a shock," she said. "But you are nothing like him. Believe me. I knew him. And now I know you."

Rob inhaled theatrically, and then gave a little laugh. "I'm so relieved."

"As am I." Olga allowed a small smile but dropped her hand. "I need to ask you the same question. Your father blamed my parents for helping Rasputin. He couldn't forgive them, not after what the man did to your mother. Can you?"

"That man caused enough pain in his life. I won't let him continue to cause pain from his grave."

Olga had to catch her breath. A glimmer of hope ignited inside her once more. "If only I didn't have to go."

"Don't go," he said. "If you don't wish it. Return to Marlingham."

"I plan to do so. Until we leave for San Francisco."

"I mean permanently," he said. "Keep Joy with you. He can't possibly make it to California. Hasn't he traveled enough?"

Olga was thinking something along those lines when Tom suggested she take Joy, but she hadn't wanted to decide without consulting her sisters. "He does seem happy here," Olga said, glancing over at Joy as Conall chased him.

"My father already spoke to you, did he not? He is happy to have you remain, should you choose. You can work with me. You can work with Celia. Not as a maid anymore."

"I don't mind being a maid," she said.

"Perhaps not, but I mind," he told her. "As long as you remain a maid in our household, this doesn't feel like it will ever be quite right."

She hesitated. "What will never be right?"

She had to hear him say it.

"I wish to court you," he told her. "Properly."

Olga touched his cheek again while her other hand slipped into her coat pocket. There, something flat and velvety surprised her. The jewelry box. She'd left it in this coat pocket ever since Easter, thinking she shouldn't wear it, but also reluctant to part with Rob's gift. She clutched the box tightly and then withdrew it from her pocket.

"Give me a moment," she said, lowering her hand.

She opened the box and removed the pendant, showing it to Rob before unclasping the chain she wore around her neck. She strung the Lilies of the Valley egg onto it: his gift to her before he had known its significance.

"Does that mean you agree?" he said, eyes wide.

The risk was worthwhile as long as she could be with Rob. She practically jumped into his arms.

Her sisters would search for happiness in California. They would remain close in her heart forever. But Olga had found her new home here.

EPILOGUE

HOLLYWOOD 1922

A na Marlowe pushed the chair back from her desk and snorted, a sound that once would have earned her a stern look from Tatiana or Olga. But Ana couldn't help herself. This latest batch was worse than the ones she'd reviewed before.

Mr. Amherst had taken her on as a story reader—the bottom rung of the studio's ladder. Ana considered herself fortunate to be on the ladder at all. But well over a year later, she still spent her days reading unsolicited scripts and scenarios, reviewing settings, actions, reactions, and title cards. They were all neatly stacked and clipped on her desk, some professionally typed, others scrawled by hand. Each had a personality of its own, that of an aspiring writer who wanted to make a career in the pictures. Ana had developed a keen eye for what worked on screen and what didn't. She wasn't about to risk her career by giving some schmuck with a sloppy story a chance. If someone's script wasn't up to snuff, they could try again until they got it right.

After all, she had revised her entire life. She had become Ana Marlowe, complete with an American accent and newly red hair styled in a chic bob.

When Ana first arrived in Los Angeles, at Central Station, she'd caught a citrus scent in the light breeze, tempering the fumes from the train. She'd tilted her head up to the warm sun, taking in the brilliant sheen of the station's walls in that light. So different from the grayness in England and the fog-gloom of San Francisco. Tatiana and Maria found the fog charming, but Ana craved sunshine. She was right where she belonged.

But Ana Marlowe needed to learn how to hold her liquor. Massaging her temples, Ana's thoughts wandered back to the previous night when she'd hit the town. At least to the extent she dared. She'd gone out for a stolen drink at one of the speakeasies along Franklin Boulevard. Not mingling. Ana knew better than that. Only sitting by herself at a corner table, eyes hidden under the brim of her hat, enjoying a Bee's Knees with extra honey syrup. How daring she'd felt. And how much better it would have been if she'd been able to talk to one of the fellas swaggering around the bar, all dapper and enticing in their swanky suits and fedoras.

Her headache had improved since morning, but she still wanted to crawl back into bed. It was too early, though. A dark blue haze permeated the sky as the sun dipped below the horizon. Ana's bungalow had many windows, allowing her to appreciate the beauty outside. Palm fronds and cactus leaves were bathed in the now gentle light.

When she finally forced her attention back to the open script on her desk—a coppers and robbers story she'd already seen some version of a million times over—she couldn't bring herself to read through to the ending. Instead, she started rifling through the remaining papers, hoping a clever title might capture her attention.

A manuscript near the bottom of the pile caught her eye.

The Missing Princess: A Tale of Revolution

Inspired by True Events

Two writers took credit, one of whom was named Anna Anderson. But that had to be wrong. When she first picked up the manuscript at the studio, Ana saw a different name on the return envelope. She found that envelope stacked in a separate pile opposite the scripts and checked again. Sure enough, "Anna" was listed, but with the last name "Tchaikovsky." Like the composer. Anna Anderson must have been a pen name.

Her chest grew cold. If Anna Anderson was Anna Tchaikovsky, then Ana Marlowe was in trouble.

Anna Tchaikovsky lived in Berlin. A few years back, she'd jumped into the Landwehr Canal, trying to end her life. After her rescue, doctors diagnosed her with amnesia. Until Anna Tchaikovsky started talking to the other patients at the mental hospital where she'd been confined.

At first, she said she was the missing Grand Duchess Tatiana. Apparently, that had been a misunderstanding. The woman then claimed she was Grand Duchess Anastasia.

And now she wanted to tell the world her story.

AFTERWORD

I hope you enjoyed this reimagining of the Romanov sisters. Anastasia's story, *The Romanov Impostor*, is coming in January 2024 and available for pre-order. For new releases, recommendations, and deal alerts, you can also follow me on BookBub.

The first draft for this novel started prior to the pandemic. Writing and revising provided a welcome escape during the first lockdown months of 2020. I appreciate the early insights of Erin Harris and Melissa Erin Jackson on the work-in-progress, which remained my beloved "secret project" through multiple revisions. I also want to thank Julie at JS Designs for her fabulous cover art, and Lisa Woodard-Mink and the Friends of the Library at Sacramento State University for hosting me as a part of the Charles Martell author lecture series, providing an enthusiastic audience for stories about the Romanov sisters.

For research on the Romanov family, I utilized the works of Helen Rappaport, Helen Azar, and Robert Massie, among others. You can find a bibliography and questions for book clubs on my website: jenniferlaam.com

Finally, while the lives of the historical Romanov children ended in tragedy, Alexei's dog did survive the House of Special Purpose. Joy lived the remainder of his days in England, though it was said he never stopped missing his family.

ABOUT THE AUTHOR

A proud native of Stockton, CA, Jennifer Laam resides in Sacramento with a temperamental tabby cat named Jonesy. When not reading or writing, she enjoys planning cosplay for the next San Diego Comic-Con, experimenting with vegetarian recipes (to mixed results), cooing at Baby Yoda, or obsessing over House Targaryen.

ALSO BY JENNIFER LAAM

The Secret Daughter of the Tsar
The Tsarina's Legacy
The Lost Season of Love and Snow

Printed in Great Britain
by Amazon